T0305024

DEFENSE
PROTOCOL

TOM CLANCY

A JACK RYAN NOVEL

DEFENSE
PROTOCOL

BY ANDREWS & WILSON

SPHERE

SPHERE

First published in the United States in 2025 by G. P. Putnam's Sons,
an imprint of Penguin Random House LLC
First published in Great Britain in 2025 by Sphere

1 3 5 7 9 10 8 6 4 2

Maps by Jeffrey L. Ward

A CIP catalogue record for this book
is available from the British Library.

Hardback ISBN 978-1-4087-3285-4
Trade Paperback ISBN 978-1-4087-3284-7

Printed and bound in Great Britain by Clays Ltd, Elcograf S.p.A.

Papers used by Sphere are from well-managed forests
and other responsible sources.

MIX
Paper | Supporting
responsible forestry
FSC
www.fsc.org   FSC® C104740

Sphere
An imprint of
Little, Brown Book Group
Carmelite House
50 Victoria Embankment
London EC4Y 0DZ

An Hachette UK Company
www.hachette.co.uk

www.littlebrown.co.uk

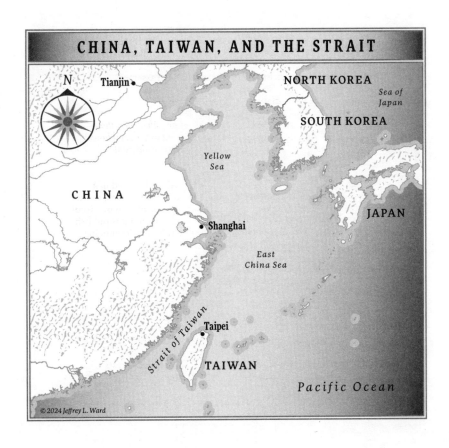

CHINA, TAIWAN, AND THE STRAIT

N

Tianjin

NORTH KOREA

Sea of
Japan

SOUTH KOREA

Yellow
Sea

CHINA

JAPAN

Shanghai

East
China Sea

Strait of Taiwan

Taipei

TAIWAN

Pacific Ocean

© 2024 Jeffrey L. Ward

PRINCIPAL CHARACTERS

WASHINGTON, D.C.

Jack Ryan Sr: President of the United States
Arnold "Arnie" van Damm: White House Chief of Staff
Mary Pat Foley: Director of National Intelligence
Scott Adler: Secretary of State
Robert Burgess: Secretary of Defense
Admiral Lawrence Kent, USN: Chairman of the Joint Chiefs of Staff
Major General Bruce Kudryk, USA: Joint Chiefs of Staff

CHINA

Li Jian Jun: President of the People's Republic of China
Qin Hâiyû: Minister of Defense
Cheng Kai: Minister of Foreign Affairs
Qiū Léi: The Night Spider
Scott Kincaid: Deputy Chief of U.S. Mission, Beijing

TASK FORCE 25

Lieutenant Commander Katie Ryan: ONI
Intelligence Specialist 2nd Class "Bubba" Pettigrew: ONI
Lieutenant JG John Conza: ONI

PRINCIPAL CHARACTERS

Andrew "Drewski" Miaoulis: Ground Branch
Ted James: CIA
Simran "Sam" Bakshi: CIA
Ben Hart: Ground Branch
Lori Tengco: DIA
Lou Donatelli: DIA
Commander Beechum: Navy SEAL
Master Chief Hurley: Navy SEAL
Senior Chief Max Harden: Navy SEAL
Chief Reed: Navy SEAL
Skip Anderson: Navy SEAL
Scott Todd: Navy SEAL

CNS *NANCHANG* TYPE 055 DESTROYER

Captain Shen Huaqing: Commanding Officer
Colonel Sun Ching-Kuo: Political Commissar

USS *JASON DUNHAM*

Commander Jeffrey Kreutz: Commanding Officer
Lieutenant Commander Karen Cook: Executive Officer
Lieutenant Commander Mitchell Horrillo: Combat Systems
    Officer

TASK FORCE 99

John Clark
Ding Chavez
Daniel Wu
Lee Hyori
Wilhelm Bauer
Charlotte "Charlie" Adams
Henri Toussaint

PROLOGUE

S omething was wrong.

Cheng Kai, minister of foreign affairs, could feel it in his bones. As he walked through the jaw-dropping, eighty-meter-tall atrium—with its arboreal-style pillars and *shan shui*–inspired design—he couldn't shake the sense that he was being watched. No, not watched . . . judged. But when he scanned the faces of the staff and other residents milling about, nobody was paying him any mind.

I'm being paranoid, he told himself. *It's the stress of the job, that's all.*

Still, something was *definitely* off. The frequency of people calling and messaging him had dropped noticeably below the daily baseline he'd become accustomed to in the job over the past two years. He was still getting directives, updates, and communications from the Foreign Affairs Commission and from the Central Committee, but the questions and requests for direction

1

from staffers in his own office had almost dried up completely. This was odd, because he'd gradually come to believe that nobody did anything in the Ministry without his prior assent.

If not me, then who is authorizing the daily decisions?

In the bureaucratic machine that was the Chinese government, a single misstep—not necessarily even a mistake—could end a man's career.

Or worse . . .

As the nation's top diplomat, a position analogous to the United States secretary of state, Cheng was responsible for overseeing the Ministry of Foreign Affairs for the People's Republic of China. In addition to negotiating treaties, advising the State Council on international affairs, and representing China in the United Nations, his Ministry's mandate was to formulate, communicate, and administer China's foreign policy abroad. In today's complex geopolitical world, a world driven by communication and messaging, his position made him one of the most recognizable and powerful men in China, second only to President Li Jian Jun.

Cheng would never boast about this fact, to do so would be unwise, but his power was real and everyone knew it.

His thoughts took him to the moment two years ago when President Li had offered him the position. Li's words played back in Cheng's mind with all the clarity and poignancy as if the man were speaking to him now:

"In accepting this position, you will be the face and the fist of China's foreign policy. You will be the hand world leaders shake first, and the mouth that delivers the ultimatums and unpleasant truths behind closed doors that I cannot. For the next five years, you will be my wolf warrior—barking, snarling, and howling. You will defend the people against the hostile rhetoric of the West. You will defend the

nation's honor when China is disrespected by foreign governments and foreign press. And you will defend me when dirty lies and propaganda try to sully my name and reputation. Are you up for the challenge, my friend?"

Cheng had agreed immediately and unequivocally, without giving the gravity or true meaning of Li's words much thought. *That* version of Cheng had been hungry for power and opportunity. He'd had eyes on the foreign affairs minister position for over a decade and had worked tirelessly to prove and endear himself to the Chinese president. He'd obediently and aggressively tried to demonstrate his skill and willingness to implement Li's political vision at every opportunity. And for this tireless effort, obedience, and loyalty, he had been rewarded.

But recently, he had doubts that had begun to plague him.

No, "doubts" was too strong a word. Second thoughts . . . he was having second thoughts.

After all, words matter.

Diplomacy was a profession defined by words—both spoken and unspoken. He'd witnessed the power of words firsthand over the past two years, as other nations' foreign policy was both made and unmade by the power of his words. As foreign minister he spoke for China. He spoke for the Party. He spoke for President Li. But speaking for the latter, unfortunately, had proven to be more challenging and precarious than he'd ever imagined.

President Li was a difficult man to please.

Pulling his roller suitcase behind him, Cheng stepped out of the lobby and under the covered porte cochere, where his driver and car were waiting. The black Hongqi H9 luxury sedan sat idling at the curb just ahead, waiting to deliver him to the airport for his trip to Laos to represent China at the upcoming East Asia Summit. This would be his fifth time attending the EAS, his second as foreign minister. The eighteen-nation convention was held annually to dialogue about political, environmental, and economic topics related to the stability and prosperity of East Asia. The original membership had only included East Asian countries, but the United States and Russian Federation had muscled their way into the mix in 2011 with dramatic effect. This summit would be no different than the last, Cheng presumed, with the U.S. contingent exerting their influence at every turn to challenge China's hegemony in setting the agenda and controlling regional policy.

Cheng paused momentarily beside the car to make sure he was seen, but the driver did not get out to load Cheng's bag and open the door, as was the normal practice. Instead, the trunk popped open while the driver remained in the driver's seat, not turning to even look at Cheng. Annoyed, Cheng rolled his suitcase to the rear of the vehicle, placed it in the trunk himself, and shut the lid. He then walked to the rear passenger-side door and let himself into the vehicle. Once he was settled into his seat, he looked toward the driver, who had yet to greet him, and that's when he noticed this H9 was not like the regular fleet of black cars that served the upper echelon of China's government ministries. This one had a tinted-glass divider between the passenger and driver compartments like one would find in a fancy limousine.

Or a police car, said the voice in his head.

Without a word from the driver, the H9 pulled away from Chaoyang Park Plaza and glided into Beijing traffic. Cheng was about to knock on the glass divider and tell the man to lower it, when his mobile phone chimed with a text message. He retrieved it from his pocket and glanced at the screen. The sender was his wife. She'd forwarded a hyperlink with no accompanying message. Normally, he would have ignored something like this, but his wife was a good partner. She understood the stress and difficulties of his job, and she had always supported him without complaint. She knew her place, and long ago had ceased calling or texting him during working hours, only contacting him with urgent matters that she was not equipped to deal with herself. Because this was out of character, he clicked on the link.

A web page opened on his mobile browser for the *Global Times*—China's international propaganda and daily tabloid newspaper. The headline article read "Foreign Minister under Investigation for Corruption and Infidelity," and was accompanied by the most unflattering picture of Cheng imaginable—a picture that was digitally altered. In the photograph, he was sitting at a lavish dinner table with his arm around a Caucasian woman's shoulders. His expensive suit looked disheveled and his eyes bloodshot—as if from a night of drinking. But worst of all was his laughing expression, which somehow looked maniacal and pathetic at the same time.

A wave of heat flushed his cheeks so hot that his head suddenly felt like it was mounted atop a stovepipe. The picture was an expertly constructed deepfake—his visage grafted onto another man's body. He knew this with absolute confidence because he'd never seen the woman in the picture before in his life, nor had he sat at that table. As foreign minister, he only drank alcohol in a ceremonial capacity, and he never, ever let himself get intoxicated. In his profession, drunkenness was an occupational hazard. The outrage he felt barely eclipsed the second- and third-place emotions of shock and humiliation. He'd been completely blindsided by this political assassination piece. And make no mistake, that's *exactly* what it was . . . a journalistic kill shot.

"I'm going to have your head on a platter, Guo," Cheng growled, calling out the paper's editor in chief by name. "How did you do it without me catching wind first?"

Then, as if someone had just poured a bucket of ice water down the stovepipe, his neck and chest went suddenly tight and cold with realization. The reason it had happened without warning was because the hit job had been sanctioned. Guo wouldn't authorize a story such as this in a vacuum; that's not how the *Global Times* operated. The paper was an instrument of the Party. To run this smear campaign, Guo would have had Li's blessing first.

Or be operating on his orders . . .

Cheng had never experienced the medical phenomenon known as hyperventilation, but felt pretty sure he was experiencing it now, as his breaths came in small, rapid, unproductive gasps. He felt the mobile phone slip from his grip and fall into the footwell. Panic overwhelmed him, and he lowered his head between his knees in primal reflex to try to catch his breath and stave off the wave of vertigo.

This is it . . . I'm out . . . Oh shit, God help me, I'm out. But why?

His mind went back to the warning his close friend Qin Hâiyû had given him about speaking his mind too freely about controversial things. Perhaps Qin had been right?

His phone chimed from the floor.

Head still between his knees, he glanced at the screen. It was another text from his wife. A three-word message that simply said: *Is this true?*

"It's not true," he muttered in between gasps. "It's not true . . ."

While he stared at it, the screen on the phone flickered once, then went black.

A moment later, the car braked to a hard stop. Both rear doors opened simultaneously and two men in black suits, neither of whom he recognized, got in, the one on Cheng's side shoving him forcefully toward the middle.

"What's going on? Who are you?" he said, the adrenaline dump magically restoring Cheng's breath and some measure of mental clarity.

The man on his left pulled a candy bar–sized white plastic cylinder from his suit coat pocket. Gripping it in one hand, the man jammed the bottom end of the tube into Cheng's thigh and pressed a button with his thumb. Cheng felt the needle from the auto-injector punch through his suit pants and puncture his flesh. A sharp burn followed as the delivery system injected him with whatever drug these men had been ordered to dose him with.

Wide-eyed with fear, Cheng met the eyes of the man holding the injector.

"Why?" he heard himself ask as his eyelids began to close.

The enforcer in the black suit answered, his hard, cold words echoing from very far away: "President Li thanks you for your service, Minister Cheng," the man said with a malevolent smile. "But your service is no longer needed . . ."

PART I

"All war is deception."

—Sun Tzu, *The Art of War*

1

Jack Ryan ground his teeth as he looked at the carnage inflicted on his Atlantic fleet. If only he could unleash a salvo instead of having to fire one damn shot at a time, then he might have a chance.

So much destruction. So much red . . .

If he didn't get a hit soon, the battle would be lost.

"C8," he said with certitude, looking up from the board at his daughter Katie, who sat opposite him at the dining room table.

She glanced down at her grid. "Miss."

"Seriously?" he said, tilting his head down to look at her over the top of the pair of reading glasses perched on his nose. "Check again."

"I don't need to check again, Dad, it's not rocket science. C8 is definitely a miss," she said with a grin. "My turn . . . J1."

He shoved his glasses back up on his nose and looked down at the gray plastic grid, where his fleet sat arranged in what he'd felt

11

certain to be an unbeatable naval configuration. Boy, how wrong he'd been. He picked up a little red peg, stuck it into the last remaining hole at the stern of the little plastic ship, and said, "You sunk my battleship."

"Woot, woot. USS *Missouri* heading to the bottom of the sea," she said, pumping her hands in the air overhead. "That makes four down and one to go. The only ship you have left is your submarine."

He narrowed his eyes playfully at her. "A submarine is all I'll need to finish you off. Fear the *Blackfish*."

"Nuh-uh, no way. *My* sub is the *Washington*. I called dibs when we started. You gotta pick a different boat. Yours can be the *Indiana*."

"Hello? Commander in chief, here," he said, raising his right hand and pointing his index finger at the crown of his head. "Last time I checked, that means I am, *literally*, in charge of the U.S. fleet. So, if I want to designate my flagship as the *Blackfish*, then there's nothing you can do about it, Lieutenant Commander."

"Sorry, Dennis," she said, wistfully looking down at her little gray submarine and referencing the real-life XO of the USS *Washington*. "I got outranked, which means you're the enemy now."

This wasn't the first time he'd heard his daughter mention Dennis Knepper, who she'd met while riding in the elite Virginia-class fast-attack sub during a near-fatal standoff against the rogue Russian submarine *Belgorod* a few months ago. Jack's Spidey sense told him there might be a budding connection between them, but he'd not heard any mention of them dating. Of course, the *Washington* had remained on station long after his daughter's return from the crisis in the Atlantic, so at best they'd be working on a long-distance thing. He made a mental note to ask Cathy about it. Katie and her mom were thick as thieves when it came to relationship gossip. But in the event his wife decided to be tight-lipped on the matter, as commander in chief he was privileged to know the USS *Washington*'s location at any given time . . . so keeping tabs on this potential suitor was not going to be a problem.

"What's that conniving look for?" she said, shaking him from his rumination.

"Oh, I was just thinking about how this game is nothing like naval warfare in real life. If only it could be so simple."

"If it was this simple, we wouldn't need any ship captains, or even sailors for that matter. I, for one, am glad that real life isn't controlled by a couple of callous, detached puppet masters sitting behind computer screens in the shadows. The strength of our military has always been rooted in leading from the front. It started with General Washington's tent in the Revolutionary War, and the tradition has carried on ever since."

He stared at her a moment and, feeling an upswelling of great pride, said, "In case I haven't told you lately, Katie, I love you. And I'm very proud of you. You're a fine naval officer, and one hell of an intelligence analyst."

Her cheeks went a little rosy at the comment. "Ahhh, thanks, Dad . . . But if you think flattery is going to save your fleet, then you've grossly misjudged your adversary."

They both chuckled at this and played the rest of the game out. He did manage to dispatch her aircraft carrier, but as expected, she showed him no quarter and soon found and sunk his submarine, ending their epic, father-daughter game of Battleship.

"Two out of three?" she asked as they both went to work pulling the white pegs out of the grid and depositing them in the molded containers on the sides of their iconic gray plastic clamshell game boards.

"Heck yes," he said, and momentarily stopped pulling pegs to refill their wineglasses.

"You know, sometimes I still can't believe you're the President of the United States. It's strange—almost like this is some fantasy we're making up and everyone else in the world is just going along with it. Do you ever feel that way?"

"All the time," he said with a self-deprecating smile.

"How do you make that feeling go away?"

"By trying to ground myself in the institution of the office."

"You mean like when you're sitting at the Resolute desk in the Oval?"

He nodded. "Yes, the physicality helps, but it's more the people running the government and military who I interact with every day who make it real. I see it in their eyes. Hear it in their words. Feel it from their presence. Everybody is looking to me with . . . expectation. Presidential expectation. They're counting on me to lead, and that makes it real. It's not a fantasy for them, I can tell you that."

"I've always wondered what that must feel like. I don't know how you do it, Dad. I would wilt under that kind of pressure."

"No, you wouldn't," he said with a confident shake of his head. "I've seen you under pressure, and wilting is not in your DNA."

"Thanks, but I don't know about that. Let's just say I'm glad that I'm not the Ryan in charge of representing the nation and making decisions that will affect the lives of millions. No thank you. I'll take my little office at ONI and a stack of reports to analyze and leave leading the country to you."

Your time will come, daughter, he thought, but did not say. *If there's one thing I've learned in this life, it's that Fate laughs at any man who thinks he has a choice over which battles he'll have to fight.*

Thankfully, for the moment, the seas were calm and the sailing smooth. In the months since the *Belgorod* incident, calamity had taken a sabbatical and the world had been granted a reprieve from global conflict, pandemics, terrorism, and natural disaster. He knew, of course, that this reprieve would be temporary—that the maligned forces of evil and entropy were already conspiring to unleash their next plot to bring chaos and death to the world. But tonight, the Ryan family was safe, and he would savor every second of this opportunity to sip wine and play Battleship with his daughter. Sure, he *could be* working. His presidential to-do list was a mile long and his inbox flooded with messages and briefs waiting to be read.

But the work could wait until tomorrow.

That was something else he'd learned over the years.

When a moment like this presented itself, sit back and enjoy it. Which was exactly what he intended to do.

2

XINHUAMEN GATE
MAIN ENTRANCE TO THE ZHONGNANHAI GOVERNMENT
  COMPOUND
174 CHANG'AN AVENUE
BEIJING, CHINA
0740 LOCAL TIME

Defense Minister Qin Hâiyû crossed his legs in the comfortable leather seat of the black Hongqi H9 luxury sedan, his index finger tapping on the center armrest. It was a bad habit he'd picked up to dissipate nervous energy, all the way back to his junior officer days in the PLA Navy. Even when he'd commanded the Luyang III–class destroyer *Guiyang* almost a decade ago, his left index finger would tap out its little cadence on the armrest of his captain's chair in the bridge. Back then, he'd thought the burden of commanding a warship was the pinnacle of pressure.

Oh, what I wouldn't give to return to those simpler days . . .

As a ship captain, the pitfalls of command were clear and identifiable. Running aground, collision at sea, personnel problems, failing to achieve or execute mission parameters . . . and so on. In

16

those days, he'd spent his time worrying about the people *beneath* him. Negligence, lapses in judgment, or mistakes borne from inexperience or poor communication—these were the problems that plagued commanding officers. Such things ended careers— but rarely *lives*. But this job, with its secret agendas and knives behind backs, was a viper's game and filled him with anxiety the likes of which he'd never thought possible.

Not anxiety . . . paranoia.

"A few more moments, Minister Qin," the driver said, looking at him in the rearview, interpreting his tension as concern for being late. "The traffic around the complex is heavier than usual."

"Thank you, Da," he said.

His thoughts went to Cheng Kai and the dubious fate of the minister of foreign affairs.

I warned him that his arrogance would be his downfall . . . but did he listen? No, he did not.

The last time Qin had visited privately with his friend, Cheng's family had been on vacation in Singapore, which had given the two men a rare opportunity to speak frankly and unencumbered. Cheng, who only drank in private, had imbibed heavily that night. As the two men got drunk, the conversation had shifted to President Li's growing desire to "reintegrate" Taiwan into China. Plumbed by alcohol, Cheng had let his true feelings be known on the matter:

"Li is a fool if he thinks the Americans will do nothing. General Su thought that a few years ago. President Ryan crushed those plans.

"We risk everything to gain little. Ten years ago, it made sense. But today, there is nothing that little island can do that we cannot. This is about Li's ego. Nothing more."

Unfortunately, the recent reelection of the troublemaking president of Taiwan had provided a megaphone for independence rhetoric on the global stage. And predictably, it had only amplified the almost manic obsession President Li harbored to reintegrate the island, even if that reintegration required military force. Devising a comprehensive military plan for reunification of the belligerent island had been Qin's professional charter since day one of his appointment as commander of the PLA Navy. Cheng believed it was Qin's plan that had prompted Li to select Qin as the replacement for Defense Minister Zhao Fu. Zhao Fu's "retirement" had been swift and sudden and taken *almost* everyone by surprise.

But not Cheng.

"Zhao agreed with me. Now is not the time for reunification," Cheng had said. *"We were working behind the scenes to build a coalition so we would have strength in numbers when confronting Li about the danger and hubris of his plan, but now Zhao is gone . . ."*

In the aftermath, the inner circle understood—although never discussed—that Zhao had been eliminated. Qin did not have history with his predecessor like he did with Cheng. Zhao had been Qin's boss, on paper, since Qin had been the head of the PLA Navy at the time, but Qin had personally interacted with him very little. And, frankly, Qin had not wanted to. Zhao had been a pompous ass. His disappearance, and later his announced retirement, had opened the position that Qin now filled.

Qin had been elated at the time.

If only I knew then what I know now . . .

Qin glanced at his watch. Plenty of time to make the meeting in Conference Room Number One in Zhongnanhai North. The very fact that such a meeting had been called on short notice, and at such an early hour, was cause enough for concern. Perhaps he would learn something of Cheng Kai's disappearance. Maybe the foreign minister had been the victim of some foreign plot and it had not been his reckless mouth that had led to his disappearance.

And then I would have much less to fear myself.

It was known that he and Cheng were friends and socialized often.

Could this connection be enough to spark Qin's own fall from favor?

For Qin, what had happened to Cheng felt like déjà vu. Just like Zhao, Cheng had been disappeared by President Li Jian Jun's secret police. Otherwise, there would have been immediate and frank discussions about the foreign minister's supposed corruption and infidelity. There would have been arguments about his fate and whether damage control was necessary. But none of that had happened. They'd had two cabinet meetings since Cheng's disappearance, and no mention of him had occurred, not even with the glaring diplomatic fallout at the East Asia Summit.

No, there was no mistake. Cheng Kai was gone.

Qin had warned him not to voice opposition to Li's designs on Taiwan, and now he was gone.

"You worry too much, Hǎiyû. I am a respected man whose voice matters . . ."

Qin chased away the memory from their last evening together and glanced out the window. As Da circled the black sedan around Taiye Lake, Qin saw the Hanyuan Temple, situated on the Yingtai Island in the "Southern Sea," the southern part of the ancient, man-made lake. That lake, and the one to the north, separated by a sliver of land now the site of the rebuilt Qínzhèng Diàn Hall, had been constructed in 1421 from the basic outline of the complex emerging during the Ming dynasty. It had been the de facto center of government since the Empress Dowager Cixi and, later, Prince Regent Chun had built residences there instead of inside the Forbidden City. Zhongnanhai had been the center of government ever since, first as the Republic of China under Yuan Shikai as the Beiyang government and later as the People's Republic under Mao Tse-tung. Most of the "real" government business occurred on the north side of the complex, on the lake known as the Northern Sea, where the Party chair and other government complexes now sat. The southern area was for show and entertaining visitors more than anything.

So much history.

Da maneuvered right, around the shore of the Northern Sea, slowing at an additional checkpoint, where they were quickly waved through, the uniformed guard snapping a sharp salute to the darkened windows, behind which Qin sat, tapping his left index finger on the armrest.

They were nearly there. Qin slipped his phone from his suit pocket and dialed his wife.

"Is everything well, Hâiyû?" she asked, subtle urgency and concern in her voice. "We are at the airport and about to board."

"Yes, yes, all is well," he said, a hint of a smile forming at the sound of her voice. "I simply miss you already. You and the girls."

He could almost see her relaxing at this. "We understand, my love. Your work is very important. Do you know if you will still be able to meet us?"

They had been planning this family vacation to the Maldives for months. They had a wonderful suite waiting at the Four Seasons Resort and a week to enjoy one another, but the call last night for this meeting had put a brake on the plans. Not knowing what might be happening, he'd insisted she take their daughters and go anyway, that he could meet them there. No reason for everyone to miss out because of his work commitments. His teenage girls would be living at home for only a short time more. Soon, his precious twin girls would graduate and be busy with their own lives.

"I very much hope so, Caiji," he said. "I am arriving at my meeting now and will let you know as soon as I can. I simply wanted to say I love you before you board your plane."

"We love you, too, *xīn gān*," Caiji said, sounding reassured.

Qin ended the call as the car arrived at the front of the headquarters for the State Council. His driver parked and then hustled around to open the door for him. Qin disliked the pampering, but it would be a sign of weakness to be seen here, of all places, opening his own door, and in any case, his young driver seemed to relish the opportunity to serve in such a way.

"Would you like me to wait for you, sir?" Da asked.

"Yes," he said, and the young man bowed. Normally he would send Da to have a coffee or something, but he had no idea how long this meeting might take. It was not unusual for Li to assemble everyone and share something that might have easily been sent in an unclassified email. The record for the shortest unscheduled meeting in conference room one was three and a half minutes.

Moments later he crossed the expansive room that served as a foyer of sorts, but had truly been transformed into a museum of artifacts dating back to the Ming dynasty, and entered through the floor-to-ceiling wooden doors into the room where State Council business was discussed. The seats around the expansive conference table were filled, with most of the attendees coming from offices within the complex. The deputy secretary general gave Qin a solemn nod, while Secretary General Xu Chao didn't even look up. There were no military officers present, which was not unusual, but their presence always served to make Qin feel less like a political impostor.

Each place at the table was marked by a leather binder, which many of the assembled were already perusing. In addition to the binder, everyone had a cup and saucer for hot tea.

All places save one.

The seat normally occupied by Cheng Kai had no folder and no tea service setting . . .

"We are assembled?" said President Li Jian Jun as he entered from the door to Qin's left.

Clearly, Li had been waiting to make his entrance only once Qin arrived, though a glance at the clock on the far wall validated that Qin had arrived a full six minutes early. Qin quickly took his seat and opened the leather folder as Li stopped behind his own chair, but remained standing. Qin fought the sudden urge to glance again at the empty seat. He stared a moment at the intimately familiar document inside the folder—a document he had prepared—then looked up, hoping the shock he felt was not evident on his face.

Operation Sea Serpent: Reunification of Taiwan

Now I know why Cheng is not here, and why I will never see my friend again . . .

"Gentlemen," Li began, "we are quite fortunate that our current minister of national defense, Admiral Qin Hâiyû, is not only an expert on naval and marine operations but is the architect of the plan you see in front of you. This is a plan that has been in evolution, has in fact evolved as often as the changing winds of the South China Sea, as the threats to our sovereign claim have evolved—as has the threat to our security. Minister Qin, in the interest of brevity, give us a five-minute overview of this battle plan."

"Of course, Mr. President," Qin said.

He rose, and in general terms outlined the plan in the nearly one-hundred-page document in the folder. He did not need to glance through the pages, of course. The operation was like a child of his own, one that had started as a flirtation, then became a wish, and over the last two years had grown into something he was quite proud of. But it was a theoretical plan only, born of the intersection of mandates from his superiors and the intellectual curiosity of a man who'd dedicated his life to naval warfare. It was a war game—one that he had, in his mind, waged time and time again into something that now was an operational plan that he believed to be not only possible but almost guaranteed to be successful.

If one measured success as simply the achievement of an objective.

Taking Taiwan was like taking a hill in a war zone—given enough resources and the desire to succeed, any stronghold could be taken. But stratagems rarely contemplated the aftermath. There was risk in the *having*, not only in the taking. Nowhere was this more true than in the reunification of Taiwan by force. Could China take Taiwan? Yes, of course. Could they hold it? Almost certainly. Would there be other costs to the People's Republic of China?

Without a doubt . . .

Such was the conversation he'd had with Cheng, the last time he'd seen him alive. It had been Cheng's intention to speak his mind to the president.

It had been Qin's advice that he hold his tongue.

He felt his eyes tick over to the empty seat and hoped the look went unnoticed.

"It is a brilliant plan, and one that you can see is absolutely achievable," President Li said when he'd finished, and Qin gave a humble bow.

There were murmurs around the table.

"Who has questions for our minister of defense?" Li posed, finally pulling out his own, much taller chair and taking a seat, crossing his legs at the ankle, and pouring some tea from the pot beside his cup.

"That we can defeat the traitorous ROC forces of Taiwan is not in doubt, I should think," Secretary General Xu said, looking at Qin with a critical eye. "But surely this plan takes into account an inevitable American response, Minister Qin?"

"It does," Qin admitted, unwilling to look over at Li for fear his eyes would betray how deep this concern was. "After war-gaming this scenario out many times, it is our conclusion that American and NATO forces, but certainly the American fleet, would move assets into the area as a show of force—"

"Sabre-rattling, nothing more," Li interrupted, sipping his tea. "Minister Qin is the expert on military operations, but it is my job to estimate the will of our enemies. The Americans are weary of war. After two decades of war against terrorism, the American people have no appetite for more military conflict. Look at their willingness to give up Crimea to our Russian friends, rather than actually *using* the power they seem willing to project. President Ryan is a worthy opponent, but he rules at the whim of his people and they will never support military action that would risk war with a nation as mighty as ours."

The secretary general now gave Qin a softer look.

"Is it your estimate that the Americans would give up Taiwan without firing a shot of their own?"

"Possibly," Qin said, couching his words, the empty seat across from him shouting its warning. "But there is danger in even a limited engagement. We would expect a very short-term conflict with United States naval forces within the South China Sea, if only due to the inherent dangers of escalation when our forces operate in very close proximity. However, as our president has said, we do not believe that the Americans would risk an all-out war. The strength of this plan is the speed with which it unfolds. By the time the Americans arrive at the decision point of if and how to intervene, the Taiwan islands would all be in the hands of our forces. Thus, intervention means an offensive attack against China, which we do not believe the Americans would have the stomach for."

But this says nothing of the enormous geopolitical pressure they could exert if they had the sympathy of the world. It could be a cata-strophic blow politically and, more immediately paralyzing, econom-ically.

As he'd discussed with Kai, it was a mistake to underestimate the will of the Americans if blood had been spilled. They had a country song in the States that painted the Americans as a big dog who bit if you rattled his cage.

This, he believed, was a true metaphor.

The secretary general leaned back and studied him.

"So, we would expect no direct resistance from the American forces," Xu pressed.

Qin chose his words carefully. While this was all just a theo-retical war-gaming plan, it was best to not fill this room with too much confidence in the plan, lest it become a reality. By the same hand, he saw what could happen when you went against the view of the president, evidenced by that damn empty chair.

"It is very possible that, while the attack on the island would be bloody indeed, no shots with the Americans would be directly exchanged. Our absolute worst-case scenario would be very brief military conflict at sea in the region, possibly resulting in damage to the American fleet."

"Damage?" the secretary general pressed.

Qin clenched his jaw, but there was no hiding it. Hell, the BDEs, or battle damage estimates, were in the damn document if they chose to read the whole thing.

"At the extreme, there could be the loss of an American naval vessel," Qin said. In fact, the BDE estimated this to be a real possibility and that, in fact, the most likely loss would be an American aircraft carrier. But there was no need for him to press this point and upset President Li. No need, because the assembled leaders would read it for themselves. It was all clearly outlined in the extensive and sobering battle damage estimates in the paper they each had in front of them.

Let the numbers speak for themselves . . . As many as two to five thousand Americans could perish.

Secretary Xu's eyes widened a moment, but then he got the reaction under control before glancing at the president and giving him a nod.

"I see," he said.

"And that is an absolute worst-case estimate," Li said with a smile.

"You are to be congratulated, Minister Qin," the deputy secretary general said with a bow of his head and a sympathetic look. "It sounds like your operational plan is a tremendous tool to have in our toolbox."

"Thank you, Mr. Deputy Secretary," Qin said.

"Or perhaps more," President Li said, leaning in and placing his teacup on the table. Qin felt his pulse pounding in his temple. "Operation Sea Serpent is a large-scale naval and Marine landing-force exercise taking place in just two weeks. This is an exercise planned for some time, and one that has been leaked intentionally to the American intelligence apparatus."

"Why?" the deputy secretary asked, then blushed at the misstep of interrupting the president. For Li's part, he ignored the overstep and instead smiled at the deputy secretary. "I am glad you asked," he said. "For the better part of two years, we have harassed the American Navy and conducted frequent, large-scale, and aggressive exercises. The result has been that the United States Navy has become numb to such prodding, and therefore has become complacent. Despite our leaking information about Sea Serpent, we have seen no increase in naval activity or hints about what they like to call 'force projection.' Sea Serpent, it would seem, will go ahead unchallenged by the Americans."

Qin felt a knot form in the pit of his stomach.

"Minister Qin, can you provide for us what type of Marine and naval presence would need to participate in this exercise, this Operation Sea Serpent, were it to be modified into the execution of the real Operation Sea Serpent—the operation you created to defeat the Taiwan forces and reunify Taiwan to the homeland? I would like to see a summary of this as soon as possible."

"Of course, Mr. President," Qin said, bowing and then returning to his seat.

"Are you suggesting that we intend to invade Taiwan in two weeks?" Xu asked gently.

"I am suggesting that, eventually, the timing will be such that we can reclaim the island of Taiwan and reunite the patriots living there with the homeland. We can reclaim our rights to the strategic position of the island in the South China Sea. We can reclaim our rights to the rich minerals available and the technology production that competes now with our own. Taiwan has always been a part of China. I want us to be prepared for that opportunity, whenever it might come along."

"I will provide you with my assessment as soon as possible, Mr. President," Qin said.

"Tomorrow," Li said, reaching again for his tea. "You were made minister because you bring extreme value and experience to this position, which has been lacking. I assume you can brief us on these details by tomorrow morning, say . . . ten o'clock?"

"Of course," Qin said, but his mind went to the Chinese 055-class destroyer *Lhasa*, operating this very moment in the northern part of the Strait of Taiwan. A brilliant and deadly modern warship.

"It will be my honor, Mr. President," Qin said.

"Wonderful," Li said, and was on his feet already. "Then we are adjourned until tomorrow at ten a.m."

Qin rose, as they all did, and watched him go, tasting bile in the back of his throat.

President Li couldn't possibly be considering this for real. President Ryan would never fail to respond to threats against his people. Qin's worst-case BDE showed the loss of multiple aircraft, damage to several American vessels, and the potential loss of an American aircraft carrier from the Seventh Fleet in the ensuing naval showdown.

More than five thousand American lives.

Qin had no doubt that the Americans, most especially with President Ryan at the helm, would indeed go to war over such a loss.

The impact to China would be immeasurable and would set back their geopolitical and economic gains by decades.

Surely someone, tomorrow perhaps, would say something.

He glanced again at the empty chair where his friend once sat.

What am I prepared to do for my country and my family?

Mind reeling, he followed the others out of the conference room and headed across the foyer.

The artifacts of the warrior nation they had once been, a warrior nation many would argue fell from its own hubris, called out to him as he walked, shouting warnings.

How could he agree to be the instrument of such a fall?

3

OFFICE OF NAVAL INTELLIGENCE (ONI)
NATIONAL MARITIME INTELLIGENCE CENTER (NMIC)
4251 SUITLAND ROAD, WASHINGTON, D.C.
0847 LOCAL TIME

Katie Ryan's new office at ONI looked as Spartan as the day she'd moved in two months ago. She'd fully intended on tastefully decorating the space and making it her own, but like so many things in her life that she'd *fully intended* on doing, it hadn't happened. At present, her office had only two decorations. The first was a framed 8×10-inch photo of the Ryan family together at Christmas from three years ago, which was the last time they'd all been together in the same place at the same time. The second was an orchid that had arrived just after she'd moved in with a personal note from retired CIA officer Matthew Reilly.

Reilly had been hugely instrumental in helping her crack the *Belgorod* case—*if you could call it that*—and she credited the sentimental spook with helping her understand and outwit the rogue Russian submarine commander behind the plot. The handwritten note, which she'd kept, had simply read:

30

Thank you for helping me find peace.
I can finally sleep at night.
M. R.

The orchid, a yellow-petaled phalaenopsis, aka moth orchid, had been in bloom when it arrived—with six flowers on one stem and five on the other. She'd watched a YouTube video on how to care for orchids and was following the guidance to the letter. Josie, as she'd instantly decided to name the plant for some reason, was starting to lose her blooms now, but Katie had been assured this was normal and that with proper care it would rebloom up to several times a year. According to Reilly, the key was not over-watering and he recommended putting an ice cube in the pot every other day instead of watering as usual. Katie had been doing just that, religiously, with what appeared to be success. At least, she'd not killed the thing *yet*. Katie found herself looking at the little plant often and felt like Josie's adopted mom now.

The rest of her mementos from the glorified cube she worked out of before her promotion and transfer to the Brooks Center at ONI sat in a box in the corner. After "her" success during the operations to find and stop the madman at the helm of the *Belgorod*—something she suspected was little more than her being in the right place at the right time—Katie had worried her next billet would be to take on more responsibility at SWORD. While she felt like she'd made contributions working at the Submarine Warfare Operations Research Division, she was not a submariner or an undersea warfare expert. But, like all Ryans, she prided herself on rising to meet challenges rather than finding excuses to shirk them. She would swim a mile in whatever fins the Navy needed her to wear and not complain.

That's when fate threw her a curveball she didn't see coming. The director of naval intelligence, or "little DNI" as the insiders called the three-star in charge of all the Navy's intelligence programs, to differentiate him from the director of national intelligence, moved Captain Ferguson from the Nimitz Warfare Analysis Center over to lead the Brooks Center—the office at ONI involved in processing human and signals intelligence pertaining to global maritime threats. When Ferguson had offered to take her with him, she'd said yes.

Brooks was definitely her jam.

And now she had an office appropriate for a lieutenant commander. She hadn't particularly minded working in a cube, but multiple times a day she'd found herself wishing for a door so she could shut out the din and think clearly. Ironically, now that she had a door, she couldn't stand having it closed. On the few occasions that she had shut it, she'd felt so disconnected from the energy of the building and her peers that she'd gotten up and propped it open.

Humans are strange creatures.

She tapped her trackpad to wake up her computer, logged in, and checked messages.

The first one made her smile broadly. It was from the low-side email account of one Dennis Knepper, naval officer, submariner, and current XO of the USS *Washington*, known to her crew as the *Blackfish*.

> Hi. Wanted to say happy day in advance. I know you'll be
> celebrating two weeks from today. I'll be raising a glass
> with you!
> DK

She chuckled, and did her own "decryption" of the "coded" message. Ever since they'd shared a dinner in Spain, Dennis had messaged whenever he could, which was infrequently at best for a submarine officer. They'd decided they would celebrate his return to Norfolk at the end of the deployment and she'd told him she was looking forward to that day.

His message was pretty clear.

The *Blackfish* would be home two weeks from today and, apparently, he had not gotten cold feet about a real date.

> That will be a happy day indeed! Looking forward to it
> very much.
> KR

Next, she scanned the classified and unclassified intelligence feeds, stopping when a *non*-update entry caught her eye:

> Chinese Minister of Foreign Affairs Cheng Kai whereabouts
> remain unknown. Last observed fifteen days ago before
> Cheng failed to appear at the East Asia Summit in Laos . . .

Intrigued, she clicked to expand the entry:

> China's Foreign Affairs Ministry did not release a
> statement. When addressing reporters at the summit, the
> deputy minister who attended in Cheng's stead stated that
> Cheng's absence was due to unspecified health problems.
> However, the *Global Times* ran a piece the same day
> claiming that Cheng was under investigation for corruption
> and infidelity.

Cheng's first two years in the five-year post have been characterized by DOS as an escalation rather than a departure from his predecessor's practices. Cheng's more aggressive "wolf warrior" style of diplomacy was believed to be favored by President Li. Lack of details as to Cheng's whereabouts has fueled speculation of an unexpected falling-out with President Li or Chinese Communist Party leadership that may have arisen over recent rhetoric concerning Taiwanese reunification and maritime policies governing naval activity in the South China Sea.

Cheng's duties have been taken over by the deputy foreign minister, Lu Jing. It is rumored that Cheng's predecessor, Yang Xi, who has been serving as leader of the CCP's Foreign Affairs Commission, will return to run the Ministry. Yang held the foreign minister role from 2016 to 2021.

Katie leaned back in her task chair and spun around in a circle, thinking . . .

During her tenure at SWORD she'd closely monitored the Chinese submarine community, but it had not been her charter to track East Asian geopolitics beyond their relevance to the western Pacific theater of maritime operations. That said, a good analyst doesn't stick her head in the sand when it comes to news and current events. Katie was no ostrich. She liked having her finger on the pulse of world events. This was not the first time she'd heard of someone "disappearing" from the upper echelon of the Chinese political machine.

"Oh, I see how it works," said the familiar voice of her enlisted intelligence specialist, IS2 Pettigrew, from her open office doorway. "They give you an office, and then you get to pretend you're riding a merry-go-round all day. Must be nice."

Using her foot, she abruptly stopped her spinning chair so she was facing him. Pettigrew, who insisted that everyone call him "Bubba," laughed and shook his head, clearly enjoying himself at her expense. She smiled back as she tried to think of a clever comeback, because smack talk—not nuclear power or jet fuel—was the stuff that powered the U.S. Navy.

"That's right," she said. "And you should know that if you're going to interrupt my ride, you better come bearing a funnel cake, or a snow cone, or some other tasty treat to get yourself back on my good side, because your southern charm and goofy face isn't going to cut it."

At this, they both chuckled, and she waved him into her office.

He took a couple of steps past the threshold and stopped.

"What's on your mind?" she asked, gesturing to the chair opposite her desk.

"I'm not here to talk shop, ma'am," he said, remaining standing. "I was wondering if it would be all right if I left early this afternoon. Cindy booked one of them 3D ultrasound things and I'd like to go. They say we'll be able to see what the little man looks like. I figured that was probably a good idea . . . That way, if he looks like me, we can start the paperwork for a return or an exchange at the hospital."

The last bit got her laughing so hard she choked on her saliva.

"You gonna be all right there, boss? I ain't never seen your face turn that shade of red before," he added, which only made things worse.

Finally able to breathe after a few gasps, she said, "You made me laugh so hard I choked on my own spit."

"Yeah, we Pettigrews tend to have that effect on people."

"The answer is yes, you absolutely can punch out early, but only if you promise to text me a picture of the ultrasound screen. I can't wait to see baby Bubba," she said.

"Roger that, but if he's ugly, don't say I didn't warn you."

"He's going to be beautiful," she said, feeling a warm glow just thinking about Bubba holding his soon-to-be-born son.

"Thank you," he said and turned to leave.

"Hold up a second," she said, stopping him. "I want to get your opinion on something."

"Sure, fire away."

"What do you know about the mysterious rash of Chinese elites disappearing without warning or explanation?"

He considered the question a moment, then said, "Well, I'm no China expert, but I don't think there's any mystery here that common sense can't solve."

"What do you mean by that?"

"They're Communists, ma'am. It ain't no different than Russia during the Cold War. In Russia, if you pissed off the wrong person, then the next day the KGB would show up and haul your ass off to the gulag. I think it's pretty much the same thing with China today. It don't matter if you're a billionaire or an admiral, the Party doesn't tolerate dissension in the ranks."

She turned her laptop screen to face him. "They just disappeared the minister of foreign affairs two weeks ago, and they weren't shy about it, either. It happened the morning before the East Asia Summit in Laos, which is arguably the most important political economic event for China of the year."

Pettigrew nodded. "I wonder what he did?"

"Me too," she said, her mind churning through what-if scenarios.

"Oh no . . ."

"Oh no, what?"

"I know that look," he said.

"What look?"

"The look that means you're not going to let this go until you know what happened to this dude and why. Last time I saw that look I had to fly on a death trap that landed me on an aircraft carrier facing off with the Russian Navy . . ."

She smiled at him.

"Boss, in case you've forgotten, we work for the Office of *Naval* Intelligence, not the State Department. I do not see the word 'Navy' or 'Naval' anywhere in this man's title, which means this definitely falls outside our wheelhouse."

"I know, but I'm curious." She turned her computer back so she could see the screen. "It says here: 'Lack of details as to Cheng's whereabouts has fueled speculation of an unexpected falling-out with President Li or Communist Party leadership that may have arisen over recent rhetoric concerning Taiwanese reunification and maritime policies governing naval activity in the South China Sea' . . . Did you catch that last bit? 'Maritime policies' and 'naval activity.' So, I have to disagree with you, Bubba. Cheng's disappearance could very much be related to something that pertains to this office."

"They have people who are paid to look into this, ma'am. Those people are called case officers, and they work at the CIA."

She stared at him blankly.

"You're going to pull on this thread anyway, ain't ya?" he said.

"Yep." She waved goodbye to him with just her fingers. "Have fun at the ultrasound."

Shaking his head, he turned to leave.

"And don't forget to send me a screenshot of the baby," she called after him. "That's an order, Bubba."

4

Qin paced back and forth in the living room of the home that his family had occupied for only the last sixty-seven days. It was modern and well-appointed and not at all his taste, and while it didn't yet feel like home, it did feel familial. Perhaps because, despite the work he had to do to prepare for his meeting tomorrow morning, his mind was fixated on his family. Right now, Caiji and their twin daughters, Diedie and Beiye, were enjoying a lovely dinner at the Four Seasons in the Maldives.

Qin wondered who was in more danger in the coming days.

Me or them?

Should he decide to challenge President Li, it would not only be his life in jeopardy. But if he did nothing and the president invaded Taiwan, tens of thousands would pay the price.

And not just those serving in the PLA, but also the civilians, who could suffer decades of social and economic impact. The global reaction to such a brazen move was impossible to know

38

with certainty. The worst-case scenario would have China follow North Korea into hermit nation status. Its people isolated, impoverished, and miserable because of their leader's arrogance.

"What is wrong with me?" he asked aloud of his reflection in the floor-to-ceiling window. He allowed himself a slight smile. He'd not been alone with President Li in conference room one this morning. He'd been with a half dozen others, including the secretary general and his deputy, the deputy foreign affairs minister, who unsurprisingly had seemed shaken, and senior policy and military advisors. Yes, he'd been reluctant to share the potential costs of Operation Sea Serpent during his summary, distracted by the glaring absence of Kai, but he didn't need to, right? Each member of the meeting had a nearly one-hundred-page detailed briefing on the war-gamed operation and each would be poring over it today and tonight in preparation for the meeting tomorrow. Li himself would refresh his memory by reading through it, surely. They would read for themselves the battle damage estimates, but even more, there were pages and pages of follow-up data, brainstorming out the American and global reaction to a military action. Li would see for himself, and if not, others would find a way to help him concede that the risks were too great.

Qin strode to the dining room table and recovered the leather folder from his briefcase. Then he poured himself a short glass of Kweichow Moutai Baijiu, sat at the table, and opened the folder. He wanted to review the details of the BDEs, but also reassess how conservative his team had been in estimating the post-invasion military response. He knew they had sanitized much of the projected geopolitical fallout, knowing that it was best to stay in their lane and focus on military-specific projections.

He skimmed through the document, looking for the section

titled "Projected Foreign Military Response," which fell right after the section on estimations of not only the Taiwan ROC troop strengths and assets but willingness to engage. He skimmed the pages, sipping his drink, then got to the end, his mouth dropping open. He set his drink down with a trembling hand and whispered, "Oh my God."

This was not the document he had authored.

The details of the operational plan, from the taking of Kinmen Island to the covert insertion of PLA special operations forces onto Penghu, to the subsequent Marine landing after missile and antiaircraft had been neutralized by the PLA special operators were just as he remembered. Ship placements, aircraft deployments supporting the ground and amphibious invasions, the naval blockade to the north and south—all were as he'd written.

But the section on BDEs had been heavily edited. Not only were the new casualty numbers grossly below his estimates, but the three scenarios for foreign military engagement had been massively diluted.

In fact, they were now more of a childish fantasy.

The worst-case estimate was now written to be damage to an American vessel due to an inadvertent collision at sea. The section on military and geopolitical response had been removed completely.

But why?

Because Li intends for Operation Sea Serpent to be an exercise in name only.

Qin closed the folder and reached for his drink. He drained the glass, then refilled it from the bottle.

Li's words from that morning came back to him: "*It is my job to estimate the will of our enemies.*"

"You arrogant ass . . ." he growled.

Li was flat-out wrong to underestimate the American response and their will to defend Taiwan. Yes, Americans were lazy and entitled. But the one thing, throughout history, that brought Americans together was a common enemy. They had lost three thousand in a terror attack on 9/11, and had as a nation rallied behind a war in two countries that had lasted two decades. What would they do if they lost five thousand sailors in the Pacific when Li invaded Taiwan?

They would wage war.

Even against the nation of China, they would send their sons and daughters into battle. And they would wage a political war that would ostracize China from the global community. And they would wage an economic war, which would ravage the Chinese people, whose lives depended completely on world commerce.

There was no way that Qin could let that happen. The damage to the country he loved was inevitable, but President Li refused to see that. He'd become so fixated on reunification that he believed his legacy depended on it. He was going to make it happen, BDEs be damned.

He slammed the glass on the table hard enough he was shocked it didn't shatter. Then he rose and walked over to the adjoining living room to pace in front of the couch.

The only person with the authority to alter and edit my report is Li himself. Which means he did it to deceive the other ministers and Party leadership. He's going to force me to lie and validate the erroneous projections.

Now there would be no paper trail showing that Qin had predicted that much more dire outcomes were possible from a reunification campaign. By altering the report, Li had laid the groundwork to blame Qin for any "unforeseen" disaster or negative outcome. Qin would be the scapegoat, his life's work ruined.

But what could he do? He was stuck between two choices that both ended badly. He knew the right thing to do was to stop this war before it began, but the cost to him personally would be swift, severe, and irreversible. Had Kai not tried to talk sense into Li on this very topic? And look what had happened to him.

But how can I do nothing?

He dropped onto the low sofa—stately and modern, but not terribly comfortable—and leaned forward, his face in his hands. Qin was a man who loved his country, loved it dearly, and had dedicated his life to service. He had, from the first day he proudly donned his Navy uniform at the Academy, gladly taken on the risk of losing his life for China and its people.

But was he willing to sacrifice Caiji, Diedie, and Beiye as readily?

And what would that sacrifice even accomplish?

"I can't do *nothing*," he mumbled. "I simply can't let Li plunge us into war, no matter the value of Taiwan."

The truth was, he did believe that Taiwan should be part of China, that the Chinese people deserved the security and economic advantages that the island held. He also believed that being part of China was best for their brothers and sisters in Taiwan, whom had fallen prey to the propaganda and false promises of the West. But in the end, the advantages of reintegrating Taiwan did not nearly rise to the risks of military action that would result in the deaths of Chinese on both sides of the conflict.

I am thinking in circles. What am I to do? There is only one best answer to any problem. How can I serve both my family and China at the same time?

He sighed and stared out the living room window into the neatly manicured garden out back.

What if the Americans knew of the plan? What if they knew an invasion was imminent?

The thought felt filthy in his mind. What he was considering was treason against the nation he loved and had sworn to protect.

But what if it stopped a war that would destroy China? Is that not noble, even patriotic?

Still, the risks were incredible. If he were discovered, he would be executed swiftly and publicly. If he stood up to Li and voiced his concern, then he might only be sent to a reeducation camp. Life as they knew it would be over, but not their literal lives, right?

In his mind, he pictured again Minister Kai's empty seat. His friend and colleague had not been sent to a reeducation camp. He was certain of that.

Risking his own life was one thing, but his family should not have to pay for his decision.

I could warn them.

Long ago, Caiji and he had set up their own secret, coded language for when someone might be listening in on a call. At first it was to protect their intimacy, but as Chinese politics and ambitions had evolved and changed, so had their secret language. He could text her to call him from the "other" phone. Caiji and the girls could slip away from the Maldives and travel somewhere obscure and safe.

But as a senior cabinet member, Qin and his family rated a security detail. This was for their protection, of course, but now it was a double-edged sword. If they tried to disappear and were detected, how would they explain things? And whatever he wanted to do next would be tainted. No, it was too risky for the girls, not without some sort of exit plan.

And what does such an exit plan mean that I am considering?

He shook the thought away.

I am no traitor. I just need more time to think . . .

At the Academy, his last-year roommate was a brilliant young man named Dong Jun. Jun had been his closest friend for many years, a friendship that had stood up despite their different paths—Qin pursuing a life at sea as a surface warfare officer and Jun serving China in the naval intelligence command. While they'd not stayed in touch nearly as much as either would like, especially now that Dong Jun was an executive-level leader at the MSS, they still had dinner or drinks a few times a year.

Dong Jun was back in Beijing, after a three-year tour in Shanghai.

Qin found his mind pulled to the memory of a cryptic conversation they'd had about the infamous spy that everyone called "the Spider." The Spider was said to be a Western agent with connections deep into not only the Central Committee but also the MSS itself. Legend had it that she was a woman who had helped the West extract not only numerous state secrets but on more than one occasion citizens who had betrayed the CCP and escaped alongside those secrets, some to America. He'd heard many conflicting stories. Some said the Spider was not Chinese at all, but an American CIA operations officer who'd lived in Beijing for decades undetected. Others said that she was a fiction invented by the MSS to justify the massive mole hunt and purge of 2013. He'd ribbed his friend, after a few drinks, about the legend that it seemed the MSS could never quite bury and the mysterious woman that had bested them, and Jun had just grinned.

But if the Spider was real, could she be a conduit for him to warn the Americans?

Maybe this is the answer . . .

He glanced at the clock on the mantel—not even seven o'clock.

It was too early to call the girls, whose voices he suddenly, almost desperately, needed to hear. They would still be at dinner. If he called now, Caiji would worry for sure. *I should let her call me at the regular time.* But it was not too early to make *another* call. He fetched his phone from where he'd left it on the kitchen counter, scrolled through his contacts, and tapped the call button.

Dong Jun picked up on the second ring.

"How is it that I am finally hearing from you, old friend? Are you not too busy for a lowly bureaucrat such as myself?"

Qin closed his eyes and embraced the warmth of the familiar voice.

"Ah, how I have missed your bullshit, Jun. And anyway, I hear you are the one keeping us safe at night, with your James Bond exploits."

"If only it were so, like in the movies," Dong Jun said through a laugh. "Then I would now be sipping a drink in a tuxedo, a beautiful girl in my lap."

Qin chuckled at that. He'd been sad when he'd heard about Jun's divorce. Theirs was a difficult life of service, and not every woman was as strong and independent as Caiji.

"We must catch up, my friend."

"Any time," Jun said.

"How about tonight?" Qin asked.

"Tonight?" Jun said, surprise and concern in his voice.

"It has been too long," Qin said, "Caiji and the girls are in the Maldives, and I'm a terrible cook."

"In that case," Jun said, now clearly reading between the lines, "how about that restaurant in Langfang you like so much?" Jun knew this was where Qin liked to go when there was something important—and private—to discuss.

"That would be the ideal place," Qin confirmed.

"Great," the Chinese spy said after a moment. "Eight o'clock?"

"Perfect," Qin said.

"I will see you there," Jun said, and the line went dead.

Qin set the phone beside him on the uncomfortable couch. Perhaps he was driving himself mad for nothing. But if nothing else, a conversation with his old friend might set his mind at ease. For any invasion of Taiwan, the MSS would have advance knowledge. But if Jun confirmed his worst fears . . .

Then I will have to act.

He turned his attention to the clock on the wall and tapped his finger in cadence with the second hand as he waited impatiently for Caiji's call. Hopefully, she would call promptly at seven, giving him just enough time to talk to his girls before leaving for one of the riskiest dinner conversations of his life.

5

Katie stepped into the McLean Family Restaurant, took off her cover, and scanned the tables for her contact. She was wearing her "guacamoles" so . . . he wouldn't have any problem spotting her. The same could not be said in reverse. The restaurant was packed, with ninety percent of the patrons middle-aged or older.

Heavy on the *older.*

A wave from a white-haired man with a goatee and eyeglasses sitting in the back corner booth along the left wall caught her attention.

She didn't miss the eye roll that came with it, either.

Larry Sexton, one of the CIA's senior China experts, had been recommended as "the guy you want to talk to" by Captain Ferguson. The CIA man sat with his back to the wall, so he had a view of the entire restaurant. Given her family history and pedigree, this tactical approach to restaurant seat selection was something

Katie was intimately familiar with. Jack Junior had it so bad he wouldn't be able to make it through the meal with his back to the entire restaurant like she would be forced to do for this lunch.

But she wasn't there yet.

Maybe someday, but hopefully not.

She walked up to the table and smiled at him. "Katie Ryan."

"Larry," he said and stuck out a hand without rising from his seat. She shook his hand before sitting down in the cozy diner booth with its maroon-colored Formica table.

She set her cover on the seat cushion beside her left thigh and shifted her weight to get comfortable. "Thanks for meeting me on such short notice."

"Like I had a choice," he said, and followed it up with a too-late chuckle.

"What's that supposed to mean?" she said, her brain-to-mouth filter down for maintenance today.

"You're the President's daughter—what am I supposed to say? No?" he said with a laugh, but this time the sentiment was real.

"I'm also a naval officer and intelligence analyst at ONI," she said, feeling her face flush with irritation, "so I would think that counts for something?"

"Ahhh, I'm sorry. I can be a real pill until I'm sufficiently caffeinated. Feel free to ignore fifty percent of the things that come out of my mouth. That's what my wife does, and apparently it works for her, because we've been married thirty-five years."

She appreciated the walk back and self-deprecating apology. Then she made a show of glancing at her watch. "It's after noon, Larry. Are you saying you wait until lunch to have your first cup of coffee of the day? That's discipline."

"Hell, no. Details, Ryan, details. You gotta pay attention to the words. I said *sufficiently* caffeinated. This is my fourth cup of coffee . . . One more and I'll be sociable."

A male server wearing a white apron appeared table side. "Are you ready to order?"

"I'll have the eggs Benedict with extra hollandaise sauce," Sexton said, not even bothering to give her a chance to weigh in or look at the menu.

Adapt and overcome, her big brother's voice said in her brain with a mocking laugh.

"Breakfast all day, every day—that's why I love this place," Sexton said as Katie hastily scanned the laminated menu. "I recommend the eggs Benedict, obviously, but the pancakes are good here, too."

"Mm-hmm," she said, scanning for something *not* that. "I'll have the Greek salad with grilled chicken, and a glass of water."

The server finished jotting their order down in a notepad and left.

"Should've got the pancakes," her lunch companion said with a judgmental smile. His eyeglasses had slid halfway down his nose, but instead of pushing them back up, he just looked at her with judgment over the top of the frames.

"Yeah, well, I'm not eight," she said, leaning into the strange dynamic that had quickly developed between them.

"Fair enough," he said. Then getting straight to the point he asked, "So, what are we here to talk about, Commander?"

"I wanted to pick your brain about Cheng Kai, the Chinese minister of foreign affairs who disappeared two weeks ago."

"What specifically do you want to know?" he said, still not pushing his glasses up, which was beginning to annoy her.

"What do you think happened to him?"

The CIA man's lips curled up at the corners just a touch. "Probably been sent on an all-expenses-paid vacation to Beijing's finest 'reeducation' resort and spa."

"Is that real? Do such places really exist?"

He shot her a look that she translated to *Oh, please, what rock have you been living under?*

"Absolutely they do. They've spent over a hundred million dollars building detention and reeducation centers all across Xinjiang province alone."

"But those are for the Chinese Uyghurs and Kazakhs," she said. "Cheng was their foreign minister, for God's sake."

"Which makes his offense even more egregious in the eyes of the president and Party. Religious dissident, cultural dissident, political dissident—do you really think the distinction matters? 'Dissident' is the common denominator. In China, you either drink and promote the Kool-Aid or you're labeled a troublemaker, and the one thing they don't tolerate is troublemakers."

"Okay, I hear you, but from all the research I've done, Cheng was the furthest thing imaginable from a troublemaker. He was a loyal, competent, and effective foot soldier for the Party his entire career. As foreign minister, he spoke directly for President Li. You don't put a dissident in charge of your country's foreign policy."

"You're absolutely right, Commander," Sexton said. "So, the question we need to be asking is what could Cheng have done or said that was so egregious that it would get him removed from his post and punished? In my opinion, the answer is simple . . . he must have committed the number one cardinal sin in China."

"And what's that?"

"He broke rank and defied either the Party or the president," the CIA man said. He sat back and she thought he would fix his glasses, but he didn't. "Most likely the latter."

Her glass of water arrived and she took a much needed sip before lowering her voice and asking, "Do you think he's still alive?"

Sexton's glasses slipped farther down his nose. "Did you see the piece the *Global Times* ran on Cheng?"

"I did."

"Did you notice how they fingered him for both corruption *and* adultery?"

"Yeah, so?"

"I call that a double-barrel blast. Condemning him both professionally and morally is their way of discrediting him across the spectrum of public opinion. I would not be surprised if the next article reports that former foreign minister Cheng has taken his own life."

"So, you think Cheng is already dead?"

He nodded.

Their food arrived and Katie's gaze was drawn to the twin bulges of eggs Benedict on Sexton's plate that were hidden under what had to be a half-inch-thick layer of hollandaise sauce.

"Good God, Larry, that's a heart attack on a platter," she said. "Are you really going to eat all that?"

On this cue, and to her great relief, he pushed his glasses back up onto the bridge of his nose, lest they fall into Lake Hollandaise.

"I had a triple bypass two years ago. Doc said I'm good for another decade." With a smile, he plunged his fork into one of the mounds, releasing a lava slide of golden egg yolk.

She shook her head while spearing a piece of chicken, a slice of cucumber, and some lettuce.

They both enjoyed their first couple bites in blissful silence before he said, "What else do you want to talk about?"

"I want to talk more about Cheng."

"Why do you care so much about Cheng?" he asked, still chewing his last bite. "More importantly, why does naval intelligence care about him?"

She finished chewing her own bite, then said, "My gut tells me his disappearance matters. He's not the only one. The previous defense minister, Zhao Fu, also disappeared, and hasn't resurfaced in four months. Taken together, it feels like a precursor to me."

"A precursor to what?"

"I don't know, that's what I'm trying to figure out."

Sexton wiped his mouth with his napkin and in a low voice said, "Fu is dead."

She sat back against the backrest and stared at him. "You've confirmed this?"

"Not me personally, but yeah, it's confirmed."

"Okay, well, can you confirm what happened to Cheng for me?"

"As soon as I hear something, I'll let you know. Does that work for you?"

"I'd rather find out sooner than later," she said. "Can you put in an RFI or whatever the spooky term is for shaking trees in your HUMINT network?"

The CIA man pressed his lips together in annoyance and looked around, as if to check whether someone was listening. "Look, Ryan, I gotta be honest. I feel like you're bowling outside of your lane on this one. It kinda feels like a personal interest project rather than something related to your charter over there at Brooks."

He wasn't wrong, but the comment still pissed her off. "Captain Ferguson told me you were the guy who could help me, but I guess he was mistaken. Don't worry about it, I'll find somebody else instead."

"Oh, come on, don't be like that," he said.

"I came here asking for your help. Either you agree to do it or not. I don't see how there's a middle ground."

He sighed with what she took as exasperation, then went on a diatribe. "Twenty-five years as the China guy and nobody wants to listen to me. I tell them we're making a mistake focusing a hundred percent of our attention on counterterrorism. I tell them to snap out of their fugue because China is the future threat. I tell them Beijing is playing the long game, that the Chinese Navy will surpass our own in twenty-five years, that Li's bluster about reunification of Taiwan is not just bluster but telegraphing . . . But does anybody listen? No. Now, six months before I'm supposed to retire, my phone won't stop ringing. Everybody wants to know what I think, including ONI, apparently. Fucking typical."

She stared at him a long moment before saying, "Do you feel better now?"

"No," he grumbled and, on that cue, his eyeglasses slid halfway down his nose.

"Are you sure about that? Not even a little?"

"Maybe a little," he said, and at this they both laughed.

He took another bite of eggs Benedict.

She took another bite of salad, resigned not to break first in what she hoped would be the final standoff.

"Fine, I'll shake some trees," he said at last. "Will that make you happy, Commander?"

"Very," she said and fixed him with a genuine smile. "Thank you, Larry."

"You're welcome."

6

President Ryan glanced at the wall clock.

Despite the long day he had ahead of him, he felt pretty good. When the daily security brief took less than an hour, it was a sign that all was well in the world—or as well as he might dare hope. Top that off with the fact that his wife and best friend, the First Lady, would be joining him for dinner with the Russian ambassador and this would count as a good day for any American president.

"So . . . there's nothing you can think of that might become a grenade tossed in my lap tonight?" he asked his secretary of state, Scott Adler.

"Nothing we're tracking, Mr. President," the SecState said, uncomfortable with the metaphor. "It would seem that the Kremlin—and even President Yermilov himself—are playing better with others these days. And not just us. We expect the oil deal with Finland to wrap up in short order and under much better terms than anticipated."

"Great work you and your team did on all fronts," Ryan said.

Of course, Adler didn't realize that Yermilov would be on his best behavior for a while *not* because of Adler's brilliant diplomatic skills but because of the leverage Ryan possessed over the Russian president. After the incident with the *Belgorod*, Yermilov was *beholden* to Ryan personally, which meant he owed the President a favor.

"I suspect President Yermilov has seen the light regarding cooperation with the West," Ryan said with a cagey smile. "I fully expect to see the Russian government continue to be more reasonable and compliant."

"That would be . . . *refreshing*, sir," Adler said. "From your lips to God's ears."

"Last item," said Mary Pat Foley, the DNI and Ryan's longtime friend. She nodded at CIA director Ben Stephens, giving him the floor.

"Our update on the disappearance of the Chinese minister of foreign affairs is a non-update," Stephens said as a picture appeared on the screen—Minister Cheng Kai staring at the camera during a state dinner. "Since his failure to appear at the East Asia Summit and the subsequent release of information about the scandal involving him, there have been no sightings of Cheng, public or otherwise."

"By otherwise you mean what?" Ryan pressed.

"We still have limited assets inside Beijing, Mr. President, and they confirm that Cheng has disappeared. Interestingly, it does appear that the accusations against him were fabricated—a propaganda hit job. Our priority now is to find out what he may have said or done to fall out of favor with the Party or President Li, but, as you know, our in-country network is not as robust as it once was."

"Understood," Ryan said. And he did. Since the purge undertaken by President Li's predecessor, the rich network of both organic and managed intelligence assets inside China had dried up significantly. Ryan was well-versed in the dangers of the espionage business, and the problem of getting reliable intelligence out of China was a very real one. To make matters worse, America had fallen behind the CCP in cyber and signals intelligence these days.

"You're reporting this at the end of the brief, so I assume there is nothing to indicate that Cheng's disappearance is a prelude to something more . . . *nefarious?*" he asked. He glanced at the clock again. If the day kept going this way, he might even have time to get in a workout.

"Not at present, sir. There does seem to be an increase in naval activity in the South China Sea—particularly in and around the Strait of Taiwan—but that's not that unusual these days. Li has been quite aggressive flexing his maritime might over the past eighteen months."

"Larry, your thoughts?" Ryan asked, turning to Admiral Lawrence Kent, chairman of the Joint Chiefs.

"Stephens isn't wrong," Kent said. "The Chinese Navy has been a total pain in the ass lately. You'll remember last week they had two destroyers frustrating our carrier flight operations. The *Reagan* was operating well outside any contested areas, so they were doing it just to harass us, it seemed."

"They've been dangerously aggressive of late," General Bruce Kudryk chimed in. "Damn near caused a collision when the *Robert Smalls* and the *Sharp* transited the strait a few weeks ago.

Flanked them danger close and flew jets across their bows nearly at water level. Thankfully, our Task Force 70 commanders and ship drivers have been highly professional in the face of the provocation."

Kent looked from Kudryk to Ryan. "We're expecting more of the same aggressive behavior, Mr. President, when they kick off Operation Sea Serpent, their big naval and amphibious landing exercise. This one is definitely meant to shake up the Taiwanese ROC. We're keeping Task Force 70 on station to show that we have Taiwan's back, which means our forces will be in close proximity to the exercise . . ."

"Okay," Ryan said, but his thoughts drifted back to Foreign Minister Cheng's disappearance. "So, let's see what we can shake loose about whatever Cheng did that displeased President Li."

He knew it would be a mistake to ignore this completely. Li might appear more reasonable and in control than his predecessor, Wei Zhen Lin, who had nearly brought them to war by bowing to the power-hungry general Su Ke Qiang a few years back. But Ryan knew that, while Li's weapons of war may have changed Su's missiles and ships to economic policies and attacks with technology, he shared a vision for the expansionist plans of General Su from the earliest days of the Jack Ryan presidency.

As the CIA director finished up, Ryan found himself unable to shake the news of Cheng's disappearance or label it as unimportant. The smear job that followed suggested the man was *not* spending a few punitive months in "reeducation" before reemerging from some health scare. No, this guy had crossed President Li in some major way.

But over what?

He realized that all eyes were on him, expectantly waiting.

"All right, well thank you, everyone. And, Ben, I'd like you to take a hard look at Cheng's disappearance. I think there's more to this story than meets the eye," Ryan said as he rose, ending the meeting.

"Yes, Mr. President," Stephens said, a bit of surprise evident in his voice.

While the national security team gathered their things and headed out the door, Ryan walked over to Mary Pat to have a private conversation with his director of national intelligence.

"Something got your antennae up, Jack?" she asked when the door had been closed behind Admiral Kent. "Do you know something about Cheng Kai that I should know about?"

Ryan shook his head, but remained pensive. "What's the name of their new national defense minister again?"

"Qin Hâiyû," Mary Pat said.

"Navy man, wasn't he?" Ryan asked. The intelligence analyst inside was trying to move the scattered pieces around and form them into some sort of picture. But there weren't enough pieces.

Not yet.

"That's right, Jack," she said. "He was head of the PLA Navy before being asked to assume the duties of the minister of national defense after Zhao Fu's exit."

"Who also vacated his post under dubious circumstances . . ."

"That's correct," she said.

"What did Qin do before this job—not the Navy career, but in the Li government?"

"Nothing," Mary Pat said. "He came over from the active-duty Navy, as I recall."

"That's unusual, isn't it?" Ryan asked.

She shrugged.

"A little, I guess," she said. "Li does tend to bring people up from within the cabinet. Test of their abilities, but also their loyalties. Not a perfect system, I suppose, in light of what sounds like a removal of his minister of foreign affairs. Cheng was inside the Li cabinet from the beginning."

He nodded.

"What are you thinking, Jack?"

Ryan gave her a smile. "I'm not sure. Nothing, I guess. Hard to take off the analyst hat, even after all these years."

"For sure," Mary Pat agreed, but he felt her watching him carefully now.

"Still," Ryan added as he led her to the door. "Make sure Stephens does a deep dive on this one, Mary Pat. Not just on Cheng, but also on Qin. Maybe even his predecessor . . ."

"Zhao Fu," Mary Pat said, helping him.

"Right. Zhao Fu. Let me know if you find anything interesting."

"Yes, Mr. President," Mary Pat said, and followed him out of the room. "And enjoy your dinner tonight."

He cocked an eyebrow at her. "I can add another place setting if you want to join us? I told Bobby to serve meatloaf, dinner rolls, green beans, mashed potatoes and gravy. And for dessert, apple pie and vanilla ice cream."

"Are you serious?" she said with a chuckle.

"Dead serious. Diner food in the State Dining Room. They're even going to laminate the dinner menu," he said, grinning at her. "I can't wait to see the look on Darmatov's face . . ."

7

Qin folded his hands behind him in case they might be shaking as he glared at the aide to the deputy minister of foreign affairs. If the goal over the next seventy-two hours was to draw as little attention to himself as possible, then what he was doing now was not the way to do it.

"This is highly irregular, Minister Qin," the young man said, obviously annoyed. "You were not on the original guest list for the weekly meeting."

"Are you suggesting that I, the minister of defense, need your permission to sit in on a weekly meeting with the lead diplomat of our most formidable adversary and largest trading partner?"

"No . . . no, of course not, sir . . ." the man stammered, looking around the room for anyone who might help him. "I'm only saying . . ."

"Hûyâi, it is such a pleasure to see you," a familiar voice called

60

out, and he looked over to see Deputy Minister of Foreign Affairs Bai Ming angling toward him, the smile on Bai's face discordant with the suspicious look in his eyes. Qin understood completely. It was not Qin himself that aroused suspicion, but rather the hidden "why" behind the reason he'd come to a meeting he did not regularly attend. After all, Bai certainly didn't want to meet the same fate as his predecessor.

Qin shook the soft, moist hand of the smaller man in the expensive suit, who nodded dismissively to his aide.

"The pleasure is mine, Ming," he said, his best disarming smile on his face. "I hope it is okay for me to attend. I am here of my own accord, I assure you." He leaned in, proceeding in a conspiratorial whisper. "You were at the cabinet meetings yesterday and the day before, my friend. Our leader has given me a most dangerous and difficult task. I had hoped to sit in today and see if the U.S. ambassador might reveal something—anything—of value regarding the American naval posture ahead of our 'exercise.'"

"Ah, of course," Bai said, seeming relieved, but perhaps just playing along. "This is why it was wise to replace Minister Zhao with an experienced military officer. I said as much to—" He hesitated, and glanced around, as if uttering the name of his previous boss might bring the same fate down on his own head. "Well, to the committee, and also to the president. You are a shrewd one."

"Thank you, Ming," Qin said. "We serve the people. If it is quite all right, I may want to speak during your meeting? I had hoped to say a few things to see if I might get a rise out of the ambassador, perhaps trick him into revealing something."

"We can play at what the American movies call 'good cop, bad cop,' if you like," Bai said, relishing having an ally in the room, Qin thought. "But you should know that Ambassador Mitchell will likely not be here. We meet today with his aide, Mr. Scott Kincaid."

"Even better," Qin said. "His underling is probably more likely to give something away as I press him. He will be less experienced in the American techniques of deception and slipperiness."

And far better for Qin, since Kincaid was likely CIA, if his friend Dong Jun's assessment was correct.

"Yes, yes, I see," Bai said, and gave him a conspiratorial wink, just as the door opened and the deputy to the ambassador, Scott Kincaid, entered the room with a woman in tow, both wearing gray business suits.

"Thank you for coming, Mr. Kincaid," Bai said, gesturing for the two to take a seat as he took his own seat at the head of the table, his young aide beside him. He also gave a nod to Qin, indicating he should take the seat beside Bai, to his right.

"Perhaps you have met Minister of National Defense Qin Hûyâi?"

"I have not," Kincaid said, rising again.

Qin folded his arms across his chest to abort shaking hands, and simply made a gruff sighing sound.

Kincaid gave a tight-lipped smile and returned to his seat.

"We appreciate your willingness to continue these weekly meetings with us, Minister Bai," Kincaid said, all smiles again. "It is of great value to both our nations that we continue a close working relationship."

"Perhaps," Bai said, sounding bored. "Minister Qin has a few things to say at the end, but why don't we go through the agenda items Ambassador Mitchell sent over, shall we?"

Kincaid gave a pleasant nod, but his eyes ticked over to Qin. There was no fear or concern in the brief glance, but Qin definitely saw curiosity.

Dong Jun was right. I know the eyes of an American spy when I see one. Scott Kincaid is CIA, just as Jun said.

The two diplomats took the lead, working through the agenda, sharing already well-publicized talking points from their respective bosses in a boring sparring match over trade, intellectual property rights, foreign real estate investment, and oil trade with Russia—all things that, if Li had his way in two short weeks, would be completely and utterly meaningless.

While they yammered, Qin's mind drifted back to the two-hour dinner he'd had with Dong Jun last night. Qin had let his intuition serve as his lodestar during their conversation. Despite their yearslong friendship, Qin had decided to err on the side of caution. Jun was a good man, and an even better friend, but he was a spymaster in the MSS. His loyalty would be—*should* be—to the CCP and President Li, no matter how strong his friendship and history with Qin. So, instead of confiding his true concerns about Operation Sea Serpent, Qin had taken a very different tack.

Swearing Jun to secrecy, Qin shared how President Li had approved the plan to convert the exercise into a real-world operation, code-named Sea Serpent, to "repatriate" Taiwan. Then, instead of voicing doubts over the plan and its repercussions, Qin feigned the opposite. He touted the plan as brilliant and timely, bragging it would be a swift and unprecedented success and that Taiwan would be conquered in a matter of hours under the operational plan he'd designed.

"Before the Americans even know what is happening, Taiwan will be a part of the CCP," he boasted.

"But surely they will retaliate?" Jun asked, leaning in and speaking in a hushed voice on the terrace of their favorite steak house. "How can they not?"

Qin smiled and shook his head, then regurgitated President

Li's assumptions—assumptions he knew with all his heart to be folly.

"They won't dare retaliate," he said, sticking to the Li script, "as to attack us after our victory would be an attack on China itself, and an act of all-out war. They have no stomach for such a war after decades in the Middle East."

"Taiwan is not my area of responsibility. I must confess, I've not heard anything regarding this operation. Which means the OPSEC surrounding the plan has been robust and effective. Reunification was a goal I believed would forever remain ten years in the future," Jun said, and Qin could see both hope and fear in the other man's eyes.

Qin seized the moment to exploit his friend for what he needed. Expressing deep concern about American intelligence assets getting wind of the plan in advance, which he told his friend would allow them to position their fleet in a way to make success very difficult and guarantee losses on both sides, he asked for his help in understanding the American intelligence machine operating inside China.

"It is weak and ineffective," Jun bragged. "The purge a decade ago resulted in a decimation of American and other foreign intelligence operations inside China. Not only did we uncover the traitors within our ranks—all of whom were arrested and summarily executed—but we were able to unmask and destroy the American and British intelligence operations that were fed by them. We believe that intelligence operations between us and the West are now asymmetrical, practically a one-way street."

"Surely the Americans still have intelligence operations within China. It would be naive to believe otherwise," Qin pressed.

"The American diplomatic mission in Beijing is staffed with CIA personnel posing as FSO and State Department officials. As in their embassies throughout the world, they exploit the access that diplomacy provides—the same as we do. But we know who they are and where they travel. We know who they meet with and when. And, most importantly, we have completely disassembled their ability to interact with Chinese government and business officials without our knowledge."

Qin smiled and toasted his classmate's great success. Then he leaned in closer and, taking a conspiratorial tone, asked, "The ambassador—is he a spy?"

"No, but his deputy, Scott Kincaid, is a CIA operations officer."

"I've heard rumors," Qin said softly, "of a legendary double agent, thought to be a woman, that people call the Spider. She is said to have duped the Americans and been the mastermind of the purge . . ."

Avoiding the trap of potentially trusting the wrong agent was of key importance to Qin's survival if his plan were to work. He needed to know which narrative about the Spider was truth and which was fiction—did she work for the Americans or was she a product of the MSS?

Dong Jun laughed at this. "One of the greatest operations of all time, and one for which I can boast—secretly to you, of course—to being the architect."

"So the Spider is a fiction?" he asked.

"Better," Jun said. "The Spider is real, but we created a narrative around her to make her ineffective. You see, the Spider is not an MSS agent, but rather she is a traitor and spy, run by the CIA, who uses old-school spycraft and stays completely off the grid, which made her impossible to catch. So, we created the legend that she was actually an MSS asset, used during the purge to unmask traitors and Western spy networks. We credited her for most of the arrests and subsequent executions. As a result, no *would-be* American collaborators will go near her now, fearing that she will betray them to the MSS."

"Genius indeed," Qin said.

Now Qin heard his name, which snapped him back to the present. He refocused his gaze from the middle distance to the American deputy chief of mission. "Excuse me?"

"Do you care to comment, Minister Qin?" Kincaid asked.

He stared at the man with what he hoped to be deadly serious eyes.

"I have no interest in these matters, Deputy Kincaid," he said, waving a hand in the air as if shooing away an annoying gnat. "I have but one purpose here today, and that is to avoid missteps that could lead to war."

Kincaid's eyebrows shot up, and he glanced at the woman beside him, who had been silently taking notes as Kincaid and Bai Ming had sparred.

"Well, you certainly have my attention," Kincaid said, folding his hands on the table in front of him.

Qin rose, standing in front of his chair to lord over the table in a position of dominance, only barely glancing at Kincaid as he spoke. He clasped his hands behind his back again, fearful that they might shake. But he knew his face and voice would betray nothing.

"We have notified all relevant nations of our scheduled Sea Serpent military exercise. The tensions between our naval fleets, especially in the South China Sea and the Strait of Taiwan, have become untenable recently. The presence of American warships in Chinese territorial waters is both reckless and dangerous." He felt the eyes of the CIA man on him, but still gave Kincaid only a glance as he spoke, staring out the window at the lake instead.

"This exercise is vital to our national defense. In recognition of the hostility of the American fleet in the region of late, I feel a need to emphasize to you now how dangerous it would be to interfere in any way with Sea Serpent. American naval forces are prohibited from entering Chinese territorial water for forty-eight hours before to forty-eight hours after the completion of our exercise. Reckless interference with our training would reasonably be considered an act of war, especially should injuries occur as a result."

He leaned in now, palms on the table, and glared at Deputy Scott Kincaid. To his credit, the American reacted with a patient smile.

"As I know *you* are aware, Minister Qin, your nation's claims to territorial rights encompassing the South China Sea and the Strait of Taiwan are disputed by many, including the United States. However," he said, raising his hands with palms up in a gesture of deference, "we respect your need for military training and we agree it is best for all parties that our forces not come in close contact. We have made this same point through diplomatic channels frequently, as needed, when Chinese naval forces have interfered with our own naval exercises and training operations in international waters . . ."

"The CCP does not recognize the United States Navy's right to conduct exercises near our territories in areas of vital strategic importance," Qin said through a growl.

"I understand that," Kincaid said with a gentle smile. "What I can assure you is that Ambassador Mitchell will most certainly pass on your concerns to President Ryan. The United States wishes only peace and prosperity for both our nations. I can assure you that we will never do anything to unnecessarily provoke conflict with China."

Qin held the eyes of the American CIA operative, hoping that his own eyes now conveyed another, secret message along with his words.

"Mr. Kincaid, I will personally do anything it takes to avoid war between our two nations," he said, then blinked, straightened up, and again put on the mask of a warrior. "But we will not tolerate interference."

"I understand," Kincaid said, and something in the other man's eyes suggested perhaps he did.

"I must return to work," Qin said, striding around the table, passing behind Bai so that the palm of his hand would be turned away from the acting minister of foreign affairs.

Qin stopped in front of Kincaid, who rose from his seat and extended his hand. Cupping a wafer-thin packet in his palm, Qin gripped the American's hand and shook it. They locked gazes, and something flickered in the CIA man's eyes as Qin made the transfer.

"I can assure you that we understand each other perfectly," Kincaid said, dropping his hand to his side. He then disappeared the item with the fluid grace of a trained magician. "I appreciate your attending the meeting in person to share these sentiments."

Qin turned to Bai, who smiled at him approvingly.

"Minister Bai, I trust you can wrap up these discussions without me. I think the Americans now understand our position," Qin said in Mandarin.

"Thank you, Minister Qin," Bai said, rising and giving him a slight bow.

Without another word, Qin turned and paced quickly out the door.

Striding down the hallway, it took all the self-control and discipline Qin had built over a lifetime of military service not to stop and lean against the wall with emotional exhaustion. There were cameras everywhere in this building. His handshake with Kincaid would most certainly have been recorded, but would the technicians viewing the footage notice the transfer? He did not think so. And why would they want to look in the first place? Who would suspect him, of all people? He loved China, the military, and his work. Everyone who knew him understood this.

His reputation was beyond reproach.

Which may well be the only thing that kept him alive in the coming days after the act of treason he had just committed.

8

Qiū Léi (Autumn Thunder) finished her warrior katas and bowed to her opponent. Then she dragged the Wing Chun practice dummy back into the corner of her living room, where he would wait in stoic wooden sleep until their next session. Her late father, Qiū Língbīn (Autumn Radiance), had been a practitioner of Wing Chun, the southern Chinese style of kung fu made famous by Bruce Lee. Remarkably, both Qiū Língbīn and Bruce Lee had studied under the form's originator, a grandmaster known around the world simply as Ip Man. Léi had not had the privilege to meet Ip Man or Bruce Lee—as both the grandmaster and the icon died before her birth—but her father had once remarked offhandedly that she was skilled enough to spar with either man.

That had been the greatest compliment he had ever given her.

He'd begun her training at age six.

At age eleven, she overheard him tell a neighbor that she was a prodigy.

And yet despite her skill and potential, he had not let her participate in the sport publicly. Her mastery of kung fu was to be a private and personal affair, just like her sexuality. *Education* . . . this was where her father mandated that she excel and shine in the light. Mathematics, science, history, rhetoric—these, he said, were the skills that would allow her to dominate her opponents in the battlefield of life.

"With your mind and body aligned, you will accomplish great things, my Autumn Thunder. My only regret is that you must face all of life's challenges as a woman," he once said. But the most stinging comment of all had come on his deathbed, when he'd hugged her tight and tearfully lamented, "I'm sorry, Qiū Léi, that you were born a girl."

Dripping with sweat, she bowed to the framed photograph of her father, which hung on the wall beside the practice dummy.

"Don't be sorry, Father . . . I'm not."

But she hadn't always felt that way.

Her father's words had profoundly shaped her worldview and self-perception during her formative years. Being a woman in China—a culture where femininity was often equated with weakness and masculinity with dominance—was not easy. Which is why her father had dedicated all his spare time to instructing and training her, his only child, with a warrior ethos. In his mind, to survive and thrive as a woman in a male-dominated culture, she needed to be like China's legendary folk heroine, Hua Mulan. As if to immerse her in this mindset, her father spent nearly a year painting a sweeping mural depicting "The Ballad of Mulan" in Léi's childhood bedroom.

The unspoken message: *To compete against a man, daughter, you must become one.*

Qiū Léi walked to the freestanding soaking tub in the other corner of the room, which was heated to thirty-seven degrees Celsius. She removed her hair tie, stripped naked, stepped over the tall lip of the basin, and gingerly lowered herself into the steaming water. She reclined, closed her eyes, and let the heat flow through her skin into her joints and muscles, all the while imagining the water healing and rejuvenating her deep tissues. After sufficient time soaking, she picked up a piece of dried loofah sponge from the bath side table and methodically scrubbed and exfoliated her body from head to toe. A regular routine of exercise, meditation, rejuvenation, and exfoliation was the key to health and longevity.

At fifty years old, Léi had the body and skin of a woman fifteen years her junior. If not for her graying hair, which she refreshed with black hair dye regularly, no one would be able to guess her age. Unlike almost all of her contemporaries, Léi had never married and she'd not had children—a difficult and sometimes sorrow-laden choice, but *her* choice nonetheless. Her body, unchanged and unmarred by gestation and childbirth, had mostly retained her adolescent proportions. This, in combination with her longevity routine and girlish face, only amplified the dichotomy between her biological and chronological age.

Nowhere was the contrast more stark than when she was out in public with Fa Héng. With increasing frequency over the years, strangers had begun mistaking her long-term lover for her father. Héng, a university professor who was five years her senior, looked very much his age. Instead of this bothering her, she embraced it. She loved him for his mind and spirit, not the package they resided in. Unlike the other Chinese men she'd dated, Héng was the only one who'd ever treated her with the deference and respect she deserved.

With her bathing ritual complete, she stepped out of the water and dried her body and hair. Next, she applied lotion to her arms, legs, and trunk, then dressed to begin her *second* workday. Tonight, she would sleep here, in her apartment. Tomorrow she would spend the night with Héng at his place. As for the night after next, well, they would decide that when the day after tomorrow came around. That was the beautiful thing about true love—it meant finding the perfect balance between autonomy and dependence.

Like her romantic life, her professional life was a yin and yang existence. As Qiū Léi, she spent her days running the taxicab business she'd inherited from her father. This was her *yang vocation*—white, light, and open. With the setting of the sun, however, she became Yèjiān Zhīzhū (the Night Spider). Subverting what the state had become was her *yin vocation*—black, dark, and hidden . . .

She had not intended to become a CIA asset. Like so many things in life, it had happened almost by accident. Thirty years ago, an American expatriate living in Beijing had flirted with her at the vegetable market. She'd found him handsome, charming, and exotic; their attraction had been mutually instantaneous. They'd become lovers during the two years he'd lived in China. Six weeks before he was due to return home to America—after a particularly passionate night together—he'd divulged that he was an American spy. Instead of feeling betrayed, the discovery had excited her. As a university student with no influence or access to military secrets, she had *not* been his mark. He'd confessed as much when she'd asked him: "You were simply too beautiful to resist. I did this for me . . . not for my country." Then he'd apologized with tear-rimmed eyes for having selfishly put her in mortal danger.

"In danger?" she'd asked. "How have you endangered me? I've provided you with nothing of interest or value to the Party. Just my heart and my body."

He'd smiled at her naivety. "It doesn't matter, Léi. You don't want to know what they do to Chinese nationals who collaborate with the enemy. If your government were to pierce my cover, the repercussions for you would be too terrible to imagine."

And therein lay the irony, because the next five weeks with him had been the most thrilling and tantalizing time of her young life. Leading a clandestine existence made her feel alive. And so, five days before he left to return to Virginia and the CIA, she told him that she wanted to work for the CIA, too. To her surprise, he said no. But it wasn't Larry's decision to make, it was hers.

That night the Spider was born . . .

In tradecraft terminology, Léi was *not* a spy. Nor was she a double agent. She didn't work inside a Chinese government agency, the Ministry of State Security, or the PLA. She didn't have access to government or military computer systems, have a clearance to attend classified briefings, or network with rich and powerful men she could bribe or seduce for information. Acquiring state secrets was not what she did.

She was a *support asset*.

Her specialty was providing logistical services to aid the CIA's human intelligence collection activities, such as scouting dead-drop locations, vetting safe houses, and providing temporary lodging for assets moving under cover. Her most frequent contribution, however, was providing safe and reliable transportation using her taxi company. None of these activities were "sexy," but they were essential. The contribution she was most proud of, however, was when she had the opportunity to assist with the exfiltration of political dissidents. In her heart of hearts, she was an idealist who loved the citizens of her country, while despising the ruling caste of cold, corrupt, cruel men in charge.

They rule with fear and an iron fist. But like Hua Mulan, I am not afraid.

She'd honed her craft in the days before computers, and mobile phones, and satellites. These days, signals intelligence, or SIGINT, served as the backbone of the Chinese and American espionage apparatuses—vacuuming up billions of digital communications every day. But this was not her area of expertise. Yes, her taxi company used computers, but she didn't use one for her covert activities or communications. She owned a mobile phone, but not the smart variety, and she rarely carried it with her. As her American handler was fond of saying, Léi did things *old-school.*

It was her disciplined "sticks and bricks" approach to tradecraft that she credited for her longevity. She'd survived the Ministry of State Security's infamous dragnet and purge that decimated the CIA's spy network in China during the years 2010 to 2013. According to Scott, her current CIA handler, she was one of only two serving assets to avoid arrest and execution during the purge. Also, she held the record for the longest tenure of any active Chinese asset by a whopping fifteen years. But in a strange twist of irony, she could thank the Ministry of State Security for her survival the past decade.

By rounding up and dismantling the CIA's HUMINT network, the MSS had obviated the need for her services. Directed and supported clandestine activity in Beijing had dropped and hovered near zero for nearly five years. During that period, she'd contemplated retiring many times. But in addition to being an idealist, she was also an adrenaline junkie. Take away the Night Spider, and life as Autumn Thunder became boring and unfulfilling. Every Chinese knows that yin cannot exist without yang, and vice versa.

An unbalanced life is an unbearable life . . .

Then, to make matters worse, she learned that the MSS had corrupted her legend—rebranding the Night Spider as one of *their* agents and celebrating her as the architect of the great purge. According to the propaganda, she used her web to catch the CIA flies and suck them dry in service of the state. This bastardization of her legacy had angered her and stoked the fire of defiance that had convinced her to stay in the game. It had taken all of her handlers—and she'd had many over the years—to convince the CIA director that she was not, in reality, a double agent. But most of her gratitude was directed at Larry, who Scott said had battled tirelessly as her champion to ensure her reputation remained unsullied at Langley.

Nevertheless, it has been months since I have received any tasking.

With a deep and cleansing exhale, she blew the poisonous thoughts about what was and what was not true from her body. She sat down on the bench by the front door of her apartment and laced on her athletic trainers. Walking the city is how she serviced her web. Tonight's route had six stops and would take her between two to three hours to complete with SDRs and taxi hops. Even now, thirty years into the routine, *walking her web* still gave her an adrenaline rush.

Every patrol was dangerous.

Despite the propaganda, she knew the MSS had not lost interest in her. They'd been trying to penetrate her web and trap her for years, and she suspected that her eluding their dragnet for so long had only made her a more desirable and high-value target.

She was not so arrogant or ignorant to believe that she couldn't be caught. So long as she refused to retire, getting caught was inevitable. One day she would make a careless mistake, an informant would sell her out, or an MSS counterintelligence agent would outsmart her. And when that day came, she would go down in a flurry of fists, feet, elbows, and knees that would make Ip Man, Bruce Lee, and her father smile down from heaven.

But not tonight, she told herself as she stepped out the door into the dark. *Not tonight . . .*

9

U.S. EMBASSY
55 ANJIALOU ROAD, CHAOYANG DISTRICT
BEIJING, CHINA
2011 LOCAL TIME

S cott Kincaid locked the door to his office.

As the ambassador's deputy chief of mission, his daily schedule was filled with actual State Department work in service of the embassy's mission and supporting the ambassador. If he didn't work for the CIA, his job would have been exhausting enough. But throw his *collateral* duties into the mix and his workday rarely ended before nine or ten o'clock at night. The ambassador was read in on Kincaid's official cover, or OC, but the same could not be said for the majority of the employees working at the embassy. This was for both his and their protection, and the way it had been since the earliest days of the CIA. Everyone knew this was how the game was played, including the Chinese. The trick was sorting the actual foreign service officers from the spies posing as them.

Veil piercing was serious business, and so Kincaid took precautions even inside the embassy itself.

From a hidden pocket inside his suit coat he retrieved the tiny opaque plastic object that Defense Minster Qin had passed to him during the meeting today. It had taken all of his willpower not to open it until now, when he was certain he would not be seen or interrupted by the organic State Department mission staff. He was confident his windowless office was not bugged or under micro-camera surveillance. Access to his office was both controlled and limited, but more importantly he had both active and passive countermeasures in place.

Significant countermeasures.

He collapsed into his leather task chair and held the item up for inspection—which appeared to be one of those tiny plastic cases that SD memory cards were sold in.

I hope whatever Qin put inside is not laced with poison, he thought with a grim smile.

Being covertly assassinated by the MSS, while unlikely, was not out of the realm of possibility. The fact that the idea even crossed his mind was upsetting enough, but that he gave it one-in-ten odds was beyond disturbing.

"Too bad I don't keep a pair of rubber gloves in my office," he quipped as he flicked the tiny plastic clasp on the side of the case and opened it.

Inside the slot, where an SD card would normally be, sat a tightly folded square of white paper. Printed neatly in black ink on the face was a single Chinese logogram:

禮

He stared at the Hanzi character, which he did not recognize.

"Hmm," he murmured and grabbed his phone, which had a Hanzi lookup app that used his phone camera as a scanner. He opened the app and centered the character in the guide square until the app detected and deciphered the symbol:

禮 Li (Traditional Chinese Character)—Origin Confucianism,
    Chinese Philosophy.
Traditional definition: A ritualistic sacrifice. A gift, but not an
    object. The transformation of the invisible into the visible.
礼 Li (Simplified Chinese Character)
Modern definition: Decorum, good form, rules of propriety.

"Holy shit, I hope that means what I think it does," he said, and goose bumps stood up on his forearms as he gently removed the prize from the little plastic clips inside the case.

Fingers trembling with anticipatory adrenaline, he carefully unfolded the little piece of white paper, expanding it into a two-inch square. Despite being a young man of only thirty-two, Kincaid needed a pair of magnifying glasses to read the tiny Chinese characters scrawled on the paper. Thankfully, Qin had written this message in simplified Chinese, rather than traditional logograms. Kincaid was well-versed in the former, but not the latter.

He translated the message aloud: "'All war is deception. Sea Serpent battle plan. Drop 2100 tomorrow. Liulichang. Protect my family, Maldives.'"

He set the paper down, leaned back in his chair, and exhaled slowly.

Is this real?

"Because if this is a dangle and I send the Spider, then she's screwed," he muttered, looking at the ceiling. "And if that happens, then *I'm* screwed . . ."

But it feels . . . real.

He grabbed the little square of paper and turned it over to look at the single Hanzi character again. His first thought was a question. Why had Qin used the traditional logogram 禮 instead of the simplified Chinese character 礼?

"Clearly he did it on purpose," he said, looking back at the translation app on his phone and talking himself through trying to decipher the note. "Because he must have been signaling the traditional definition—a ritualistic sacrifice. A gift, but not an object." He blew air through pursed lips, hoping. "So, Qin is making a sacrifice. Giving us a gift and in doing so making visible what has been invisible."

He looked back at the app and the modern definition for *Li*.

Good form. Rules of propriety? Maybe he intends it to mean both? That makes the message even more powerful.

He stood and began to pace.

"Or maybe I'm overcomplicating this. What if *Li* simply refers to *President* Li?" Kincaid said out loud, agitated by the logic of the thought. "But then, why not write the logogram for President Li?"

He flipped the paper over to read the message another time. "'All war is deception'—that's from Sun Tzu's *Art of War* . . . but what is Qin telling me?"

He let out a long, annoyed growl.

Think, think, think . . .

He let his mind drift back to the meeting and Qin's stern words to him from across the table to keep the Navy clear and away from Operation Sea Serpent, the big upcoming PLA Navy exercise.

"'All war is deception . . . Sea Serpent battle plan.'" His heart skipped a beat. "Oh shit. He said 'battle plan,' not 'exercise.' They're going to take Taiwan! Qin is warning us. He's giving us time to prepare. And he *expects* to get caught, that's why he ends the note with a demand to protect his family . . . Because he's going to give us the battle plan at a drop tomorrow night!"

He balled his fists to keep his hands from shaking.

Oh my God, oh my God . . . this is huge. The biggest intelligence coup since . . . since I don't know when.

Mind racing, Kincaid glanced at his watch. He had less than twenty-four hours to run this up the chain of command, contact the Spider, and prep contingencies in case the drop went bad. And he had to do it all without tipping off the rest of the mission staff.

This was why he'd joined the CIA.

This was how legends were made.

With this intel, Kincaid would be giving the White House and Pentagon a head start to circumvent an invasion. Which meant potentially stopping tens of thousands from dying in the forced reunification of Taiwan.

If I can pull this off, it will be the operation of the century.

10

John Clark shuffled barefoot across the gray wood tile floor of the kitchen toward the coffee maker, wishing he'd either put on some socks or relented to Sandy's insistence that they put in heated floors when they'd redone the kitchen last year. The thought made him grumpy, but in a self-amused sort of way. It was the thought of an old man, and while he felt older than ever before, he believed he remained a long way from "old." Still, the John Kelly from his SEAL team days and even the John Clark from his more recent exploits with the CIA, then the Rainbow international counterterror task force, and now the director of operations for The Campus, wasn't the kind of guy who worried about socks on his chilly feet as he made coffee in his kitchen, right? Hell, it had only been weeks since he'd infiltrated Russia by swimming to a waiting trawler in the freezing waters of the White Sea . . .

Clark laughed out loud at himself and dug out a filter for the old coffee maker sitting beside the new Italian espresso machine Sandy had bought him for Christmas. He claimed he liked the old coffee better, but the truth was he was just too damn lazy to figure out how to use the new-fangled machine.

Another old man thought . . .

He watched as the old Mr. Coffee machine gurgled to life with a puff of steam. He rubbed his hands together and thought about whipping up some eggs and bacon. His grandson and namesake, John, would be here later. JC, as they called him, was on leave from the Marines. Like any good leatherneck, he would dig in, but John had no doubt Sandy would give him "that" look—the look that meant she'd seen his last cholesterol level and still loved him enough to want him around for a while more.

Clark intended to take his grandson fishing and he was looking forward to it. Spending more time with his family was a growing priority and thoughts of retiring were ever on his mind lately.

A rap on the back door, which led from the kitchen to the fenced-in backyard, made him raise an eyebrow. Seeing Ding Chavez's familiar silhouette through the frosted-glass panel brought a different kind of concern. He took a sip of the black coffee, spun the two dead bolts on the reinforced door, and opened it. The air was unseasonably cold for this time of year. It made him shiver as it whipped around his bare legs beneath his boxers.

"What the hell are *you* doing here?" he asked Ding, taking another sip of coffee and letting the heat chase away the chill. "You're supposed to be giving my beautiful daughter the romantic getaway you both need."

"Yeah, don't I know it," Ding said, slipping past him into the warm kitchen as Clark shut the door behind him. "Nowhere I'd rather be, especially since you are no doubt aware Patty handles disappointment with all the grace of her old man."

Clark snorted at that.

"What's going on?" he asked his senior operations officer, son-in-law, and friend.

"There's been an event," Ding said, finding himself a mug in the cabinet and pouring himself a steaming cup of coffee. "Well, maybe. If it turns out to be true, Jerry thinks we'll almost certainly need to get involved," he added, referring to The Campus's chief of strategic planning, Jerry Rounds.

"What's going on?" Clark asked a second time, slipping on the familiar skin of the President's most effective and lethal black ops team leader like a favorite coat.

"The Chinese foreign affairs minister has gone missing."

"Yeah, so what?" Clark said with a shrug. "They lose ministers like I lose socks on laundry day."

Clark set his coffee on the counter, but honestly he still didn't see why Ding was here and not on his way to the Eastern Shore. A few months ago, Zhao Fu was fired from the minister of defense position, the announcement of his "firing" coming after he had disappeared from public for more than three months. The CIA had confirmed he'd been killed by the CCP regime. He guessed that maybe the foreign affairs minister—Cheng Kai, he thought he remembered—had been "fired" in a similar way. It sounded like President Li couldn't find good help.

"Okay," he said. "So one more minister failed to please the CCP. What does the shake-up have to do with us?"

"Rick thinks there may be more to it. He thinks the new minister of defense, Qin Hâiyû, wants to defect," Ding said, referring to Rick Bell, the head of intelligence for The Campus.

Clark felt himself getting annoyed.

"That's more interesting, but still sounds like a CIA thing to me. Besides, I'm on vacation this week."

"I know," Ding said, "but Jerry says that this Qin guy, actually former *admiral* Qin, has something pretty nice he's offering up."

"Fine, I'll bite," Clark said. "What?"

"The detailed plans for China's invasion of Taiwan—a plan Qin claims is imminent."

Ding folded his arms on his chest and gave him his best *You're interested now, aren't you?* look.

"Holy shit," Clark breathed. "Are you serious? And Jerry thinks this is for real?"

"We don't know, to be honest," Ding said, "but they think there's a fair chance it's real, or I sure as shit wouldn't be in your kitchen. Turns out that Admiral Qin is the architect of at least the naval portion of the plan, if not the whole damn thing. Before being assigned to the position of minister of defense, he was the commander of the Chinese Navy. And, before that, he was deputy commander of the Southern Theater."

Clark sighed.

Why would a true believer, as Qin must be to have risen through the commands, suddenly want to defect and turn over battle plans? The whole thing seemed fishy.

"Don't give me that look. The intel is legit," Ding said.

"Is it out in the general IC?" Clark asked, his concern deepening a touch.

Ding shook his head.

"Not yet. We intercepted the intelligence through the CIA and NSA. As you can imagine, they're all going crazy, but they're still vetting the intel before chasing it up the chain."

Clark let out a long, slow breath. If this wasn't bullshit, they'd be getting a back-channels communication from Mary Pat very soon.

"We should head to the office," he said.

If we go in now, caucus with Jerry and the analysis team, I can still spend the afternoon on the Bertram fishing with JC.

"What's going on?" a soft, feminine voice asked.

Clark looked over at where his wife stood at the swinging door to the kitchen, arms wrapped around herself to keep a fuzzy robe in place. "I thought you were taking JC out on the boat," she said, her eyes boring into Clark before turning to Ding. "And you, young man, are supposed to be wining and dining your wife."

"Yes, ma'am," Ding said. "I am still planning to, but . . ."

"Something's come up," Clark said, hoping his eyes sent a message of both love and apology. Whatever Sandy saw, her look softened. "But it shouldn't take long. I'll be back for our fishing expedition by early afternoon."

"Well," she said, walking to the espresso maker she'd gifted Clark—the one he never used. "It must be pretty damn important for both of you to risk pissing off your wives." She pressed the start-up button and the machine blinked to life. Then she returned to wrap her arms around her husband's neck. "I'll hold down the fort," she said. "I'd like some time to catch up with JC myself, but call when you can to tell him when you'll be back." He kissed her, now hoping his eyes gave her the thank-you she more than deserved. "And put on some damn pants, John."

"Give me five," Clark said to Ding. "We'll ride over together." Then he hustled out of the kitchen, heading for the stairs, praying that this time he'd be able to actually keep his promise.

11

SITUATION ROOM
THE WHITE HOUSE
WASHINGTON, D.C.
0740 LOCAL TIME

A request to defect and asylum from a cabinet minister in the CCP and I'm just learning about it now?" Ryan demanded. "How is that possible?"

"It took time to vet the information, Mr. President," Mary Pat said. "We have to be extra careful these days. This could easily have been a dangle by the Ministry of State Security. We can't afford to unmask any of our operatives or burn assets in Beijing. We don't have many left."

Ryan turned to General Kudryk. "And what does the Pentagon believe about the validity of Qin's signaling an imminent move against Taiwan?"

"Obviously, this is an eventuality we've been concerned about for some time," Kudryk said, unable to contain himself before yielding to the chairman of the Joint Chiefs, Admiral Kent.

Kent leaned in and spoke directly to Ryan, as he always did.

"Over the last month, the PLA Navy has been conducting nearly constant exercises in the Strait of Taiwan, Mr. President—"

"Over the past *year*," Ryan said, correcting him. "But that didn't answer my question. I'm looking for something that could confirm Qin Hâiyû's assertion that an attack is imminent."

"Of course," Kent said, seeming flustered, something way out of character for the admiral. "But that's the point, isn't it? I mean, maintaining this almost constant state of readiness and harassment of our assets, we've grown numb to the aggression. My worry is that this year of posturing, which we long thought to be for political show and leverage, may in fact be positioning more of a 'not if but when' scenario, where we become complacent and when the right opportunity presents itself they go."

"What would that opportunity look like?" Ryan asked, but he had his own ideas. And he knew that this new information from the IC would also create assumption bias in even the most intelligent military minds—and Kent and Kudryk were certainly two such minds. No amount of intellect seemed ever to trump human nature.

"Well," Kudryk began, "it would have to be something where they could generate some degree of sympathy from their allies at least."

"And produce some claim of legitimacy on the global stage. Something they could spin as a security issue for mainland China . . ." Kent added. Clearly they'd brainstormed this out together.

"A false flag of some sort," Kudryk continued, "even if only superficial, to reduce the likelihood of a global condemnation and response."

"That would be an absolute requirement," Mary Pat agreed.

"Because China's future is tied up in the global economy and that means global opinion matters. They need to present a case compelling enough that most countries would look the other way rather than take the economic hit of doing the right thing and sanctioning China directly."

"Not hard to do in the current world climate," Ryan pointed out. Not many countries existed that wouldn't feel the economic impact of a failed Chinese state or even a crippled Chinese economy—at least not First World countries. Ryan had seen the growth of worldwide Chinese dependency for years, and had long held the belief it represented a serious threat. Their dominance in technology, their cheap manufacturing, their precious metals and semiconductors . . . Business was war, and China waged that economic war with precision and might.

"Indeed," Kudryk agreed. "We've been war-gaming these scenarios more than ever the last six months. We have several scenarios, which, having been vetted through the lens of what we know thanks to ONI and the broader IC, seem the most likely . . ."

Ryan held up his hand, but turned to Mary Pat as he spoke. "I appreciate that, Bruce, and I'm well read in on the war-gamed scenarios, thanks to the great daily intelligence briefs. But what we need now"—he held his eyes on his DNI—"is intelligence to show us what *will* happen rather than a half dozen gamed scenarios of what could happen. But, before that, we need to validate the intelligence from Qin, starting with whether it really is coming from him and if so whether they're just pulling our chain. What are your people coming up with, Director Foley?"

Mary Pat sighed, and Ryan got it. He'd been on the receiving end of such urgent demands for actionable intelligence his whole life—well, until this job came along. Still, he needed to know.

"We have nothing concrete," Mary Pat said. "At least not yet.

We've engaged ONI, and the broader community is laser-focused now."

"There is one obvious solution we can use to fill the intelligence vacuum," Kudryk offered, trying and failing to wear a diplomatic hat for once. "Let's get Admiral Qin out of China and let him tell us what he knows. He authored the damn battle plan, after all."

Mary Pat sighed as she continued.

"We are exploring that possibility, obviously," she said patiently. "But extracting a Chinese national, much less a ranking member of the CCP, out of mainland China is no easy feat. And the only evidence we have that there even is a plan is Qin's claim."

"If we're even sure this came from Qin," Ryan added.

"We know the request came from Qin, sir," Mary Pat said. "He executed a bump at a meeting. Very ballsy. Very risky."

"With who?"

"Scott Kincaid. He's our deputy chief of mission in Beijing."

"And it would seem that Minister Qin knew he was CIA," Ryan said.

"Not necessarily," Mary Pat couched, but seeing his look she shrugged. "But probably."

Ryan held her eyes. His look, he knew, would tell her everything. "Use whatever assets we need to get answers quickly."

"Already working on it," she assured him, her eyes communicating the unspoken details he needed.

"Larry and Bruce, what are you recommending for defense?" Ryan asked.

"Task Force 70 and the *Reagan* strike group is in the area, Mr. President," Kent said. "We recommend she steam north and conduct operations east of Taiwan. In addition, the *Makin Island* is operating with her two LPDs on an East Pac deployment with the

Nimitz strike group in the eastern Pacific, sir. She has the 13th MEU aboard. We can steam them west to augment and have expeditionary Marines at the ready."

Ryan considered that a moment. Force projection was always a good thing and made bad players take pause. But he didn't want to provoke something here, especially if it might play into whatever narrative President Li was scripting.

"Move them west, but not directly into the AOR—not yet. Have them within a day or two away, however," he said, hoping he wasn't playing right into President Li Jian Jun's game plan.

"Sir, I'd like to get Raptors in the area," Kudryk said, referring to the lethal F-22 fifth-generation fighters. "We can deploy a det from Langley."

"Why not from Hickam?" Ryan asked, but he knew the answer and it annoyed him.

"Sir, the 19th has a det in Nellis right now, and can't provide the ground support and maintenance for a second det that this would require. The First Tac can give us more reliability right now." The F-22 program had originally called for nearly eight hundred aircraft, but eventually had been whittled down to barely two hundred. When a detachment deployed, the maintainers and other support needed to accompany them degraded the remaining squadron by nearly sixty percent, even compromising the ability to train. It was a problem that needed fixing. "We can get a Langley detachment from the 94th Fighter Squadron in Japan in the next few days by diverting the planned deployment to support contingency operations over Syria."

Ryan nodded. That made sense. The F-22 provided far more capability then the CENTCOM theater needed right now.

"Do it," he said to Kudryk.

"Mr. President," Kent said, "we also have a special operations exercise planned for Taiwan for six weeks from now. SEAL Team Five is conducting joint training exercises with the Taiwanese SEALs and DEVGRU was to provide a red force challenge. We can consider moving that up, or at least moving the two Special Warfare units into place now under the guise of exercise planning."

Ryan liked that idea—a lot.

"Do it," he said. "And can we embed elements from NSW Group Eight as well?"

This time he looked at Mary Pat instead of his Department of Defense heads. A few years ago, Group Eight had been established to absorb Group Three and Group Ten. Group Three had spent a decade as Special Warfare's undersea-focused command, operating the Dry Combat Submersibles, SEAL Delivery Vehicles of SDV 1 and 2, and the new technology including UUVs, the underwater drones that had become important to advanced intelligence and communications operations. With changing technology and its importance in intelligence, it had made sense to combine that unit with Group Ten. In addition to the HUMINT capabilities and Reconnaissance Teams One and Two, Group Ten had also evolved to cover cyber warfare, electronic warfare, and multi-domain unmanned systems spaces. Putting the two groups together under a single umbrella had been brilliant.

For this mission, Ryan was looking to bring all the intelligence elements of the new Group Eight to bear.

"That's a great idea," Mary Pat said, and Kent echoed his affirmation.

"We'll send a team from the SRT as part of the 'exercise.' That will be a tremendous help on the ground in Taiwan, but also for the Seventh Fleet."

"My thinking exactly. We need time," Ryan said, feeling a headache coming on. "We need time to unravel what's really going on and, if this proves to be real, get ahead of whatever false flag operation President Li may be planning."

There were nods around the room.

"We need answers, people. We can't risk a war over a gut feeling. If Minister Qin is to be believed, then things will go to hell very, very quickly." He turned to Mary Pat. "We need the entire IC on this. I assume that's in the works already?"

"It is," she said, and he could tell from her look that would include their go-to and most deniable assets. "And we're putting together a joint, interagency task force to work in the region . . ."

Ryan turned to his defense team, looking back and forth between Bruce Kudryk and Lawrence Kent. "We need to be prepared, gentlemen. We need our presence in the region reinforced for the predictable response. No American in the region gets harmed or there will be hell to pay. Make it clear, gentlemen."

"Will do," Kent replied.

"We need to reconvene at the end of the day to update the situation," Ryan said, "or sooner if events warrant. But let's get things moving." He turned to Mary Pat. "I have a few meetings this morning, but I need to be in the loop on this."

With that the room began to empty, and Ryan pressed a thumb into his left temple where the brewing headache had begun.

He looked up, and found himself alone again with Mary Pat.

"Tell me straight, Mary Pat, if this is real, is defecting Qin even viable?"

She didn't answer for a long moment. "Difficult, but not impossible."

"Do you have a plan?"

"I'm working on it."

Ryan sighed. He needed ibuprofen for his head, and a coffee would help as well. "Tell me about this interagency task force."

"Of course. We're mobilizing a team with representatives from the FBI out of the joint counterterror task force, CIA of course, and we'll roll the elements of Special Warfare Group Eight in, just in case. And, anticipating your Navy force projection, Admiral Kohler has reached out for an ONI presence on the task force, which I agreed with, so they'll round out the team. That gives us inside, real-time intelligence for the fleet as tension mounts and the predictable chaos from China's response to our presence."

Ryan nodded. The Chinese belligerence and aggression toward U.S. ships in the region had been a pain in the ass, but now a misstep could lead to war. The last thing he could risk doing until they knew more was unintentionally giving President Li a reason, if he was looking for one.

Ryan wanted to ask who was coming from ONI, but resisted. That was a call for the director of naval intelligence, and Mary Pat may not even know yet.

"I'll be opening a dialogue with our allies in and around the region," he said. "I wish we still had Rainbow up and running. This would be a perfect mission for an international group with sanctioned autonomy."

"Funny you should say that, Jack," Mary Pat said. "I spoke with a close mutual friend who was thinking the same thing. I was about to propose that you authorize the ODNI to work with our partners to stand up a joint international task force modeled after Rainbow to respond quickly if and when the violence begins. I would like to propose inviting John Clark to come out of retirement to head the group up, if you think our partner nations would be interested."

Ryan smiled. He, of course, knew John Clark was not *really* retired and that he remained a go-to asset for his director of national intelligence—including the operations to stop the *Belgorod* and unravel the Russian cabal behind it.

"And you believe his private-sector employer would be willing to let him go?"

"I'm sure it can be arranged," Mary Pat said with a wry grin. "It would only be temporary. A response to a real crisis. And my understanding is that his employer at the financial firm he works for is a real patriot. I can make it happen."

"Let's do it," Ryan said. It would be nice to have a sanctioned relationship with the man he trusted more than anyone in the world. "Let me see the details on the structure and I can float it to our partners—especially in the UK, Germany, Australia, and South Korea. We need representation from Taiwan, of course."

"I'll take care of it, Jack."

Ryan rose, gathering his leather notebook and the notes he'd taken.

"And Jack?"

He looked over at Mary Pat, an eyebrow arched.

"I know you won't ask, so I'll just tell you. The admiral is tapping his rising star to head up the ONI contingent. Katie will be receiving orders this morning to deploy to Taiwan."

Ryan kept the gut punch from showing on his face, but he wasn't surprised. Katie had proven herself as a star analyst during the *Belgorod* "incident." She was the perfect choice. And he was commander in chief today.

"Let Admiral Kohler know that you and the White House believe that's a perfect choice," he said. "And get your joint intelligence task force and this new international team heading into theater immediately. We need to get out in front of this thing, Mary Pat. I don't want to get stuck playing catch-up."

12

K atie rapped with two knuckles on the door frame, after peering in the open door to see Captain Ferguson at the small table he used instead of his desk, two laptops open and his reading glasses on the tip of his nose.

He looked up from one of the laptops. "Come on in, Ryan, and close the door behind you."

She did as instructed and took a seat opposite him, then waited to be addressed by her boss. He'd summoned her just minutes ago, telling her to come to his office at her "earliest convenience," which she'd learned long ago meant ASAFP.

"There is a situation brewing in the Pacific requiring ONI's attention," he said, and pushed a tablet computer across his desk toward her. "Take a look."

With anticipatory butterflies in her stomach, she picked up the tablet and looked at the screen, which had a classified memo that had been forwarded to Ferguson from the director of ONI, Vice

Admiral Matt Kohler. She quickly read the text, which summarized how the Chinese minister of national defense had contacted a CIA case officer on the American embassy staff outlining his desire to defect and what he was willing to trade for that privilege. He'd also signaled that Operation Sea Serpent was not an exercise but a battle plan for an actual invasion.

She set the tablet down on Ferguson's desk and looked up. "Well, shit, that's not good."

"My reaction exactly," he said, removing his reading glasses and laying them on the table.

"The timing, coinciding with the disappearance of the minister of foreign affairs, certainly is concerning, but this feels out of character for someone like Qin," she said, her brain having moved on almost without her permission, past the face-value shock of the report to considerations like veracity, motive, and strategy. "Are we sure this is real? Qin has been vetted at the highest levels and I would assume is a true believer to be in the position he is. Plus, he's a former naval officer."

I imagine that his predecessor was a true believer as well, and we know how that ended up . . .

Ferguson nodded. "I agree, which is why I've decided I want you to head up an ONI team to represent us on a joint interagency task force stood up to investigate what the hell is going on and, in the case of the ONI contingent, to keep the Seventh Fleet commanders well-versed on gathered intelligence. If you want my personal opinion, the defection of Minister Qin is a pipe dream. We'll never get our hands on that battle plan, and even if we do, it will be too late. Which is why your charter is not only to gather and analyze intelligence but to provide scenario-based predictions and recommendations to U.S. naval forces in the region. Leadership needs to understand how to mitigate risk and proactively maintain maritime stability and our tactical advantage in the Seventh Fleet AOR."

She didn't answer immediately, because she couldn't. Her brain was too busy reeling from her boss's pronouncement . . .

He cleared his throat. "Shall I take your silence as a yes?"

"Um, sorry, sir," she said, blinking him back into focus. "It's just, there's quite a bit to unpack in what you said."

The left corner of his mouth curled up into the hint of a crooked grin. "Understood. But, of course, I only ask the question as a courtesy. That's why they call them orders, Ryan. But look, Katie, this is a short-fuse mission because the President and the Joint Chiefs desperately need to know what's happening with the announced Sea Serpent exercise. Is it an exercise or a cover story for an invasion of Taiwan? We need you to uncover the truth, gather real-time intelligence, and feed it to our fleet."

She nodded as a new, almost discordantly ironic thought occurred to her. Then her brain-to-mouth filter glitched and what she'd been thinking leaked out. "All due respect, sir, but why me? I'm not the East Asia expert. Why not send Hollister or McMahon? They know the region, PLA order of battle, and politics way better than I do."

He chuckled. "Because what we need is someone who thinks outside the box. Someone with a track record of identifying tactics and strategies that are being employed by our adversaries that other people miss. That person is you, Ryan. If I need to know how many missiles a Type 055 destroyer carries, I'll call Hollister or McMahon. Admiral Kohler was beyond impressed with your performance during the *Belgorod* incident, and so was I. We talked and decided that you're too valuable of an asset to keep holed up inside the walls here at NMIC. We want to take the Katie Ryan show on the road."

On the road? Just awesome.

What came out of her mouth next was both embarrassing and absurd. "But, I like my new office . . ."

To her relief, he took this as a joke. "I'm not taking away your office, Ryan," he said through a laugh. "I'm just letting you know you're probably going to be spending the next few weeks away from it."

She forced a smile on her face, hoping to hide her displeasure with her new tasking. What he'd just proposed was precisely what she wanted to *avoid*. She'd pursued a career in intelligence because she *wanted* to work in an office. She didn't want travel. She didn't want to be a field agent—forward deployed and on the pointy tip of the spear. That was her big brother Jack's gig.

I'm an analyst, her inner voice grumbled. *And who's going to look after Josie?*

"Earth to Ryan," Ferguson said, waving his hand to get her attention. "Are you all right?"

"Sorry, sir," she said, having to be snapped back to the present for the second time in as many minutes. "I was just thinking."

"I thought you'd be excited about this."

"I am," she lied.

"Good, because this was a by-name request from the admiral and we don't want to let him down."

She exhaled slowly. "So, who are the other members of the unit or group, or whatever you're calling it?"

"Task force," he said, "and in addition to an ONI officer from the Kennedy Center, you'll take along an IS from the shop. Our contingent from ONI will partner with representatives from the CIA and I expect someone from the DIA to be there as well. And, of course, whoever else Director Foley from the ODNI sends."

"Oh, okay. So, when do I meet the officer from Kennedy?" she asked, referring to the ONI center tasked with warfare analysis for Naval Special Warfare and Cyber.

"Today. The task force is being mobilized immediately."

"Does this new unit have a code name?" she said, trying to psych herself up and channel her inner 007. "You know, something cool like Task Force Firefly or Operation Kraken?"

Apparently, he found this question extremely amusing because he shook his head and grimaced playfully as he shoved a folder across the table to her. "Yeah, it's really cool—we call it Task Force 25."

Red-cheeked, she changed the subject.

"I'll put my team together," she said after a beat, "and meet with the Kennedy Center officer . . . What did you say their name was?"

"I didn't," Ferguson said and leaned back in his chair. "His name is Lieutenant John Conza."

"Captain Bellamy is sending an O-3?" she asked, surprised. She felt under-ranked as an O-4 for something like this.

"O-2," Ferguson corrected. "He's still a junior grade. But he makes up for it with his background. Conza was an enlisted SEAL for eight years before his injury. Lost a leg from an IED in Syria while assigned to SEAL Team Five. You can get to know him better on the plane," he said, picking up the pair of reading glasses and putting them on—his signature move to signal that the meeting was over and he was ready to get back to work.

She met his knowing gaze. "On the plane? What plane?"

"You're heading to Taiwan. You leave in five hours."

"You're kidding?"

"Do I look like I'm kidding?" he said, tilting his head down and looking at her over his glasses.

"No, you do not," she murmured.

"You fly out for Norfolk, where you'll meet with the SURFLANT and brief him on the situation from our perspective. Then you'll join the rest of the task force on the flight out of Virginia Beach to Taiwan. Your orders and flight details are in the folder," he said, sliding an interoffice mail folder across his desk and then returning his attention to his computers. "Task Force 25 is operating under an OC of preparing for an already scheduled exercise with the Taiwanese 101st Amphibious Reconnaissance Battalion—their version of our SEALs—so that will place your team on the Penghu island base."

She swallowed hard, resisting the urge to ask again if he was kidding. The Taiwanese had established forward operating bases for their Special Forces units on both the Kinmen and Penghu islands in the Strait of Taiwan. The former was only a stone's throw from mainland China, and Penghu wasn't much farther.

"If you're bringing Pettigrew with you, I recommend you tell him straightaway. I hear he's a slow packer," Ferguson said, signaling, again, that they were done.

She scooted her chair back, stood, and tucked the folder under her arm. Feeling very much like someone who'd just been told they were going to need a root canal, she said, "Thank you, sir, for this . . . *opportunity.*"

The hint of a smile returned to Ferguson's face, but he didn't look up. "Good luck, Ryan, and don't be afraid to give 'em hell if somebody tries to put you in a box, especially the spooks from the three-letter agencies. You're the face of ONI in the field on this, and that means Admiral Kohler is loaning you his big stick to carry. Just be smart about who you decide to whack on the head with it."

"Yes, sir. Understood."

"Leave my door open on your way out, Ryan," he called to her back as she walked out.

The folder—which in reality weighed only a few ounces—might as well have been a hundred-pound dumbbell her boss had ordered her to carry around.

"Why me?" she grumbled. "I hate the field . . ."

A flashbulb memory of being lowered by cable winch out the back of a hovering Osprey onto the sail of the broached USS *Washington* Virginia-class submarine popped into her mind—something she still couldn't believe she'd done and never wanted to do again.

Ferguson's words echoed in her head: *"You're the face of ONI in the field on this . . ."*

Wonderful, she thought, shaking her head as she made her way to Pettigrew's desk to give him the bad news. *Just friggin' wonderful.*

"You must be Ryan," a friendly voice announced, and she looked up to see a naval officer in khakis striding toward her in the hall. "I'm John Conza," the man said, extending a hand.

Then it all clicked into place. The man was handsome, dark hair, dark eyes, Hollywood fit. But the partial sleeve tattoo on his right arm and the ribbon stack far too tall to be a lieutenant JG, topped with a gold Navy SEAL Trident, confirmed her guess.

"You're my new teammate from Kennedy," she said. She glanced down at the man's feet, then closed her eyes in horror at the obvious glance at his disability. She released his powerful handshake, then looked back up into his eyes, aware her face was burning and no doubt crimson. Worse, it had been pointless, since both khaki pant legs ended at the top of polished black shoes—though not the high-sheen patent leather most intel officers wore with khakis.

Good God, Katie, what did you expect—a peg leg?

Conza, to his credit, ignored the faux pas.

"My teammates always call me JC," the officer said. "I was on my way to meet with Captain Ferguson, who is giving me a quick brief and my orders, apparently."

"Yeah," she said. "You're gonna love it. Just got mine. Guess we're working together on this one."

"Looking forward to it, Commander," Conza said. "Heard you're the genius over here at Brooks. Single-handedly destroyed a rogue Russian submarine or some such shit."

Katie couldn't help but laugh out loud.

"Don't believe everything you hear, JC," she said. "Especially an urban legend like that. And call me Katie. I can hold my own running a PowerPoint presentation, but I'm sure no Navy SEAL."

"Well, Katie," Conza said, studying her, but still smiling. "My experience has been urban legends are usually based on something. I look forward to working with you."

"You too," she said. "I'd wait and chat more, but I need to tell my best IS that he's heading with us to Taiwan—which he will not be thrilled about—and then I need to go pack a seabag."

"Right," Conza said. "Guess I'll be seeing you soon."

"Sooner than you think," Katie said, glancing at her watch and shaking her head.

She continued down the hall, hustling toward where Pettigrew would be at his desk, but her new teammate hollered after her.

"Hey, Commander Ryan," Conza called out, and she turned to find him grinning at her. "It's the left one," he said, pulling up the left pant leg of his khakis to reveal a polished black prosthetic that ended with several inches of articulated stainless steel, which extended into his black shoe. "Got my dress leg on today."

"Thanks," she said, regretting that she couldn't think of a single other thing to say. She felt the heat of her blush.

"I'm totally just messing with you," Conza said, laughing and dropping his pant leg back down. "You can't even imagine the shit Team Guys give each other."

"Right," she said. "I'll see you later."

Then she put her embarrassment behind her.

She had a lot to do in the next couple of hours.

13

John Clark leaned back in his comfortable black leather chair, a huge grin on his face.

"I'm glad you see the utility in the idea, at least," he said on the encrypted line on which he spoke with America's chief intelligence officer.

"I have no doubt the boss will support the idea, John," Mary Pat Foley said. "If the present situation proves to be what we fear, it could be an incredibly valuable asset. And," she added, and now he could almost picture her wry smile, "I'm sure the President will be as thrilled as I am at the thought of having you out of retirement and back in the game, even if only for a short time."

"Well, I certainly appreciate that, Madam Director," he said. "But I'll wait for your call with approval before I start putting together a team."

"Don't wait, John," she said, her voice now deadly serious.

"Start your outreach and vetting now. I am confident President Ryan will approve this, so move quickly. I'll authorize space at the Farm for you to train up your team on a short fuse so you can get right to work."

"Sounds great," Clark said, though the weight of this brought mixed feelings. Coming in out of the dark had its advantages, but also carried some downsides. The idea he'd pitched for an international task force based on the Rainbow model couldn't happen without high levels of sanction, which meant trading the safety of the shadows for greater visibility in the light.

"It's great to have you back, John," Mary Pat said, and then the line went dead.

He looked up to see Ding leaning against his door frame.

"Sounds like that went well," his teammate said.

"It did indeed," he replied.

"You sure about this?" Ding asked. "I'm not gonna lie, man. There is comfort in the dark."

Clark let out a long sigh. He totally got it. In this case, coming out of the "dark" of the deeply covert, unsanctioned activities of The Campus, where not a single politician had a shred of paper or money trail to their activities, carried an even bigger risk. Because, in the Rainbow model, they were putting trust in the security not only of the ODNI but in the sister organizations of the international community.

"I get it completely, brother," he said. "But to get the depth of support from partner nations we'd need if this shitstorm really starts to blow, I don't see a better way."

"Okay, well, I'm in," Ding said. "Who else from here? Jack will be back in a day . . ."

Clark shook his head.

"Not for this one," he said. "We need him on standby here for whatever next short-fuse crisis crops up. It's just you and me this time."

"Roger that," Ding said.

"How was your meeting with Jerry?"

"All good," Ding said. "Hendley signed off and we are now on official sabbatical from our investment firm duties. Whoever you choose, which it sounds like is just the two of us."

"Actually," Clark said, rising from his desk. "Check and see if Rick is willing to come along and help us translate whatever intelligence streams we get access to. We need a brainiac, now that we're going to be on the receiving end of a firehose of intel."

"On it," Ding said. "Where are you going?"

"Home," Clark said. "After you chat with Rick, you should do the same. Take my daughter out for a nice dinner, and we'll watch the kids." He slung his leather briefcase over his shoulder by its strap. "I expect we'll head to Williamsburg tomorrow and get set up to receive our teammates, if all goes well. And, if this whole thing is as real as Mary Pat thinks it is, we may not be home for a while."

14

Katie followed the driver, whom she'd expected to drop them at the front of the terminal rather than escort them through the small, tile-floored reception area to the private room, where they were meeting the rest of what Conza kept calling their "stick." The former SEAL followed behind her as she dragged her wheeled duffel across the floor, where it made a *click . . . click . . . click* sound as she walked. The driver, Petty Officer Deneen, was eyeing the coffee kiosk in the lobby of the air terminal, rubbing his hands together.

"Gotta get caffeinated, ma'am," he said sheepishly when she glanced at him.

Pettigrew and Conza had, predictably, hit it off immediately. She wasn't being a misandrist, and it wasn't because they were both men. It was because Pettigrew and Conza were both country outdoorsmen, hunting, fishing, and camping types.

Is it uncool to think of them as rednecks?

She didn't think so, since Bubba always referred to himself as a redneck with great pride, and Conza had already referenced himself as a redneck with a degree.

"Here you are, ma'am," Petty Officer Deneen said, gesturing with a hand at the door he opened for her. She had no idea if he was from NOB Norfolk, the AMC terminal, or perhaps from the ONI office.

"Thank you, shipmate," she said, and the sailor spun on a booted heel and hustled back across the tiny terminal, making a beeline for the coffee kiosk.

She entered the room, which turned out to be a combination conference room and lounge, complete with a government surplus–style conference table across from a well-worn, faded leather sofa, matching love seat, and two matching chairs surrounding a square coffee table. She met the eyes of the man seated at the head of the conference table. He was flanked by two men on one side and a woman on the other, all wearing blue jeans, sports shirts, and hiking boots.

Our CIA contingent . . .

"You must be the ONI gang," the man at the head of the table said, shooting her a pleasant-enough smile.

"What gave it away?" she asked, reaching out a hand and laughing, since her team was all dressed in the Navy's latest iteration of BDUs—the Type III uniform, which had a camouflage pattern that shared a color palette with guacamole. "I'm Lieutenant Commander Ryan."

"Ted," the man said after a short, firm handshake.

"John Conza," Conza said, shaking the case officer's hand next, and then introducing Bubba. "This is Petty Officer Pettigrew."

"People call me Bubba," Pettigrew said.

"I'm sure they do," Ted said, gesturing for them to have a seat

110

at the table and then glancing out the row of windows, where the ramp sat empty. "I don't see our ride, so we may have a little time to kill."

Katie took a seat at the opposite end of the modest table, with Conza and Pettigrew flanking her as Ted made introductions to the rest of the CIA team.

"This is Andrew and Ben," he said, indicating the two men beside him, who both gave small waves.

"Call me Drewski," said the handsome man on the left, whose long and unkempt curly black hair and patchy beard made him look more like a blues singer than a CIA case officer.

"Good to meet you, Drewski," Katie said.

"And this is Sam," Ted added, gesturing to the woman beside him—whom Katie decided must be a triathlete, based on her build.

"Simran Bakshi," the woman said with a nod to Katie, smiling with both her mouth and her mocha-colored eyes. "*These* guys call me Sam."

"Why?" Conza asked.

"I suppose because my name wasn't Beth, or Jessica, or Amy, but mainly because they're morons," Sam said, delivering the line perfectly.

The laughter that followed broke any ice remaining in the room.

"So you're the OGA team," Conza said, using the other-government-agency acronym usually reserved for CIA. "Where is the DIA contingent?"

"Arriving with the plane," Ted explained. "No sense hiking down to Virginia Beach to meet up when Andrews is so much closer."

"Aren't you guys up in Northern Virginia, too?" Bubba pointed out as he slipped a can of Copenhagen from his blouse breast pocket and an empty soda bottle from his cargo pocket.

"Yep," the man called Drewski said as Bubba packed a dip into his lip. Katie watched Conza raise a finger and an expectant eyebrow, and Bubba slid the can of smokeless tobacco across the table to him. She might be in charge, but she was already feeling the odd man out with the blossoming bromance. "We were in the area already, if you know what I'm sayin'."

"Williamsburg?" Conza asked, packing his own lip with a generous helping of tobacco.

Operated by the Department of Defense as the Armed Forces Experimental Training Activity, Camp Peary outside of Williamsburg was the world's most poorly kept secret. In its current incarnation, Peary hosted the CIA's covert training facility known as "the Farm," used to train CIA officers from the Directorate of Operations, as well as the DIA's Defense Clandestine Service. The CIA also planned and trained for specific operations at the facility, with partner organizations such as the DIA, FBI, and the SEALs and Army Special Forces from the JSOC.

"That was convenient," she noted.

Ted just smiled.

"I understand that you'll be heading up the intelligence section of our little task force here."

Katie studied the man carefully, but he remained smiling and relaxed. She expected there might be some sort of turf battle over who had authority over what, but hoped that wouldn't be the case. Teams worked best when they put mission over whatever political rice bowls might exist outside of their mission, especially up north "inside the Beltway."

"I'd like to approach this as a collaboration, Ted," she said. "Each of our task force components bring unique skill sets to the team, but we also have our individual charters from our parent commands. I say we take a team approach here to make sure everyone shares intel and collaborates on analysis, but also gets what they need so we can complete all aspects of our individual missions."

"That's cool," Ted said. "Glad to be working with a famous sub hunter. I've heard, well, *read* a lot about you."

She felt herself blush. Surely there was some wall of secrecy around her exploits in the covert mission to stop the *Belgorod* that had not been penetrated. The idea of people at the CIA reading *about* her felt horrifying.

"The most important thing for us to be successful is the unfiltered sharing of both information and opinion. Do you agree?" she asked.

"Completely," he said. "And I know Lou Donatelli, our DIA lead, very well. He's a former Army JSOC guy, so he knows about how things need to work in a joint task force environment. And his teammate, Lorie Tengco, is a total badass, but also a solid team player. I deployed with her before."

"That thing in Mariupol?" Sam asked, and Ted nodded. "I heard she's the real deal."

"And I heard Mariupol was a total shit show," Drewski said, and then fist-bumped his partner, Ben, as they laughed at some inside joke.

"Well, sounds like we've got the perfect team," Katie said, hoping the lovefest continued once they got in the thick of things.

"The challenge will be working with the Group Eight team," Ted warned, his voice lowering after glancing over at the closed door. "They're talented and professional, but I hear they tend to stay a little more to themselves."

"Group Eight, like Naval Special Warfare Group Eight?" Katie asked, surprised, keeping her own voice low. "I wasn't briefed they were part of Task Force 25."

"Technically, they're not—not formally," Ted said. "They're going to be with us at Penghu, working with the Sea Dragon frogmen and the other NSW elements. But we'll want to loop in close with them for information sharing."

"I can help with that," Conza said, and then dribbled some tobacco juice into a Styrofoam cup he had fetched from the small coffee station beside the table. "When Big Navy folded SRT 1 and 2 in with the intel collection elements from Group Three, they became an intel gold mine. Their charter might be to provide signals, HUMINT, and covert ops to prep the battlefield for JSOC and Navy elements, but they are very much team players in the joint environment, I promise. More so probably than the DEVGRU guys, who are highly compartmentalized because they're all direct-action oriented."

"Sounds like you're a frogman?"

"Former," Conza said with a shrug. Katie knew that was like being a "former" Marine. "I have a close buddy over at SRT 2 and I augmented at DEVGRU for a time. By the way . . ." He glanced over at Katie. "The details of their work is obviously SCI-level shit, but the *existence* of Group Eight is open-source, so it's okay to talk about them."

"Where did the orders for Group Eight come from?" Katie asked, feeling annoyed now. It seemed odd that Captain Ferguson hadn't briefed her on the NSW covert intelligence team joining them. She was the ONI component, for crying out loud, so why was she hearing about Group Eight from the CIA?

"We heard about it from our ODNI brief," Ted said. "So, my guess is it came from the White House."

"Gotcha," Katie said. Ferguson may not have heard until they were already departed, and that was the kind of information not best shared on a phone call. She'd be grateful to arrive at their final destination and have access to a TOC for information sharing.

"We can discuss more details of how to structure the team during the flight over," Ted said, maybe reading her mind. "We're traveling on an agency asset, so it's basically an airborne TOC. The aviators are organic to us, so they're both TS/SCI cleared."

"Great," Katie replied, and meant it. "We should probably settle in and then get intel updates from our various head sheds, and then we can share information and brainstorm out an approach to . . ." She hesitated to say it out loud. ". . . Our mission."

"By mission, you mean supporting the joint special operations exercise with Taiwan's Navy and the Sea Dragons?" Ben asked, his eyes twinkling with amusement.

"Exactly," she said. The rest would have to wait, and not much longer, it seemed, since the executive Boeing 777 that taxied now onto the ramp in front of the terminal was painted all white, with no markings except a civilian aircraft registration number, in this case beginning with a C, meaning it was registered in Canada.

That plane could literally only be CIA.

"JC!" a voice boomed from her left as the door opened. She looked over to see a mountain of a man standing there, a large duffel over his shoulder. Dressed in gray cargo pants, a flannel shirt, and a Hurley ball cap, he grinned through a bushy red beard as he stared at Conza, who was already on his feet and hustling over to the door.

"What's up, bro?" Conza said as the SEAL operator dropped his duffel and they wrapped each other up in a bear hug, the new arrival lifting Conza off the floor.

"Oh shit, dude," Conza laughed.

The burly SEAL stepped back and inspected Conza's left leg, then put his hands on his hips, shaking his head in apparent disappointment. "Bro, you promised you'd do a peg leg, like an honest-to-God pirate."

For no good reason, Katie blushed, remembering the thought she'd had about a peg leg when she'd been caught glancing at Conza's prosthetic.

"No, asshole," Conza said. "I promised if I lost an eye, *then* I'd get a peg leg and a black eye patch. If I can't be a SEAL, then pirate is the only other viable alternative."

"So . . . looks like I'm crashing y'all's party," the SEAL said, looking past Conza—whom he towered over by eight inches—into the flight lounge.

"Come on in," Katie called out from her seat. "I'm guessing you're here to join us on the flight for Task Force 25?"

"Can't say, ma'am. But if so, we'll have to connect on board," he answered with a wink. "My team is staging gear. If we're on the same plane, I look forward to meeting you all." He turned to Conza again and pointed a finger at him. "Don't drink the ginger ale, dude."

"I won't," Conza said, and they both laughed at some inside joke.

"And keep that peg leg greased, bro," the SEAL said as he turned to leave. "You never know when you might need to jam."

"I hear that," Conza said, and closed the door behind the operator.

She watched her new teammate's face fade from joy to something else. She wondered just how hard it had been for the man to transition from a man of action with the elite SEAL teams to sitting at a desk analyzing intelligence data.

The human toll—it reaches everywhere . . .

"Commander Ryan?" a new, far-less booming voice called as the door opened again. Katie turned and saw a young female sailor standing at the door with a clipboard.

"Yes?" she answered.

"Ma'am, your aircraft is here. If I could get you to confirm the passenger manifest and have everyone present their CAC cards, please?"

"Of course," she said and rose.

"We can then tag all of your bags and get them on the ramp."

"Well," Ted announced and stood as well. "Let's show IDs to this charming young lady and then assemble our gear outside." He looked at Katie. "We'll get into a deeper conversation once we're in the air."

"Sounds good, Ted," she said. "And please call me Katie."

"All right, Katie," the CIA officer said.

Her thought went to the burly SEAL they'd just met, and just outside the open door she saw him with more than another half dozen similarly clad men and one woman, though none the size of the man who'd hugged Conza. They stood surrounding a mountain of gear—duffels, backpacks, and two stacks of what she surmised were weapons cases.

Her thoughts drifted to her comfortable new office, swivel chair, and Josie sitting on the windowsill. She shook her head.

Just what the hell has Captain Ferguson gotten me into?

15

Zhīzhū (the Spider) walked her web, the strands invisible to everyone but her.

Like an actual orb weaver, Léi had designed her tapestry with diverging meridians tied together by a spiral that began at the front door of her apartment and expanded outward. And, just like a real spider, she'd committed every node and filament to memory. She'd lived in the same apartment, in the same neighborhood, for twenty-five years. Getting lost or turned around was impossible for her. Her mental map and ability to geolocate within her domain would give even the best satellite GPS program a run for its money. She knew and recognized every sign, building, street corner, and alley. She knew hundreds of locals—from business owners to bartenders, baristas to beauticians—and she interacted with them regularly and in meaningful ways. She patronized their shops and salons. She learned the names of their

spouses and children. She tipped often and generously and performed thoughtful favors that made people like and appreciate
her. And in the doing, she had slowly and methodically built a
network of genuine allies who would, if ever called upon, recip-
rocate her kindness. Their shops, restaurants, and apartments all
served as safe, highly vetted, and inconspicuous signal nodes and
drop locations.

In the espionage business, operating "in pattern" was critical to
an asset's survival, but, of course, patterns had their own risks and
she sought to find that balance as the world changed. Over the
past two decades, the number of cameras in Beijing had increased
exponentially. The Ministry of State Security and Beijing police
watched everyone, everywhere, all the time. More troubling than
the cameras themselves, however, were the powerful data-
processing servers the cameras fed. Léi was no computer expert,
but she didn't need to be a hacker to appreciate the threat.

According to her current CIA handler, Scott Kincaid, the Chinese government used artificial intelligence and machine learning
to perform facial recognition, movement tracking, and pattern
recognition. Everywhere she went and everything she did was
monitored and studied by the computer network. So long as her
behavior wasn't flagged, she was unlikely to warrant the attention
of a dedicated human surveillance team. However, there was no
way for the CIA, or for Léi herself, to know if she'd been flagged,
so the recommendation was for her to always operate under the
assumption she was under active surveillance. This didn't frighten
or unnerve her. It had been her default mindset her entire career.
Assuming she was being watched is what kept her on her toes and
focused.

Paranoia was her best friend.

Paranoia kept her alive.

"Hi, Ping," she said, greeting a street cart vendor at the location she thought of as node nineteen.

"Léi! It's wonderful to see you. How are you?" the middle-aged man asked with a wide smile on his face.

"I'm well. How is the bun business today?"

Ping sold homemade *baozi*, aka bao buns. He only sold one variety, a steamed bun stuffed with a savory BBQ pork filling that was so delicious that she actually daydreamed about them often.

"The business of *baozi* is a steamy one," he said, laughing at his own joke, which he repeated each and every time they crossed paths. Then he made small talk as he used a pair of bamboo tongs to select a fresh bun from the tray and wrap it in paper for her. She used the moment of his distracted attention to check her six and scan for watchers. "On the house, for the most beautiful woman I know."

"Ping, if you give them away for free, your wife is going to be furious with you," she said, graciously accepting the culinary gift.

"She's furious with me no matter what I do," he said and tapped his cheek. "But at least this way, I get a kiss from a pretty girl and end the day happy."

She chuckled, leaned in, and gave him a peck on the cheek.

This was their routine, fifteen years in the making, and they both looked forward to it.

"Thank you, Ping. My stomach is already grumbling," she said, stepping back.

"I hope you have a nice walk. Good night, old friend."

She glanced at the side of Ping's cart, looking for a mark, and saw nothing. Then she unwrapped the paper to expose the steaming-hot bao bun and took a bite. "Heaven," she said, grinning with food in her mouth as she turned to leave.

Conducting SDRs, or surveillance detection routes, was a critical component of every "web walk." The purpose of SDRs was twofold: first, to make it more difficult for any would-be surveillance team to effectively track and trail her; and second, to provide multiple opportunities for her to conduct countersurveillance to spot any would-be tails, or *ticks*, as they were known. Typical SDR maneuvers included route variations, random stops to allow visual scans, and speed changes. Advanced SDR techniques included unexpected reversals of direction, clothing changes, vehicle swaps, and employing confederates to distract, delay, or confuse any watchers.

Léi's taxicab company was one of her greatest SDR assets. She employed sixty percent women and made an effort to hire girls who resembled her in build and appearance. She put herself in the rotation of drivers, taking shifts every week. This not only created a pattern of her behind the wheel, but kept her driving and navigation skills sharp. She also patronized her own taxi service regularly, hailing rides from dispatch many times a week.

Location "jumps" by taxi during her walking SDRs were a backbone maneuver.

Using central dispatch, she would pre-stage a pickup at a particular intersection or alley so that her driver would be ready and waiting *before* her arrival. That way, she never had to wait on a ride and any ticks following her on foot would be forced to hand her off to a partner in a vehicle, which would almost certainly be out of position. If she wanted to really level things up, she would use multiple taxis to play a shell game—swapping cars in covered locations like parking garages and tunnels. For shell games, she only used her most senior and trusted employees. To explain this odd behavior, she confided in one that she had a secret romance with a person of importance and let the office rumor mill take care of the rest. The knowing smiles and blushing cheeks were all the proof she needed that "her girls" were fully invested in helping her "get a little action on the side."

The first five blocks of her SDR involved three stops to check her six, two direction changes, and one prolonged loiter at a local grocery store, where she bought a few items. During that first leg, she checked for signal marks in designated places—signposts, curbs, building corners, and the price placard for scallions in the produce section of the grocery. If a mark was present, it would indicate that a drop awaited her at a different location. Every signal node was tied to a specific dead-drop location, and that one-to-one relationship never changed. She compartmentalized this information carefully. No source was aware of any other source's signal or dead-drop locations, and she served as a firewall between her CIA handler and her sources.

Having successfully completed her SDR without spotting any tails, she began leg two of her web walk. On reaching the third signal location—a noodle shop—she saw a panda sticker stuck on the bottom left corner of the shop window. Her heart rate instantly spiked, followed by a surge of adrenaline. Scott Kincaid used three different stickers to communicate with her: pandas, dragons, and butterflies. The panda sticker signaled a drop with tasking of the highest priority.

Kincaid had never used a panda sticker before.

Feeling the most alive she'd felt in months, she centered herself to contain her emotions. She could not risk letting any of the excitement she was feeling impact her demeanor, body language, or the pace at which she walked. The drop location she'd selected for panda events was Club Icon, a high-end bar, gastropub, and nightclub frequented by Westerners. A place where the very Caucasian and closely watched Scott Kincaid could visit without drawing too much attention. She'd never actually met Kincaid face-to-face, but she knew what he looked like because his head-shot was on the U.S. State Department's Chinese embassy web-site. Kincaid was supposed to go to Club Icon biweekly to establish a pattern of patronage.

Hopefully, he'd kept this promise.

She walked the remainder of leg two, completing the route as she normally would, before hailing one of her trusted drivers for a ride to Club Icon. When the cab arrived, she climbed into the back seat and greeted the driver, a woman named Biyu. During the drive, Léi transformed her appearance by applying dramatic mascara, eye shadow, and lipstick, letting her hair down, and ditching her sweatshirt and track pants for the yoga pants and exercise bra she already wore underneath. In the dim club lights, she would fit in just fine. In fact, the last time she'd gone to Club Icon, she'd had men half her age hitting on her all night long.

Flattering, but also annoying.

"Biyu, can you please take my groceries and outerwear back to the garage at the end of your shift?" she asked when they arrived at the club.

"Yes, madam. Do you have a hot date tonight?" Biyu asked.

"*Very* hot," Léi said with a mischievous grin, and climbed out of the back seat of the taxi.

"I wish I could be so bold as you. I live vicariously through your adventures. I want to hear all about it tomorrow," Biyu said, grinning back.

"That's a deal," Léi said, and shut the door.

She took a deep, centering breath, imagined herself twenty years younger and as the sexiest woman in Beijing, then walked with confidence to the entrance of Club Icon. The bouncer at the door looked her up and down, then waved her inside without making her pay the cover charge. It was still early, two hours before Icon transformed into a dance club, but the bar and dining areas were packed with the after-work crowd.

The hostess, standing beside a podium just inside the door, greeted Léi with polite disinterest—as if to say, *I'm better than you, but you're also a paying customer I'm supposed to serve.*

"All of our tables are spoken for," the young woman said, not even bothering to make eye contact with Léi, "but you're welcome to look for a seat at our bar."

Léi fantasized about dropping the woman with a four-beat, four-strike Wing Chun combination to the face and neck. Then, without a parting word, she left the pathetic thing behind the hostess stand and made her way to the reverse U-shaped bar twenty meters away.

The Icon Bar, as it was known colloquially, was truly a sight to behold. Somehow, the designer had managed to suspend colorful crystals in a fifteen-centimeter-thick block of clear resin that formed the bar top. The "floating" crystals were then illuminated by UV strip lighting that ran the perimeter, causing the floating crystals to glow like stars in a purple sky. It genuinely looked to Léi as if someone had miniaturized a vast chunk of outer space and trapped it in glass.

"It's beautiful, isn't it?" a male voice said behind her as she stepped up to the right corner of the bar. "The entire universe, trapped in amber."

She turned to see a tall, thirty-something Chinese man, whom she didn't recognize, smiling at her. He was dressed in a hipster suit with a starched white shirt that was open at the collar.

"Yes, it is," she said, taking a measure of his motives—noting his posture, pupil dilation, and nature of his smile.

"Can I buy you a drink?" he asked, moving into position beside her. He placed both his hands on the bar top where she could see them.

"I like cosmopolitans," she said, wondering whether this was a random pickup or something else. He could have been sent by Kincaid. Or . . . he could be an MSS agent. "I'm Qiū Léi, by the way."

"Wang Disung," he said and extended his hand to her.

She looked at his palm, smiled, and nodded, but did not shake it. Instead, she leaned against the bar and fixed him with a sultry gaze.

"Disung. I don't hear that name often. What does it mean?" she asked, but she already knew the answer.

"It means 'one who can be trusted,'" he said, then flagged down a bartender and ordered her cosmopolitan and a bourbon for himself. He returned both his hands to the bar, again where she could see them. She noted he wasn't wearing a wedding band. "What does your name mean?"

"Autumn Thunder," she said, looking up to meet his gaze.

He nodded, as if trying to decide what to say next.

"Do you like whiskey?" she asked him.

"Bourbon," he corrected.

"Oh, I didn't realize there was a difference."

"Yes, an important one. For a whiskey to be called bourbon, it must be distilled in the United States with fifty-one percent corn content. So, you see, to call yourself bourbon, you must first be American," he said, speaking in Mandarin with the exception of the last word. "American," he spoke in perfect English with an American accent.

He's signaling me, she thought, but still needed to be careful. She would wait and see if he passed the final test, something only Scott Kincaid would be able to instruct his proxy on how to do it.

"I did not know that," she said with a smile before adding, "I wonder what other useful facts and information you know about the world."

"I'm full of information," he said. "I could bore you to death with trivia."

"Oh really? Try me. You might be surprised."

"Okay, here's a nature fact. Did you know there are over three thousand species of orb weaver spiders, making them one of the most successful nocturnal predators in the natural world?"

This sealed the deal. Disung was definitely here as Kincaid's proxy.

"That's fascinating," she said, and let her hand drift until the outside edge of her little finger was touching his. "Did you know that orb weaver spiders are the longest-lived species of spider, and that their resilience is directly related to their unparalleled ability to weave and service their web?"

Before he could answer, the bartender arrived with their cocktails, which Disung instructed be charged to his tab. The barkeep nodded and turned to the next customer. The proxy picked up his bourbon as she picked up her cosmo.

"To new opportunities," he said, meeting her gaze.

"To dangerous liaisons."

They clicked glasses.

With the vetting complete, the next fifteen minutes was a ballet of countersurveillance scans and overt physical flirting in preparation for the handoff. When the moment finally arrived, he placed his hand on the small of her back, and she let him. He turned her so her back was to the bar and his torso shielded her from most of the other patrons in the room. Then she felt him slip something slim and flat inside the waistband of her yoga pants. Her clothing options for this impromptu drop had been limited and what she wore lacked pockets, but Disung had found a way to make it work.

"Thanks for the drink, but I should be going." She tipped up on her toes, wrapped her arms around his neck, and whispered in his ear, "Check node thirteen for my reply."

When she let go and stepped back, she watched him blink once in acknowledgment before he said, "Wait, can I at least get your number?"

She shot him a coy smile as she turned to leave. "Sorry, I'm not into younger guys."

16

Q in checked his watch.

Two minutes until the meet, and his heart was pounding so hard in his chest that he worried he might be on the verge of a heart attack. Making the initial handoff with Scott Kincaid at the embassy meeting had been nerve-racking enough, but this . . .

Feels like waiting for the firing squad.

In his note, Qin had dictated the time and the place for the drop. He'd done this unilaterally, not giving the American CIA any say in the matter. The reason was *not* because he was experienced or skilled in the ways of clandestine tradecraft, but instead because he wanted control. At the time, having that control had felt important and comforting. Now he was second-guessing himself terribly.

What if I've chosen badly? What if this location is predictable and obvious? What if Liulichang is the type of place that an inexpe-

rienced and naive person would think satisfied all the right criteria, but the MSS knows this and has cameras and plainclothes agents everywhere?

He stuffed his shaking hands in his pockets as he plodded slowly along the nameless street known locally as "antique row" that cut through the heart of Liulichang. The artsy antique market and tourist trap had seemed like the perfect location for a clandestine meeting. Located in the bustling Xicheng district, the traditional Chinese neighborhood, with its tightly packed stone houses and shops, dated all the way back to the Ming dynasty when glazed tiles were mass-produced for the imperial palace, temples, and the homes of wealthy ministers. To the uninitiated, navigating Liulichang was a daunting proposition. Not only did the neighborhood cover a large area, but it was also a warren of shops and alleys, packed with locals and tourists day and night.

For Qin, Liulichang felt safe and familiar. Maybe, subconsciously, that had factored into his decision to pick this place. His wife—who was a lover and collector of artisan crafts and antiques—made him bring her here regularly to shop and bargain hunt. In keeping with this history of patronage, he had arrived an hour early to browse shops and studios. Ten minutes ago, he'd bought a hand-painted ceramic teapot as a gift for her—a gift he knew she'd never receive—which he carried now in a shopping bag in his left hand. In his right front pants pocket, he carried the same kind of plastic SD memory card case he'd passed to Kincaid. Only this time, the little plastic case contained an actual memory card with ten gigabytes of data about Operation Sea Serpent. Despite having virtually no actual weight, the psychological and emotional weight of the thing he carried was practically unbearable. He wasn't sure how much longer he could last if he didn't unburden himself of the thing.

He checked his wristwatch: 2117.

Anger—born of impatience, guilt, and fear—flared in his chest. *They're late. Where the hell is my contact?*

He scanned faces in the crowd of people walking in the opposite direction on the narrow street between the shops, looking for anyone who might appear to be watching him.

But would I even be able to pick them out? They would be professionals. My God, what have I done?

He clutched the tiny plastic case in his right hand inside his pocket, ready to pass the material to whatever American the CIA sent to retrieve it. But would they send an American? One of the reasons he'd picked Liulichang was because it was a place frequented by Western tourists. A Caucasian could blend in here more easily than most places in Beijing.

But they could send an ethnic Chinese. At least half of the American embassy staff have ethnic Chinese roots. My contact could be anyone in this crowd, he told himself.

As the minutes ticked by his frustration grew at his own foolishness for leaving so many unknowns to contend with. In trying to show dominance and exert control over the meet with Kincaid, Qin had actually done the opposite. All the variables Qin had left undefined would, by default and necessity, be defined by the Americans.

That was stupid of me, he thought.

But then, as quickly as he'd thought it, another voice came to his defense: *You had no choice. Repeated contact and communication with the Americans was not an option. You did the only thing you could do without raising suspicion.*

He resisted the urge to check his watch again and forced himself to take a deep, centering breath. It was imperative that he stay focused and not allow himself to be distracted by negative thoughts. He could not afford to miss the handoff. Maybe he already had. Having never done this before, he wasn't exactly sure how it was done. In his mind, a stranger walking toward him and in the opposite direction would make prolonged eye contact and vector to pass shoulder to shoulder. Hopefully, the agent would be carrying a large paper shopping bag or basket with an open top and Qin could drop the SD card and case into the open mouth of the bag as they passed side by side.

That is how I would do it, he told himself. *And I will walk the streets and shops of Liulichang all night long if that's what it takes.*

17

LIULICHANG

From her outdoor table at the tea shop, Léi frowned as Defense Minister Qin checked the time on his wristwatch for the second time in five minutes.

He has no idea what he's doing, she thought with exasperation. *Worse, he has no idea that he's being watched.*

An ethnic Chinese man in a black coat had been trailing and observing Qin since his arrival at the Liulichang market. Whether Qin's tail was MSS or PLA intelligence she did not know. She'd conducted a thorough SDR en route to this location and felt confident she was tick free. Unfortunately, she was not sure if the man watching Qin was the only observer or if an entire team had been put on the defense minister. If the MSS had any reason to suspect Qin as a potential traitor or turncoat, then the agency would devote considerable manpower to his observation.

Léi's hope was that tonight's surveillance of the high-ranking officer was routine. Trust was nonexistent in the upper echelon. President Li operated with the default mindset that everyone would betray him eventually. It wasn't a matter of if, only a matter of when.

What a terrible way to live, she thought as she clocked a second possible observer.

A woman, who'd been walking behind Qin for half a block, had just followed him into an antique store. Under normal circumstances, with this much heat, Léi would abort the op. But Kincaid's instructions had made it clear that tonight would be their only opportunity with Qin. Given his rank and stature, the admiral would most likely not risk a second encounter. In fact, Kincaid had given only fifty-fifty odds that Qin would show up tonight at all . . . But here the man was, bumbling his way through the market, risking both their lives.

Léi gritted her teeth.

To pull this off, she would have to be perfect.

To succeed, she would have to risk everything.

Last night, she'd transformed her appearance to look like a young, club-hopping party girl before entering Club Icon. Tonight, she'd accomplished similar magic, but in the other direction. The gray wig, eyeglasses, frumpy clothes, and stooped posture made her look like a woman in her sixties or seventies. This was her favorite of all disguises.

No one paid attention to women aged past their prime.

Especially men.

She'd not made a move to approach Qin. She couldn't. Not yet. The problem with this entire situation was that Qin had dictated the time and location of the handoff. Worse, by not allowing for two-way communication, he had eliminated the safest option, which was a dead drop. She'd built her web specifically for dead drops—safe and anonymous transfer of information that did not require her to meet face-to-face with agents or assets. Because of Qin's misguided need to dictate terms and control the handoff, she would be required to make physical contact with him. With one observer, she might be able to pull it off without being made.

With two . . . *impossible*.

Which meant she had a terrible decision to make. She could abort and tell Kincaid that the handoff was compromised, or she could attempt to disappear Qin underground. She was certain the defense minister was operating under the belief that he could pass top secret data to the Americans and get away with it, but this was delusional. The MSS was too good and too persistent. Even if the handoff were successful and Léi managed to get away, the MSS would eventually figure it out and Qin would be disappeared. The man had to know this. His predecessor had been eliminated for what—Léi imagined—had certainly been a far lesser infraction than high treason.

Kincaid's message had made it clear that defection and exfiltration were authorized if that was what Qin desired. The Americans were planning to secure Qin's family and give them new identities. If the defense minister wanted to join them and defect to the West, the CIA would make it happen.

I can give him this future.

The question is . . . will he let me?

She thought about her own life—as a business owner, as a spy, as a sometimes lover and companion to a man she adored but did not wish to marry or bind herself to.

If I do this, my life in China will be forfeit. I will have to defect as well. What will my life become in America? Can it be more than this? Will I find more challenge, more excitement, more fulfillment?

She looked down at her hands.

They weren't pretty hands. Decades of hard work and thousands of strikes against a wooden Ip Man practice dummy had transformed them into hard, calloused things. Her hands were tools . . . but the ironic thing was, that's what she loved about them.

A sad smile stretched across her face.

I would probably not be happy in America . . .

She looked up and found Qin mulling around in the antique shop. As she watched, her perception of him morphed. She noted his courage, his honor, his determination. Tonight, he was not the defense minister, he was a husband, a father, and a man of principle trying to do the right thing. In her heart of hearts, Léi was an idealist. The desire to help tip the scales in the direction of what was good and right was why she'd become the Spider in the first place.

Damn.

Her heart took the lead and made the decision.

I'm going to save you, Defense Minister Qin . . . even if it means saying goodbye to my life in China.

A bolus of adrenaline flooded her bloodstream in preparation for the dangerous game of hunter and hunted she was about to play. Using her mobile phone, she sent instructions to reposition three of her taxis in preparation for the complex, multistep exfiltration she was about to attempt.

18

LIULICHANG

Q in hadn't even noticed the old woman standing beside him until she spoke.

"We have a private collection in the back room not open to the public. Would you like to see it?" the woman asked in an almost playful conspiratorial voice. Qin was about to rebuff the woman and shoo her away when she added, "I will show you some very nice pieces that Caiji might like."

She just used my wife's name. That's the signal, he thought.

"Um . . . yes, I would be interested in seeing the private collection," he said, meeting her eyes.

"Excellent. This way," she told him, and shuffled toward the rear of the antique shop.

She passed through an open door, which she shut and locked behind him after he'd entered. The rear of the shop did not contain a private collection, rather it served as junk storage and a tiny office space for the proprietor. The "old" woman seemingly transformed before his eyes as she stood up straight and tall, with her shoulders square and back like an athlete or soldier.

"Did you bring it?" she asked, her eyes suddenly as sharp and focused as a bird of prey.

"Yes," he said, and placed the SD card case in her outstretched palm.

She disappeared it inside the tunic-style top she wore, undoubtedly slipping it inside her undergarments.

"You're being watched. I identified two tails, but there may be more," she said, her tone serious with a hint of reprimand. "You have a choice to make in the next ten seconds, Admiral Qin—come with me and disappear, or face your comrades in the Guóānbù."

His reflexive and immediate reaction to her ultimatum was to bristle, followed a heartbeat later by denial. "I was careful."

"Not careful enough, it would seem," she said, holding firm despite his six inches height difference and hard stare. "Time's up, Minister Qin. You must choose now. Both paths are dangerous, but I will not let your indecision determine my fate."

His emotions morphed yet again, this time to something that felt a lot like panic—which was something that up until recently he had never experienced. "If I go with you, what will happen to me?"

"We will disappear, and after . . . I will attempt to reunite you with your family."

"*After* what?" he pressed, not liking the vagaries of this plan.

"No more questions. Choose now," she said, glancing over his shoulder at the door.

In his mind's eye, he imagined MSS agents positioning on the other side, about to burst through any second with guns blazing. It should not have been a hard decision. If she was telling the truth about being watched, then it meant the gambit was already up. He knew exactly what his comrades in the MSS would do to him. The fate of his predecessor and Foreign Affairs Minister Cheng Kai were all the proof he needed.

"Okay. I'm going with you," he said, and felt like his body temperature dropped ten degrees with the decision.

She acknowledged with a curt nod and instructed him to do *exactly* what she said until they were safe. "Power off your mobile phone and leave it on this table."

He did as instructed, then followed her out the back of the antique shop to where a black taxi was waiting at idle.

"Get in and lie down on the floor behind the front seats," she said.

He started to protest, but she shoved him hard toward the idling vehicle. "Do it now."

A flare of anger surged in his chest at being bullied by this small, impetuous woman whose name, professional identity, and history he did not know. Was she the infamous Night Spider? His gut told him the answer to that question was an unequivocal *yes*.

"You're going to kill us if you keep this up," she said and shoved him again, this time keeping her hands on his back and pushing him into the back seat of the car.

Grudgingly, he lowered himself into the footwell space in the back, disgusted by the dirty floor as he laid horizontally behind the front bench seat. She climbed in after him and sat in the back seat, but at least had the curtesy to curl her legs underneath herself on the cushion rather than put her feet on top of him. The driver departed immediately without instruction from her.

"Where are we going?" he asked.

"Quiet," she snapped as the taxi bounced and bobbled along

the cobblestone alley before finally transitioning to smooth pavement.

Qin hated not being able to see. He also hated how the hump in the middle of the floor was hitting him in the lower section of his rib cage. With a grunt, he tried to prop himself up on an elbow to relieve the discomfort, but it only made it worse, so he instead tried to arch his midsection.

Several long minutes passed before anyone spoke.

"We have a tail," the taxi driver, a woman, said.

"Are you sure?" the Spider asked.

"Pretty sure."

"Stick with the plan."

The taxi driver drove the car smoothly and normally, making no obvious attempt to outmaneuver or outrun the vehicle following them. This had the paradoxical effect of making Qin feel more confident and more nervous at the same time. How was it possible to escape observation by the MSS in Beijing?

His mouth went dry as he imagined what would happen to him if they were captured.

They will pull out my fingernails. They will hang me upside down by my feet and pour capsaicin and vinegar in my nose, filling my sinuses until my skull is on fire from the inside out. They will douse my body in frigid salt water and electrocute me until my muscles contract so badly that my ligaments pop and tendons rupture. And then they will beat me until all my bones are broken and my teeth are knocked out . . .

He felt the vehicle slow and turn.

"Get ready, Admiral," the Spider said, her voice tense but confident.

The simple act of showing him respect by using the honorific of his naval rank in this moment of terrible tension and dependence served as a strange but much needed salve to his ego and nerves. He took a deep breath, steeled himself, and resisted the almost pathological need to ask questions.

The taxi's tires clunked over a grate of some kind, then he felt it turn, creep forward, turn again, then accelerate rapidly. After two more turns and straightaways, the taxi braked to a stop.

"Thank you, Gi," the Spider said to the driver as she opened the door.

"Good health, and good fortune," the driver said.

Qin crawled backward out of the taxi's passenger compartment and got to his feet. They were inside a parking garage, parked tight next to a stairwell in the corner. The Spider closed the taxi door, then jerked him by the arm toward the stairwell. She moved quickly and elegantly, like a woman half the age she presented with her disguise. He followed her into the stairwell and eased the door shut quietly. They paused on the concrete landing, where two small duffel bags were waiting—one pink, one blue. He watched her as she stripped down to her underwear, doffing her gray wig, tunic-style top, and traditional pants to reveal a lithe, athletic body thirty years younger than he'd first imagined.

"Hurry. Change quickly," she barked as she emptied the contents of the pink bag and stuffed the clothing she'd just removed in its place.

He nodded and did as instructed.

The garments inside the bag were simple and casual—a black hooded sweatshirt, gray cotton slacks, and athletic shoes. Her outfit was casual, blue jean bottoms with a cream-colored sweater top. She let her black hair down from the tight bun that she'd been wearing under the wig. Next, she took him by surprise by pulling a pistol with a suppressor from the duffel and stuffing it inside the waistband of her jeans. She hid the pistol grip by draping her long sweater over it in the front. Last, she retrieved a pair of eyeglasses.

"Put these on," she said, mussing his hair and handing him the spectacles. "They are plain glass and won't affect your vision, but they will make facial recognition more difficult for the algorithms."

He slipped on the glasses and stuffed his old clothes into the duffel as she had done. On the other side of the steel door, he heard the squeal of tires on smooth concrete inside the parking garage.

"Are they coming for us?" he asked, his heart pounding fiercely in his chest.

She grabbed the pink bag and headed down the stairs. "Let's go, hurry."

Qin slung the blue bag over his shoulder and ran after her as she descended the switchback steps, their footfalls echoing like a stampede of horses inside the concrete stairwell. On reaching the bottom, they ditched their duffels in a trash bin. Then she exhaled sharply, forced a smile onto her face, and hooked her right arm around the crook of his left elbow.

"Pretend we're a couple," she said and pulled the door open to exit the stairwell.

He was beyond impressed as she transformed from the serious Spider into a woman on a date having a grand time. She laughed loudly as they stepped out into the cool night air. A silver sedan waited, idling at the curb fifteen meters ahead.

"I sure hope that's our taxi," she said, stumbling a bit as if she were tipsy from a few too many cocktails. "I'm in no condition to drive."

He wasn't sure who exactly the show was for because there was nobody within thirty meters of them. But no sooner had he said that than the parking garage door they'd exited only moments ago swung open and crashed into the concrete wall with a resounding clang. She whirled, shielding him with her body, to face the threat behind them—a young, powerfully built man dressed in street clothes. What happened next unfolded so fast Qin didn't have time to react. Their pursuer shouted for them to stop while reaching inside the flap of his jacket. The Spider, who'd pulled her pistol on the spin, fired two suppressed rounds and dropped the agent.

"Run!" she said.

This time he didn't argue or hesitate. In a flash, they reached the idling sedan. He pulled open the rear passenger door and dove headfirst inside, going down into the footwell without being told. She followed a heartbeat later, slammed the door, and laid flat on the rear bench seat. The taxi took off, this time speeding through the streets of Beijing.

"Plan A or plan B?" the driver, a woman, asked from the front.

"Plan B," the Spider said.

He hated not being able to see what was happening or where they were going, but he understood that the need for proper tradecraft must trump his pathological need for control. Fresh perspiration already soaked the armpits of the sweatshirt. He gritted his teeth and forced himself to trust that the Spider knew what she was doing. After all, she'd evaded capture by the Guóānbù for two decades, so there was that . . .

Several minutes later, the vehicle braked to a hard stop.

"We've arrived," the driver said. "Good luck, Léi."

"Thank you, good fortune and good health," the Spider—

whose name he'd now learned was Léi—replied as they both scrambled out of the back seat.

The silver sedan sped away, leaving them alone and crouching low beside a dumpster in a back alley. The Spider scanned left and right, then grabbed his hand and tugged him toward a door a few meters away. She knocked three times and the door opened. She pulled him inside and quickly shut and locked the door behind her. He scanned the space and identified it as the rear service entrance for an apartment building. The person who'd opened the door, a middle-aged woman, stared at them with a worried look on her face.

"What is going on, Léi?" the woman said. "I got a message from Gi saying to be here to meet you and not tell anyone or to leave until you arrived."

The Spider took the other woman by the hands. "Thank you, Jia. My brother has done something very foolish . . ." she said and shot Qin a nasty look. "He stole money from a triad, and now we're running for our lives."

"Oh God, you are in trouble. What can I do to help?" the woman asked, clutching the Spider's hands and shaking them imploringly.

"I need you to hide us. Just for a couple of days. That's all, I promise."

"Of course. Do you want to stay here in my apartment?"

"No. I want to stay in the cellar beneath your restaurant."

"Oh, Léi, it is awful down there. It's dark and cramped. It's where I keep the onions and dry goods. You will smell like onions," Jia said.

Léi smiled. "No one will look for us there. You can drive us in your delivery van."

"Are you sure this is what you want?"

"Yes. Wait for us in the drop-off circle in front of the south building."

"Okay," the woman said.

The Spider hugged her friend, whispered something in the woman's ear, then turned to Qin. "Let's go."

He followed her to an elevator that they rode down one level to the basement, which housed the building's mechanical equipment, cage locker storage, and janitorial services offices.

"You killed a man," he said, trotting to catch up to her as she strode quickly through the maze of machines and lockers.

"Yes . . . I had no choice."

"If they catch you, you'll be executed for that."

She laughed at this. "If they catch me, I would have been executed anyway. Killing that agent changes nothing."

He considered arguing the point and telling her that killing one of their own would only motivate the MSS, but in the grand scheme of things she wasn't wrong.

Something hot and wet dripped on the top of his head.

He reached up and touched the spot with his fingers and they came away moist with clear liquid.

"Condensation from the steam pipes," she said. "Don't look up or it will drip in your eyes."

He thought about reminding her that he was wearing glasses, but didn't.

"All the people helping you are women," he said.

"Yes. Women care and they are dependable . . ."

He nodded. This was true in his experience.

"They are also incredibly brave when it comes to helping a friend," she added.

"You have many good friends, it would seem."

"I do," she said, her voice cracking.

They walked in silence for several minutes, the Spider stopping occasionally to peer around corners before proceeding.

"I think I made a mistake coming with you," he said, confessing this truth for some reason now, after it was already too late.

"Watch your head," she said, tapping a rusty pipe that was lower than the others as she walked under it without ducking.

If she hadn't warned him, it probably would have hit him squarely in the forehead.

When she didn't answer or acknowledge what he'd confessed, he asked, "Did you hear what I said?"

"Yes, I heard you," she said without turning to look at him. "But it's too late for such sentiments now, Admiral. What's done is done."

He stopped.

It took her several strides before she *chose* to notice and stop. He watched her shoulders rise and fall with a heavy, exasperated exhale. Finally, she turned to face him. "What do you want me to say? Do you want me to challenge your regret? Do you want me to tell you that you made the right choice? Well, I'm not going to do that because it would be pointless. You're not the type of man who cares what someone like me thinks."

He stared at her, angry. Not because she'd challenged him, but because she was right. In this moment, she was strong, and he was weak. She was the officer in charge, and he was the foot soldier taking directions. How could the defense minister of the world's largest military have fallen so far so fast?

Her expression softened only slightly. "I understand what you are feeling. I can empathize with your regret, your fear, your uncertainty . . . because I am feeling those same emotions, too. By helping you, I've given up my life and my friends in China. I did it because it was the right thing to do, but also because you have a wife and two daughters who need you. In choosing this path for yourself, you've also chosen a difficult and dangerous path for them. You have a duty to stay alive because they will need you in the future you have forced upon them."

A lump had formed in his throat. He tried to swallow it down, but it persisted. "Wise words," he said. "You're the Night Spider, aren't you? The infamous spy working with the CIA who has defied the Guóānbù for decades."

She bowed her head in acknowledgment.

"How did you do it? How did you accomplish such a thing?"

"My father raised and trained me to be a strong and powerful woman. He put dreams of Hua Mulan in my head and I became her—a woman warrior fighting for the right and the righteous. I fight for the China that *should* be. Now you must instill the same ethos in your daughters. They will be hunted. You need to make them strong and invisible so they can survive, as I have."

He'd been so busy thinking about himself, he realized he'd outsourced the fate and safety of his family to the Americans. He'd signaled to Scott Kincaid that safeguarding his family was a condition of the information trade, but this was nothing more than an assumption on Qin's part. The American had made no such promise or guarantee. And how could he? The flow of information had been entirely one-way . . . until now. The Spider's words were confirmation that the Americans had not only gotten his message but communicated to Léi that protecting Qin's wife and daughters was a priority. And Léi was taking it one step further by demanding that Qin promise to raise, support, and train his daughters.

Her profound words echoed in his head: *You have a duty to stay alive . . .*

"Thank you," he said with a humble bow before meeting her gaze. "Your words are what I needed to hear."

"You're welcome. Now we need to go. There will be plenty of time to talk and make plans while we hide in Jia's restaurant cellar."

"Ah yes, where we will wait with the onions and the spiders," he said, trotting to catch up to her.

"I can't do anything about the onions," she said, smiling for real for the very first time, "but I promise to put in a good word for you with the spiders."

19

President Jack Ryan shot an apologetic smile to his secretary of agriculture, who sat across from him on the matching gold and white sofa, and leaned over to press the intercom button on the end table.

"I am so sorry, Sheila," he said as he made the buzzing stop, but Sheila Barnes just waved her hand, shooing away the apology, though he knew it was for show. She'd waited nearly a week to get on his schedule. "Yes, Kevin?"

"Mr. President, I'm sorry to interrupt," the President's secretary said from the outer room, "but I have the DNI here, who says it is quite urgent that she speak to you, sir."

"Send her in," Ryan said. He gave Secretary Barnes a tight smile, hands up in surrender. "Corporate subsidization co-ops to family farms really is important to me, but . . ."

"No apology necessary, Mr. President," she said. "I look forward to sharing our progress, but I can't imagine the DNI came over here unannounced without something quite important in the works."

"It's possible Mary Pat's update will be quick. If you have the time to wait, we can pick back up . . . but I wouldn't want to throw off your day."

"Happy to wait, Mr. President, and no issue at all if we wind up rescheduling."

The smart-as-hell and tough-as-nails political appointee gathered her leather binder into her shoulder bag and headed for the main door, just as the director of national intelligence entered, holding the door for her. Ryan rose to greet Mary Pat.

"Apologies, Sheila," Mary Pat said with a sincere smile.

"Not at all," Barnes said, and then shut the door behind her.

"Sorry, Jack," Mary Pat said when the door had been closed, "but I knew you'd want to hear about this right away."

"What's happened?" Ryan asked as they took seats on the facing sofas. His many years of intelligence work and time now in the Oval Office prevented him from meeting a crisis with anything but calm, but the serious look on Mary Pat's face had him concerned.

"It's Chinese minister of national defense Qin," she said, getting right to the point.

"Don't tell me he's been disappeared, too," Ryan said. President Li clearing his cabinet was a bad sign.

"I'm afraid so, but not in the way you may think. Scott Kincaid set up a meet with Qin last night, based on the request Qin had passed him. It was a test drop as much as anything, to validate if Qin was the leading edge of another mole hunt. He arranged a meet with a very reliable asset we're managing over there, one of the few still in the game after the purge."

"The Spider," Ryan guessed. Using the aging asset was the

smart choice, since her utility had diminished to the point where, if she were burned, the fallout would be highly containable.

Smart—but cold-blooded.

"That's correct," Mary Pat confirmed. "We have no idea whether Qin was compromised and they used him as a dangle to lure out the Spider, or if there's a leak within Kincaid's network, but . . ."

"Qin is dead?" Ryan asked, clenching his jaw.

"No, Jack. Not dead."

"Captured, then?"

"In the wind," she said. "The MSS moved in on the meet, but Kincaid had assets watching from close by, recording with parabolics in case something went south. They were able to provide some distraction just in time to allow the Spider and Qin to slip away. We have a mess to clean up, but Kincaid assures me that the managed assets he used have a few degrees of separation, even if they get swept up—which so far has not happened."

Ryan stood, unable to contain the energy from the intense emotions he felt. While Mary Pat filled him in on the details of Kincaid's after-action report, his mind reeled and also took him down myriad rabbit holes. But then a singular and focused thought sliced through the din in his head.

"Qin is what he said he was, Mary Pat," he declared, turning back to her from where he had paced a few steps away. "Otherwise, why would he go underground with the Spider?"

"Maybe that's part of the plan. The Chinese are smart, Jack, and they are always playing the long game. They could be tracking Qin as we speak, intent on going after the larger prize of unmasking what we've rebuilt of a Beijing network, not just nabbing the Spider."

"Using the minister of national defense as the bait? That seems like a helluva risk."

"But a risk that someone as calculating and brazen as Li might embrace," she countered.

Ryan rubbed his chin, considering. "The only way we're going to know for sure is when we see the goods. We need to know what Qin is selling. The data will answer the question. I want a full brief on Kincaid's take and any follow-up signals, cyber, and HUMINT out of Beijing."

"I could be ready in two hours to brief the NSC in the Situation Room," Mary Pat said, but then let out a long, slow breath. "But I won't be able to address the *real* question we both need answered: Is Qin's defection real or is it a ploy? Unfortunately, Qin and the Spider have gone dark. And now that the hunt is on, our only chance of getting the battle plan for Sea Serpent is probably going to be if we proceed with Qin's extraction . . . The exact thing we wanted to avoid without first validating the veracity of Qin's offer."

"Damned if we do, damned if we don't," he muttered.

"It looks that way," she said.

He shook his head. "Why is *that* the situation we always seem to find ourselves in, Mary Pat?"

She chuckled. "I don't know, Jack. Probably has something to do with the type of people we're constantly up against . . ."

"Or the type of people we are," he replied grimly.

Silence, thick and heavy with the weight of the decision that needed to be made, hung in the air between them.

"Is there anyone in country we can use to get them out?" Ryan asked, finally breaking the quiet.

Mary Pat frowned. "My gut says we don't dare use regular assets because we don't know if or how our network is compromised . . . But there is another option. They may not have a lot of experience working together, but the international team Clark has put together is the crème de la crème. They were my backup plan to get Qin out of China if the Spider was unable, or unwilling, to help. None of the members should be on the MSS's radar because none of them have history of operating in China."

"That's a double-edged sword," Ryan said. "Their inexperience in China is a liability."

"Yes, which is why they were my plan B," Mary Pat said, "but running deep-cover missions on foreign soil is Clark's bread and butter."

Thank God for plan Bs, he thought with an ironic smile, *or I wouldn't be here having this conversation right now.*

"Are we calling this new task force Rainbow Seven or something?"

"Nothing so exciting, Jack. We're calling it Task Force 99."

"And how, exactly, would Task Force 99 get Qin out of Beijing?"

"That's a work in progress, and something I imagine will require flexibility and modifications on the fly."

"You didn't answer my question, Mary Pat."

"I know," she said. "Because the truth is, I don't know."

Ryan picked up his gone-cold cup of coffee and took a sip. "Why is it that hot coffee tastes good, iced coffee tastes good, but room-temperature coffee tastes terrible? Can somebody please explain that mystery to me?"

Mary Pat chuckled again. "I'm not sure its unique to coffee. I think our taste buds prefer variation from the baseline."

He set the cup down and looked at her, grateful that she was willing to be the rock he got to lean on time and time again. "Do it," he said, the decision made. "Send TF 99 to get Qin out. Like you said, this is what Clark does best."

She hesitated for a beat, then said, "Yes, Mr. President."

"What?" he said. "You have that look on your face you get

whenever I get something wrong. And, you did just call me Mr. President . . . ?"

"Can I speak frankly?"

He narrowed his eyes at her. "Since when do you need to ask me permission for that?"

She nodded. "It's just that this is different. We're not talking about an op in Europe or the Middle East. Hell, it's not even Russia, where he can blend in. This is Beijing without a support network of assets he can leverage. If I send Clark and his team, we both need to go into the decision with eyes wide open, knowing that there's a better than fifty percent chance that he will fail and one or more members of his team might not make it out of there alive."

"It's Clark, Mary Pat," he said, thinking of all the seemingly impossible missions the man had pulled off over the years. "You know, as well as I do, what he's capable of."

"I do, but this *is* different, Jack," she said, holding his eyes. "I want you to understand the stakes. If this goes bad, he won't be coming home. And if the MSS take him, and break him . . . Well, let's just say the knowledge he has about this government, our covert capabilities, and you and me personally would be beyond devastating were it to fall into Chinese hands."

He'd not considered either point in his calculus. His confidence and faith in Clark was so absolute he'd not really contemplated the hard and soft costs of failure.

Am I being too cavalier? Have I finally become a Napoleon who sends his best soldiers to fight an unwinnable battle?

But there was more at stake than just John Clark and his team. Reunification of Taiwan by force appeared to be on the table. Was that something he could allow to happen on his watch? If defecting Admiral Qin was the key to preventing the fall of Taiwan, then didn't he have an obligation to try?

The good mood he'd been in just ten minutes ago was obliterated.

"Workup time is over. Get Clark's team ready and into position," he said.

"Is that a green light, Mr. President?"

"No. It's exactly what I said it was. I want to know the plan before I give the green light. You were right about what you said before. We need to be sure the potential payoff justifies the risk."

"Understood. And for what it's worth, I agree with that call," she said, meeting his gaze. "Oh, and just so you know, Task Force 25 is arriving shortly in Taiwan. They'll be operating out of Penghu."

"Thanks, Mary Pat," he said. "Let's convene the NSC in two hours. All the principals need to know what's potentially at stake."

Mary Pat rose and held his eyes a moment before heading for the door.

Ryan knew what his friend was really telling him.

Lieutenant Commander Kathleen Ryan from the ONI was heading up Task Force 25.

And right now, it looked like he had just deployed his daughter into the eye of a brewing storm.

20

C lark dropped his backpack onto the floor at the head of the table and then stood at the front of the room, arms across his chest, as his team shuffled in. He locked eyes with Ding Chavez, who gave him a satisfied nod as he took a seat. This team was going to work out just fine, should the need arise to get them in the field. Either Ryan or Foley had done their job in soliciting talent from their partner nations to form the small, elite Task Force 99, and had been able to fulfill all of his requests where he had some. The afternoon in the kill house had proven they were all solid, experienced shooters, and the interviews with each of them the day before had proven they were all smart, creative, and confident.

Now they just needed a few days to train as a team so they could gel into a unit.

He wished that the sixth member, Tsai Akio from Taiwan, could be here for that crucial piece. But unfortunately, the National Security Bureau operative and former Airborne Special Service Company officer would be joining them in Taiwan after he finished up "other vital commitments." Clark had rejected the idea, feeling that living and training together for even a short time was a vital part of the preparation, but he'd been overruled by his friend, the DNI. They needed someone from Taiwan on the task force, and Tsai Akio was who they were getting. The man was impressive on paper, and Clark had no doubt he would be a fit for the team based on the man's TS/SCI file, but he hated not training together.

"How did you think that went?" Clark asked when everyone had gear stowed and seats taken. Weapons had been secured in the armory assigned to them, a base regulation at Camp Peary. Clark preferred to keep teams armed while in training evolutions, but that wasn't an option here, at least not on this, the guest side of the training base. On the organic side, things were different. He held his eyes on Daniel Wu, the SBS operator assigned to the unit from the UK.

"Balled it," Wu said in a thick East London accent. "Charlie and I are clearly the A team 'ere." He gave a fist bump to Australian Special Air Service intelligence officer Charlotte "Charlie" Adams.

"We 'ate that," Charlie agreed, and the room chuckled.

"The kill house is rudimentary training, Mr. Clark," Wilhelm Bauer from the international counterterror cell within Germany's Bundesnachrichtendienst, or BND, said. Clark knew the man had a decade in Special Forces with the German Kommando Spezialkräfte before joining their spy agency.

"Perhaps," Henri Toussaint said, his French-accented tone suggesting he did not agree at all. "But how would you suggest we train, Wilhelm? In DGSI we insist that teams go to the range together frequently. Doing fire and move drills is absolutely imperative if we are going to be together in . . ." He looked up in the air, searching for the word. "How do you say it, Mr. Chavez? The spit?"

"The suck," Ding corrected with a laugh.

"Yes, yes. In the sucking, of course," Toussaint said, but the twinkle in his eye suggested to Clark that he knew the lingo and he was just having a little fun.

"What did you think, Lee?" Clark asked Lee Hyori from South Korea's WARFLOT, the ally's version of the Navy SEALs. Clark liked the South Korean frogman, who was very quiet, but always seemed to be in deep thought. Hyori had been on his short list, having met the seasoned officer once before when working in the Pacific Rim.

"I think we have very talented shooters who will handle themselves well in a firefight," he said softly. "Both individually and as a team. I am very interested in finding out where it is we might find ourselves where such skills will be necessary."

Clark glanced at Ding, who raised an eyebrow at him, clearly in agreement with their South Korean colleague.

"Let's debrief the course of fire in the kill house," Clark said, pulling a laptop from his bag and opening it on the table as he took his seat. "And I promise, as soon as the time is right, I will tell you everything about . . ." He trailed off as a dialogue box opened at the top of the screen on his heavily encrypted computer as it connected to the high-side server via the yellow cable he'd plugged into the port.

Qin missing

Attacked by MSS during drop with asset

Believed alive and in hiding

Need to mobilize 99 to AOR ASAP

Contact immediately for full brief

Eyes only

-MPF

Clark leaned back in his chair and shot a look at Ding, then a smile crept onto his face.

"Everything all right, mate?" Wu asked.

"It seems," Clark said, leaning forward on his elbows, "that the time is right now. Things have escalated and we'll be heading into theater immediately."

"Which theater?" Bauer asked.

"We have a full brief on the mission parameters coming in a few moments," Clark said, typing a reply into the text box that he was ready for a brief now. It would take a few minutes before a reply came through and a briefing happened, he imagined. "In the meantime, does the name Admiral Qin Hâiyû mean anything to you guys?" he asked.

"Of course, he is the Chinese minister of national defense, is he not?" Toussaint said.

"Very good," Clark said.

"Qin is the boner who replaced the last minister, who fell from favor after not supporting President Li's growing lust to reintegrate Taiwan," Charlie Adams said, pulling the hair band from her ponytail and letting her auburn hair fall onto her shoulders. "He was head of the Navy before this, and our people believe him to be the architect of the PLA's military contingency to seize Taiwan by force."

Clark gave a satisfied look to Ding. This was going to be a helluva team.

"That is all correct, Charlie, and consistent with the CIA and ONI assessment here in the States as well. And so," he said with a conspiratorial grin, "we're going to take him."

"Kidnap the defense minister from inside the bloody PRC?" Wu, the Brit with the Chinese name and heritage, said. "Are you mental?"

"Not kidnap," Clark said. "Extract. Qin has signaled a desire to share intelligence with us and may be looking to defect."

Assuming he's still alive with all his limbs and faculties intact.

His text box chimed and populated again and Clark read the message quickly.

> Briefing in 2
> You and Chavez
> Aircraft en route to you
> Team should be ready to depart within 2 hours
> -MPF

"Looks like things are happening quickly," he said to the group. "Pack your gear and secure our loadout from the armory. Then reconvene here in one hour for a full brief. We have a plane to catch. We'll brainstorm mission parameters in the air."

The team hustled out of the room, brisk conversation stopping when they crossed the threshold of the doorway. This was a disciplined group of seasoned professionals. He might miss having Jack Junior at the tip of this spear, but these operators were not likely to disappoint.

Clark clenched his jaw. He hoped he would be able to bring them all back home.

A video box opened on his laptop and Mary Pat Foley's serious face filled the screen.

"Hi, John," the director of national intelligence said.

"Director Foley," he said, feeling the formality of the moment. "I'm here in a SCIF with only Colonel Chavez. It sounds like we're headed to China."

"Afraid so, John," she said. "This is incredibly short-fuse, so we need you in Beijing quickly if this is going to work. We're building out a nonofficial cover for the team as we speak. We'll need to stagger the arrivals once we get you into the area. But we need to keep you together as a group initially because you have a stop to make first."

"A stop?" Clark said, his curiosity piqued. "Where?"

"Maldives," Mary Pat said. "Unless we're too late, we have a different Qin rescue mission for you to execute first . . ."

PART II

"*Let your plans be dark and impenetrable as night, and when you move, fall like a thunderbolt.*"

—Sun Tzu, *The Art of War*

21

I want him found," President Li Jian Jun shouted, pounding his fist on the conference room table hard enough to cause the tea sets to chatter. The fearful expressions on the faces of his cabinet ministers were precisely what he wanted to see. He'd summoned them well before dawn from their beds for this tongue-lashing. Defense Minister Qin's disappearance was an absolute catastrophe. "I want him hunted down, taken alive, and executed on state television as a traitor."

He watched as the men around the room exchanged silent glances, but it was Deputy Minister of Foreign Affairs Bai Ming who, to Li's surprise, spoke first, after glancing at Secretary General Xu Chao for encouragement. Beside Xu sat Li's chief of intelligence, Minister of State Security Deng Su Wei, who watched the proceedings with a stone-faced expression. It was clear to Li that Bai and Xu had discussed the situation and developed a strategy ahead of this emergency meeting.

163

"President Li," Bai said, his voice controlled, but hands visibly trembling. "We do not know with certainty that Defense Minister Qin *is* a traitor. The last time we spoke, he not only expressed confidence about Operation Sea Serpent, but he seemed highly motivated to see it through. He has always supported a reunification agenda. I think we must consider the possibility that Qin was taken, Mr. President."

"Taken?" Li said, his rage giving pause enough to be curious. "What do you mean?"

"Mr. President," Deng Su Wei now chimed in. "From the reports I have heard from my agents and asset managers, all evidence indicates that Minister Qin was in Liulichang shopping for his wife—he bought her an antique teapot, in fact. He did nothing to suggest he was preparing for a meeting and nothing has been out of the ordinary with him leading up to this event. I have shopped for my wife on this antique row many times."

"If Qin's shopping trip to Liulichang was so innocent, what was the MSS doing surveilling him in the district?" Li asked, but he knew the answer already.

"We are currently surveilling all the key members of the cabinet leading up to Operation Sea Serpent," Bai said softly. "This is standard protocol, Mr. President."

"For the safety and security of our key members," Deng added, but his tone suggested he knew Li's real reason for watching everyone so closely.

"An agent was shot and killed!" Li said, and slammed his fist down on the table. "That does not suggest this was a mere shopping outing for Defense Minster Qin."

"Yes, Mr. President, that is true, but we do not have surveillance video of the event. It is unlikely that Qin is the one who pulled the trigger. We believe Minister Qin may have been taken at gunpoint."

"Let's suppose I indulge the theory that Minister Qin was kidnapped," he said, his voice a tight cord. "Who took him?"

"We are analyzing data at this very moment," Minister Deng said, "but logically, we should assume the Americans had a role in it."

"Qin recently attended a routine weekly meeting with the U.S. ambassador's chief of staff," Bai said.

"I heard," Li said, and made a *pffttt* sound. "Kincaid is CIA. It's obvious based on his pedigree."

"We agree," Minister Deng said, "but so far we have seen no indication Kincaid was working Qin, nor did he seem to be recruiting him. We know of only one interaction between the two men, and it was at this meeting with Deputy Minister Bai. Qin and Kincaid's interplay was quite adversarial. I reviewed the video personally and observed nothing suspicious. Qin was the perfect wolf warrior with the Americans, demanding that they keep their fleet far removed from the upcoming exercise and threatening consequences if they did not. Perhaps the Americans saw an opportunity and decided to take Qin. Maybe they're blackmailing him to extract state secrets or learn the details of Operation Sea Serpent."

"This would be an unprecedented and brazen move by the CIA," Li said, his mind looking at the problem from every angle. He had never had reason to suspect Qin. In fact, the man's loyalty and patriotism, combined with the genius with which he had crafted the plans for Operation Sea Serpent while in charge of the Navy, were exactly why Li had appointed Qin to the position he now occupied after removing the feckless Zhao Fu. He'd had only fleeting concerns when he'd learned of Qin's friendship with

Cheng Kai, but nothing had made Li suspect Qin as someone capable of betrayal. Still, with all that was at stake, it would still be safest—and most expedient—to remove Qin from the equation, permanently.

"While I don't know Minister Qin on a personal level, Mr. President," Xu said, "he does have a long and solid life of service to the Party. He also has a reputation as being a dedicated family man. It seems unlikely he would defect, but especially unlikely he would leave his family behind."

"And they are home?" Li asked.

"No, sir," Deng said. "They are vacationing in the Maldives. Minister Qin was supposed to be with them, but they went without him when our new operation made it necessary for him to remain here. I have spoken personally with both their security team and our MSS agents in charge of monitoring their movements. They are lodging at the Four Seasons. Qin has made no effort to contact them. And there is nothing at all in their behavior to suggest they are in any way under stress. I do not believe they even know he is missing."

"We should pick them up and interrogate them immediately," Li said. "Then we hold them for leverage."

"I propose a different tack, Mr. President," Deng said softly, but with great confidence. "We have both Qin's family security team and our MSS surveillance team on the ground in the Maldives. We are listening to all their communications and monitoring their activities. They cannot escape from our surveillance. The Four Seasons is on a very small island in the chain, accessible only by boat. Where is it that they could go without our notice? I suggest we leave them for now. Should Qin contact them, we will discover his location and whether he's working with the Americans. If we pick the family up now, this opportunity is lost."

"Do you think Qin is a traitor?" Li asked pointedly, watching his minister of state security very carefully.

"I honestly do not know, Mr. President," Deng said, wisely choosing not to put himself at risk for Minister Qin. "But I do know that if he is, we will find him and he will face your justice. If he is not, we must find those responsible for this, an overt act of war, and bring them to account."

It was the best and only answer Deng could give, and Li nodded his approval.

"Very well," Li said. "Leave Qin's wife and children in the Maldives for now. But if there is any reason to suspect Qin has betrayed us, bring them back to Beijing immediately. They can be used to leverage his recovery. And if not, they can pay the price for his sins."

Deng gave a sharp and deferent nod.

"Of course," he said.

"And what are we to do about the exercise?" Xu asked, his voice suggesting he'd rather not be bringing it up. "Obviously, we must now reconsider our plans, but I suggest it would show weakness to cancel the exercise. I feel it is more important than ever to proceed and show our strength."

"Why would we reconsider our plans?" Li asked, eyeing Xu with suspicion. "I would argue that this brazen move by the West is the very cover we are looking for. Might there not even be an opportunity to blame operatives from the West for Qin's disappearance, or even link it all to Taiwan? Would this not be the very justification we need to act? This, with the cover of the secret false flag already part of Operation Sea Serpent, makes our chances of success even greater."

Instead of nods of approval, he was met with stunned silence, but he'd expected as much. This was why he ruled with an iron fist. So few men could see such opportunities for what they were, much less have the fortitude to grasp them.

"But, sir, with all due respect," Bai said, a slight tremor in his voice. "Whether Qin was taken or defected hardly matters now. If the plans and knowledge he possesses about Operation Sea Serpent fall into the hands of the West, especially the Americans, then the results would be catastrophic."

"You lack vision, Deputy Minister Bai," Li said, and took the opportunity to cross his legs at the knee and reach for his teacup, demonstrating his calm and his strength. "Are you a gelding or a stallion? The former, perhaps, which is why you are a *deputy* minister. Minister Deng will tell you, I am sure, that after the purge we have complete control of the flow of information, but most especially the flow of people, in and out of the homeland. If Qin is a traitor we will find him and kill him. If he is a victim of the West, we will find him and rescue him. Either way, neither he nor the knowledge he has will ever leave China." He took a sip of tea, then replaced his cup gently on the saucer. "Isn't that right, Deng Su Wei?"

The minister of state security, to his credit, did not even flinch, but did again nod his deference. "Yes," Deng said. "That is absolutely correct, President Li."

"Good," Li said, leaning back in his leather executive chair, which was four inches taller than the other chairs in the room. "Then we are in agreement. Minister Deng will handle finding Minister Qin and taking care of what must be done once the truth is discovered. Secretary Xu and I will manage the optics of the situation to our benefit both geopolitically and militarily, and you, Minister Bai"—he leaned forward, folding his hands on the table, aware of the effect the dark smile he had perfected would have on the deputy minister of foreign affairs—"you will coordinate with Admiral Long to be sure that he and General Liu are taking all steps necessary for Operation Sea Serpent to execute as scheduled." He rose from his chair, standing for full effect, leaning in again, his palms on the table. "Regardless of what happened to Qin, Sea Serpent is two years in the making. All the chess pieces are in place and this is an opportunity we will not squander. We will bring Taiwan home and China alone will have full control of the strait and the South China Sea."

"Yes, Mr. President," Bai said, nearly leaping to his feet, then bowing in supplication.

Li struggled to contain a laugh. "I want to know where Qin is, Minister Deng, and no matter what the truth turns out to be, the next face he sees after yours will be mine, either to praise him or inform him of his impending execution."

Deng bowed. "I will see to it, Mr. President."

Anything else he said now would diminish the moment, so Li spun on his heel and left the room.

22

Katie stepped out of the SUV and into the morning sun, which was reflecting off the blue waters of Liaoluo Bay. The air was warm, at least twenty degrees warmer than back home in Maryland, but comfortable. She inhaled the sea breeze as she took a measure of the place.

"Hmm, so this is what it looks like on the opposite side of the world," Bubba said, stepping up beside her.

"Well, technically Penghu island isn't D.C.'s antipode," she said.

"Antipode?" he echoed, cocking an eyebrow at her.

"The geographic opposite coordinates of a location on the globe," Conza said, joining them.

"Fine, I'll bite, since y'all are obviously dying to tell me," Bubba said, popping a piece of chewing gum into his mouth. "Where is the antipode for Washington, D.C.?"

"Probably somewhere near Australia," Conza said, using his

170

fingers in the air to mark points on some imaginary floating globe nobody could see.

"Helpful visual there, JC," Bubba said.

"Must be a SEAL thing, generating mental holograms that only other SEALs can see?" Katie asked, unable to resist piling on.

"You guys can't see this?" Conza said, screwing up his face. "Weird. Must be a SEAL thing."

They all laughed.

Looks like Conza is going to fit right in with us, she decided.

The CIA/DIA contingent that had flown over with them pulled up in a separate SUV and parked behind their vehicle. She mentally matched up names with faces, trying to commit everyone to memory: *Ted James, Andrew "Drewski" Miaoulis, Ben Hart,* and *Simran "Sam" Bakshi* were unloading gear from the back. The two DIA officers, *Lorie Tengco* and *Lou Donatelli,* emerged from the front seats. They were dressed in blue jeans and casual shirts like their CIA colleagues, and carrying oversized, coyote-tan backpacks.

"Comms gear?" Katie asked, gesturing to the large hard cases that Drewski and Ben were lugging.

"Among other things we may need," Ted responded for his group.

Katie assumed she knew what that meant, but couldn't imagine needing weapons while secure on the Taiwanese base— especially with the Group Eight operators, visiting JSOC SEALs, and the Taiwanese Sea Dragons who were garrisoned here. She looked over her shoulder, expecting to see the third Suburban pull up that had been behind them carrying the Group Eight folks, but it must have taken a different turn once on base.

She turned to Conza. "Where's the other SUV with your buddies heading?"

Conza shook his head. "They're not *with* us, if you know what I mean."

Having never worked in the WARCOM side of the house, she wasn't particularly familiar with special warfare and covert operations, so wasn't actually sure she knew what he meant.

"But we'll be sharing information with them, I assume?" she asked, sounding less commanding and more hopeful than she intended.

"Yeah, of course," Conza said. "Team before self, bro . . . I mean, ma'am. We'll set up daily intelligence briefs with Lieutenant Temperley from Group Eight to make sure all information flows both ways. We got this."

"Perfect," Katie said, feeling relief at his reassurance.

If the Group Eight team had the sophisticated signals and other intelligence-gathering tools she expected, then Katie wanted full access to what they learned, even if they did have some collateral mission she wasn't read into.

"Are we ready to go?" asked their escort, an ROC soldier named Fa, who'd met them at the front gate of the base. Fa was a soft-spoken man who only stood about five foot seven, but he had thick arms beneath the rolled-up sleeves of his cammies.

Katie nodded and grabbed the handle of her roller duffel.

They followed Fa, lugging their gear toward a low building— the design rounded like a miniature airplane hangar. Behind the building she could see a volleyball court, and a collection of benches and charcoal grills, all overlooking Liaoluo Bay. Beside her, Conza was in a light conversation with the CIA officer Sam about college football.

If Ferguson hadn't shared Conza's pedigree with her, she would have never guessed he was a former SEAL, other than the sleeve tat, which wasn't uncommon throughout the Navy these days. He

was smart, super social, and funny. She wasn't sure what precon-
ception she had of the Navy's elite warriors, but she supposed it was
tainted by the brooding, serious, and violent caricatures of SEALs
she knew from film and television. The SEALs had kept to themselves in the back of the plane, laughing, watching movies, and
playing cards. Now a part of her couldn't help but wonder how
many "former" operators from both the Navy and Army JSOC elements had lateral-transferred into other billets inside the intelligence community. It was a strange thing to think that the easygoing
Conza, as well as all of his SEAL colleagues on the plane—who
looked so *ordinary*—could kill her with their bare hands.

"You will be staying here," Fa said with a nod. "We can drop
your bags and gear and then I will show you where the gym and
the food services are located, as well as the headquarters building
and our tactical operations center. We will have CAC cards for
you to access the TOC shortly. After you look around, our task
unit commander, Major Yang, will meet with you to explain our
operations and security procedures, as well as to see that you have
everything you need. Welcome to the home of the Sea Dragons."

"After you," Conza said, holding the door open for her.

Katie had expected Spartan, barracks-style accommodations,
but instead found herself in a large lounge, complete with a small
mini-kitchen and a pool table. Beyond, a hallway led to their
sleeping quarters.

"Two persons to a room. There is a bathroom with showers at
the end of the hall," Fa said, gesturing. "I will wait outside while
you get settled. Five minutes or less, please."

"I'll share a room with Ryan, if you want to go solo," Sam said
to Lorie Tengco, the senior-ranking CIA female.

Tengco shrugged. "I'm happy to have a room to myself, but
Ryan's the task force commander. Your call, Ryan?"

Katie hadn't thought of it that way, really. More like a team with division heads, but she was the officer in charge of whatever *this* cross-functional, joint-operation boondoggle was.

"I'm fine to room with whoever," she said with a gracious smile.

"Dibs on top if it's bunk beds," Sam said, but then gave a sheepish look. "I mean, if that's cool with you. Lorie's right—you're the task force commander."

"Fine with me. I'd prefer the bottom if it's bunk beds," Katie said.

It wasn't.

Katie and Sam snagged the last room on the right, down the hall from the common area, next to the two sets of bathrooms and showers, where one now had a hand-drawn female silhouette on a piece of typing paper taped to the door. Katie tossed her seabag on one of the twin beds and her briefcase-style shoulder bag onto the desk beside it after letting Sam pick her rack first. Lorie moved into the room next to theirs, on the same side of the hall, and the men split off into groups of two, with Conza strategically grabbing a room with Ted.

Moments later their group assembled back outside, where their ROC Sea Dragon escort, Fa, was waiting. The small but incredibly fit soldier led them across the volleyball field, pointing out the chow hall on their left and the gym on their right as they crossed, both buildings identical to the others from the outside.

"The general wishes to first meet only the Navy personnel," Fa said to the group.

Katie turned to the head of the CIA contingent, Ted James.

"Fine by us," Ted said. "We'll go check out the quality of the chow hall while you sort out the Big Navy stuff."

"Meeting with some Sea Dragon general doesn't sound all that chill to me," said Drewski with the sly grin he seemed to wear for sport. The handsome spook gave Katie a wink and a little two-finger salute, then followed Ted, who led the contingent of spooks, four CIA and two DIA, out the door.

Fa held the door open for Katie's team and they shuffled into a cramped lobby of the new building where, to her surprise, an American naval officer was waiting, hands clasped behind him.

"Commander Ryan?" the man asked, vectoring toward her specifically and extending a hand for her to shake. "I'm Commander Endicott, aide to Admiral Urban, the Task Force 70 commander, but you can call me Hank."

"Katie," she said after shaking his hand, and then gestured to her ONI teammates. "And this is Lieutenant Conza and IS2 Pettigrew."

"Great to meet you, fellas," Endicott said, turning to shake hands with Conza and Bubba. "Admiral Urban came over from the *Reagan* for two reasons. First, he wants me to brief you on our intelligence needs and open lines of communication with our N2 shop aboard the *Reagan*, and second, to get a briefing on anything you may have to share with us that impacts our mission."

Katie shifted uncomfortably. "Wait . . . Admiral Urban is here on Penghu?"

"He's waiting for us right now, together with General Wu Akemi, the ROC commander of the 101st, who is also here on the island."

"Um . . . nobody told me about this. What I mean is," she said, fumbling for words, "we didn't prepare a brief for the admiral."

Endicott waved a hand. "I know, I know," he said, apparently trying to reassure her. "I think the admiral just wants to meet you guys personally to see how and where you'll add value to our mission. The alarm bells appear to be ringing in D.C., but we're not read in at the strike group level on the details of what has everyone so spooled up."

"I'm happy to brief the admiral," she said, relenting while glancing at Conza, who gave her a *Better you than me* look. "I don't have anything definitive, but I'll certainly share everything I know."

"Great, that's all we ask," Endicott said, and gestured for them to follow him down the hallway to the right. "The general and his team have graciously provided us a SCIF here in the building for our use."

"Roger that," she said, butterflies growing in her stomach.

Like at home, the room at the end of the hall had bins for electronics, but no one had any to deposit, so Endicott punched a code into the heavy door and opened it for them.

The admiral, a tall, thin, handsome man with dark brown hair and a face that kind of reminded her of the late-night host Jimmy Fallon, sat leaned over in conversation with the ROC general, his close-cropped hair flecked with gray. In his current billet, Rear Admiral Urban had multiple titles: commander of Task Force 70, commander of Strike Group Five, the CSG associated with the USS *Ronald Reagan*, and, unlike the other CSGs in the fleet, he wore the hat of air wing commander, or CAG, for CSG 5, as well. She had no idea how one man managed all that, but she suspected it involved surrounding himself with very talented men and women, like Commander Endicott. She had already noted that Endicott, unlike the naval aviator wings on the cammies of the one-star flag officer he served, wore the "water wings" of a surface warfare officer—a warfare designation she was proud to have earned herself during her fleet tour in the N2 shop aboard the *Eisenhower.*

Smart, when your strike group contains all of those surface ships surrounding the carrier . . .

The admiral looked up.

"Welcome, Commander Ryan. Your reputation precedes you," he said, rising and shaking her hand, which only made the situation more awkward and uncomfortable for her.

"Thank you, sir," she said, and took a seat at the table when he gestured she do so.

"All of you . . . please," Urban said, looking at Conza and Pettigrew.

"Sir, if you prefer, I can wait outside," Bubba said, his voice flecked with uncertainty.

"No, shipmate," the admiral said to the second-class petty officer. "Team approach here."

Reluctantly, Bubba took a seat on the other side of Conza, who didn't seem uncomfortable at all.

"This is General Wu," Urban said, gesturing to the Taiwanese warrior beside him.

"It is a great pleasure to meet all of you," the general said in flawless English, peppered with just a hint of a British accent, she noticed. Or Australian, perhaps. "We are honored to have you here, working with us toward our mutual defense goals. The warriors of the 101st Sea Dragons are at your service, and I know you will meet Major Yang later, the Penghu task unit commander. Anything you need, you have but to ask."

"Thank you, sir," she said.

"We know that your task force—what are they calling it, Hank?" he asked, looking at his aide.

"Task Force 25, sir," Endicott said.

"Yes, Task Force 25," Urban said, but she suspected he hadn't really forgotten. "I'm sure Task Force 25 has many hats it will be wearing while here in the Pacific, Commander Ryan. But, while I wear a lot of hats in my position with Task Force 70, I have but one mission—the defense of America's interests in the region and the protection of our sailors on the pointy tip of the spear."

"Of course, sir," she said.

"Maybe you can help this simple bush pilot from Indiana understand why the *Reagan* battle group is extending on station and why she needs augmentation from the *Nimitz* and Carrier Air Wing Two? We've been briefed that this elevation of readiness is due to increased Chinese aggression in the South China Sea, but frankly we're not sure where that assessment is coming from. We watch the Chinese fleet very carefully, as you might imagine, Commander, and if anything, they seem unusually quiet." He folded his arms across his chest and stared at her, and she felt General Wu's eyes on her as well. "I'd hate to think we're being kept in the dark about something."

She took a long, slow breath.

"We hear you and understand your concerns, Admiral," she said. "From a naval intelligence perspective, our primary goal in being here is to augment your existing resources and provide real-time analytical support to help anticipate and mitigate negative outcomes from any rising threats that would jeopardize maritime stability in the Seventh Fleet AOR."

But was that their primary goal? She wasn't so sure. Everything had happened so fast that she wasn't exactly clear on what the "little DNI," Admiral Matt Kohler, expected from her. Hell, she wasn't sure what "big DNI," Mary Pat Foley, expected of her. So, she'd parroted back to the admiral what she'd heard as his primary concern as a reassurance. But that didn't mean she and the task force would be able to add real value. Her presence here felt almost like a cover for intelligence-gathering efforts surrounding what was happening on mainland China. But if the latest compartmentalized intelligence she'd received about the possible defection of Minister Qin prior to an imminent move on Taiwan was true, both men at the table needed to know about the threat.

"Sir, the truth is, there is something going on in mainland China. I simply don't have all the facts right now, which frankly is a big reason why we're here. But, it is possible that, if events unfold like we fear, the quiet you see in the South China Sea is the calm before the storm . . ."

"Commander Ryan, does your intelligence indicate that Operation Sea Serpent is a smoke screen for a possible invasion of Taiwan?" Wu asked, getting straight to the heart of the matter.

She looked at the calm face of the general, his hands folded on the table in front of him. She didn't know what hell might break loose if she shared her suspicion—or was it just a fear? That's why she'd phrased her comment like she had—to provide *analytical support* and to *mitigate negative outcomes*. It wasn't meant to be a hedge; rather, she simply wanted to avoid any misconceptions about the threat until they knew more.

She decided to go with the absolute truth.

"The truth is I honestly don't know, General," she said. "Right now what we have is a series of indicators that are raising that suspicion, but we don't yet have any real proof that this concern is valid . . ."

"Although the commander in chief is concerned enough to extend the *Reagan* and move the *Nimitz*, as well as the 13th MEU, to within a day of striking distance," Rear Admiral Urban said. "Even as we speak, the Pentagon has authorized movement of a Fifth Fleet DDG, the *Jason Dunham*, to redeploy from her

CENTCOM AOR to augment the Seventh Fleet where I'm light on destroyers for this deployment. Someone is worried about something, Ryan. So, what do we know?"

Thanks to her performance during the *Belgorod* incident, people's opinions of her had risen dramatically. Which, on the one hand, was a good thing. The higher-ups were now interested in her opinion and her opinion had weight to it. But on the other hand, she wasn't wearing a blue and red spandex suit with a giant S on the chest underneath her cammies.

I'm an analyst, not Superwoman.

"Sir, all I can give you right now is my word that as we learn more we will share it directly with you in real time. My only goal is to properly inform and prepare the fleet for the scope, scale, and nature of whatever the Chinese PLA is orchestrating. Is Sea Serpent an exercise or an operation? That's what we're here to find out."

The admiral seemed to like her response because he nodded and said, "I suppose that's why you brought an army of spooks with you." He leaned forward now, elbows on the table. "The lives of a lot of very important people, young sailors from all over our great country, hang on my ability to make good decisions. I'm trusting you to give me the tools to do that."

"Yes, sir," she said, her throat now impossibly dry.

"Well," the admiral said, leaning back in his chair, "I'm heading back to the *Reagan* this afternoon, but Commander Endicott will remain behind for a few days to have a seat at your table. Are you okay with that?"

Realizing suddenly that Urban meant her, not Endicott, she replied, "Oh, sure. Of course, sir. Happy to have him here with us."

Her mind went through a thousand little things she needed

done five minutes from now, not the least of which was checking with Captain Ferguson on the offer she'd just made to give the admiral's aide a "seat at her table," and just what that might look like.

"Sergeant Cheng Fa is still in the lobby and will show you the communications center we have set up for you over in the building housing our tactical operations center," General Wu said, and she wondered if he had somehow read her mind.

Or maybe she was just generally that easy to read.

"I appreciate that, sir. Thank you."

"Good luck, Ryan. The fleet is counting on you," Urban said, and she rose next to Conza and Bubba.

Her gaze ticked to Commander Endicott, who was watching her, possibly glaring, as he stood behind the admiral, arms crossed—undoubtedly not thrilled at the prospect of being left behind on Penghu with a possible war brewing.

Minutes later they followed Sergeant Cheng across the field between buildings, where now a platoon of soldiers in black PT gear were doing calisthenics.

"Bubba, can you head over to the chow hall and grab Ted James and the others?" she asked. "Meet us at the TOC."

"Yes, ma'am," Bubba said, and gave her a two-finger salute.

She looked over to find Conza's face deadly serious.

"Are you thinking what I'm thinking?" he said.

"That we need an update on the Qin situation ASAFP?"

He nodded.

"Then yes, I'm thinking *exactly* what you're thinking."

23

Lieutenant Commander Mitchell Horrillo loved his job.

As the combat systems officer on the USS *Jason Dunham*, his role was to oversee and manage the operation and maintenance of the ship's combat systems. And given that the *Dunham* was an Arleigh Burke–class guided-missile destroyer, that meant a whole lot of critical hardware and software to be responsible for. But he didn't mind. Quite the opposite, in fact. If the ship's combat systems weren't operated and supported to their design specifications and capabilities, then that put the lives of the entire crew at risk. He slept better knowing that he was the person making sure that happened.

He wasn't afraid to put in the work.

And the Navy was paying him good money to do it.

Sometimes, however, the needs of the Navy involved the occasional curveball . . . like the one the crew of the *Dunham* was dealing with right now. With forty-five days left on their deployment to the Fifth Fleet AOR, orders had come in repositioning them from the Middle East to the Pacific. They'd been retasked to support Task Force 70 in the South China Sea, but in what capacity Horrillo did not know. According to the skipper this was one of those "we'll find out when we get there situations."

A mental picture formed in Horrillo's mind of President Ryan moving little plastic boats around on a Battleship board while he sipped wine and ate cheese.

It's not that far from the truth, he thought with a chuckle, and couldn't imagine having that kind of power.

"TAO, can you take a look at Track 82342?" said the surface warfare coordinator from his workstation on the starboard side of the combat information center. "This dude has been running parallel to us for about an hour at a five-nautical-mile standoff, but he turned and now he's closing on an intercept course."

Horrillo currently stood watch as the tactical action officer (TAO), which meant he was the senior watch stander in Combat and responsible for the weapons, sensors, and tactical posture and propulsion of the ship in the captain's stead. Given the late hour, the ship's captain—Commander Jeffrey Kreutz—was asleep in his stateroom.

But if things started to get hairy, the CO would be Horrillo's first call.

He looked up from his workstation at the LSD, or large-screen display, at the front of CIC. The port panel showed a bird's-eye view of the ship's surface contact picture—a 360-degree representation of every surface or air contact being tracked by the *Dunham*'s Aegis Combat System (ACS). Presently, the display was set at a range of sixty-four nautical miles and the screen was littered with contacts. This was hardly surprising, since the Malacca

Strait served as the main shipping corridor between the Indian and the Pacific oceans—linking the powerhouse economies of China, Japan, South Korea, and Malaysia with India, the Middle East, and Africa. Forty percent of the world's maritime commerce, roughly fifty thousand ships, passed through this narrow corridor. But it wasn't the commercial ship traffic that had Horrillo concerned.

No, he was worried about pirates.

Or, to be more specific, terrorists moonlighting as pirates.

The Strait of Malacca had a long and storied history of piracy. The five-hundred-nautical-mile-long passage, with its countless islets and unpatrolled harbors, provided ready hiding places and sanctuary for pirates. Raids on commercial vessels got so bad in the early 2000s that a coalition of nations—Malaysia, Indonesia, Thailand, Singapore, and eventually India—banded together to patrol the strait and stamp out piracy. The effort took time, but over the next decade they got control of the problem and saw the number of attacks plummet.

Until recently . . .

Taking a cue from the Houthis in Yemen, terrorist groups in the region—GAM and Jemaah Islamiyah, both from Indonesia—had begun to step up maritime terrorist attacks. Before entering the strait, the XO had briefed the emerging threat and cautioned that all watch standers needed to be vigilant. The crew of the *Dunham* was no stranger to such attacks, as they'd fended off three drone attacks from Houthis while operating in the Red Sea. But . . . this wasn't the Red Sea and it was night. As much as a part of him might like to take a shoot-first-and-ask-questions-later approach to the situation, Horrillo couldn't do that. Blasting an unidentified surface contact out of the water just because it *could* be a threat wasn't an option.

He watched the dotted square-shaped icon—unknown surface contact—for Track 82342 closing on a zero-bearing rate course toward the *Dunham*. When a contact was closing, but the bearing to that contact didn't change, it was a red flag. Not only did a zero-bearing rate indicate an intercept course, if neither vessel changed speed or heading, it also indicated an inevitable collision. Collisions at sea, no matter who was at fault, were always bad. The *Dunham* had never suffered a collision at sea and Horrillo fully intended to keep it that way.

The surface contact was being tracked by the ship's highly accurate AN/SPS-67 surface-search maritime radar, as well as the powerful SPY-1D. Both radars independently processed raw data using mathematics and logic—along with human input—to generate a track with bearing, range, angle on the bow, speed, and closest point of approach (CPA) for every contact. The remarkable system was capable of tracking over a thousand targets simultaneously and air contacts as small as a hummingbird at ranges over a hundred nautical miles. Track 82342 was no hummingbird, but it wasn't a big lumbering merchant vessel, either. The MK-99 fire-control system had the target moving at twenty-eight knots, at a range of nine thousand yards, with a CPA at zero yards.

"Bridge, Combat—we hold an unknown surface contact of interest, designated Track 82342, bearing two-one-seven, range nine thousand yards," Horrillo said into the boom mic of his headset, which connected him to the ship's Net 15 communications circuit. His call to the bridge notified the ship's officer of the deck—the CO's representative on the bridge in charge of the ship's navigation and noncombat operations—that they were tracking a contact of concern. "Track 82342 is making twenty-eight knots and is on a collision course."

"Combat, Bridge, aye. Any ES?" the officer of the deck, Lieutenant Sara Cullinan, replied.

Horrillo glanced left at the electronic warfare shack in the port forward corner of Combat, where ET2 Merryweather manned the SLQ 32 console. Known as the "Slick 32," it was the *Dunham*'s electronic warfare system, capable of locating, intercepting, and identifying electronic transmissions from civilian and military aviation and maritime platforms.

"Merryweather, whatcha got on 82342?" he called.

"Just a commercial navigation radar, sir," the ET2 called back.

"Roger that," Horrillo said, then into his mic said, "Bridge, Combat—only ES is a commercial nav radar. Recommend hailing them on the bridge-to-bridge and querying their intentions."

"Combat, Bridge, aye. The JOOD is doing that now," came the OOD's response, referring to the junior officer of the deck.

"Surface—cover Track 82342 with Guns and man the Mark 38," Horrillo said, out of an abundance of caution, to the surface warfare coordinator, who acknowledged the order and repeated it back, as was protocol.

In this case, "Guns" referred to the ship's five-inch, .54-caliber deck-mounted cannon, whereas the Mark 38 was the ship's 25mm remote-controlled machine-gun system, which was capable of firing 25×137mm ordnance at a rate of up to 180 rounds per minute. Horrillo was taking the "belt and suspenders" approach to the situation. Most likely a couple of salvos from the Mark 38 would do the trick, but if he needed to take the tango out of the game, he would not hesitate to use the big gun. The five-inch cannon would blast the inbound craft to smithereens and therefore was his solution of last resort.

At night and in low-vis conditions, pirates sometimes mistakenly decided to go after a ship they held on radar *before* they could make visual identification. In this case, if Track 82342 was a pirate vessel, they might have targeted the *Dunham* not realizing it was a U.S. Navy destroyer. And that's where the radio call that the JOOD was making factored into the picture. In attempting to hail the inbound vessel, the *Dunham* would overtly identify itself as a U.S. warship. Any pirate captain with a head on his shoulders would abort the ill-intentioned assault immediately. But if that didn't happen and 82342 kept coming . . . that would tell Horrillo everything he needed to know.

The CIC was located inside the ship's forward superstructure and pilothouse. Unlike other spaces on the ship, Combat was kept dimly lit day and night to promote easy viewing of the numerous computer monitors and wall-mounted displays. CIC had no windows or portholes with a view of the outside world. Just like the tactical operations centers at bases on land, Combat was the communication and data information nerve center of the ship. Over a dozen personnel stood watch in Combat during normal-readiness conditions. At battle stations, also known as Condition Zebra, that number doubled. Prior to the surface warfare coordinator alerting Horrillo to the possible threat posed by Track 82342, the mood in Combat had been chill—with his shipmates working, chatting, and bullshitting each other like sailors love to do. But the minute the threat level had elevated, the atmosphere changed instantly. Now everyone was locked on and the only noise in the compartment was the whir of air-conditioning vents, which kept Combat at temps so frosty that everyone wore jackets or sweaters.

"Combat, Bridge—we hailed 82342 five times. No response," Lieutenant Cullinan reported on Net 15.

"Bridge, Combat, aye. Keep trying," Horrillo said and glanced at his workstation monitor, where he'd pulled up a tracking window on the inbound contact and checked the critical details:

Range: 6,800 yards

Closure rate: 1,215.2 yds/min

CPA: <5 yards

Time to CPA: 5:32 min/sec

Five minutes wasn't much time. The CO's standing orders required that the OOD maintain the CPA for all vessels outside three thousand yards and Track 82342 would cross inside that threshold in less than three minutes.

The OOD ordered the helmsman to reduce the bell from "turns for seventeen knots" to "turns for ten knots," and Horrillo felt the ship slow. This action would accomplish two things. First, it would extend the distance to CPA and add valuable time to reaching it. Second, it would provide them with tactical information. If Track 82342 was *not* a pirate or a terrorist—just some non-English-speaking ship captain driving his vessel fast and loose and cutting across the *Dunham*'s track—then this would open up a gap to safely do so. However, if 82342 reacted to the *Dunham*'s speed reduction by adjusting heading to maintain an intercept course . . . well, then the riddle of the other ship's intentions would be made clear.

Horrillo watched the calculated CPA quickly grow to several hundred yards on the track window, then slow, peak, and begin to march back toward zero.

Looks like we got our answer.

"RCS, interrogate Track 82342," Horrillo said to the watch stander, who was sitting at the ship's MK20 Electro-Optic Sighting System console. EOSS provided high-resolution imagery in both the visual and thermal bands to augment the ship's radar with target acquisition, identification, and tracking. More important, EOSS beat the hell out of binoculars.

The petty officer repeated the order and put the imagery from the system up on one of the auxiliary flat-screen monitors near the front of Combat for Horrillo to view.

"God, I love the EOSS," he muttered as the approaching vessel came into view. Despite the three-nautical-mile-range and the darkness, in thermal imaging mode he could make out that the craft looked like a modified fishing boat, which he guessed was approximately thirty to forty feet long. He counted at least four personnel, but because of the angle the pilothouse blocked the stern.

He picked up a handset and called the captain in his stateroom.

"Captain," the ship's skipper answered on the second ring.

"Captain, TAO—we have a situation, request you in Combat."

"Track 82342?" Kreutz asked, undoubtedly looking at the monitor in his stateroom, where he could mirror any of the displays in Combat.

"Yes, sir," he said. "The vessel is not responding to hails and is on an intercept course."

"On my way."

Horrillo called the OOD next. "Bridge, Combat—just notified the CO of the situation. He's on his way to Combat."

"Combat, Bridge, aye," the OOD said.

"TAO, Surface—the Mark 48 console is manned on the bridge and tracking the target. Guns is covering Track 82342. Three-round KE-ETs salvo is prepped and loaded," the surface warfare coordinator, Lieutenant Junior Grade Higgins reported.

"Very well," he said, watching his own ship's speed level off at ten knots.

The Mk182 five-inch Kinetic Energy Electronically Timed, or KE-ET, ordnance, was the Navy's version of a giant shotgun shell. Inside the payload portion of the .54-caliber round, behind the expelling charge, sat nearly ten thousand, 13-grain tungsten alloy pellets. Similar to how a cloud of bird shot allows a hunter to hit a small, fast-moving target that would be almost impossible to hit with a single slug, the KE-ET round transformed the *Dunham*'s five-inch gun from a long-range bombardment weapon to a lethal, close-in fire-support tool. If the Mark 48 machine gun didn't do the job, the KE-ET round most definitely would.

"XO in Combat," a watch stander announced as the executive officer entered CIC via the portside hatch.

The ship's XO, a blond dynamo named Lieutenant Commander Karen Cook quick-stepped through Combat to stand in between the TAO's console and the captain's console in the very center of CIC. Hands on hips, she studied the wall of monitors on the forward bulkhead. After looking at the EOSS visual feed, she shifted her attention to the bird's-eye-view plot. He knew exactly what she was analyzing—*course change options*. He'd already performed the same assessment, as had, undoubtedly, the OOD on the bridge.

The *Dunham* was currently on course 140, steaming in Sector 4 Undan, which placed them roughly in the middle of the strait that cut between the Malaysian Peninsula to the north and Indonesia to the south. The eastbound traffic traveled on the south side of the scheme, while westbound traffic transited on a track to the north. Presently, the *Dunham* was eastbound with an oil tanker ahead at nine thousand yards and opening and a merchant behind at twelve thousand yards and closing. Enough room to maneuver, but not enough to screw around with course reversals. At their current speed of ten knots, they were operating below the transit speed of the other vessels in the strait. The ship behind would overtake them if they stayed this slow and the last thing Horrillo wanted was a big civilian merchant trying to pass them while they were in a firefight with possible terrorists.

"Did you call the captain?" Cook asked, turning to Horrillo.

"Yes, ma'am. He said he's on his way."

"Good." She put on a headset. "Bridge, CDO—any luck hailing 82342?"

"CDO, Bridge—no, ma'am," came the reply.

"What channel are you using?"

"CDO, Bridge—VHF 61."

"Did you try 88? Sometimes these guys forget to switch channels when they move through the sectors."

"Yes, ma'am, we tried 88 and 84. No response."

She turned to Horrillo and he read her mind.

"Man the LRAD?" he asked, annoyed with himself he'd not already done this.

She nodded and he gave the order to the bridge. The LRAD, or long-range acoustical device, was an acoustic hailing device implemented Navy-wide after the bombing of the USS *Cole*. The system installed on the *Dunham* worked like a super-power, highly focused megaphone—generating long-range, clear voice transmissions and warning tones at volumes up to 160 dB at a range of two miles. The LRAD served a dual purpose. First, it provided a way to communicate with an approaching vessel not responding to radio hails. Verbal instructions and warnings could be given clearly at a distance before proximity demanded taking more aggressive measures. Second, the transmitting power of the LRAD was strong enough it could serve as a nonlethal deterrent to ward off a potential suicide attack.

"Just so you know, we're covering 82342 with Guns and the Mark 48," he said before she could even ask the question.

"Good," she said, then into her mic, "Bridge, CDO—make turns for twenty-five knots. Hail using the LRAD. Use our standard identification protocol and instruct the vessel to change course and maintain a standoff range of two nautical miles."

"XO, Bridge, aye," the OOD said, then repeated back the order.

"All right, TAO, the captain should be here any second, but in the meantime, do whatever we need to do to keep the ship and crew safe. I'm heading to the bridge."

"Roger that, ma'am," he said with fire in his chest as she turned to leave. Per protocol, the ship's captain and the executive officer—in tactical situations and casualties—never occupied the same space at the same time. If the skipper was coming to Combat, then LCDR Cook would take station on the bridge. That way if, God forbid, a missile strike or RPG made it through the *Dunham*'s defenses, the chances of it killing the ship's CO and XO in a single strike were minimized.

The *Dunham*'s commanding officer, Jeffrey Kreutz, was the best skipper that Horrillo had served under, and that was saying something because his previous two captains had been damn good. Horrillo respected how Kreutz put the needs of the ship and the crew ahead of his own, and his ego never factored into the decision-making process. The same, unfortunately, could not be said for all officers and senior NCOs. Kreutz was a delegator, not a micromanager, which fostered a sense of empowerment and self-determination among the crew.

Just like right now.

Whatever decision Horrillo made as TAO—even if ex post facto that call turned out to be wrong—the captain would have Horrillo's back.

"Tripwire, Track 82342 crossing inside four thousand yards," the surface warfare coordinator announced.

"Surface, redesignate Track 82342 as suspected hostile," Horrillo ordered, and the icon on the port large-screen display changed from a dotted square to a dotted diamond.

"Track 82342 redesignated as suspected hostile," Surface replied.

"Bridge, Combat—sitrep?" Horrillo queried on Net 15.

He shifted his gaze to the EOSS feed on the aux display. He could see several men in the approaching craft covering their ears, but 82342 was not deviating from an intercept course.

"Combat, Bridge—LRAD transmitting, but no change in the target's course or speed," Cullinan answered.

"Bridge, Combat—crank up the volume to maximum and keep at it. I think we know their intentions, let's not make it easy on them."

"Combat, Bridge, aye."

"Captain in Combat," a watch stander announced as Commander Kreutz entered CIC.

"Bring me up to speed, TAO," the skipper said as he fell in beside Horrillo at the captain's console.

But as the words left the captain's mouth, Horrillo saw—on the EOSS feed—one of the men on the inbound vessel hoist a boxy rocket launcher onto his shoulder and point it at the camera. The aux display screen momentarily washed out as the missile launched, then showed a streak of fire screaming toward the *Dunham*.

24

THE *LADY ELIZABETH*
LAMBERTI 80 LUXURY MOTOR YACHT
DHONFANU THILA DIVE SITE IN THE BAA ATOLL CHAIN
ELEVEN KILOMETERS FROM THE FOUR SEASONS RESORT
LANDAA GIRAAVARU, MALDIVES
2334 LOCAL TIME

While the dive had been purely for show, Clark had to admit he had enjoyed himself immensely. He had only very rarely been diving for sport, but their recreational night dive on the reef, as part of their cover to position for the infil, had no objectives other than appearances, so he'd taken a moment to actually enjoy the beauty of the sea life. As a former frogman, diving was a tool for stealth infiltration or a means of escape. SEALs embraced the ocean that most people innately feared. But the night dive—from the luxurious Lamberti 80 they had chartered out of Kamadhoo—had been beautiful, the waters warm, and the reef full of color and life.

He slipped his fins onto the aft swim platform of the boat, where British SBS frogman Daniel Wu grabbed them and slid them up onto the main deck as Clark maneuvered up the ladder. Behind him, his "dive buddy," Ding Chavez, held on to the ladder in the calm and gentle but very dark waters of the Indian Ocean. Clark never worried about the predators in the sea, not in all his time as a SEAL. He was fatalistic when it came to such things, but the Indian Ocean was rather famous for sharks, so he knew Ding would be eager to get up on the deck.

It's different when you're underwater than bobbing in the waves like bait.

Moments later, they were all aboard, wetsuit tops pulled down to their waists, and theatrically gushing about what they'd seen on the dive. Clark wouldn't usually bother with all the playacting on a chartered boat at sea, six miles from the X in the middle of the ocean. But this was the Chinese they were up against and they were at the top of the food chain when it came to signals intelligence, perhaps only slightly behind the United States.

Or maybe even ahead . . .

"One more dive?" he asked, pouring bottled water over his head to wash away the salt.

"I'm game," Ding said.

"We have four more tanks with three thousand pounds of air," Wu said with his thick British accent. "Why not?"

"Something shallow," Lee Hyori said with a perfect American accent. "We're at the edge of the tables tonight and I want to be able to dive with the manta rays tomorrow."

"Sounds good," Clark said. "We can do the shallow reef near Landaa Giraavaru and then anchor overnight. We'll grab breakfast when we wake up at the Four Seasons."

"Sounds lux," Wu said.

Clark climbed the inboard stairs to the flybridge, where he

took the helm of the Lamberti 80. From the fly he had a better view of anything that might be around them. Blocked by the bimini top from any curious satellites or drones above, he donned a pair of night vision goggles enhanced with the latest X27 full-color technology. Instantly the world outside came to life in crisp, full color that looked for all the world like midday, but without the glare. The calm ocean was empty, their luxury dive boat alone on the calm sea, at least this far from Landaa Giraavaru, where the Four Seasons sat. There were no other boats, and the only light he saw were the hazy lights of the island just under seven miles away, which looked slightly artificial in the night vision.

Clark engaged the key and pressed the start button and the twin 650-horsepower Volvo Penta D12s growled to life. He tapped the twin throttles, and the engines grumbled as the yacht crept forward, taking the tension out of the anchor chain as Lee Hyori worked the controls for the electric winch at the front of the bow. Once the anchor was secured, he watched Hyori head aft along the gunwale. Hyori gave Clark a nod, and Clark nodded back.

With the anchor stowed, Clark advanced the throttles and the Lamberti accelerated smoothly. He removed the NVGs, tossed them on the seat behind him, and angled the bow toward the lights of the Landaa Giraavaru. Below, Ding and Hyori would be preparing their combat loadouts, weapons and gear that would be attached to the anchor line in long, slick bags. If anyone was watching from the sky, they'd be unlikely to detect the loadouts dropping into the water on the anchor line. The divers on the swim deck would be the focus, and those divers would be dressed out in standard dive gear.

"Hey, man," the voice of Daniel Wu called from behind him.

Clark accepted a bottled water from his make-believe friend, out on the guys' trip, dive vacation of a lifetime, then watched the British SBS operator take a seat on the matching captain's chair beside the one he stood in front of. Effortlessly, the man slipped into his NOC and began to talk about his fictitious work, wife, and kids. Clark bantered back with him, aware that this dude was going to be great in Beijing. Despite only limited time operating deep under a NOC, Wu was a natural. Even if there was no Chinese signals technology listening in on them, this was good practice for the next stage of their operation.

As they chatted, the Lamberti cut through the gentle waves effortlessly, and with a check of his watch, Clark pulled the throttles back and slowed the yacht to seventeen knots, glancing at the large screen of the marine GPS, which gave his ETA as a minute or two early. They needed to be precise and perfect with the schedule milestones because there would be zero electronic comms between Clark's four-man team and Bauer, Adams, and Toussaint, who were on the island already and preparing for their part in the operation to liberate Mrs. Qin and her twin daughters. The Chinese security presence at the Four Seasons would be robust, and would include the Qin family security detail as well as agents from the MSS. Clark couldn't risk communications between his team and other TF 99 members being intercepted because it would alert the Chinese they were coming.

And that would mean losing the element of surprise . . . the only meaningful advantage TF 99 had tonight.

Clark savored the opportunity to pilot the expensive Lamberti, breathe in the salty air, and feel the cool breeze on his face as he chatted with Wu during the twenty-minute drive to the next site. The fact that these things even registered in his mind told him something—something potentially important. He was enjoying the manufactured recreation of the job tonight more than the actual job.

Maybe I am ready for retirement, he thought, scanning the sea.

He eased off the throttles as they approached the next dive waypoint. Hyori returned to his post at the bow anchor well. Clark caught a glimpse of long gray bags fixed to the anchor chain just above the anchor as it splashed into the sea. He tapped the throttles out of neutral and into reverse as the chain played out, then secured the engines and slipped the key into the pocket of his wetsuit. Just off the port side of the bow, he could now easily see the lights of the Four Seasons and make out the details of the resort. The long pier at the eastern edge of the island resort was well lit straight ahead, and to his left he could see the winking lights of the luxury bungalow-style accommodations, each with its own plunge pool, where Qin Caiji and her twin daughters were staying. Beyond, and just a hundred yards to the west, was the dive center, where, if all went well, Bauer, Adams, and Toussaint had already secured a boat for their exfil. The swim to the beach from the dive point was only four hundred yards.

What could possibly go wrong?

"Ready for one more dive?" he asked his teammate.

"Totally," Wu answered, but the fire in his eyes didn't match the casualness of his voice. "Then a good night's sleep."

They descended from the flybridge and joined Hyori and Ding, who were already donning their tanks, and a minute later, geared up, masks on, and fins in hand, they shuffled to the swim platform and one by one entered the warm Indian Ocean.

Clark led Ding beneath the yacht, descending as he did, and encountered the anchor line, which he then followed to the bottom, thirty-five feet down. His flashlight illuminated the first of the four gray bags lashed to the anchor line, and he tore the Velcro open to access his gear as the others did the same. After swapping his Sea Pro dive mask for the military-grade mask with embedded night vision, he clipped his flashlight on the anchor line. The bobbing of the boat would make the lights move around, simulating divers exploring the reef around the anchor. They wouldn't move out much from the anchor, but that wasn't unusual for recreational divers on a night dive, fearful of getting lost or swept away by the current.

After securing the Wilson Combat SBR Tactical assault rifle tightly to his chest over the body armor he donned, he checked the programmed navigation computer on his wrist and then kicked off the swim, taking the point position of their diamond formation. He could *feel* his team beside and behind him, but he focused on keeping them on track, following the nav guidance for the route programmed on his wristwatch dive computer. He hugged the bottom, which morphed rapidly from reef to scattered brain coral formations, and then to soft white sand. As they moved north and west he watched the depth grow shallow, marking their approach to Landaa Giraavaru and the Four Seasons resort beach.

He'd planned to hit "feet dry" just short of the arrowhead-shaped western edge of the resort island, putting the large pier and its U-shaped floating dock to their right and the row of beachside cabanas to the left. Given the late hour, the beach should be empty, hopefully, and more important, it would be dark, blocked from the resort lights by a row of palm trees and still a good seventy yards from the first in the row of cabanas.

They arrived three minutes early, so he held his team, in about six or seven feet of water just outside the surf. Better to wait here, under the water, than on the beach, where someone might stumble upon them. Clark made eye contact with each teammate in the eerie artificial light of the night vision masks and held up three fingers.

We wait three minutes . . .

His operators each flashed an OK sign, and together they waited, kneeling on the soft sand, the gentle waves above moving them back and forth like trees in the wind. When the time ticked down, Clark finned forward until they were in just a few feet of water, then got one foot and a knee under him, and slowly raised his head above the surf until just the top of his head and his mask broke the surface.

He scanned the beach, satisfying himself that it was empty. Beyond the beach, the long pier also seemed unoccupied, and to his left, no late-night walkers, stargazers, or skinny-dippers out tonight, thank God. He counted from left to right and found the fourth cabana from the east to be totally dark, save a single dull light on the rear patio by the pool.

It seemed the Qin family was fast asleep.

Clark descended back to the bottom, gave the team a thumbs-up, and in seconds they all slipped out of their dive gear. Then they were back in a diamond formation, rifles up, moving out of the surf onto the beach. Clark led them rapidly across the open stretch of sand and into the shadows of the row of palm trees, where he took a knee, each member of the team scanning their sector from the formation for threats. He glanced at his watch, wishing like hell he could make a comms check with the other half of the team.

But the micro-transmitter/receiver in his left ear canal was silent, and that was a communication of sorts. If there was a problem, then Bauer would break radio silence and warn them off, right? So the silence was a good thing.

Unless they're captured or dead . . .

He glanced again at his watch. Adams would arrive at the Qin cabana door in two minutes.

Time to go.

Clark circled a hand over his head and led his four-man team west along the tree line.

25

T he anti-ship missile screaming toward the *Dunham* had just removed the biggest uncertainty that had been handcuffing Horrillo. Track 82342 was not a civilian merchant vessel. Nor was it a fishing boat or an Indonesian maritime security patrol craft. None of those vessels would fire on a U.S. Navy destroyer. From a geopolitical perspective, sinking any vessel in the Strait of Malacca without provocation would create a big, hairy incident for the U.S. Navy and the captain and crew of the ship.

That scenario was off the table now.

Any actions the *Dunham* took would be in self-defense and authorized under the U.S. Navy's rules of engagement governing anti-terrorism.

Horrillo looked at Commander Kreutz and said, "Captain, I intend to kill Track 82342 with Guns."

"Do it," the skipper said.

"Surface—kill Track 82342 with Guns," Horrillo announced, using his command voice.

The surface warfare coordinator acknowledged the order. Two seconds later the Mark 45 on the forecastle boomed as the five-inch gun sent a KE-ET round barreling toward the terrorist-attack boat.

"TAO, Air—looks like they got off another shot. We have a second anti-ship missile inbound," the air warfare officer announced. "First inbound vampire, designated Track 82351. Second vampire is Track 82352. CIWS is tracking 51."

The ship's Phalanx CIWS, or close-in weapon system, was the ship's last line of defense against close-range airborne threats such as RPGs, anti-ship missiles, and kamikaze drones. The six-barrel, Gatling-style machine gun fired 20mm, armor-piercing, tungsten penetrator rounds at a rate of 4,500 rounds per minute. Designed and built by General Dynamics, the CIWS was capable of both manual and fully automatic operation and designed for rapid response against threats inside five nautical miles. In this case, the instant the shoulder-mounted missile launch was detected, the RCS watch stander was trained to switch CIWS from HOLD FIRE ON (safe) to HOLD FIRE OFF (safety disengaged). The CIWS's radar and processing system would take care of the rest.

Inside the sound-insulated walls of CIC, Horrillo couldn't hear the distinctive and unmistakable *brrrrrrrttttttt* sound the CIWS made when it sent a kill volley at the incoming terrorist-launched anti-ship missile, but he was able to observe it on the RCS terminal. Horrillo watched with satisfaction as the inbound missile got ripped to shrapnel by the bullet barrage.

"TAO, Air—Track 82351 destroyed," the air warfare officer announced. "CIWS now tracking 52 . . ."

A heartbeat later, the EOSS feed—which was trained on the terrorist fast boat—showed the KE-ET projectile explode and annihilate the aggressor vessel with ten thousand pellets traveling at supersonic speeds.

"TAO, Surface—Guns scored a hit on Track 82342. Performing visual battle damage assessment," the surface warfare coordinator announced.

"Very well," Horrillo said simply, but his heart was pounding like a bass drum in his chest as the second anti-ship missile screamed toward the *Dunham*.

He, along with the captain and the rest of the watch standers in Combat, watched helplessly to see if the CIWS would hit another home run for them . . . or, would this be *the* missile that slipped through their defenses and hit the ship? The robo-Phalanx was an incredible defensive weapon, but it wasn't perfect.

Time slowed to a crawl as he waited . . .

"TAO, Air—Track 82352 destroyed!" the air warfare officer announced triumphantly.

"Way to go R2-D2!" the RCS operator whooped at his console, using the ship's nickname for the CIWS. "Saved our ass twice in one night."

Commander Kreutz turned to face Horrillo. "Good job, Mitch, you kept the ship safe. Any other threats I need to know about?"

"No, sir," Horrillo said, hoping that statement held true for the rest of their transit through the Malacca Strait.

"Very well. Tell the XO to ring me in my stateroom. We're going to need to draft a message and report this to the task force."

"Yes, sir. Thank you, sir," he said, then added, "I assume that means you don't want me to set Condition Zebra?"

"A little late for that, don't you think?" Kreutz said with a chuckle.

"Well, I was just thinking, sir, there could be more of these guys out there. What if this is just the first of multiple planned attempts along our track through the strait?"

The CO paused to consider this a moment, then said, "I have a feeling after what just happened to that boat, the other terrorist captains—if there are others—are going to think twice about taking us on. The Mark 45 is one helluva hammer . . . But you never know. One thing you gotta give martyrs credit for—they are committed."

"Yes, sir, they are indeed."

The CO put a hand on Horrillo's shoulder. "You did everything right. If it happens again, rinse and repeat, TAO. Rinse and repeat."

"Yes, sir. Understood."

And with that, the CO yawned and headed out of Combat without a backward glance.

How the captain could even consider going back to sleep after all that was a mystery to Horrillo, but that was how the man operated. As far as Kreutz was concerned, they'd faced the threat; they'd beat the threat; the threat was over.

Not Horrillo. He was so jacked with adrenaline that falling asleep after he got off watch at 0300 was almost certainly out of the question.

"TAO, Surface—completed battle damage assessment. The threat is neutralized. No visible survivors and the craft is sinking," the surface warfare coordinator said.

"Very well. Good shooting, Guns," he said.

"Thank you, sir," said the first-class petty officer seated at the GFCS.

"Bridge, Combat—Track 82342 is neutralized. Both inbound anti-ship missiles have been destroyed. Inform the XO that the captain wants her to contact him in his stateroom," Horrillo said into his boom mic.

"Combat, Bridge, aye. The XO wants to know if you discussed setting Condition Zebra with the CO?" came Lieutenant Cullinan's reply.

"I did and he does not."

"Roger that. Combat, Bridge—slowing to turns for seventeen knots."

"Roger that."

"Do you want us to keep the Mark 48 manned?" she asked, referring to the 25mm machine gun, which was controlled from the bridge.

They'd not used the Mark 48 this time because of the way the situation had played out, but it was the lower-impact option. "Maintain the Mark 48 manned as well as the LRAD for the remainder of the watch," he said. "We'll reassess with the CDO at shift turnover."

"Maintain the Mark 48 and LRAD manned, Combat, Bridge, aye," the OOD replied.

He exhaled long and slow and felt the tension ebb from his neck and shoulders.

This was the second time in as many months that the *Dunham* had been attacked by terrorists at night. The previous encounter in the Red Sea they'd anticipated and had manned battle stations before the engagement—putting every sailor in the role that they were optimally trained and suited for. If the *Dunham* was a professional football team, the battle stations watch bill was equivalent to their starting lineup. This time, an unseen terrorist threat had caught them by surprise in a normal readiness posture, and the on-watch team had responded with nerves of steel and expert efficiency.

Feeling suddenly very proud, he congratulated everyone in Combat on a job well done.

Horrillo didn't know what maritime mission awaited them beyond Singapore in the South China Sea, but whatever the threat was, whatever tasking the Navy needed them to execute, the officers and crew of the USS *Jason Dunham* would answer the call.

26

Charlotte "Charlie" Adams, intelligence officer for the Australian SAS and now some sort of bloody spy on an international task force, glanced at her watch and clenched her jaw. Timing, she knew, would be everything. In the SAS, there was never room on a team for baggage.

For tonight's op, the last thing she wanted to be was baggage.

Despite not being an operator she'd trained extensively with the SAS and had real-world experience in the Middle East planning and coordinating operations much like this one. But this was the first time she might be forced to have to pull the trigger. If it came to that, she would be ready.

She closed her eyes, executed a quick round of four-count tactical breathing like the badasses in the SAS had taught her, and then opened them again.

Let's do this.

She grabbed the room service cart, feeling both comforted and anxious at the knowledge of the Wilson Combat AR-9 compact machine pistol secured to the underside of the main service tray by a magnet. She let herself slip into character—a room service attendant who was weary from working long hours waiting hand and foot on wealthy guests, but had no choice but to smile and bear it. She began her stroll toward the pathways connecting the main campus pool area to the more exclusive beachside cabanas.

The wheels of the cart chattered, but then she wasn't really intent on a stealthy approach. In fact, drawing some attention was rather important, as it would distract from the approach Henri and Wilhelm would be making to the cabana just west of unit number four, where Qin Caiji and her daughters, Diedie and Beiye, now slept. That unit, number five, was occupied by a four-member Chinese security team assigned to the defense minister's family. Wilhelm Bauer identified the security force earlier that day as he wandered the grounds of the resort as a registered guest. Unit three, on the other side of the Qin cabana, was presumed to house a second four-man team. But unlike the security detail that followed Caiji and the girls everywhere, these men rarely left their cabana. These men, she assumed, probably served as the security detail's eyes and ears and had transformed their cabana into a tactical operations center. Henri, whose NOC had him as a wealthy French architect, had found little luck determining what other Chinese assets—MSS or PLA—were embedded at or surveilling the resort.

Theirs was a business of imperfect information.

When she walked past cabana number one, the lights brightened in unit three, as she had assumed they would. As she passed number two, the wheels of her cart making all kinds of squeaks and racket on the pebble path, the front door to number three opened. A Chinese man dressed in a black suit and tie, despite the late hour, stepped out to confront her.

ANDREWS & WILSON

"May I help you?" the man said in clipped English, the main language of the Maldives, since it was the language used in schools, despite the use of Dhivehi script on most signs. She noticed that his right hand was at his belt, just inside his suit coat.

"No thank you, sir," she said. "I am delivering a room service order to another unit. I am so sorry if my squeaky cart disturbed you."

"Which unit?" the man demanded.

"Pardon me?" she said, and let her hand slip beneath the main tray of the cart, tickling the pistol grip of the AR-9. "Did you have a room service order you are expecting, sir? I can check on the status for you if you like."

"No," the man said, eyeing her suspiciously and moving his right hand deeper inside his coat. "I asked where it is you are taking this order. I am the head of security for another guest here."

"Oh, I see," she said, and made a show of looking at the order ticket on top of the cart with her left hand as her right now wrapped around the pistol grip of the AR-9. "Let me have a look here," she said. Had the guard not confronted her, she would have wheeled her cart up to cabana four and rung the bell, but this guy wasn't going to let her get anywhere near that door.

A soft, dull *whump*—which she knew instantly was suppressed fire from one of her teammates—echoed down the path toward cabana five. The Chinese agent heard it, too, because he turned to his left, yanked his pistol, and took a step to move around her. Unsuppressed gunfire from inside the cabana broke the quiet and the windows flashed from muzzle flares. With the man's attention on the raid, she pulled the pistol from the cart and took a step back, and sighted. With the dot of her Aimpoint holographic sight on the back of the guard's head, she squeezed the trigger. The pistol kicked and the whisper suppressor on her short AR-9 kept the discharge to a dull burp. The 9mm bullet tore through the man's skull and he collapsed in the shrubs beside the manicured path.

She heard footsteps moving from inside cabana three.

Stealth didn't matter anymore, as a second burst of gunfire now shattered the peaceful quiet of the luxury resort.

So much for sneaking off undetected into the night.

She darted left for cover, disappearing into the shadows of the bushes beside the entrance to cabana three. Any second, the other guards would charge from the cabin, like hornets from a rattled hive. She raised her compact machine pistol to drop them from behind as they did, all the while hoping Clark had a contingency for getting the team out of here alive.

27

C lark saw the unsuppressed flashes of gunfire from cabana five just a microsecond before he heard the unsuppressed retort.

"Shit," he breathed, and spun his left hand over his head as he kicked off a sprint, still in a low combat crouch, toward the cabana on the far side of the target, where another crack of gunfire now erupted. He wanted to demand a sitrep, the element of surprise clearly lost, but the radio silence was about more than that—any signals collected by the Chinese could implicate the United States in an operation where it now appeared some Chinese nationals from the security team were going to die.

God, I hope it's Chinese bodies I find and not a French and a German operator . . .

He kept his team tight against the tree line, keeping to the shadows, though the Chinese MSS team would certainly have night vision capabilities.

A voice sounded in his earpiece, brilliantly in Arabic instead of English.

"Khamsat wadih," came Toussaint's growling voice.

Five is clear . . .

"Sabea . . . aithnan fi almabnaa sifr," Charlie Adams said next, picking up the cue and also speaking in Arabic, alerting them of two shooters still in the building between them and the target house containing the Qin family.

"Shukran," Clark said, thanking her.

He took a knee beside the three wooden steps leading up onto the deck and plunge pool of the luxury cabana, sighting into the rear sliders as Ding, Wu, and Hyori took positions for the assault. Then he was up, taking the stairs and moving forward across the deck, sweeping his SBR Tactical across the deck, looking for targets.

A man in dark clothes crossed to the glass slider from inside, a compact submachine pistol in his grip, and pulled the slider open. Clark dropped the green dot of his IR laser designator onto his forehead and dropped him with a single muffled shot. As he did, a second man emerged from behind the curtain and he heard the dull whump of Ding's rifle as it spat a .308 round center mass and the shooter fell dead.

"Clear the house with Ding," he whispered to Wu after muting the VOX on his radio. "Hyori, you're with me."

Clark leapt off the deck, boots digging into the sandy beach, leading Lee Hyori toward the target building, where a light now came on inside the master bedroom to the west of the great room. As he reached the deck a dark figure crossed through the poorly lit living room, heading toward the master bedroom. Was it a security agent, or just one of the twin girls heading to Mommy's room, frightened by the gunfire outside?

He chopped his hand left, indicating Lee should position himself on the far side of the sliders, then took a knee to the right, just as a light came on over his shoulder—the children's room, he assumed.

Damnit, who did I see?

He glanced over his shoulder, watching Hyori do the same, clearing their six before the breach. Then he pulled a flashlight-sized laser generator from his kit with his gloved left hand, positioned it above the latch, and pressed the button and shielded his eyes, dragging the thin beam up and down as the acrid smell of burning metal filled his nostrils. Then the lock latch separated with a dull snap, and he slid the door open with his left hand, scanning left and right as he breached the room.

The dark figure was a man, beside the door to the master bedroom, who turned toward him as he dropped his green designator on the man's temple and squeezed. The man collapsed, his fall louder than the suppressed .308, just as two voices reached him.

"*Shéi zài nà'er?*" Qin Caiji called out in a frightened voice, asking who was there, just as her daughter called out from the room to his right.

"Mama!"

"*Nǐ hěn Ānquán,*" Lee Hyori called out from behind him in a commanding voice. "*Bāochí nǐ yuán yǒu wèizhì!*"

You are safe. Stay where you are.

It was good thinking. The Qins would be used to orders from their security detail. Clark surged forward and dragged the body behind the breakfast bar. As he did, the front door opened and Charlie Adams slipped in, closing the door behind her and disappearing the submachine gun under her uniform apron.

The master bedroom door opened and a frightened eye peered out at him as he approached. Clark lowered his weapon, flipped his NVGs up on his head, and smiled as best he could. He spoke in English.

"Qin Caiji, your husband sent us. Qin Hâiyû wants you to be safe. You are in very real danger."

The woman behind the door stared at him with her one visible brown eye, then opened the door, tipping her chin up bravely. She was small, but Clark immediately knew she was a powerful and confident woman.

"Hâiyû said you might come," she said, her English crisp and clear, with a hint of a British accent. "I do not know what it is that has happened to him, but we have a secret code we use . . ."

Clark nodded and held her eyes.

"I have the same with my wife," he said. "I understand."

"When last we spoke it was clear something was happening. He signaled he would send someone for us. Is that you?"

Clark admired her frankness and hoped his eyes showed her more than his words could.

"I do not know your husband, Qin Caiji," he said, "but I am a friend. It is my job to get you out of here, but more than that, it is my job to make sure you and your daughters, Diedie and Beiye, are safe. It is a promise that was made to your husband."

She stared at him and then her shoulders dropped. "Is he . . . Is he dead?"

"No," Clark said quickly. "No, he is still in China and we are trying to get him out. But right now we need to move, and very quickly. Leave your things, but get your girls and come with us."

She stared at him a moment, uncertain.

"Caiji, I can't promise you we will reunite you with Hâiyû, but I can promise that we will fulfill our promise to him and that if we can get him out, we will. Please—call your girls."

She held his eyes and he saw she believed him.

"Diedie . . . Beiye," she called loudly. "Come quickly."

The girls came from the second bedroom, looking at the strangers in their resort room in terror, and ran to their mother, wrapping arms around her waist. He watched Charlie clear their room and then they were hustling out the back door, Clark in the lead, Charlie beside the terrified family, and Hyori clearing their six.

To his shock, they were not met with more agents as they sprinted across the beach to the west, toward the dive shop, where already he heard the sound of a boat roaring to life. Clearly Wilhelm and Henri had made it to the exfil site and were preparing their escape.

Moments later, he took a knee beside Hyori at the end of the long pier, scanning for approaching threats, as Charlie hustled the family to the waiting boat. Headlights suddenly appeared on the small access road behind the dive shop, and moments later the source presented as a large golf cart, loaded with security guards. Three of the four had the rent-a-cop appearance of resort security, but a larger Asian man leapt with grace and speed off the back, a long gun in his hands, and Hyori dropped him expertly with a double tap to the chest.

"Do we kill the others?" Hyori asked. His voice held the same thought that rattled in Clark's head.

"Only if we have to," he replied. "Let's see if they're a threat."

Clark fired three warning shots wide of the golf cart, into the ground just to the left of where it had careened to a stop. Instantly, all three uniformed guards sprinted away in terror.

Clark grinned and motioned with his head to Hyori.

"Let's get the hell out of here."

He covered the rear as they moved rapidly up the dock to the waiting dive boat, whose lines were already cast off, held in place by Wu's expert control of the helm.

Clark followed Hyori into the rear of the boat, which instantly accelerated away from the dock, heading south with the running lights out. In a moment, he knew Hyori would correct left, heading toward the waiting yacht.

Then, if they were lucky and the Chinese had no maritime asset standing by—or at least no asset that had been notified of what went down—they would board the yacht, abandon the dive boat, and head north, where an Indian Navy ship waited to intercept them and whisk them to safety.

Better to be lucky than good.

Clark let out a long sigh, then glanced over at where Qin's wife held her two daughters tight against her from either side as they leaned back on the bench seat in front of the empty row of scuba tank racks. The girls were crying, and shivering in the cool air, still in their nightgowns.

"Henri, see if there are any blankets or towels we can wrap the girls in," he said to the Frenchman, who stood beside Hyori at the helm, dressed all in black with a black beanie on his head and a compact machine pistol on his chest. He looked for all the world like a caricature of a World War II French Resistance fighter.

"*Oui, monsieur,*" Toussaint said and headed forward.

Clark listened as one of the girls said something he couldn't make out in Chinese and Qin Caiji answered her in English.

"It will be fine. Be strong like your dada."

"What did she say?" he called to Qin Caiji over the roar of the twin outboard motors.

"She is sad that she left her doll. It was a gift from her father . . ."

"This one?" Charlie asked, rising from the bench across from them and pulling matching dolls from inside her server's uniform. Clark smiled at her and she shrugged. "I saw they had matching dolls on their beds and thought it might help if they had them."

"Thank you," Caiji said. Then the emotion and stress finally got the better of her and she began to weep, holding her children to her chest.

"It's going to be all right," Clark said, leaning in and placing a hand on the woman's shoulder. "And this team will do everything in our power to bring your husband to you."

"Okay," she said softly.

"You're safe now," he added.

Then he rose, moving to the stern of the wide boat, and snapping his color-enhanced night vision goggles back into place to scan the sea behind them. Because if the Chinese *did* have a maritime asset in the area that they had not detected, then none of them were safe.

It was a long way to the Indian frigate waiting for them.

28

K atie sat on the rear bench seat of the open-cabin, military Humvee beside Conza. The sun felt warm on her skin and the air cool as they headed back to base. The tour had not only been informative but it had opened her eyes to the critical role that Penghu played in the defense of Taiwan.

Penghu "island" was a bit of a misnomer, as it was actually an island chain. The base housing the 101st Amphibious Reconnaissance Battalion, aka the Sea Dragons, was located on the southern tip of the main island of Magong, which was only five miles long. This was the base where Katie and her team were currently housed and operating out of. A second base was located across a bay in the center of Magong and was home to the Army units responsible for the myriad of air and sea defense units spread throughout the island chain.

Katie and Conza had spent the day inspecting a shocking

number of heavily guarded military installations on Magong as well as the other two islands accessible by bridge. They'd toured the island of Baisha to the north, via Highway 203, and viewed three heavily fortified compounds containing advanced anti-air and anti-ship missile batteries. Afterward, they'd driven west to Xiyu, a seahorse-shaped island four miles long, but mostly only a half-mile wide or less, where they saw Taiwan-produced Sky Bow II and III mobile missile batteries. They had been told that the myriad of smaller islands, accessible only by ferry, contained numerous air and sea defense batteries also. And, of course, the mainland of Taiwan was rich with U.S.-sourced Patriot missile defense systems to augment the fighter aircraft of the ROC Air Force.

"More than you expected?" Conza said over the din of the road noise from the Humvee's engine and tires.

She turned to see him studying her as they passed Jigang Road, forking off to their left and leading into the quaint village of Suogang with its shops, bed-and-breakfasts, and fishing village. The entire chain of islands felt like a bizarre mix of peaceful little coastal villages and military posts and weapons that advertised an urgent defense against an impending invasion.

"Yes and no," she said. "I mean, I've seen it on paper, but it doesn't prepare you for the stark reality of the fortifications. And the people all seem so content and happy going about their day while hundreds of missiles are on standby waiting to repel an invasion. It's weird."

"Yeah, a strange fatalistic pragmatism. Living in the shadow of war . . ."

She nodded.

"The gun batteries, lined up along the south end of Xiyu, gave such an old-school, World War II vibe, you know?" Conza said.

"Yeah, I hear you," she said. "I thought they were just historic, left in place as a memorial or something, when I saw them on the satellite images."

Conza shook his head. "Old-school, but effective," he said. "Good luck breaching the mouth of the bay and getting into Magong Harbor with those bad boys on duty."

"Still," she said. "How long could such an antiquated system survive a war with China? I mean, they would just target those guns with ballistic missiles ahead of any amphibious assault."

"In theory," Conza said with a shrug. "But remember, with the MIM-23 Hawk missiles, the TK II and III Sky Bows, as well as the newer Sky Sword anti-ballistic missile systems, are backed up by the Patriot systems. We know historically and through war-gaming models that amphibious-landing success is below twenty percent if you don't control the air."

"But China's Air Force is vastly superior," Katie argued. "Air superiority is impossible for Taiwan against the Chinese. Hell, even with U.S. involvement directly from our carrier strike group, it would be a struggle at best."

"Right," Conza said. "Due to proximity to mainland China, among other things. But that's why the defense doctrine here isn't superiority—it's denial. These modern air defense systems we've seen can theoretically do that. They can counter not just aircraft but ballistic and even hypersonic missiles from China, both from the mainland and from ships and aircraft. Your question about the gun batteries at the mouth of the bay are the perfect example. China would try to take out those sites with ballistic missiles—but they would fail, at least at first, because of the rich and intricate network of missile defense against both aircraft and Chinese missile attacks. I'm not saying that China couldn't take Penghu and mainland Taiwan if they're truly committed, but doing so would exact an enormous toll on their forces."

Katie thought about that as they now made their own left turn just short of the coastal, touristy village of Jing'an. The driver, a fit ROC soldier with sleeves rolled up over thick biceps, looked at her in the rearview mirror of the open truck.

"Have the ID cards we provided ready, please," he said in clipped English. She dug hers out of the breast pocket of her uniform blouse as they maneuvered left and right between the staggered cement barriers meant to slow an approaching vehicle to a crawl.

"Do you think Taiwan could rebuff an all-out attack?" she asked Conza, aware that the driver of their vehicle could probably hear her.

"No," Conza admitted, glancing at the driver. "Not without our help. But between the air and sea defenses, the Army and Marines on Taiwan proper, and the badass warriors in the 101st here on Penghu, they'd put up a helluva fight."

"What about with our help?" she asked the former SEAL, handing her ROC ID to the fully kitted-up soldier at the gate.

"With our help—with Task Force 70 and our special operations augmenting—that would be a very different story, but with far more variables," Conza said as they were waved through, the barricade lowered into the ground.

"Such as?"

"Such as, what price is China willing to pay? What plan do they have in place to manage the world condemnation that would follow an unprovoked strike? And how much resolve do the American people and our leaders have to defend Taiwan?"

They finished the drive in silence, circling around the southeast end of the airfield runway to reach their compound. Katie found herself drawn again and again to Conza's second point. Was Li willing to risk isolating his country's image and economic status for a reunification dream that the majority of the citizens of China and Taiwan didn't see as a priority? Would he risk the devastating economic sanctions that would be levied by the West after an unprovoked war and invasion?

He must have a plan for that . . .

And how much resolve did the American people have to protect an island thousands of miles away that the average citizen didn't know much about?

How much resolve did her *father* have?

He had been challenged in the past by other Chinese leaders, but this time was different. Today's threat was more direct.

She stared west, out across the water, toward where President Li's massive military nation sat just seventy-five miles away. President Ryan had enough resolve to form a task force and send her team here. He had enough to send a team of spooks into mainland China to find Minister Qin and to put the Pacific Fleet on alert to defend Taiwan. Her father was a black-and-white—*right and wrong*—leader. She couldn't imagine him letting Taiwan be forcibly taken without a fight.

Because it would be the wrong thing to do . . .

The Humvee braked to a stop and she climbed out of the 4×4, feeling stiff from the hours of being bounced around. She arched her back, then thanked the driver, and agreed with Conza to meet up in the conference room with the team in ten after a bathroom break.

When she arrived, Conza was already inside, seated at the table with a fresh cup of coffee, leaned over and apparently making some sort of adjustments to his prosthesis. He looked up as she entered and pulled his pant leg back down over the sleek and modern robot-looking prosthetic limb.

She took a seat and watched Bubba place his laptop in front of him and then slide a can of smokeless tobacco across the table toward Conza without even being asked this time.

Conza slid a second coffee cup toward her.

"Thanks," she said.

"You're gonna love it," Conza said with a grin, and she took a long swig, then her eyes opened wide.

"Wow, that's a good cup of coffee. I almost hate to ruin it with cream." She rose to head to the small coffee kiosk set up in the room, where individual packets of sugar and creamer sat in a paper cup. "Where did you get this?"

"Brought it with me," Conza said. "It's called Goat Locker."

Katie laughed as she added just a splash of cream. "You gotta be kidding me. So this is for-real Navy coffee." The goat locker, she knew, was the slang term used for the chief's mess on all ships and Navy stations.

"Made by the Bonefrog Coffee company. Former SEAL buddy of mine started it when he retired. Donates a portion of profits from every bag to Navy SEAL charities. He's good people."

She raised her mug, then headed back to the table.

"Bubba, can you put up the map of the Penghu chain with all of the missile batteries and other military positions?"

"Sure, boss," Pettigrew said, and plugged an HDMI cable into the side of his computer. The monitor on the wall beside the table came to life with the entire island chain, each of the numerous batteries labeled with colored icons.

"Scroll out so we can see Huayu and Wangan and Cimei, too," she said, and Pettigrew did, additional sites popping up on the islands south of the Penghu chain. "Let's war-game out what an amphibious invasion might look like."

"The best way onto the mainland of Taiwan," Conza said, "is from the southwest, away from the rich defense network extending down from Taipei and away from the American carrier strike group, which is north in the Sea of Japan. The whole purpose of this network we see here is to make that impossible, or at least damn difficult. The sites on Wangan and Cimei to the south complete the wall of missiles that the PLA Air Force and Navy will have to penetrate to conduct an amphibious assault. Taiwan's strategy is a doctrine of denial using missile strikes—both offensive and defensive—to target maritime, airborne, and land-based assets on mainland China. Taiwan's missile network rivals Israel's Iron Dome."

Katie nodded, but that wasn't what was tickling around inside her mind.

"Right, I get all that," she said, studying the map and looking for a clue to what her subconscious was telling her. "You said something on the drive that I can't shake. Something like, what plan do they have to manage the world condemnation after an unprovoked strike? Something like that . . ."

"Well, sure," Conza said. "The biggest risk other than military losses is the impact on China's economy in terms of boycotts and sanctions, which would seem inevitable, even with the global supply chain monopolies they've managed to establish. But . . ." He leaned in, his forearms on the table. "If I were Li, I'd capitalize on the disappearance of Qin. I'd make a big fuss and blame America. Use propaganda to claim we had something to do with it. Maybe he thinks that provides him enough cover?"

Katie rose from her chair, too much energy from the racing thoughts energizing her, especially after a day spent seated in the uncomfortable Humvee.

"For sure," she said in response to Conza's theory, which was undeniably in play. "But two things bother me about that. First, it doesn't seem like it's enough to justify the invasion. Taking

Taiwan as retaliation for Qin's disappearance . . . I don't know, unbalanced and poorly measured. In my book, it doesn't rise to the level of justification that gives them the cover they need on the global stage."

"That kinda bothered me, too, now that you say it out loud," Bubba said. "I've been waiting for the announcement where Beijing links Taiwan as an accomplice, assisting the evil Americans in the assassination plot somehow."

"Maybe," Katie said, staring at the map. The answer was on the damn map somewhere, she felt sure of it.

"And the second?" Conza asked.

"What?" she said, turning.

"You said two things bothered you about the Qin disappearance being the false flag they need to justify the invasion."

"Qin's disappearance was opportunistic. They could not have predicted that. Li would have had to have another plan in place to address what I see as the biggest risk of taking Taiwan by force. Something that shifts the narrative. A false flag, for example, that would rally international support for his invasion—or at least limit the economic fallout."

"Unless he always intended to whack one of his cabinet members and blame us, and we unwittingly helped foster that plan by supporting Qin's defection," Bubba said.

"Qin didn't want to defect," she mumbled, turning back to the map. "His goal was to prevent a war."

As she studied the map, she began to imagine Chinese ships and planes in the battle space. She pictured the amphibious assault ships, their air cover, the Chinese destroyers that would try to neutralize the Taiwan defense network. She could see the missiles in the air, ROC Hawks and Sky Bows knocking Chinese missiles from the sky. She pictured the Feng IIIs streaking toward their targets, destroying Chinese ships . . .

"Where is the exercise that the Chinese Navy is conducting supposed to be centered, Bubba? Operation . . ."

"Sea Serpent," Bubba said, leaning over his computer. "It's a naval operation in the strait, south of Xiamen. It culminates with an amphibious landing here . . ." He used the computer pointer to indicate a small island, just outside the Futou Bay, due east of the peninsula separating it from the Dongshan Bay.

And due west of the Penghu island chain.

"JC," she said, feeling the thrill of the chase now. "You were a SEAL and you augmented DEVGRU, right?"

"All true," Conza said, crossing his arms on his chest.

"Bubba, take off all of the air defense batteries from the map and leave only the sites with Feng II or Feng III anti-ship batteries."

Bubba tapped the keyboard and two-thirds of the sites went away, leaving a string of sites along the western edge of the chain.

"So, as a former Navy SEAL," she said, turning to Conza now and smiling. "If you were going to plan an operation, a supercovert operation to take control of one of these missile batteries, where would you go and how would you do it?"

"Okay," Conza said, and the fire in his eyes suggested he now understood where she was going with this. He stared at the map for a long moment. "Everything on Magong and Xiyu are out," he said. "And you can remove those along the northern edge of Baisha as well."

Bubba tapped, and the multiple sites on the two islands disappeared.

The remaining sites were located on the string of islands

extending south including Hujing and Tongpan to the north, and Wangan due south and Cimei further south still. Conza rose and walked over to the flat-screen monitor and tapped a finger on a smaller island southwest of Wangan.

"I'd insert my team right here, on Huayu isle. It's south and the farthest west. It's small and it's very remote, with not much infrastructure outside the missile battery sites. I'd use a very small team and infil at night. I'd secure communications first, then take the battery. Then I'd conduct the false flag operation and exfil immediately."

"What false flag?" Bubba asked.

"You'd be seen coming and going? Taiwan and the U.S. have robust satellite coverage," Katie said, ignoring Bubba for a moment.

"True," Conza conceded, "but I would conduct a covert maritime infil. China has special missions submarines just like we do."

"So, scuba infil and exfil via a loitering submarine?"

Conza nodded.

"What false flag operation?" Bubba asked again, insistent this time.

Conza turned to Bubba. "I believe Commander Ryan is theorizing that the Chinese will conduct a covert operation to take control of a Feng III site on one of these perimeter islands. The black ops team will then fire an anti-ship missile at one or more Chinese Navy ships during Operation Sea Serpent. *That* would be the act of aggression needed to justify a full-scale invasion of Taiwan, and they would already have the naval and Marine assets deployed and conveniently in position to do just that, thanks to the exercise."

"Wait," Bubba said, his voice conveying his disbelief. "You're suggesting Li would be willing to destroy one of his own ships? That he would murder his own sailors?"

"Yes," Katie said, her conviction absolute.

"Hold on," Conza said. "I said that's how *I* would do it. That doesn't mean that's what Li will do."

"Or that it's the plan at all," Bubba pointed out.

"That's his plan," Katie said. "And it'll happen on Huayu island. We need to get a team on Huayu to prevent it."

"Which the Chinese will see," Conza said, "and pick another island."

"Then we need to figure out how to get a team in place without being seen," she said. Her confidence was audacious, she knew, but she felt it in her bones. Just like when she'd figured out the mission for the Russian submarine *Belgorod*.

"We'll need more than just a hunch to get authorization to do anything about it," Conza said.

"We'll need to prove it," Bubba said.

"Well," Katie said, her hands on her hips now. "Then I suggest we get the team together and get to work."

29

Footsteps woke Léi.

Flush with fear, she tensed and lay stiff as a board on her sleeping roll.

The ceiling of the cellar where she and Defense Minister Qin were hiding—the floorboards of the restaurant above—flexed and creaked as someone walked past overhead. Dust and grainy particles trickled down onto her face. She wiped her eyelids, then opened her eyes, but saw nothing but the pitch black. Paranoid thoughts harried her as she waited and listened.

Do they know we're here? Have they come for us? Has our luck finally run out?

The footsteps stopped.

A moment later, they started again.

Only one pair of feet, she decided.

She lifted her arm and checked the time on her wristwatch: 0823.

Jia's late.

Time passed slowly and strangely in the always-dark cellar, which was more of a crawl space than basement. With only a little over a meter of vertical clearance, it was impossible to stand, so she and Qin spent both day and night lying down.

She exhaled, not realizing until that moment that she'd been holding her breath since the first footfall had woken her. The person upstairs was *probably* her friend, Jia, the restaurant owner who had given them sanctuary. Jia had done everything she could to make them comfortable, providing them with sleeping rolls, pillows, blankets, flashlights, as well as food and bottled water. She'd also thoughtfully offered scented candles to help mask the sweetly rancid smell that came from years of housing food stores and produce—mainly onions—some of which invariably spoiled. Léi's nose had acclimated to the stench after the first day, but her companion complained endlessly about it.

Léi had noticed yesterday that Qin's nerves were beginning to fray. In more than one moment of self-induced agitation, he threatened that they should part company. He vowed to make it to the American embassy on his own, and she could go back to her old life. They both knew this was folly, and she'd told him so.

"You wouldn't make it within three blocks of the embassy without being grabbed," she'd said, her voice as hard and cold as the concrete floor of the cellar that had become their home.

As for me, my old life is over, she thought with a frown. *There's no going back . . . Not ever.*

She'd used her taxicabs, driven by her girls, to run the shell game on the night of Qin's escape from the Liulichang market. They'd been followed that night, and Léi had shot an agent, so the MSS would be in full manhunt mode by now. She knew with absolute certainty that the driver of the first cab, Bai, would be arrested, interrogated, and probably tortured. The second cab-driver, Zena, might have escaped notice, but Bai would eventually break and give up the names of the other employees at the company. They would all be questioned. Hopefully, they would not all be tortured. Léi compartmentalized everything, and not even her most trusted employees knew the truth about who and what she was.

My girls have nothing to give up, which will only infuriate the interrogators and push them to more extreme measures.

Guilt, and the self-loathing that accompanied it, weighed heavy on her heart.

"I'm sorry," she whispered in the dark, her eyes rimming with tears.

"Do you think that is Jia upstairs?" Qin whispered from where he lay on his sleeping roll a few meters away.

"Yes," she said, "but we wait for the knock."

"Obviously."

They both laid still behind the stack of wooden onion crates and bags of rice, which they'd stacked from floor to ceiling to block their hiding place. At eight o'clock Jia would come to the restaurant and open the cellar so they could climb out, use the washroom, stretch and eat breakfast, before returning to their cramped little refuge for the rest of the day. This morning, Jia was late.

More footsteps above, this time the cadence was faster. They seemed . . . hurried.

Léi's heart rate picked up again as fear and uncertainty crept back into her consciousness.

In silence, they waited . . .

Waited.

Waited . . .

She could hear Qin breathing and felt that he was nervous, too.

They had all agreed that Jia would always knock before unlocking and opening the cellar door. If the cellar door was opened without a knock, then the unspoken message would be that Jia was opening the cellar door under duress.

Finally, the coded "all clear" knock came: *knock-knock . . . knock-knock-knock.*

Léi exhaled the toxic negative energy—breath laced with fear and doubt—to center herself. Then she rolled onto her hands and knees and worked side by side with Qin to move the center stack of onion crates to clear a path. The cellar door creaked as Jia opened it, and dull gray light filtered in through the hole in the floor.

She let Qin go first, and he crawled on hands and knees to the half flight of wooden stairs that led up and into the rear of the Purple Lotus restaurant, where the kitchen was located. Léi followed, her joints stiff and achy from inactivity, as she crawled to the stairs and straightened into a standing position. Not exercising and performing her daily katas was taking a toll on her fifty-year-old body.

Most of all, she missed her soaking tub.

When she stepped out of the cellar and into the light, she could tell immediately from the look on Jia's face that something was wrong.

"I'm sorry I was late this morning," Jia said with an apologetic smile. "I needed to go to the market."

"What's wrong?" Léi said, taking her friend's hands in her own. "You look worried."

"I wasn't going to tell you this, but since you asked, your taxi business has stopped operating. The dispatch phone number is not working and both your website and app are offline."

A lump formed in Léi's throat as Jia confirmed that Léi's worst fear had become a reality. The Chinese authorities had connected her to Qin and now they were busy prosecuting her network, starting with her employees first. It was only a matter of time before they broadened the search and started investigating her outer-orbit contacts like Jia.

We're running out of time.

Qin, who'd been listening to the conversation, said, "It won't be long before they connect all the data points. We can't stay here much longer. What is taking your contact so long?"

Léi had not been completely honest with Qin about their situation. Hiding in the cellar of the Purple Lotus had been her plan B scenario, but Scott Kincaid was not read in on this location. In the event the extraction became compromised, she needed a safe location with zero chance of being compromised. A place known to her and her alone. The Purple Lotus had served this function perfectly. The only problem was, to complete phase two of the extraction she needed to coordinate with the Americans, and to do *that* required communication.

She met Qin's bloodshot gaze. The defense minister had dark circles and heavy bags under his eyes and looked like he'd aged ten years over the past few days.

Time to come clean.

"Jia, will you please excuse us for a moment?" Léi asked her friend with a smile.

Jia nodded and left the kitchen.

Once they were alone, Léi exhaled slowly, centering herself, and said, "My contact doesn't know we're here."

"What?" he said, his face going red.

"You were surveilled. When we couldn't proceed to the primary safe house location I had to change plans. This is the backup location—a place known only to me."

He laughed. "Wonderful. And how long were you planning for us to live in the onion cellar, Léi . . . Forever?"

"I could have left you in that market," she said, not appreciating his sarcasm. "And if I had, you'd be dead . . . Or strapped to a table having your body parts systematically removed. I'm tired of you questioning my methods and decisions. If you really believe you'll be better off on your own, then go." She pointed to the back door of the kitchen.

He glared at her, his ego clearly bruised by having a woman dare speak to him as an equal, but she didn't care. She was done catering to his self-importance.

"Maybe I will," he snapped.

Even though Jia had left the kitchen, Léi suspected she was eavesdropping on the other side of the door. So far, Qin had not slipped up and said anything to overtly contradict the story Léi had concocted about Qin being her brother and cheating the triads, but the argument they'd just had pushed the boundaries. Jia wasn't experienced in matters of state and espionage, but she was no fool, either. The triads were dangerous, but their reach and resources were nothing compared to the Ministry of State Security.

Before Léi could respond, in a calm, measured tone Qin said, "I'm sorry, Léi. The fear and stress are getting to me. Couple that with the physical discomfort of being holed up in the cellar has made me . . . well, not myself. If it wasn't for you, the triads would have already found me. I owe you my life, sister."

Then he pulled her in for a hug.

She hesitated, wooden in his embrace, and completely surprised by this perfectly timed and executed pivot. But her wits quickly caught up to the situation and she returned his hug.

"It's okay," she said, patting his back.

On that cue, the door to the kitchen opened and Jia popped her head in. "I want you both to know that you can stay as long as you need to stay."

Léi let go of Qin and turned to her friend, who had obviously been listening. "Thank you, Jia. You are a good friend. I promise it won't be much longer. I don't want to put you in danger."

Jia smiled. "Enough of this, I'll make you both breakfast while you freshen up. You only get an hour out of the cellar per day. Let's not ruin it with fighting."

"Agreed," Qin said, and gave their host a respectful little bow, which took Léi by surprise.

They spent the next forty minutes eating, drinking, and refreshing themselves by the light of day. Léi used the remainder of her time for stretching and katas, which improved her mood. After a hearty breakfast and a second trip to the restroom, it was time to return to the dark, dank cellar. They both thanked Jia and descended the stairs, crawling back to their hiding place behind the bags of rice and boxes of onions. Once the wall of foodstuffs was in place, Qin turned to face her, seated cross-legged, and clicked off his flashlight. He didn't say anything for a long moment, but his posture and the way he'd turned to face her signaled he was readying himself for a serious conversation.

A serious conversation in the dark.

"I meant what I said up there . . ." he began.

When he didn't elaborate she asked, "Which part? The first part where you yelled at me and threatened to leave, or the second part when you apologized?"

"The second," he said. "I've been behaving like an asshole. And my behavior threatened to undermine the story you told Jia. I saw the fear and uncertainty in her eyes this morning when she opened the cellar door . . ."

She nodded, but then realized he couldn't see it. "I'm glad, because our survival depends on Jia's judgment and courage."

"I know . . . but I am concerned about what you told me. How can the Americans possibly find us? And if they are looking for us, how long will they persist before giving up?"

"Qin, you know that I am the Night Spider, right?"

"Yes," he said. "I figured that part out for myself."

"Okay, then you also know that I survived for over two decades in this business. When all the other assets the American CIA was using in China got captured in the purge, I alone persisted unscathed. Do you know why?"

"Because you are careful?" he said after a beat.

"Not just careful," she said. "I'm methodical. I'm patient. I'm meticulous. And I'm prudent. I don't make decisions based on emotion. I don't rush to take action, because sometimes the best action is *inaction*. Do you understand?"

"Yes, very much."

"We can't afford to make any mistakes now. One mistake and we're finished . . . So, I've been waiting and planning."

"Waiting for what?"

"Waiting for the Americans to lay the groundwork for our extraction," she said, trying not to sound exasperated. "You set an unrealistic timetable. They weren't ready when you signaled 'go.' It takes time to mobilize personnel and manage the logistics to get us out of Beijing and out of China undetected. It's going to be very dangerous for them. It's not just our necks on the line here. Whoever the Americans use to get us out will be risking their lives for us."

He grunted in what sounded like agreement, then said, "But you still haven't answered my question. How will the Americans possibly find us *here*?"

"They won't . . ." she said, and blew air through pursed lips, dreading the terrible risk she was going to have to take tonight. "Which means I have to do something I really don't want to do— go out there and leave them a message."

30

PRC Minister of State Security Deng Su Wei stared up the hill at the elaborate Yufeng pagoda, towering like a lighthouse above the city from the top of the hill, and thought about his wife. A passionate historian and professor at the Beijing university, Shiji would love the chance to see the entire grounds of Yuquanshan and explore the Jingming Garden, the Jinxing and Furong palaces, and most especially the Xiangji Temple. He imagined her excitement as she shared the history she knew so well with him, hand in hand, as they explored these ancient grounds.

But the history and sanctity of this place was not what made him think of his wife.

To the contrary, it was President Li's temper that had him concerned and the fear that any misstep on Deng's part would mean he'd never see his loving Shiji again.

That President Li was upset on learning that Qin Caiji and her daughters had disappeared in the Maldives was the understatement of all time. Far more terrifying to Deng than the raging outburst when he'd first notified the president that Qin's family had been taken, was the cold, long silence that followed his informing Li they could not be sure exactly *who* had taken them and that whoever it was had assassinated the entire security detail and the covert MSS team as well. The silence had ended with Li simply ordering him, his voice a chilling whisper, to meet him at his residence in Jade Spring Hill and then hanging up.

It seemed entirely possible that Deng would not leave the compound alive.

He was far less afraid of losing his life than of the effect that would have on Shiji. They had abstained from children, and now, as they approached the late stages of their professional lives, they were truly all each other had outside of work. She would be devastated.

Or worse . . .

Deng steeled himself and pulled his focus from the top of the hill to the heavy, ornate door, and took the two steps up as he straightened his tie and smoothed his coat. Before he could press the buzzer on the box beside the door, it swung open, revealing one of the president's security detail. On paper, the powerful-looking man from the protection division of the Ministry of State Security worked for Deng. But the cold look from the man held no deference. President Li's private army of security might come from his budget, but the handpicked cadre of stone-cold killers had loyalty to only one man, and that was the increasingly paranoid president of the People's Republic of China.

He crossed the threshold, but after two steps into the opulent foyer, the bodyguard held up a hand, stopping Deng. A second guard dressed in an identical black suit approached and indicated with a grunt that Deng should raise his hands to be frisked.

"Do you know who I am?" Deng demanded indignantly, but he complied, raising his hands so the brute could frisk him.

"Yes," the first man answered, a snarling smile forming on his lips. "Do you know who *we* are?" he asked, leaning in and staring right through him.

The pat-down done, the apparent man in charge gestured with a flourish of his arm and a condescending smile toward a heavy oak door at the far end of the foyer. As Deng approached the door, the bodyguard opened it, gesturing that Deng could enter the room beyond. Deng felt his anxiety rise as both guards accompanied him inside the president's private chambers, flanking him on both shoulders. President Li sat behind a large desk, reading glasses on his nose, studying something on a laptop, and did not even bother to look up.

Deng scanned the room and felt a modicum of relief at not seeing plastic sheets on the floor to protect the opulent oriental rug from blood spatter.

At least they don't mean to shoot me here.

He folded his hands in front of him to keep them from shaking.

Predictably, Li made him wait in agonizing silence, not acknowledging his presence, until Deng could barely stand it. Li was a master at emotional and psychological manipulation, but Deng was rarely on the receiving end of it. Finally, the president looked up, pulled his readers from his nose as if only just now noticing the three men in his office, and fixed Deng with an out-of-place smile.

"Please have a seat, Minister Deng," Li said, gesturing at the two high-back chairs that faced the desk, upholstered in fine leather. "Long Fei, please get our guest a cup of tea," he added, looking expectantly at Deng.

"Thank you, sir."

"Get it now," Li said to his security man.

The brute beside Deng gave a low growl and left, closing the door behind him. The other man moved to the side of the door, clasped his hands, and stood staring at the wall.

"Have a seat, Su Wei," Li said, using Deng's given name.

Deng did so, aware that all of his years as a covert-operations officer had given him the ability to appear outwardly calm and in control, but not the ability to control the fear he felt inside in the presence of this man, a fear driven mostly by his awareness of just how vulnerable his wife, Shiji, was in this moment. For many years, he'd expected to die in the field—a violent, warrior's death. His last few years as a bureaucrat had made him soft and senti-mental.

"Tell me . . . Who took Qin's family?" Li asked, his face a stone mask.

"Well," Deng said, crossing his legs at the knee, "it appears from archived satellite imagery that the assault team arrived by private yacht, which we then tracked to the Nautilus Beach and Ocean Houses resort on the nearby Khiladhoo, just a few miles west of the Four Seasons on Baa. We lost satellite coverage after that, unfortunately, so we have no imagery of their subsequent escape. However, we were able to trace the yacht, which was chartered out of Dharavandhoo the night before the attack. It was leased to a German businessman out of Berlin on a dive vacation with friends. Only a single name is listed on the manifest. He used a well-crafted nonofficial cover, because it withstands rigor-ous scrutiny. Only after our cyber-investigation unit dug deeper did it disappear. We have no facial imagery whatsoever, as the camera coverage in the Maldives is archaic, so we can't trace any faces back to flight manifests into the Maldives. We are digging into customs records with algorithms, searching both names and faces in the database, but nothing has come of this yet. Unfortunately, the assault team are ghosts. Four Seasons has significant privacy protocols in place, so there is not significant footage from the resort, either. We are poring through all other potential sources, including guest registrations, but so far we have nothing actionable."

The president stared at him, unblinking, hands folded on his desk.

"How did the Americans accomplish this, Minister Deng? How did they defeat your entire security apparatus and MSS surveillance teams in situ to disappear Qin's wife and daughters without a trace?"

The president's voice was calm and even, but this meant nothing. Beneath the man's stoic expression lay a volcano. Deng chose his words carefully. Li had not yet mentioned that he had asked Deng to bring Qin's wife and daughters in for questioning the other day. It was Deng who'd politely rebuffed the suggestion and recommended leaving Qin's family in play, promising his teams could handle any and all contingencies. But Deng had never envisioned a scenario like this . . .

"I agree that the Americans are on the top of the list of suspects, Mr. President, however—"

"There is no list," Li said, his fist pounding the desk hard enough that a penholder fell over, the gold pen rolling to the left side of the desk and then falling to the floor. "It was the Americans. Of this we can be certain. The only question is whether they kidnapped Qin's family as part of a defection protocol, or if they took the wife and daughters for leverage to manipulate the man. There are no other questions that need answering. Did Minister Qin defect or was he kidnapped? This is the only question that matters."

"We will find Qin. He will not escape China," Deng said, the words coming out reflexively, but as he spoke it was not lost on him that a second broken promise would mean his death, and the end of any meaningful life for Shiji in China.

That is assuming I survive this meeting . . .

"That is imperative, Minister Deng," Li said, his eyes like twin lasers boring into Deng. Li rose and walked around his desk, hands clasped behind his back. "Our plan depends on it."

"Mr. President, if Qin was taken, the likelihood of his captors escaping China with him is very small. We have security personnel patrolling every train station, airport, and bus terminal. Also, Qin would never have shared details of his work with his wife, so she will have nothing to leak to the Americans."

Li frowned, but said nothing.

The door behind Deng opened, and it took every ounce of self-control developed over a lifetime of service to not turn around.

Looking will change nothing. If the man behind me intends to execute me, I will not be able to escape my fate.

"Your tea, Mr. Deng," the security agent said, pausing beside the chair.

Deng took the cup and saucer from the killer, proud that his hands did not shake.

"Thank you," he said, holding the tea in his lap, then turned back to Li. "We will continue to pursue leads on the kidnapping in the Maldives, and the dragnet we are using to locate Qin will yield results soon."

"Regardless of Qin's fate, I want your cyber division to use any and all means to learn what the Americans know about Operation Sea Serpent and what they are planning in response."

"We are working on—"

"You misunderstand me, Su Wei," Li said, cutting him off. "We cannot wait for you to find evidence of American involvement. Operation Sea Serpent is but days away. The next stage of our response will be a disinformation campaign identifying and blaming the Americans for assassinating Qin inside the People's Republic of China, as well as kidnapping his family. Assassinating a defense minister is an act of war. Our outrage will garner support from the international community. We will announce that the American Navy is prohibited from operating in the South China Sea and the Strait of Taiwan. We will form a naval blockade of their vessels as a response to this act of war. This will provide cover, as well as motivation, for our operation to reunify Taiwan. When coupled with the attack by Taiwan on our fleet, I will have all the justification necessary to control perception on the world stage."

"Wait," Deng said, shocked. "There has been an attack by Taiwan on our fleet?"

"Not yet," Li said, a malevolent grin forming at the corners of his mouth. "But there will be, just as we kick off our exercise. The Taiwanese outpost on Penghu will launch an anti-ship missile at our fleet, thereby turning us from the aggressor into the victim. Our actions from that point forward will be justified as measured retaliation rather than instigation."

"How can you be sure they will fire on us?" Deng asked.

"Our Special Forces are even now planning their infiltration of the island to commandeer one of the Taiwanese missile batteries," Li said, his voice even and confident. "In the chaos of the attack, we will retaliate massively against the island, erasing any evidence of the covert operation. Then we will liberate Kinmen Island and move the fleet and our assault force into position to take the main island of Taiwan. With a fully justified blockade of the American fleet already in place in response to their killing of Qin and kidnapping his family, the island will fall before they can mount a response."

"It is brilliant," Deng said, and realized he meant it. For all his paranoia and brutality, Li Jian Jun was a genius tactician. "I will begin work immediately to support your vision, Mr. President."

"I know you will, Deng Su Wei," Li said. "Regrettably, I will not be able to tolerate another failure, so please, for the sake of your lovely Shiji, do not put me in the awkward position of having to make an example of you."

The president took a seat.

"You can count on me, Mr. President."

"Oh, and one more thing," Li said. "I've decided to expel the U.S. ambassador and all diplomatic mission personnel. Why should I let the CIA have any foothold in our capital?"

Deng was taken aback at this brazen move. "Permanently?"

"I have not decided," Li said. "At least until Minister Qin is found and reunification is complete. This will give your people ample time to tear the embassy building apart, remove American jammers, and install the latest monitoring technology."

Deng loved this idea. "Brilliant and bold, Mr. President. I support it completely."

"Of course you do," Li said, and waved a hand, dismissing Deng.

Deng rose and spun on a heel and headed for the door, full of energy and purpose now. At the door, he leaned close to the president's bodyguard, glared into the man's eyes, and whispered, "Do not ever place your hands on me again. If you do, I will see to it you and your entire family pay the ultimate price, do you understand?"

The man's face tightened. He glanced at President Li, who was seated at his desk, but not paying attention to them.

"Yes, Minister Deng," the man said, his voice a mix of anger and subservience.

Deng handed the man his untouched teacup.

"See to this, *nucai*," he said, referring to the man as a lackey. "I'll let myself out."

He left, crossing the foyer, new power and purpose in his step.

31

C lark let out an "old man" sigh and shifted in his intolerable seat.

Despite being exhausted from the highly kinetic mission to liberate Qin's family in the Maldives, a *relatively* short hop from their destination, he and Ding had taken military transport back to the States, to then begin the long flight to China from there, to be consistent with their NOC. The others had scattered around Asia and Europe for their own infil flights. After the long mission and relatively comfortable flight to the U.S. in the back of a C-17, he'd flown the twenty-three-hour-long haul entirely in economy class for two reasons. First, this trip was on the tax-payer's dime and he hadn't become so jaded or self-important that that didn't matter. And second, because it fit his NOC.

But dear lord was it painful.

He looked over at Ding, who'd been stuck in a middle seat be-

tween a profusely sweating, obese middle-aged man and an eight-
year-old girl who watched movies on her iPad for the entire flight
while refusing to wear headphones. Ding must have felt Clark's
gaze, because he looked up and rolled his eyes. Clark couldn't
help but chuckle at his son-in-law's expense.

At least I have an aisle seat.

He returned his attention to the screen in the seat back in
front of him, which was in flight tracker mode, showing the
plane's geo-position, altitude, air speed, and time until landing.
Only nine more minutes and this slow-motion torture session,
also known as transpacific aviation, would finally be over. Long-
haul travel was worse than a running gun battle. At least combat
was kinetic and over quickly. Flying coach on a sold-out flight was
practically death by a thousand paper cuts.

He had to laugh because before the trip his wife had made him
promise to stay hydrated and wear compression socks.

"DVT is a real thing for people on long flights," she'd said. "I
don't want you to have a stroke. You're not a young man anymore,
sweetheart."

Funny, he thought, *she's worried about deep vein thrombosis but
didn't say a thing about me not getting murdered or locked up in a
Chinese prison for espionage.*

The risk of the latter was not insignificant given the nature of
what TF 99 had been tasked to do. From the Chinese point of
view, extracting Defense Minister Qin would be akin to the MSS
kidnapping Admiral Kent, the chairman of the Joint Chiefs of
Staff, from Washington, D.C. If Clark and his team were caught,
they would not be going home. Which is why he'd instituted a
strict comms blackout policy during Phase One: Entry into China.
Other than the occasional shared glance, Clark hadn't interacted
with Ding since yesterday before boarding. Maintaining physical

separation and the appearance of anonymity between all the task force members was imperative for the operation to succeed, especially in phase one.

The Chinese government ran the largest and most aggressive cyber-intelligence operation on the planet. Clark had no choice but to err on the side of caution. Until proven otherwise, he would assume that every member of Task Force 99 could have an electronic personnel file with the Ministry of State Security, regardless of how seemingly bulletproof their NOCs might be. They were all veteran operators with experience using legends around the globe, but in 2024, that experience was a double-edged sword. From a situational awareness, tradecraft, and street smarts perspective, there was no substitute for experience. But from a cyber- and counterintelligence perspective, the more missions each team member had completed under previous NOCs, the more digital fingerprints they would have left behind in cyberspace. Facial recognition algorithms were improving at a logarithmic rate, as was the number of mobile phone and security cameras live-streaming data to the cloud.

Clark had explained the risk to the team this way:

"Let's say, for example, Charlie recently traveled to Singapore under a different NOC than the one she's using here at 99. On that trip, she cleared customs with no problem and triggered no flags. But let's also imagine that China's PLA Unit 61398 hacked the security contractor's servers that collect and maintain all Singaporean customs entry data. Thanks to that breach, they siphon off her data and feed it to their own servers. When Chinese customs at BCIA runs her passport, facial rec algos will see Charlie's new NOC as a mismatch compared to her Singaporean record and generate a flag. That flag could result in her being detained,

DEFENSE PROTOCOL

questioned, and denied entry into the country. Worse, if they are working hand in glove with the MSS, her entry might be granted but trigger a surveillance team. In that case, Charlie would unwittingly lead the MSS directly to the other members of Task Force 99, thereby scuttling the entire operation."

It was for this reason that Clark had issued a nonnegotiable standing order to every member of the team. In the event of detainment and interrogation, no contact was to be initiated with any other TF 99 members, and all tasking for the detained member would be aborted. Clark hated that he had to take such extreme measures, but this was the world they lived in today. Beijing was becoming more and more like Cold War Berlin with each passing year, and he refused to underestimate his adversary.

Been there, done that . . .

Twenty-five minutes later, the plane had landed and was unloading passengers and bags at the gate. Clark, who'd been seated in row forty-one, was forced to wait until practically everyone else on the plane had disembarked before it was his turn to gather his things and head for the forward door. Ding's side of the jet moved faster than Clark's side, and so he watched his teammate disappear through the main cabin door to the jet bridge while he was still trudging up the aisle with his carry-on bag.

They were the only two members of the task force on this flight. The others had been split up on different airlines with different routes. Half were flying into Shanghai or Guangzhou, where they would clear customs, then connect to Beijing. Like Clark and Ding, Lee Hyori and Henri Toussaint had also flown into Beijing, but they'd arrived at Beijing Daxing International— the city's newer and more modern airport. All flights were scheduled to facilitate team members meeting collectively by 2100

251

local time tonight at a safe house located on the outskirts of the Daxing district, in the southernmost suburbs of Beijing.

After disembarking, Clark made his way to passport control for nonresidents and spotted Ding in the line, twenty people or so ahead of him. Clark pulled out his mobile phone and pretended to check email while, in his peripheral vision, he watched Ding step up to the next open customs kiosk. As soon as the customs agent scanned Ding's passport, Clark knew there was a problem. The man's body language instantly changed from bored disinterest to nervous tension. Clark couldn't hear what the agent was saying to Ding, but he ticked his gaze to the man's lips, which seemed to say something like "problem with your passport."

Shit, that's not good . . . not good at all.

"Sir, counter number four is open," a female customs agent who was directing traffic said in heavily accented English to Clark and directed him to another line, where a large party had just been cleared.

He nodded and pushed his roller bag toward the now open kiosk while retrieving his passport wallet from the inside pocket of his suit coat. To his left, he saw an armed, uniformed security guard walk up to the kiosk where Ding stood.

"Passport, please," the customs agent at Clark's kiosk said in accented English.

Clark fixed the man with the closed-lip smile of a weary businessman trying to be polite and handed over his passport wallet. The agent took the leather case, opened it, and placed the photo page on a flatbed scanner. Clark's pulse rate, which rarely deviated from baseline, jumped in nervous anticipation as he waited for digital judgment. Two kiosks away, he could see Ding gesticulating as he talked with the security guard.

Clark's gaze ticked back to the passport reader.

Come on stupid machine . . . give me the green.

A heartbeat later, the scanner made a pleasant chime and a green LED flashed.

Despite the relief he felt inside, he kept his expression completely neutral.

"How long do you plan to stay in the People's Republic of China?" the agent asked.

"Nine days."

"What is the purpose of your visit?"

"I'm here on business," Clark said.

"What is your profession?"

"Agriculture equipment sales . . ." Anxiety blossomed in Clark's chest as he stole a glance at Ding, who was now being escorted away by two uniformed security guards. "I work for Jackson Combine. We build combines, tractors, and the like."

"John Deere?" the agent said.

Clark nodded and forced a casual smile onto his face despite the strain of watching his friend being led away. "John Deere is a competitor of mine, but yes, same products."

The customs agent stamped Clark's passport and handed it back to him. "Welcome to the People's Republic of China. Enjoy your stay."

"Thank you," he said with a nod and returned his passport wallet to his inside jacket pocket.

He walked fifteen paces from the customs entry kiosk, then took a knee to retie his left shoelace, creating an opportunity to watch Ding being led toward a frosted-glass door along the back wall, where security interrogation rooms would be housed. A part of him—the Navy SEAL part—wanted to rescue Ding from whatever fate Chinese security had in store for his teammate. The operator ethos of *Leave no man behind* was branded on Clark's soul, but to intervene now would be both pointless and foolish.

In the clandestine world, different rules applied.

His shoe tied, Clark stood and turned his back on his teammate.

Damn it, he thought with gritted teeth as he headed for baggage claim. *Of all people, why did it have to be Ding?*

32

Ding Chavez swallowed his anger and forced himself to remain in character as he waited for the next question from his interrogator—a Chinese man who'd introduced himself as Officer Wàn. Presently, he was locked in a simple, windowless room with a metal table, two metal chairs, and security cameras in the upper four corners. The chair he sat in was the folding variety, terribly uncomfortable and without any padding or seat cushion. Officer Wàn, whom Ding pegged for a Ministry of State Security agent, had been remarkably persistent and even-tempered for the duration of the interrogation.

Ding wasn't sure if that was a good or bad sign.

Usually, it's the calm ones who are the most dangerous.

Since being detained four hours ago, Ding had not been offered food or beverage. Not even water. Nor had Ding been permitted a bathroom break.

At least I'm not handcuffed . . . yet.

For this mission, he was Dominic Sanchez, an international contracts officer for Orion Foods. According to his NOC, he'd traveled to Beijing looking for opportunities to capitalize on China's growing export market for specialty foods. It was okay for Dominic Sanchez to be frustrated, confused, and afraid in this situation.

It was *not* okay for him to be experienced in the ways and means of resisting interrogation. For as long as he was in China, he had to forget that he was a former CIA Special Activities Division operative and an operations officer at The Campus. And above all else, it was not appropriate for him to be thinking about how badly he wanted to kick Wàn's ass for putting him through the ringer.

"If you will just admit that you work for the Central Intelligence Agency, then everything will go so much easier," said Wàn.

"But I don't work for the CIA. For the one-hundredth time, I work for Orion Foods," Ding said, allowing exasperation to creep into his voice. "Please . . . if China doesn't want our business just let me go home. I can promise I never want to come to China again after this."

"It is not a crime to work for the Central Intelligence Agency. Just as it is not a crime to work for the Ministry of State Security, like I do," Wàn continued, as if Ding hadn't even spoken. "If you admit the truth, then we can move on to discussing the conditions for your release."

Wàn's minimal accent, word choice, and knowledge of American English phonics told Ding that the man had spent considerable time living in the United States. Talking like a native American English speaker was not something a person could learn in a language class. As a multilingual individual, Ding knew this from personal experience.

Forcing a tone of fear instead of anger into his voice, Ding said, "Mr. Wàn, I'm not sure how else I can get through to you. If you want me to take a lie detector test, that's okay with me. In fact, I volunteer to take one. Maybe then you'll believe that I'm telling the truth."

Wàn's expression soured and he looked at his colleague, a woman named Tzu, who was standing in the corner. Tzu had not said anything since she entered the room, just stared at Ding with narrowed, judgmental eyes.

She shook her head ever so slightly, shutting down the lie detector suggestion.

Wàn looked back at Ding. "That is not an option, I'm afraid. My partner and I know that such machines can be fooled by experienced field agents such as yourself. Why else would you propose such a thing?"

Keep it together, Ding, he told himself. *Don't lose your shit.*

"Can I please use my phone? I need to message my wife that I arrived in Beijing and that I'm safe. She's probably worried sick, having not heard from me yet," he said, wanting to get word to ODNI that he was being held.

Ding knew that Clark had seen him detained at customs. Clark had been behind him in the queue for passport control, so the old man had undoubtedly watched the whole thing unfold.

"I'm sorry, that's not going to be possible until you cooperate with us," Wàn said.

"I *am* cooperating with you," Ding said, turning up his frustration. "I've been cooperating for hours. I've answered every question you've asked. Call my office at Orion Foods and they'll tell you who I am."

"Yes, you answer every question, Mr. Sanchez, but not truthfully," Tzu said. Her accented English was more pronounced than Wàn's and her diction not quite as perfect.

Ding met her gaze, making sure his baseline cold stare was

replaced with fear and desperation. "Please, I need to go to the bathroom. It's been over four hours that you've kept me locked in here."

"If you admit you are CIA, you can go to bathroom," she said, her face a cold slate.

"In the United States, a person cannot be locked in a room and questioned without being charged with a crime. I have committed no crimes. There are laws against this sort of thing," Ding fired back.

"You are not in the United States, Mr. Sanchez. You are in China," she said with a malevolent curl of her lips. "We may detain you as long as we believe necessary."

Ding scooted his chair back from the table and stood.

"What are you doing?" Wàn said, popping to his feet to counter any move Ding might be contemplating.

Ding turned, walked toward the rear corner of the room, and unzipped the fly of his trousers. "If you won't let me go to the bathroom, then I'm going to urinate in the corner, because I refuse to do it in my pants."

"Stop!" Tzu said, a heartbeat before Ding made good on the threat. "Wàn, take him."

Ding zipped up his pants and turned to Wàn and fixed him with an expectant look.

"This way," Wàn said and led Ding out of the interrogation room.

Ding made a mental map of his surroundings as he followed the MSS agent to the restroom, which turned out to be a single unit with a toilet and sink. To Ding's surprise, Wàn waited outside the door, giving him privacy. It didn't really matter, because there was nothing Ding could do to exploit the privacy even if he wanted to. Unlike in the movies, he had zero chance of escape, and they'd taken his mobile phone and computer, so he couldn't use the time to secretly send a message. This bathroom stop was simply that—an opportunity to empty his bulging bladder, which he did with a satisfying groan.

With the physical relief came a small, but noticeable, psychological boost. Shedding the discomfort restored a measure of his resolve and ability to focus. And as he washed his hands in the sink, he took a moment to war-game out where this battle of threats and willpower between him and the MSS was heading next.

It was highly possible that they'd pierced his NOC, otherwise why else would he have been flagged at customs and detained for questioning? The Dominic Sanchez legend was a virgin NOC, meaning this was the first time Ding had used it. There was a small, but definite possibility that the Chinese system had flagged a mismatch with his evergreen Hendley Associates official cover. He and Clark had made the intentional decision *not* to travel under their Hendley legends to provide a degree of separation in the event something went wrong with the op. Whatever happened in China with the Qin extraction could not, in any way, be tied back to Hendley because it would risk the Chinese piercing the veil for *all* the Hendley staff and jeopardize a half dozen active Campus operations around the globe.

No, if this op went south, then only Clark and Ding would pay the price.

The rest of their teammates back home would carry on the good fight from the shadows.

"Hurry up," Wàn said from outside the door.

"Just washing up," he called back, then bent at the waist to drink from the running faucet.

He drank his fill, knowing that they would likely continue to try to dehydrate him and weaken his resolve. After his last swallow, a grateful smile spread across his face. He'd been able to turn this bathroom break into a twofer, addressing both his most pressing biological needs in a single trip.

Sleep deprivation was undoubtedly the next lever of abuse they would use to try to break him down. But that was okay. Ding was no stranger to being sleep-deprived.

He turned off the spigot and wiped his mouth with the back of his sleeve.

I have to hold out, for Clark and the team, he thought, meeting his gaze in the mirror. *No matter how long it takes.*

33

Despite his best efforts to control his temper, Ryan pounded his fist on the heavy wooden conference table and watched rings of turbulence spiral outward from the middle of the tall glass of water sitting in front of him.

In a glaring breach of diplomacy, Beijing had publicly declared that the American CIA was responsible for the assassination of Defense Minister Qin and the kidnapping of Qin's family in the Maldives. In the same international address, President Li had announced that in response to "American aggression," China was implementing a maritime blockade of the Strait of Taiwan. Any American naval vessel attempting to enter the strait would be considered an overt act of war.

"What the hell is President Li thinking?" Ryan said, venting in front of the talented team assembled in front of him. "This could lead to an all-out shooting war before he even makes a play for

Taiwan. He can't possibly think that I'll tolerate a blockade of our naval forces in international waters without a response."

Essentially, Li had come an inch shy of declaring war on the United States.

"To the contrary, I believe Li might be *counting* on your intolerance, Mr. President," Secretary of Defense Robert Burgess said, his face a relief map of worry.

Ryan knew exactly what Burgess was implying, but nonetheless he wanted to hear the man out. "Explain."

"The biggest stumbling block to the PRC taking Taiwan by force is world opinion. Yes, with proper notice our forces could assist the ROC military in repelling an attack, but that's not what keeps Li up at night. It's the collapse of his economy if the world condemns the action and imposes economic sanctions. Also, if the international business community sours on China, their manufacturing and export business will take a tremendous hit."

"By forcing us to look like the aggressor, Li is minimizing the risk," Secretary of State Adler said, signaling his agreement on the theory. "By accusing us of assassinating their minister of national security and naming it an act of war, Li has already begun the narrative."

Ryan waved his hand, annoyed and angry, but not at the counsel he was receiving. No, he was upset that Li would take such aggressive steps.

"He underestimated the world stage he's performing on. Our international partners can see through his lies. He presented no evidence whatsoever," he said, gritting his teeth and seeing again in his mind Li's speech, where he accused Ryan, personally and by name, of murder. "The reality is that Qin is yet one more *disappeared* cabinet member in a string of questionable disappearances of Li's inner-circle members. The world will see this ploy for what it is—bullshit."

"But if we provoke him with military action, then it plays into his narrative," Adler said gently.

"We will not let President Li dictate how and where our naval forces can operate in international waters, and we will not abandon our allies in Taiwan," Ryan proclaimed fiercely. "The solution to this entire mess is to get Defense Minister Qin out of China and show the world he's alive." He turned to his director of national intelligence. "Give me a sitrep on our defection operation, Director Foley."

Mary Pat let out a slow sigh, then appeared to choose her words carefully. "The extraction team is in place for the most part . . ."

"What does that mean—*for the most part?*"

"One team member from the U.S. coalition was flagged on the infil and has been detained, but the remaining team members are in place as far as we know. Concerns about China's robust signals-intelligence-gathering capabilities, especially in theater, have made it necessary to limit communications, but we are still receiving scaled-down updates."

"Was it our team leader?" he asked. If Clark hadn't made it in, Chavez could certainly carry on the operation, but in Ryan's mind the probability of success went down.

"No," Mary Pat said. "It was his number two. But there has been another wrinkle, I'm afraid."

Hearing that Ding Chavez was in Chinese custody hit Ryan hard, but he didn't show it. He'd have to wait to get more details from Mary Pat later.

"What wrinkle?" Ryan said, resisting the urge to rub his temple, where a wicked headache was brewing.

"Scott?" Mary Pat said and glanced at Adler. "Do you want to take this one?"

"Sir, just as we were heading into this meeting, we were notified that Beijing is expelling the ambassador and his staff. They have twenty-four hours to vacate the embassy and leave Beijing."

"What? That's outrageous," Ryan barked. But he saw the bigger problem than this diplomatic finger in the eye from Li. Beyond the CIA personnel embedded in the diplomatic mission, America had precious few assets in Beijing. By expelling the ambassador and all embassy personnel, Langley lost their command and control. Kincaid, who had been running the Spider, would no longer be in country, which meant that Clark would now be completely on his own. Ryan turned to Mary Pat. "What are you recommending?"

"If anyone can locate Qin and pull off the extraction it's TF 99," she said, "but I'm going to be honest, Mr. President, it's mission impossible–level stuff at this point."

"Wonderful," he said through a sigh and turned to Admiral Kent and General Kudryk. "Where is 70?" he asked, referring to the *Reagan* carrier strike group. "And what's the status of Carrier Strike Group Two?"

A large monitor lit up behind Admiral Kent, showing the Pacific theater, and Kent maneuvered a pointer on his laptop to indicate a green circle labeled TF70.

"The *Reagan* and the rest of the strike group are deployed here, in the East China Sea, approximately four hundred miles northwest of Taiwan and about three hundred miles east-southeast of Shanghai. The *Nimitz*"—the admiral moved his electronic pointer to another green box much farther south and east, and, Ryan noted, significantly west of Guam—"is operating with Strike Group Five here, in the Philippine Sea, west of Guam and about seven hundred and fifty miles southeast of Taiwan. Rear Admiral

Pete Binder is the strike group commander and is already steaming the group northwest toward the AOR."

"Your recommendations?" Ryan asked, though he knew already what he wanted to do.

"We continue to move Five northwest, where they can back up 70, who I recommend repositioning here." He moved his pointer to a location midway between Okinawa and the city of Taipei on the northern tip of Taiwan. The carrier strike group would be, by Ryan's estimate, less than a hundred miles from Taipei.

"That seems awfully provocative," Adler said, frowning. "Can't we keep the carrier farther north, but still in striking distance? And maybe keep the *Nimitz* well east and outside of the South China Sea?"

"We could," Ryan said, "but we wouldn't be sending the message we want."

"Which is what?"

"That we will not have a foreign country dictate to us where we can operate our fleet in international waters." Ryan studied the map closely. "What's the green box south of Vietnam?"

Kent leaned in and studied the box for a moment, tapping on his keyboard as he did.

"Ah, that's the *Jason Dunham*, Mr. President," said the chairman of the Joint Chiefs of Staff. "She's a DDG redeploying from Fifth Fleet AOR to augment Five, whose DDG had to remain behind in Guam for repairs. *Dunham* has a great skipper and crew—one of our best. She's heading to the AOR with the HMAS *Success* from the royal Australian Navy, a replenishment ship deployed with our fleet in CENTCOM. She's providing the *Dunham* with fuel as she repositions. Our plan is to have the *Dunham* pass well south of Taiwan and then position east of Taiwan between 70 and the *Carl Vinson*'s Strike Group One."

Ryan stared at the map a moment, then felt a smile forming in the corners of his mouth.

"Li has demanded that we stay out of the South China Sea and that we are forbidden to enter the Strait of Taiwan during his exercise, correct?"

"Yes, sir," Adler said.

"President Li is such a believer in wolf warrior diplomacy, I say we see how he reacts to a lone wolf of our own. Admiral Kent, redirect the *Dunham* to join the *Reagan* and the rest of Task Force 70 east of Taipei . . . navigating the most expedient course possible."

Kent studied the map and then chuckled.

"To be clear, Mr. President," he said, "you want me to redirect the *Dunham* to travel north into the South China Sea, then cut through the Strait of Taiwan to join the strike group north of Taipei. Is that correct?"

"Yes," Ryan said, feeling satisfied.

"You're going to use the *Dunham* as a blockade buster?" Adler said, his expression incredulous.

"We're repositioning ships, Scott. I do not acknowledge their right to a blockade," Ryan said with a wily grin. Then he turned to his chief of staff, Arnold van Damm. "Arnie, get the writers working on a statement. I want a White House press release where we deny all trumped-up accusations and refute Li's legitimacy to obstruct movements in the Pacific. We won't directly accuse him of manipulating world events as a prelude to an invasion of Taiwan, but we hint like hell at it. Also, I want to publicly reaffirm our commitment to Taiwan and their right to independent sovereignty."

"Yes, Mr. President," Arnie said.

"Let's get all of this moving, people," Ryan said, and dismissed everyone but Mary Pat.

"Talk to me about Ding?" he said to her when the door had closed and the two of them were alone.

"Chavez was detained at the airport on arrival. As far as we know, he's still at the airport. We don't know why his NOC was flagged by customs, but it was. The good news is he got flagged on the way in, not on the way out. They can't charge him with espionage because he never entered the country."

Ryan shook his head. "Yesterday, I would have agreed with you. Today, the landscape has changed. I wouldn't put anything past Li. Expelling our diplomatic mission is more than just a warning show. He's signaling a severing of diplomatic ties. If you have to bargain to get Ding out, do it."

"Yes, Mr. President," she said, signaling she understood this was an order not a request.

"Spit it out, I can see something else is on your mind, Mary Pat."

"Are you sure we should leave Clark and his team in play? If they're caught, it will feed right into Li's narrative. Moreover, the price to get them back will be steep."

Ryan nodded. He'd thought of that already. He knew the risks and he knew that his friend would be bearing much of it. But sometimes it wasn't just about risk and benefit.

No, sometimes it was about right and wrong.

"We can't abandon Qin, Mary Pat. The man took an incredible risk to do the right thing. If we don't exfiltrate him, then it's a death sentence."

"Okay," Mary Pat said, but it was clear to Ryan she was unconvinced.

"Look, we're more than just doing the right thing here, Mary

CARRIER STRIKE GROUPS MOVE INTO POSITION

N

CHINA

Shanghai

JAPAN

USS *Reagan*
Carrier Strike Group

Taipei

Okinawa

Chinese Naval Blockade

TAIWAN

USS *Nimitz*
Carrier Strike Group

VIETNAM

to Guam →

PHILIPPINES

*Pacific
Ocean*

USS *Jason Dunham*

© 2024 Jeffrey L. Ward

Pat," he said. "Li is basically telling the world he is at war with the United States. If we want to prove to the world we are not the aggressor and that Li is a liar, the best way to do that is to produce the man they claim we assassinated and have him tell the world he chose to defect rather than carry out Li's orders to take Taiwan by force."

Saying it out loud convinced Ryan it was the right decision—maybe the only thing to keep their nations from a shooting war in the South China Sea.

"Come on, it's Clark," he said and gave her shoulder a little nudge. "This is what he was born to do."

"All right," Mary Pat said, rising from her chair, apparently on board. "Let's see what our team can do. Can I make one suggestion?"

"Anything," Ryan said.

She looked at the map, still up on the screen.

"With operators from Group Eight in theater, what do you think about having a submarine from Task Force 70 standing by to exfil Clark and his team—assuming they survive making it to the coast?"

Ryan smiled and nodded, reminded again of how lucky he was to have Mary Pat on his team.

"I'll talk to Kent and get it done," he said. "Good thinking."

He watched his DNI leave, then let out a long sigh before rising from his chair to get to work. For that moment, he let himself be a dad to the naval officer heading up Task Force 25 on the island of Penghu.

Because the storm his daughter was in the middle of had just gotten far more dangerous.

34

C lark checked his watch for the fifth time in the last hour as he paced a racetrack around the kitchen table, which would serve as their tactical operations center for the duration of the mission.

"Can you please stop doing that?" said Tsai Akio, the Taiwanese member of the team, turning in his chair away from his computer to look at Clark.

"Stop doing what—checking my watch or pacing?" Clark said.

"Both," Charlie, the Aussie and only female on the team, chimed in.

"No," Clark said, and kept at it.

Not only had Ding been detained, but the Frenchman Henri Toussaint and former British SAS Daniel Wu had both failed to arrive at the safe house by the 2100 deadline. The blackout communication protocol that Clark himself had mandated prohibited phone communication between TF 99 members until after phase one had been completed.

Three out of eight attrition . . . fucking terrible.

"Can we even complete the operation with five?" Charlie asked, putting words to the exact question Clark was pondering.

"We'll adapt and overcome," Clark said, projecting confidence despite harboring serious doubts about their odds of success.

Wilhelm Bauer, their German member, got up from the sofa in the living room and made his way toward the kitchen. "Does anybody want a bottle of water?"

"Yes, thank you," Lee Hyori said from where he was typing away at his notebook computer on the opposite side of the table from Akio.

No one else said anything.

Clark's dark thoughts returned to Ding.

At this very moment, Ding could be in a detention cell being sweated and interrogated by Ministry of State Security goons. With his background, SEER training, and mental toughness, Ding was not a man who was easily intimidated. Clark wasn't worried about his son-in-law breaking. To accomplish that would take months, and the Chinese would have to employ means and methods that violated Geneva Convention bans on torture. Even if the MSS harbored suspicions about Ding, subjecting him to physical torture at this stage would be an unlawful and risky course of action for a supposed businessman detained at customs *prior* to entry into China. It would be akin to arresting someone for robbing a bank before the would-be thief even attempted the heist.

However, since when did the Chinese play fair?

If the MSS had managed to pierce Ding's NOC, they could invent any narrative they chose. In this respect, the Chinese were quite Machiavellian, with the end always justifying the means. If Clark was in their shoes, the smart play would be to hold Ding. In this way, Ding could be a bargaining chip they could lord over the ODNI's head. The unspoken message was not difficult to parse:

If you disappear Admiral Qin, we disappear your man.

He shook his head. How would he explain any of this to Patsy?

There is no explaining it, he decided, *because regardless of what happens with Qin, I'm not leaving China without Ding.*

"I got eyes on Wu," Akio said from his workstation, interrupting Clark's internal battle with himself. "He's on foot, across the street."

Clark paced another half orbit around the table to get to a position behind Akio where he could look over the man's shoulder at the notebook computer screen. Akio had his display set up in a quad window configuration, streaming the live security feeds from the safe house's external cameras, all set up on old-school, hardwired feeds to reduce the risk of signals being hacked. The figure in the upper right window was definitely Wu. Clark recognized the SAS man by his gait instantly.

"About bloody time," Charlie said with a relieved smile.

Everyone's mood improved with the Brit's seemingly safe arrival. Bauer and Lee toasted their water bottles together to celebrate, and a moment later, Wu entered the front door of the apartment.

Once inside, Wu dropped his duffel bag to the ground with a thud and declared, "I need a pint."

"Sorry, mate," Charlie said, and shot Clark a stink-eyed glance. "Nothing but water and coffee here. Leave it to the Yanks to manage the safe house and an empty fridge is all you get."

"Were you detained at customs?" Clark asked, cutting through the BS to what mattered. "Were you questioned?"

"Nah, mate," Wu said. "My bag was held up in customs. It caused me to miss my next flight."

Clark glanced at Akio, who'd been tracking both Wu's and Toussaint's flights, which, according to the online tracking apps, had been on time.

"That explains it," Akio said.

Clark's eyes ticked to the duffel Wu had dropped on the floor just inside the front door. "Is *that* the bag?"

Wu shook his head. "Nah, I ditched it in Shanghai and bought this canvas one to replace it. I didn't tear the old one apart looking for a tracker, but what I did do was inspect everything I'd packed for devices and found nothing. It's possible they could have tagged something with an isotope, but, obviously, I couldn't check for that . . ."

Clark nodded. Wu was a pro and had taken the right precautions. "Any overt surveillance?"

"I wouldn't be here if that were the case. I loitered in Beijing for three hours and performed an extra-long SDR just to be sure," Wu said as he scanned the faces in the room. "Ah, now I see why everyone is bloody tense. We're missing two—Henri and Ding."

"Ding was detained by security at BCIA. We don't know his current status, but he's off the mission regardless now," Clark said.

"I can check Henri's NOC email account. It's been nearly an hour since I last logged in," Lee said, looking up at Clark from his computer.

One of the few methods available to the team members to communicate was via draft email messages maintained on international servers. Draft messages were impossible to intercept because they never got sent. To access the information, the Chinese would have to hack into the account, find the content, and copy it before it was deleted—a very difficult proposition. To further complicate matters, the messages in the draft folders were written with code words known only to TF 99 members. Even if the Chinese did manage to hack in and copy the content, they would have a nearly impossible time inferring the precise meaning of the message because the encryption was not based on a key. The only real risk, as far as Clark was concerned, was if the Chinese were monitoring every team member's specific internet traffic. Lee was using a satellite modem connection that routed all his traffic through a VPN to mask the target of the query. Could the Chinese defeat all these countermeasures?

Only fate can answer that question.

"Do it," Clark said and Lee's fingers went to work.

"There's a new message in Henri's draft folder," Lee said, his voice tense.

"Copy it and delete it."

"Done and done," Lee said, then added, "logging out and severing my connection."

"What does it say?" Charlie said, leaning forward in her chair toward Lee.

"It's an apology to his NOC's business contact in country saying that shortly after his arrival in Beijing, he fell ill with food poisoning and will unfortunately miss the morning meeting tomorrow. He apologizes for the inconvenience and will advise if and when his health improves," Lee said.

"Damn it," Clark said, and slammed his palm down on the table. "Toussaint is out."

Toussaint's draft message indicated that he'd arrived in Beijing per the schedule, but that he suspects he's under active surveillance. He would proceed with the business dictated by his NOC, in this case an investment company meeting about buying into a

Chinese tech company start-up, and then exit China for home without making further contact with the team.

"Bollocks," Wu said. "Henri was one of the few French guys I actually liked."

"So, Director Clark, it seems we have a critical decision to make," Bauer said, his German-accented English giving the statement an ominous undertone. "Do we proceed two members down, or do we abort this mission?"

Task Force 99 had just lost 25 percent of its original manpower and all they'd done so far was attempt to enter the country. As a rule, Clark wasn't someone prone to superstition, but he did believe in karma. Was the universe trying to tell him something? Was this a polite warning he was meant to heed before somebody *really* got hurt? Or did this setback mean that now they were due some good luck, which would rebalance the scales?

Clark scanned the five faces staring at him. The answer, he realized, was burning in every one of their eyes. They were all in . . . and so was he.

"We all signed on to this mission for one reason and one reason only—because extracting Defense Minister Qin would not only be the greatest intelligence coup of the decade for each of our countries, but also because it might be the only way we stop Taiwan from falling," Clark said, pushing aside all his reservations and channeling his inner field marshal. "We are proceeding, and come hell or high water, we will accomplish our mission objective."

35

A knock woke Katie.

With a groan, she rolled onto her side to face the door, which was cracked open, and saw someone peeking their backlit head in through the gap.

"Commander Ryan," a male voice said in a hushed voice. "You have a visitor."

"What? I don't understand," she said, her mind groggy and slow. Her circadian rhythms were completely out of whack, and she'd had very little sleep over the past five days.

"You have a visitor waiting for you in the SCIF. His arrival on the base is unscheduled, unannounced, and unofficial."

A surge of adrenaline instantly burned off the fog and an image of her presidential father sitting in the SCIF—dressed in jeans, a button-down, and a USS *Blackfish* ball cap—popped into her head.

Nah, it can't be, she thought as she flung back the covers and swung her feet off the side of the bed.

"I'll wait for you outside, ma'am," the messenger said.

"What's going on?" Sam asked from the other bunk.

"Not sure," Katie said. "I'm going to find out, and I'll let you know."

"Roger that," her CIA officer roommate said and rolled over to go back to sleep.

On the road, Katie slept in a pair of hip-hugging short shorts and a clean coyote-brown crewneck tee. It was both practical and expedient because she could jump straight into her guacamoles. Pop on a pair of socks and her boots, grab her cover, and she was ready to go anywhere in less than a minute.

"Can you tell me anything about who I'm meeting?" she asked the petty officer as soon as she was in the corridor.

"I'm sorry, ma'am, I cannot. I'm just the messenger," he said, striding ahead of her.

On reaching the SCIF, the petty officer badged her in and opened the door. She thanked him and stepped into the secure conference room to find a lone figure seated at the table. Although they had never met, she recognized the man instantly—Scott Kincaid, the deputy chief of mission for the U.S. ambassador to China.

The door thunked closed behind Katie and she heard the magnetic lock click.

Kincaid got to his feet, extended a hand to her, and introduced himself.

"Yes, I know who you are," she said, walking up to shake hands. Then, to cut through any pretenses or delicate dances regarding his official cover and CIA operations pedigree, she added, "And I'm read in on your OC."

"Good, that will save us time," he said and gestured for her to take a seat. He then swiveled in his chair so they faced each other. "I apologize for the nature and timing of my visit. I recognize that sleep is a precious commodity in our line of work, but given the circumstances . . . Well, let's just say I had a small window to make this happen, so I capitalized on it."

"I completely understand," Katie said. "How much time did they give you to evacuate the embassy?"

"Twenty-four hours."

"Wow," she said, raising an eyebrow. "Were you able to . . . you know, get your house in order?"

"Barely. We plan for this sort of thing, but you never actually expect it to happen. Wiping all the SSDs and incinerating docs isn't the problem. It's the non-compartmentalized stuff I worry about—you know, the unclassified shit we leave behind that seems innocuous, but with enough time and effort allows them to glean insight about our operation." He sighed. "The whole situation sucks."

"Yeah," she said in simple solidarity.

"How much do you know about TF 99 and the operation we have underway in Beijing?" he asked, pivoting hard.

"I'm read in on the objective, but not the players. Also, I've not been briefed on the current status or any specifics about Qin's exfiltration," she said.

Kincaid nodded. "I wouldn't expect you to know the nitty-gritty details because the operation is highly compartmentalized. Operating in China is—and please excuse my French—a fucking nightmare. The purge of 2013 decimated our network of assets, informants, and in-country support personnel. We simply didn't have the people or infrastructure in place to exfiltrate Admiral

Qin in an organic way. That's why we had to bring in TF 99—to do the heavy lifting of planning and executing Qin's exfiltration."

"And you're telling me all of this because . . . ?"

"Because I'm out, and there's nobody left in country who can take control of this runaway train before it goes barreling off the tracks and into the abyss."

"Hold on a second, Scott," she said, raising a hand as if to steady herself. "Are you saying you're here to pass *me* this hot potato?"

"That's right, you're the Task Force 25 officer in charge, aren't you? From what I understand, this entire operation is your brain-child."

For some reason, everyone seemed to think that the defection of Defense Minister Qin was her idea, but that was true only in the vaguest, most grandiose sense of the word. Yes, she'd sounded the alarm that something was brewing at the highest levels of the Chinese power hierarchy. And yes, she'd also set in motion the investigation into Foreign Minister Cheng's disappearance when she'd had lunch with Larry Sexton, the CIA's most senior serving China expert. But the strategizing that happened next had taken place at pay grades well above hers. She'd had nothing to do with the creation of Task Force 25 or Task Force 99, but she'd been swept up in the resulting storm anyway, and apparently someone had seen fit to name it Cyclone Katie.

"Yes, but I . . . I . . . don't have any idea what the hell I'm do-ing," she stammered. "This is the first task force I've participated in. The truth is, I don't even know what these types of task forces are supposed to do. My boss stuck me on a plane with a bunch of people I don't know and sent me here without clearly defined marching orders. I'm just winging it."

Kincaid laughed.

"What's so funny?" she asked, feeling her cheeks going red.

"Welcome to the world of international espionage, Commander," he said with a half-crazed grin. "I hate to have to be the one to tell you this, but there is no grand design. No prescient master plan. Everybody likes to think of the intelligence community like a symphony orchestra—with the DNI conducting from the podium, directing each member, who is playing their part masterfully and in time with a beautiful score that was composed by a musical prodigy. But that's not what it's like at all . . ."

A memory of sitting with her dad playing Battleship at the Ryan family home popped into her mind. In *her* mental metaphor, the IC and the DoD weren't a symphony. They were the pieces on a chessboard, and her dad was the grand master, whose guiding hand moved them. She'd always taken great comfort in this worldview. As a commissioned naval officer, she was one of the pawns in the game. But her fear and anxiety were backstopped by the knowledge that a man with unflappable courage, a highly tuned moral compass, and a tactician's intellect sat in charge of it all.

"No, not a symphony at all," he said with a chuckle, "more like trying to manage an elementary school when someone turns off the lights and pulls the fire alarm."

"That's not particularly comforting to hear," she said with a tight-lipped smile.

"Look, my point is simply that nothing ever goes according to plan. Your SEAL buddies would say no plan survives contact with the enemy, and it's every bit as true inside the wire as out. It's chaos in the dark. You never have a complete and full picture of what your adversary is doing, and most of the time, you're forced to make decisions without permission or direction from above."

She thought back to her harrowing submarine experience on the *Blackfish*, submerged and facing off against the *Belgorod* in a torpedo battle. Tactical decisions had to be made and communication with the chain of command had been impossible. For a spy behind enemy lines, the same axiom would hold true.

"Believe me, I get it," she said. "So, what is the situation with the extraction team and Defense Minister Qin right now?"

"TF 99 was supposed to be an eight-person team. We've confirmed that one member of the team was detained at Beijing Capital International Airport and is still being held for questioning. Another team member aborted when he detected surveillance on him. The remaining six are holed up in a safe house, waiting."

"Waiting for what? The green light to exfiltrate?"

Kincaid shook his head. "No, waiting for my asset—the Night Spider—to make contact and update me on Qin's status and location."

"Are you telling me nobody knows where Defense Minister Qin is right now?"

"That's correct."

"So, the Chinese could already have him?"

"Possible, but unlikely. MSS activity indicates they are engaged in an active and massive manhunt."

"Could he be dead?"

Kincaid shrugged. "Again possible, but equally as unlikely. My gut tells me the Spider made contact as scheduled and disappeared with Qin underground and has been waiting for a safe opportunity to dead-drop information to me. She's old-school. No cyber whatsoever."

"And now that you've been ejected from the country . . ."

"There's no way for her to get a message to me," he said, completing her thought.

"For all we know, she's already reached out and she's waiting on an answer back from you."

"An answer she's never going to get."

"So . . . what do we do?" Katie said, already feeling stress from the invisible ticking clock it appeared she was inheriting from this man.

"I don't know. I've only been her handler for eighteen months. I've never actually met her face-to-face."

"Wait, what? Then how can you call yourself her handler?"

Kincaid gave a little snort at this. "You have to understand the type of asset we're talking about. She's been in the spy game for three decades, operating in the most challenging countersurveillance environment imaginable, and yet she remained undetected. She survived the purge. She doesn't consider herself in our employ. In her mind, she's the one calling the shots, not the other way around."

"And you tolerate that?"

Kincaid laughed. "What choice do we have? We either play by her rules or she quits. She doesn't need us. We don't have any leverage, and besides, that's the precedent that Larry set."

She perked up at this last bit. "When you say Larry, are you talking about Larry Sexton?"

"The one and only. Do you know him?"

"We've met," she said, her mind connecting multiple dots now. "When you say that's the precedent Larry set, does that mean that he was the original case officer who recruited her?"

"Yep," Kincaid confirmed.

"Then we need to talk to him. Maybe they had a protocol in place for situations like this. Maybe they had a secret code or plan in the event he needed to get her out."

"I feel like an idiot for not thinking of that myself," Kincaid said, shaking his head. "But honestly, I would think that sort of detail would be passed on from case officer to case officer . . ."

"Did you ever play telephone when you were in elementary school?" Katie asked. "You know, where you whisper something to the kid next to you, who passes it on, and so on? Then you laugh at how unrecognizable it becomes by the end of the line?"

"I see your point," he said, clearly thinking about that analogy spread over thirty years.

"Feel free to give yourself a mulligan on that," she said, fixing him with an empathetic smile. "You've been a little busy the past twenty-four hours."

"Yeah, well, I still should have thought of it. The clock's ticking."

"What was the original exfil plan?" she asked, leaning in. "I assume whatever it was is shot now with the MSS on high alert."

"That piece of the operation is in TF 99's wheelhouse. My role was to coordinate the meetup—time and location—for the task force to take custody of Qin from the Spider. Obviously, we never got that far."

"Airports, train stations, and major highways are going to be completely out of the question . . ." she said, her mind already working the problem.

"Their video surveillance and facial rec algos are second to none. Qin cannot be seen anywhere. To get him out alive, he needs to be cargo."

"Listen, Scott, I need to get my team in here. We all need to be working this problem together," she said.

"Yes, but not until after I'm gone. There's still a chance diplomacy wins the day and the Chinese change their minds and let us back in. If that happens, I need my OC intact and well-preserved. I can't risk having your entire team read into my role," he said, his expression hard.

"Understood," she said, but wasn't sure she did. Every spy movie and book ever made had the embassy staffed with spooks. That Kincaid was, or at least *might be,* CIA was probably the worst-kept secret in Beijing.

"I assume you have a CIA contingent here with you?" the spy asked.

"Yeah, four," she said. "An operations officer, an analyst, and two ground branch—I think. They didn't hand me an org chart."

Kincaid chuckled. "No, they wouldn't, would they? Who's the team leader?"

"Ted James," she said.

Kincaid nodded approvingly. "I've never worked with him, but I've heard very good things."

"I've also got a pair from DIA and a Group Eight augment," she added.

"That's very good news, because you're going to need cyber to communicate with TF 99. There's no way you can pull this off without comms. And you're going to need logistics, and I would imagine some spooky transportation element." He cocked an eyebrow at her. "I thought you said you didn't know what you were doing? Seems to me like you already assembled all the right assets to support the exfiltration."

Apparently, but I didn't put the task force together, she thought, and the light bulb finally went on. *Admiral Kohler did . . . He predicted this would happen.*

Kincaid pulled a USB thumb drive from his pocket and slid it across the table to her.

"This is a list of all the Spider's drop locations, with geo-

coordinates and photographs, as well as a key code for the sym-
bols we use to communicate. I've taken the liberty of highlighting
in green what I believe are the most likely drops she'd use. The
ones highlighted in yellow are those I think she'll avoid. Hopefully, Larry comes through with guidance, but just in case, this is
your backup. TF 99 will have to utilize these drops to communicate with her. But be careful, doing so will be very, very dangerous."

"I understand," she said and slipped the memory stick into her
left blouse pocket.

"The challenge isn't just how to get a message to her, it's also
what to say and how to say it."

"What do you mean?"

The spook scratched his chin. "Well, you need to have a plan
in place for where she and Qin can go to intersect with your task
force team. That means having an exfil plan in place and communicating it to TF 99 in advance so they know where to pick her
up, but also where to go next. Then you have to figure out how
to code the message—old-school code I'm talking here—so that
only she will know what it means. That way, if you lose comms
with your team and the message is intercepted by the MSS instead of the Spider, it doesn't put your team at risk."

"Is that all?" she asked with a snort. She felt a tremendous
weight building on her. There were a lot of lives in play here, in
addition to the whole war-with-China thing. She wondered if she
was the right one to be heading this up. Thank God, and the
White House, that she had the talented team she did.

"I recommend coordinating with NSA to have satellite coverage over Beijing to monitor each of these sites," Kincaid continued, "and maybe they can hack into the rich network of cameras
all over the city. That could help you."

"Roger that," Katie said.

Kincaid checked his watch, then said, "Any last-second questions before I get going?"

"I can't think of any now, but as soon as you're in the air heading to Taipei I'm sure I'll think of a dozen," she said with a grin.

"That's how it works," he said, extending his hand to her.

She shook it.

"Good luck, Commander. I'll be rooting for you and your team from the sidelines."

"Thank you," she said. "Safe travels, and keep your head down."

She walked with him to the door of the SCIF, where the messenger was dutifully waiting outside in the hall.

"Mr. Smith, here, needs an escort to the helo, which I presume is waiting on him," she said, "and also I need you to wake up the rest of my team."

"Everyone, ma'am?" the petty officer asked.

She fixed him with a pitying grin. "Yep, everyone. Looks like it's going to be a long night."

36

L ieutenant Commander Horrillo stopped in front of the closed door outside the CO's stateroom. His eyes ticked to the placard on the bulkhead beside it:

Commanding Officer—Jeff Kreutz

The gravity of the title was not lost on Horrillo. Someday, if Horrillo continued to work hard, gain knowledge, and keep his nose clean, the Navy would give him the opportunity to become the captain of his own ship. As a third-tour department head and combat systems officer, he was in the middle of his journey to command. Before he could become a skipper, he would first have to finish his department head tour, select for XO, and then perform well enough that he screened for CO—plenty of time for something to go wrong and derail his career. But Horrillo didn't think that way. Worrying about screwing up or fretting about things he couldn't control created a toxic mental state. The job was hard enough without trying to take on fate, so why even try? When it came to the future, his approach had always been a simple one—keep his eyes on the road, foot on the gas, and hands on the steering wheel. The future was coming at him one way or another; best to meet it head-on and in control. The way to do that was to simply make the next right decision, followed by the next, and the next . . .

He knocked on the door frame.

"Come," the skipper called from behind the closed door.

Horrillo let himself in.

Kreutz swiveled in his task chair and greeted Horrillo with a tight smile.

"Open or shut?" Horrillo asked with a glance at the door.

"Shut, please."

"Roger that," he said and closed the door.

"Have a seat, Mitch," Kreutz said, gesturing to the open chair beside the CO's desk.

Horrillo did and felt a flutter of nerves in his stomach. He'd not been concerned in the slightest when the messenger had said the CO wanted to see him, but something felt off—like the captain was going to spring something unexpected on him. His mind shifted into emergency reconstruct mode, reviewing everything that had happened in the past forty-eight hours, wondering where and how he might have made better decisions.

"I called you here because I wanted to let you know that I was impressed with how you handled the incident in the Strait of Malacca. You faced an unexpected threat on the midwatch while I was asleep, and you kept your head under pressure and led the tactical response perfectly. Honestly, there's nothing I would tell you that you should have done differently, and with hindsight on my side you can take that as a helluva compliment."

"Thank you, sir," he said, caught off guard by the unexpected *attaboy*.

"We already debriefed the event with the wardroom, so there's no need to rehash the details now, but I wanted to circle back with you personally. When I was a JO, I remember the engineer gave me the best career advice anyone could have given me. He said, 'Kreutz, if you want to succeed in the Navy as an officer, in every situation you face, you need to ask yourself one simple question: What would my boss do if he or she were in my shoes? In other words, don't think and operate at your current rank, strive to function one pay grade above. If you want to be a captain, then you need to think like a captain.' You did that, Mitch. As TAO, you handled that situation thinking not just one but *two* pay grades above your own. You demonstrated leadership under fire, which is why I'm going to use my command appointment to send you to surface warfare tactics instructor school for integrated air and missile defense."

"You're red-chipping me?"

Kreutz nodded.

"Wow, okay," he said, suppressing with great effort a proud grin at the news that he would be going to the surface warfare equivalent of Top Gun to receive next-level training. "I don't know what to say."

"I'm not proposing, CSO. Just say yes."

"Yes, absolutely, yes. Thank you, sir."

"It's a very selfless thing I'm doing," the skipper said with a chuckle, "because it's going to leave a void when you're gone, and I'd love to keep you here, but it's what you deserve. And quite frankly, it's what's best for the Navy. I have no doubt you're going to command your own ship someday, and this will ensure you stay on that track."

Horrillo failed to suppress the giant grin spreading across his face. On his previous sea tour on the USS *Porter*, the captain had red-chipped another extremely capable officer instead of Horrillo. Mitch had thought he'd missed the window for WTI, but sometimes COs made exceptions, and apparently this was one of those times. Kreutz had just handed Horrillo the Navy's equivalent of a FAST pass card, allowing him to jump the line and hop on the ride. And what a ride it was going to be.

The IVCS phone on the captain's desk rang.

Kreutz held up a finger to Horrillo and answered the call. "Captain . . . Mm-hmm . . . Damn . . . All right, come to my stateroom and we'll discuss." The captain hung up and fixed Horrillo with a frown.

"Bad news?" Horrillo asked.

"We just got new tasking. XO is on her way to discuss."

"Do you want me to stay or go?"

"Stay, because I want to hear your thoughts."

"Yes, sir," Horrillo said, and a few moments later a knock came at the door.

"Come," the captain said, and the XO stepped in and shut the door behind her.

She handed Kreutz a folder, which he opened to look at the message inside. Horrillo watched the skipper closely and saw that whatever the man was reading, it wasn't good news. On finishing, the captain let out a *Why us God?* sigh and shook his head.

"Have you read it, XO?" the captain asked, and set the folder on his desk.

"Yes, sir," she said.

Kreutz shifted his gaze to Horrillo. "We've just been reassigned to Task Force 70 up in the East China Sea."

"Okaaaay . . ." Horrillo said, waiting for the punch line. Extending their CENTCOM AOR deployment had been a blow, but joining the *Reagan* instead of the *Nimitz* didn't feel like much of a difference.

"And we've been given explicit orders to transit *through* the Strait of Taiwan."

"What!" he said, unable to contain his shock. "Alone?"

Horrillo was well read in from the daily intel briefs on the threats made by China and her political blockade of the strait. It looked like the *Jason Dunham* had been selected to test whether that blockade had military teeth to it.

"That's insane. The Chinese Navy's maritime blockade completely encompasses Taiwan, including the strait," he said.

Horrillo, and the rest of the officers not standing watch, had been briefed in the wardroom on the unprecedented movement of ships to provide a naval blockade of Taiwan just two hours ago. The news had added some much-needed clarity as to why they'd been reassigned from Fifth to Seventh Fleet, but what they were being ordered to do now was beyond the pale.

The captain shook his head. "Apparently, it's been decided that the *Dunham* is going to be the U.S. Navy's blockade buster."

"That would take approval from the CNO, I would imagine."

"True," the XO said, "but in this case the order came down from the very top, where CNO's response would be simply 'Yes, sir,' I would imagine."

"The White House?" Horrillo asked.

"The message is explicit. It includes the words 'by order of the President,'" Kreutz said.

"Okay, but why?"

"I've never met the man personally, but everything I've heard and seen about President Ryan is that he doesn't cave in the face of pressure," Kreutz said. "When an adversary tries to intimidate him, he stands taller and reminds the world of the big stick he gets to carry as commander in chief."

"The orders are kind of poetic, if you ask me," the XO said, wearing a pensive expression. "Given our namesake, that is."

The XO hadn't been aboard long, but she repeatedly surprised Horrillo with her insights and unique perspective on things. In this case, the *poetic* reference applied to Jason Lee Dunham, a Marine corporal who'd been posthumously awarded the Medal of Honor after sacrificing his life while serving in the Middle East. Knowing Jason Dunham's story was part of every sailor's indoctrination when coming aboard DDG 109.

While serving with the 3rd Battalion, 7th Marines in 2004, Dunham went out on a patrol in Husaybah, Iraq, during which his unit was ambushed. In the ensuing engagement, he fought an insurgent in hand-to-hand combat, then deliberately covered an enemy grenade with his helmet and body to save his fellow Marines. The injuries he sustained were fatal, but *Dunham*'s action saved lives and showed valor of the highest order. Every crew member of the USS *Jason Dunham* felt an obligation to honor the sacrifice and courage of the Marine whose name the ship proudly bore.

For Horrillo, and the rest of the crew of the *Dunham*, acting as blockade buster by driving through the Strait of Taiwan with the Chinese fleet on war footing would very much feel akin to jumping on a live grenade. But for the people of Taiwan, and the U.S. servicemen and -women stationed on the island, the bold act would signal the courage of the United States Navy and America's promise of protection.

If somebody has to do it, Horrillo thought mustering his courage, *it might as well be us.*

He watched as the captain—with a look of fatalistic resignation—picked up the radio and called the bridge on Net 15.

"Officer of the deck, this is the captain—change course to new heading, north, and inform the navigator to plot a new course through the Strait of Taiwan and into the East China Sea," Kreutz said. Then, after a pause, he continued. "Yes, officer of the deck, I'm aware of the blockade . . . Very well, report when the new track is ready for me to review."

Their fate now sealed, the CO put the radio handset down on his desk and Horrillo couldn't help but notice the skipper's gaze go to the framed picture of his wife and kids that he proudly displayed on his desk.

"Well, gentlemen, if you'll excuse me . . ." the XO said after a solemn beat. Then she fixed them both with a somber gaze. "I think I'm going to go get a quick workout in, because I have a feeling it's going to be the last one I get for quite a while."

PART III

"The supreme art of war is to subdue the enemy without fighting."

—Sun Tzu, *The Art of War*

37

BRIDGE OF THE *NANCHANG* (101)
TYPE 055 GUIDED-MISSILE DESTROYER
211 KILOMETERS WEST OF TAINAN, TAIWAN
122 KILOMETERS EAST OF THE MOUTH OF RONG RIVER AT
   SHONTOU, CHINA
SOUTHERN MOUTH OF THE STRAIT OF TAIWAN
0612 LOCAL TIME

aptain Shen Huaqing crossed his legs at the knee and accepted the cup of tea brought to him by his steward as he sat in the captain's chair of the most deadly warship in the PLA Navy.

"Thank you, Fei," he said, using the mid-grade NCO's first name.

"My honor is to serve you, *dàxiào*," the steward said, folding the silver tray and giving a bow.

Shen smiled and dismissed the man with a nod, then returned to watching the beauty of the sun rising over the South China Sea. He had learned long ago that in the complex command structure of the PLA Navy, loyalty was achieved by treating your crew with respect and kindness. Shen had not risen to his current position at the command of the most prestigious destroyer in the Navy by shying away from ruling with an iron fist when needed or punishing harshly when required, but he preferred to spend most of his time leading through a position of respect and admiration. To do so required relationships with his officers and crew. While studying command philosophy at Dalian Naval Academy, his favorite instructor had once told him that a crew that feared him would obey him, but a crew that loved him would follow him to hell and back. That had struck him as the truth as he thought back to the commanders he had most admired. All ruled with an iron fist, but those who had seemed genuinely to care for their sailors had been the best leaders. Later, as vice captain of the *Zhengzhou*, he had seen such leadership demonstrated perfectly by his captain, Shi Dingfa. Before taking command of the *Nanchang*, he'd seen the opposite approach by Captain Xiao, who had been universally feared by the entire crew, including himself. In fact, he'd been shocked to learn Xiao had endorsed him as the next captain after his tour completed. Shen had thought, like the rest of the crew, that Xiao had hated him.

Just when I think I have a person figured out, they invariably surprise me.

He stared out the bridge windscreen and watched as the sun burned an orange strip of fire across the blue water of the South China Sea. The view made Shen smile. Morning was his favorite time of day at sea. Command burden was a real thing, especially at the helm of China's deadliest destroyer. The *Nanchang* was the first of the 055 class of stealthy destroyers that the West would classify as a cruiser due to its massive size and its ability to concurrently serve as a command-and-control vessel. In fact, Admiral Hu Shangfu, the commander of the massive exercise known as Sea Serpent, would be joining the *Nanchang* tomorrow to oversee the operation. But unlike some Western navies, the PLAN did not place command and control on vessels outside the fight. The *Nanchang*'s capabilities would be vital to the mission, and Shen very much looked forward to showing off his ship and her extraordinary crew.

"Helm, come right, steer course zero-six-zero degrees," Shen said, swiveling a few degrees in his seat on the bridge. He'd not given a specific rudder order with the course change, which allowed the helmsman to select the amount of rudder required. He liked to give his crew opportunities to think for themselves in low-risk situations such as this.

"Come right, steer course zero-six-zero degrees," his helmsman repeated back. "Captain, my rudder is right."

The *Nanchang* was station-keeping at the southern mouth of the Strait of Taiwan, functioning as a guard dog for the recently announced and established naval blockade. That's not what the Defense Ministry and PLA Navy was calling it, but that's what it was. Maritime exclusion zones, or MEZs, were something the power brokers in Beijing were experimenting with all over the South China Sea to expand the nation's control over their home waters, but blockading the Strait of Taiwan was the boldest move yet.

He pushed concerns about the American response to the blockade out of his mind. He just wanted to enjoy the sunrise, which was lighting up the few scattered clouds on the horizon a lovely pink. The colors made him think of his wife, Ai, back home with their young son, but in truth, as much as he missed them, he would not trade his life at sea for anything, and the new course gave him a perfect view of what he loved about the Navy. The only thing that would make it better would be the opportunity to enjoy the outside on the bridgewing, where he could feel the wind on his skin, the warmth of the sun, and smell the salt of the air. He was about to make an excuse to do just that when a voice announced a new, and unwanted, visitor on the bridge.

"Commissar on the bridge," the junior boatswain's mate announced, notifying the watch team.

Shen turned in his chair, forcing the frown away from his face, to see the ship's political commissar approaching.

"A beautiful morning, Captain," Colonel Sun Ching-Kuo said as he approached, looking out of place, frankly, in his PLA uniform.

"Good morning, Colonel," he said, annoyed that the sunrise had been ruined by the man's insufferable presence.

He didn't dislike Sun per se. It was the idea of political commissars that needled him. He would never dare verbalize as much, but that was the truth in his heart. He understood, of course, the need to ensure that philosophy was shared across the military, but the idea of the political commissar bothered him for two reasons. One, he was not a believer that there could be two leaders in any organization, much less a military combat unit. The burden of command was best executed by one, single person, properly chosen and trained, with whom all final authority rested. In the modern PLA Navy, the political commissar was a ranking military officer tasked not only with ensuring that the captain, officers, and crew had the correct outlook but, in communication with the Party committee, shared command with the ship's captain. In fact, while tactical matters were left to the captain, the commissar had authority when it came to strategic decisions.

The second thing that bothered Shen was that he could not for the life of him, especially in the PLA Navy, fathom why an officer would seek such a position.

The commissar walked over and stood beside Shen, glancing

only for a moment at the incredible view out the windscreen, as if to check a box, before leaning in.

"I believe that we are about to receive new orders, Captain Shen," Sun said, his voice taking on a conspiratorial whisper. The man then glanced around to make sure the rest of the bridge watch standers had "overheard" him. "These will be orders that will give you the opportunity to demonstrate to the world the true capabilities of the *Nanchang* and the entire 055 class, Captain."

On second thought, I do dislike Colonel Sun after all.

"And why would you know of these orders ahead of me, Commissar?" he asked, his tone a question instead of the demand he felt it should be.

Sun gave him an irritating wink and laughed. "I have my ways, Captain."

"Bridge, Radio," a voice said on the speaker at the front of the pilothouse used for station-to-station communications. "Command-level flash traffic received. Request the captain come to Radio."

Irritated, Shen snatched the microphone handset from the console in front of him. "Radio, Captain. I am on my way."

He rose from the chair and took one last forlorn glance at the now fully risen sun glittering on the sea.

"I can man the conn for you, Captain, while you are in Radio," the political commissar said, a move meant to demonstrate he already knew what the flash traffic orders were for. But all the offer really did was demonstrate Sun's lack of knowledge about ship driving and reinforce the fact in Shen's mind that the man hadn't learned a damn thing since he'd arrived on board.

"That won't be necessary," Shen said, having no intention of leaving an Army officer in control of his ship. "Commander Tong is the officer of the deck and conning officer. This is his watch station. I am in command of the ship, but I don't assume the conn every time I walk on the bridge. I would think you would know this by now, Colonel."

He spun on a heel and headed for the door.

Sun followed.

On the *Nanchang*, the ship's communications suite, aka the radio room, was located aft and just one deck below the bridge. He took the down ladder, walked ten paces aft, and punched in the code on the security lock to enter the most secure space on the ship.

"Good morning, Captain," the young communications officer said with a smile, her face changing when she saw the colonel trailing Shen. "And good morning, Commissar," she added. Nervous, she handed the already-printed message traffic to Shen, who pulled a pair of readers from his breast pocket and then scanned the document.

The orders filled him with excitement, but perhaps also some concern. As a naval officer, he was always eager to prove his warrior prowess and the skill of his crew. The Americans were a worthy adversary, but he believed with all his heart that the officers and crew of the *Nanchang* were beyond their equals.

But still, these were the types of encounters that led to war . . .

"So, you see, Captain?" Sun said, and then clapped him on the back, which Shen hated. "You have the honor of leading the charge in an action well beyond the exercise that will follow—both in challenge as well as in prestige."

"Indeed . . . I will brief my officers in the wardroom," he said, then turned to see that Sun was already at the door to leave.

"And I will be there," Sun said, then with a smug smile added,

"I'll be in my quarters. Send a messenger when the officers are assembled. I prefer to be the last to arrive."

Shen felt a flash of anger but swallowed it down. He didn't acknowledge the colonel's comment, and instead returned his attention to the orders in hand.

> Remain on station in current AOR.
> American vessel, identified as the 109 Jason Dunham, is believed
>   headed toward the strait.
> Deny them access.
> Deadly force is authorized.
> Stop.

Captain Shen Huaqing clenched his jaw. He believed the American DDG to be no match for his ship or his crew. But war with the United States could follow the use of deadly force. Of this, he had no illusions, knowing what he did about the American president, Jack Ryan.

And war with America was not desirable at all.

38

Katie turned to Conza, who sat at the opposite end of the conference table, and shot him a *Please save me* look.

Her head throbbed and her belly felt sour from the three cups of crappy black coffee she'd drunk on an empty stomach. After her one-on-one discussion with Kincaid, she'd mustered the entire team—including the Group Eight folks—for a planning and strategy session. The problem Task Force 25 was now tasked with was how to exfiltrate the members of Task Force 99 from Beijing along with Defense Minister Qin and the Chinese spy known as the Spider. And, of course, she couldn't get so distracted with this vital task that she neglected the vital task of making sure Taiwan and the United States were prepared for what she now believed would be the mission China would implement to take over the invasion of Taiwan. They had routed their concerns through the ONI to the White House, and were waiting to hear what partner agencies thought.

At the beginning of *this* life-and-death brainstorm session, Katie had made the pronouncement that "the only bad ideas were the ones people kept to themselves." She'd said this because she'd wanted to empower every member to speak their mind and not pigeonhole the team into groupthink or constrain creative solutions.

The first few hours had felt productive as they brainstormed every imaginable way to exfiltrate the team in Beijing—from an overland trek into Mongolia, to sneaking the TF 99 and defectors inside a shipping container and loading it onto a container ship bound for the U.S., to having the USS *Jimmy Carter* special projects submarine sneak into the Yellow Sea and pick them up. But as time passed, the atmosphere had become increasingly contentious as people's ideas and egos were stress-tested by the collective critique—a process that was absolutely imperative. They needed to shoot holes in each other's tactics and strategies, but leading a discussion in a room full of devil's advocates was exhausting. Right now, she just needed a friggin' break so she could collect her own thoughts.

Conza met her gaze and read her mind. He made the OK sign with his thumb and index finger, stuck them into his mouth, and magically produced a very loud and shrill whistle that abruptly silenced the din.

"Listen up, everybody," he said with all eyes on him. "I think this is a good time to take a break. Feel free to use the head, grab a coffee, get some fresh air—whatever you need to do. We'll reconvene back here at 0700."

Weary groans followed as the assembled team members got to their feet, stretched, yawned, and grumbled in a mass exodus toward the door to the SCIF. But Katie, Conza, and Ted James— the CIA lead—stayed behind for a *just the grown-ups* chat.

"Well?" she asked, ticking her gaze back and forth between Conza and James.

"Do you want my candid opinion?" James said.

"Always."

The CIA operations officer walked over to the massive flat-screen monitor on the opposite wall, which displayed a bird's-eye satellite view of the region at a fifty-mile scale. The map had Beijing in the upper left corner, North Korea in the upper right, South Korea in the lower right, and the middle was filled by the Yellow Sea and the Gulf of Bohai.

"I think they're fucked," James said, talking to the map. "The distances we're dealing with here are huge. Draw a circle of control centered on Beijing and the radius is two hundred and fifty miles. Two hundred and fifty miles of absolute primacy over the ground, air, and sea. How can we move eight people two hundred and fifty miles without detection in a modern, electronic-savvy, and paranoia-driven country and get them onto a platform we control? We've lost the element of surprise. The Chinese are already looking for them, and will use any trail we create to find them. They're already scrutinizing, analyzing, and war-gaming just like we are. Whatever we do, they're going to see us coming miles and miles away and have time to interdict."

Katie's reaction to this was a hard exhale and a tired stare.

"I know, I know, I'm sorry," James said, turning to meet her eyes. "I'm not trying to sound defeatist. I know you already know this and don't need to hear it again."

"It's not that," she said, and ran her fingers through her hair. "I just happen to believe if you approach a mission with the mindset that its hopeless at the outset, then you're destined to fail. Whatever solution we pick, we must go into it with the mindset that, no matter the odds, we're going to succeed."

"You're right, I'm sorry," James said. "That wasn't helpful."

From the corner of her eye, she saw Conza grinning.

"What are you grinning about?" she asked, feeling her own spirits lift simply because of that grin.

"I'm just thinking about this one time in Afghanistan. I was augmenting with DEVGRU at the time and this was the last mission that I still had my leg . . ." Conza said, his gaze going to the middle distance.

Katie listened as the former SEAL told the story of a seemingly impossible mission to snatch a high-value target out from under the noses of an overwhelming enemy presence. It was a classic *adapt and overcome* tale that involved battling through adversity. While she listened, she was captivated, and the imagery in her mind felt so vivid and real she felt like she was practically there with him. In the end, the story embodied all the best elements of the special operations ethos—physical sacrifice, mission before self, and courage under fire.

"I tell you this not to brag or prove what a badass I used to be—although the latter part is true," he said with a laugh. "I tell you this because miraculous things can happen when a team of highly motivated, expertly trained people are tasked with the seemingly impossible. I don't believe the situation we're up against is hopeless. As far as I'm concerned, we are going to get them out or die trying."

"And you're willing to stake your own life on that?" James said.

Conza nodded. "Absolutely. Which is why I'm going to be on the infil team and lead the rescue operation."

"What?" Katie said, truly taken aback. "No. That's what we have Group Eight for. You're part of the head shed now, John."

Conza didn't argue with her, just smiled and walked over to join James, who was still standing at the big monitor.

"Okay, look, I think we all agree that a maritime exfiltration is our best option. And while I love the audacity of bringing the *Jimmy Carter* or some other badass submarine in for a nighttime exfil, the simple fact of the matter is this entire area is just too fucking shallow. The average depth of the Bohai Sea is only sixty feet. The top of the sail would be sticking out of the water if a submarine tried to go in there," he said, shaking his head. "And to be honest, the Yellow Sea ain't much better. Looking at the bathymetry, most of the soundings are around one hundred and fifty feet. I'm no squid, but I can't imagine DEVRON 5 is going to be too excited about sending one of his six-billion-dollar submarines into what is basically a Chinese fishing pond," Conza said.

Katie thought back to her white-knuckle underway on the *Blackfish* and the sub-on-sub battle against the *Belgorod*. She remembered changing depth from five hundred feet to nine hundred feet in mere seconds. At four hundred and fifty feet long, if you stood the *Jimmy Carter* on its stern, two-thirds of the submarine would be sticking out of the water in the Yellow Sea. Conza was right, tasking an SSN, no matter how bold and capable the crew, didn't pass the commonsense test.

"I agree with you, John," she said, and shifted in her chair. "Go on."

"Which leaves two other possible options—exfil by boat or by minisub. Group Eight has an asset called the *Proteus*—a manned SDV with a dry internal compartment—that's capable of carrying eight people out and operating in the shallow depths of the Bohai Sea. But the problem is distance. It's one hundred and eighty miles from the port in Tianjin to the Bohai Strait. And another one hundred and twenty miles to get out past the peninsula into the middle of the Yellow Sea. That's a six-hundred-mile round trip. Even if the batteries could cover that range, which they cannot, at eight knots we're talking seventy-five hours of submerged travel. Like Ted said, the distances we're dealing with here are tremendous."

"It sounds like exfil by ship is our only viable option," Katie said. "But they won't have any stealth and we still have the distance problem. Even if the ship is making twenty knots, we're still looking at thirty hours of surveillance time the Chinese will have to interrogate our exfil craft during the infil and exfil."

"I know, which is why it's not going to work. A better option is to smuggle the team onto a merchant vessel or a ferry that's already scheduled to run from Tianjin *here*"—he pointed to the Chinese seaport closest to Beijing—"over to here," he said, and shifted his fingertip east across the Yellow Sea to the Korean port city of Incheon, which was located adjacent to Seoul on the west side of the Korean peninsula.

Katie looked from Conza to James. "Ted, what do you think?"

"I like the merchant vessel option better than the ferry option. Ferry access would require them to buy tickets, pass through the terminal, and be subject to visual interrogation and camera surveillance. Shipyard access is going to be a little trickier on the front end, but once they're inside the perimeter there will be less scrutiny," he said.

She laughed. "Sounds like we're back to the shipping container idea."

"But instead of spending weeks inside cruising across the Pacific, they only need to cross the Yellow Sea. We're looking at a little over a day, right?"

Conza nodded. "And they don't necessarily have to be in a CONEX box. We might be able to sneak them on as crew."

"This is a lot of logistics to plan," she said. "Do we have the time?"

"I think so," James said, "but we're going to need hand-in-glove support from the South Korean National Intelligence Service to pull this off."

"They're invested in helping us, because they've got a man on TF 99 they need to get out of Beijing, too." She checked her watch and was about to say she needed to make a pit stop before the rest of the team returned, but the secure desk phone rang. She picked up the handset. "Commander Ryan."

"Commander Ryan, I have an encrypted incoming call for you from Langley," a male voice on the line said. "Are you secure?"

She pulled the handset away from her mouth and said, "I need to take this call, guys. If you wanna take a break and keep the others out until I'm done, I'd appreciate it."

"Roger that," Conza said, and both men headed for the door.

Then, back into the receiver, she said, "I'm secure. Put it through."

"Stand by," the voice said, and she heard a series of clicks, then a change in the static.

"Commander Ryan," she said when no one spoke, in case the caller was waiting.

"Commander Ryan," a familiar, crusty voice said, drawing out both words with a superior-sounding Virginia drawl. "If I'd known you were going to go and kick the hornet's nest, I would have never agreed to meet you for brunch . . ."

"Larry, is that you?" she asked as a crooked grin curled her lips.

"Yeah, it's me," the old spook said, and she could practically hear him smiling on the other end of the secure line thousands of miles away. "And I heard from a little bird that you and I need to have another talk."

39

As Katie briefed Sexton on the dire situation with Qin and the Spider in Beijing, she silently prayed that the secure, encrypted line they were using was truly secure and encrypted. If the Chinese cyber moles had burrowed their way into the infrastructure of this ROC base, then everything discussed on this call would have the opposite effect of what was needed. Instead of providing clarity and options, it would seal the defector's fate as well as that of TF 99.

When she finished talking, Sexton said, "That's quite a pickle, now isn't it?"

"It is," she said, and was forced to wait for what felt like an eternity before he finally spoke again.

"It's funny how life works. I've spent the past thirty years trying to distance myself from Léi. You'd think seven thousand miles would do the trick, but the heart . . . the heart doesn't measure feelings in miles. I love my wife dearly, Commander Ryan. She's been a devoted and selfless life partner, and I would never, ever betray the vows we took, but to say I never think about what my

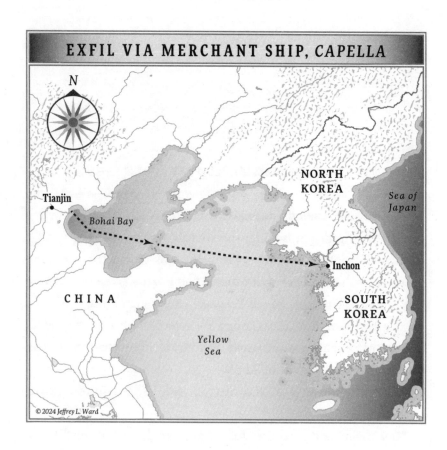

EXFIL VIA MERCHANT SHIP, *CAPELLA*

N

NORTH
KOREA

Sea of
Japan

Tianjin

Bohai Bay

Inchon

CHINA

SOUTH
KOREA

*Yellow
Sea*

© 2024 Jeffrey L. Ward

life would have been if I'd stayed in China—or if Léi had left with me—would be a lie. Maybe it's the guilt of leaving her alone in the fight as much as anything, I don't know."

"Why are you telling me this, Larry?"

He exhaled into the receiver, and she could feel the emotional burden the man carried. "I don't know. I guess because the prospect of a reunion with Léi has dredged up all kinds of complicated feelings that I'd worked very hard to bury," he said. Then, as if someone had flipped a switch, his tone changed from sentimental to all business. "But none of that is your concern. The priority is getting Defense Minister Qin and our people out of China, and to do that you're going to need my help."

It didn't matter what community someone served—whether it be in one of the branches of the military or in the IC—in the course of doing the job, relationships were forged. Katie was of the strong opinion that caring about the job also meant caring about people. That didn't mean that fraternization was something that should be encouraged or permitted, but on the flip side an *every person for themselves* mentality wasn't the answer, either. The world had enough sociopaths and egoists. The bonds of friendship, loyalty, and commitment to a higher purpose was what powered the entire apparatus. Without that, it would all come crashing down like a house of cards.

"I understand how difficult this must be for you, Larry," she said, acknowledging the delicate and heartfelt admission he'd made. "And I appreciate any help you can give us."

"The answer to your first question, even though you haven't asked it yet, is no," he said, his surly persona back on full display. "I have not been in touch with Léi, nor do I have a secret way to contact her. When I left Beijing all those years ago, I turned *everything* over to my replacement. All communications between the CIA and Léi have been managed by the chain of case officers who have served as her handlers. Thirteen case officers have managed her in the years since, and never once did I intervene. Looks like Scott Kincaid was unlucky number thirteen."

"Mm-hmm," she murmured, but she couldn't help but notice that Larry knew the exact number of handlers Léi had had. "Okay, so direct contact with her is off the table. Got it. My next question is, do you have any idea where she could be hiding with Defense Minister Qin?"

"The woman I knew back then was just a kid, Ryan. We both were. She wasn't an experienced operative and the operating environment in Beijing was completely different. The Léi of the 1990s would have tried to hide Qin in her apartment. But she's so much more sophisticated than that now—she would have to be or she would never have survived. She's built a web of contacts in Beijing that are unrivaled in the espionage business. I would not even know where to begin to tell you to look. The only thing I can guarantee is that wherever she's hiding, it's either a property she owns herself or someplace controlled by one of her most trusted contacts."

"I understand that, but maybe you could try to put together a short list of places she might consider—favorite shops or hotels or friends' apartments you visited."

He sighed. "Here's the problem with that, Ryan. Beijing has probably changed more than any other city on earth over the past thirty years. The development and expansion of the city has been off the charts. I haven't been back, but I would imagine that most of the places we used to frequent—like restaurants, shops, and favorite hotels—have changed dramatically over the years. Hell, most of them probably don't even exist anymore. As far as mutual friends go, we didn't have any."

"I was afraid you might say that," she said, deflating a little in her chair. She racked her brain for another option. "What about places that *haven't* changed since you left. There are historical and cultural sites that are immutable—like the Forbidden City, the Temple of Heaven, and the Great Wall, for example. Maybe she'd pick somewhere like that to make contact."

He chuckled. "Sure, but those would be terrible places for her to go. She might as well wear a sign on her back that says: 'Here I am, come get me.'"

A surge of frustration blossomed in her chest. "You're not making this easy on me, Larry," she snapped. "What about a secret protocol in the event of an emergency? Did you guys have something like that in place when you were together? You know, like, if bad thing ABC happens, then we'll meet at location XYZ at such and such time?"

"No," he said, and then with a defensive tone added, "I never set out to recruit her. That was never my goal. What we had just . . . *happened*. And then I left."

Static-filled silence hung on the line.

"Larry, are you still there?" she said after a long beat, wondering if he'd hung up on her.

"I'm still here," he said, his voice coarse gravel. "I'm just trying to put myself in her shoes . . . trying to remember if there was anything I said or did that she could fall back on. Damn, my old brain. It was so long ago, I'm having trouble remembering specifics."

"I know it was. Take your time . . ."

The static silence returned and seemed to vacuum up the space between them like a black hole. She was so friggin' tired that she let her mind go completely blank while she waited.

She felt her eyelids droop.

315

Her head bobbed with microsleep—

"It's just been too long, Ryan," Sexton said, snapping her awake. "I just don't know her anymore. Too much time has passed for me to guess where she might go."

Katie pursed her lips and clenched her jaw in frustration. Qin had risked a lot to prevent war with the United States over Taiwan, and he and the Spider had both given up their lives in China over this. They had to get them out somehow.

"Maybe we're thinking about this all wrong, Larry," she said after a moment. "Instead of guessing where she'll go, maybe you can help us guide her to where she *should* go."

"I thought you didn't have contact with her."

"We don't," she said. "But Kincaid believes she'll continue to monitor her network of blind drops, looking for a message from us. In my mind, the risk of leaving something is that it could be intercepted. What we need is something, a code of some sort, that only she would understand that tells her where to go. It needs to be someplace outside her network because they'll be scouring Beijing. Is that something you can help us with?"

"I got it," he said, the excitement in his voice unmistakable.

"What? What did you remember?"

"On our second-to-last weekend together, we took a trip to the Zhoukoudian Peking Man Site."

"The what Peking Man site?" she asked, completely confused.

He slowly repeated the name and said, "It's an archaeological heritage site located in the countryside outside Beijing. Some archaeologist—I can't remember the guy's name—found a *Homo erectus* skeleton there and they built a museum for it. They call it the 'Peking Man.' As far as museums go it's fine—you know, if you like that sort of thing. We looked at the Peking Man and other fossils and walked around the cave. But we spent most of the weekend trying to make sure we wouldn't forget each other."

"And you think we could leave a message that will guide her there in a way only she would understand?"

"Yes. Because we shared a moment that I still remember, and I'd reckon she does, too," he said, his voice cracking a little bit. "We were looking at the exhibits, wandering around the museum, and they have this little display of a caveman family—all naked and hairy and sitting around a fire—and she asked me, 'Do you think they were capable of loving each other like we do?' I remember thinking about that, and pulling her in for a hug, and saying, 'I don't know, but it sure would be a shame to live a life without knowing love.' And then she said, 'Do you think we'll ever see each other again?' And I remember a tear running down my face when I answered her."

When he didn't finish the story, she said, "What did you say?"

He let out a little snort. "I told her, 'I have a feeling that's up to fate.'"

She felt a sudden and unexpected upswell of emotion, and in her heart she knew with certainty that if Léi was still alive, that caveman exhibit was a place they could send her. "Thank you, Larry. That's the information we needed. I'm going to feed it to the team, and we'll give it a shot."

"Keep me posted, please," he said. "I need to know if she makes it out alive."

"I will," she said. "And, Larry, if you remember anything else that might be important or helpful, you know where to find me."

"I do indeed. Thank you, Commander."

"For what?"

"For caring," he said, then the line went dead.

She returned the handset to the cradle and pressed to her feet. The stiff muscles in her lower back and legs needed the stretch. Bladder full to bursting, she headed for the SCIF door, ready for a bathroom break.

And after, I'm getting something with protein from the vending machine.

But those plans were cut abruptly short, because as she reached for the door handle, the base-wide air-raid sirens began to wail.

40

Weariness hung on Clark like a lead blanket, but he couldn't afford to yield to it. Laziness was a killer. He forced himself to check his six one last time before turning the corner and walking to the safe house. He'd been out all night, checking the Spider's dead-drop locations and making drops of his own. Disappointingly, he'd found no notes or signals left by her, but he'd deposited four coded notes in strategic drop locations—one each of four separate quadrants of Beijing.

Hopefully, she's making rounds.

He let himself into the safe house by punching in the "all clear" security code on the door. If he had entered the alternate code, the door would have unlocked, but not before notifying the team inside that he was in distress. He closed the door behind him and trudged up the stairs to the common room, where the team waited.

"Hey, boss," Daniel Wu called out from where he was hunched

over a laptop at the dining table. "You all right, mate? You look knackered."

"I'm good," Clark said, taking a seat at the head of the table and rubbing his hands over his face, but even he knew his answer wasn't convincing.

"I've got some good news that will cheer you up, I just checked the secondary mail account drafts box and Chavez left a message that he is out of China and heading to Manila. Guessing he's standing by there in case we need help on exfil," Wu said.

Clark nodded, a wave of relief sweeping over him that his friend and son-in-law was safe.

One less thing to worry about . . .

"How did the drop go?" Bauer asked, all business. The German looked tired as well. This was a problem that needed addressing. Sleep was a weapon, and they all were operating in deficit.

"Drops—plural," Clark corrected. "And they went well. It was a long damn night of SDRs and barhopping to get into the correct positions, but the four drops were made."

"Sounds awful," Wu teased. "Having pints with pretty girls all about town while we work."

"Yeah," Clark said, and gave the Brit a Team Guy smile. "Would've been great work back in the day, but I'm not a young buck anymore." He turned to Charlie. "Any fresh guidance about what we're supposed to do next? This is one of the few times in my career I've dropped a coded message that I hadn't decrypted first."

"As a matter of fact," Charlie said, "I just finished unpacking a burst message."

That woke Clark up. Burst messages were heavily encrypted, nondirectional messages sent out via DoD satellite, intended to look like message traffic to the Navy fleet.

He cocked an eyebrow at her. "Am I gonna like it?"

"We're supposed to rendezvous with the target in just over thirty-six hours," she said, opening a notebook, where she had written out the decoded message. They were strict about using the computer as little as possible, since nowhere were cyber hacks a bigger risk than inside China. Clark looked at the chicken scratch on Charlie's notebook page and laughed.

"What the hell is that? Sanskrit?"

Charlie punched his arm, the team dynamic now fully in place, to his relief. Bringing a team up to operational readiness on short notice was always a challenge. Adding different cultures and national priorities complicated matters. But operators tended to be cut from the same cloth across cultures, and this team was no exception.

"The meet will happen tomorrow afternoon at 1600 local time at a display inside the Peking Man museum complex in Zhou-koudian," she said, reading her poor handwriting. "The message you dropped is apparently coded from a handler she worked with years ago, but the reference is one that she will understand. Or at least that's the hope. Assuming she gets the message . . ."

"And assuming she can get herself and the package there without getting killed," Bauer added, yawning.

"Where exactly is this place?" Clark asked, his weariness gone now. Beside him, Tsai Akio rolled out a paper map, again choosing to avoid the internet at all costs. He expertly folded the map, leaving Beijing at the center of a much smaller square that extended to the coast to the east and west forty miles or so beyond Beijing.

"The Zhoukoudian site is considered still a Beijing address," Akio said, and tapped a finger on the map, "but it is about thirty-five kilometers southwest of city central in a rural area in the foothills, just outside the suburb town of Fangshan, north of S320." The Taiwanese Special Forces operator turned to Wu and shot him a grin. "Thirty-five kilometers is about twenty-two *imperial* miles for you, in case you were wondering."

"How many fingers am I holding up in metric?" Wu asked, laughing as he flipped Akio the bird.

"We're looking at a forty-five-minute drive, realistically," Charlie said.

"Okay," Clark said, studying the route on the map, which was mostly highway until the smaller road that led to the site from S320. "So, we get to the site without a tail . . ."

"Theoretically," Bauer added.

"Theoretically," Clark conceded. "We meet up with the Spider and Qin who, *theoretically*, also get there undetected. And then what?"

"That's the part you're gonna love, mate," Wu said, clapping Hyori on the back, who stood beside him. "Because then we get a nice long haul to a mission impossible exfil."

"Okaaaay," Clark said, drawing it out and turning to Charlie.

"The exfil plan," Charlie began, "and there is a concerning lack of bloody detail here, by the way, is to then get the team all the way back to the coast, south of Beijing here"—she leaned over and tapped her finger on the map—"in Tianjin. This is where it gets pretty vague. All we know is we are scheduled for a maritime exfil from the port in Tianjin that night."

"So, they want a multinational group of eight officially unrelated people who don't know each other to travel . . . how far?" Bauer asked.

"About eighty kilometers as the crow flies," Akio said. "Farther, obviously, since we're not flying."

"Right," Bauer continued. "Eighty kilometers in a highly suspicious group that now includes two new people, who happen to be the most wanted people in China."

"What could possibly go wrong?" Wu asked.

Clark studied the map again and felt Bauer's concern. It did seem like mission impossible.

"And we don't know where in the Tianjin port we go or what this maritime asset is?"

"Not yet," Charlie said. "More information to follow."

"Keeping it compartmentalized for obvious reasons," Akio offered. "Until the last minute."

"Safe bet they're not sending a bloody destroyer into Bohai Bay," Wu said.

"And no submarine is coming into the Bohai," Charlie added. "Far too shallow."

"I think I can shed light on the plan," Hyori said, speaking for the first time.

Clark's joined the other four pair of eyes in turning to stare at the South Korean soldier.

"Okay," he said, prompting Hyori to continue.

"The NIS in my country," Hyori began, referring to the most recent name for the Korean version of the CIA, "has intelligence-gathering assets in and around China. Like everyone else, we suffered a brutal loss of assets in the purge. One asset we have exploited with great success the last few years, however, are civilian merchant vessels that transport goods in and out of Tianjin on a regular schedule. We have agents embedded in the crews who mostly collect signals intelligence, though on occasion they assist in moving assets—both people and material—in and out of China. There are three to four round trips per week. A vessel owned by East Star Shipping has a scheduled departure tomorrow."

"How do you know this?" Bauer asked, and looked happy for the first time since Clark had arrived.

"I have used this route myself once. I was bringing something into the country as it was, but I exfiltrated on the same ship. The *Capella*, if memory serves."

Clark nodded, feeling marginally reassured. If the *Capella* had an active and successful track record of conducting regular smuggling operations for the Korean National Intelligence Service, then that meant the vessel was probably not on the Ministry of State Security's watch list. Getting the team out of Beijing and slipping the MSS dragnet was another matter altogether. Traveling as a large group was too risky. Clark felt like he had no choice but to split the team up and he explained this to the group.

"I will proceed to Tianjin, first, alone, and in the morning to board the vessel, meet with the captain, and obtain clearances for port entry for everyone else," Hyori said.

"Good," Clark said.

"I agree with splitting up. Bauer and I are working in the same building," Wu said. "We can meet up for a business dinner, two Western guys, then proceed to Tianjin tomorrow night."

"What about me and Akio?" Charlie said.

"Akio should travel ahead and scout the Peking Man site," Clark said. "Charlie, you and I will travel together, posing as a couple. We'll pretend to meet and hit it off at Club Pink, which is a fifteen-minute walk from here off Jiuzong Lu Road. We'll book a hotel room and spend the morning together sightseeing to look like we're together before we drive to the Peking Man."

"Who would have guessed my NOC has a thing for old dudes," Charlie joked, getting a laugh from Wu.

"Keep in mind, we can't risk coming back to the safe house once we all split up."

Clark leaned over the table, palms down, studying the map.

"We have a very short time to come up with contingencies if things go wrong and a system for comms," he said as the rest of the team crowded around him. "I've done enough talking, let me hear your ideas . . ."

41

Qin woke with a start, disoriented and in pitch black.

It took the former defense minister a full ten seconds to remember where he was.

The onion cellar, he realized with a weary sigh.

Part of the reason for his confusion was that he'd not realized that he'd drifted off. He'd fully intended on staying awake until Léi returned, but staying awake and alert in the deep dark was a challenge. The mind reacts poorly to sensory deprivation and spending twenty-three and a half hours a day in an onion cellar with no windows or overhead lighting certainly qualified, if one excluded the sense of smell. For the first time in his life, Qin was struggling with depression. During his waking hours, he felt a listless apathy and hollow hopelessness. The belief that he would see his wife and daughters ever again was a candle flickering at the end of its wick.

At least he had Léi.

A grudging respect and admiration for the woman had grown in him with each passing day. In this short time, he'd become bonded to her.

Dependent is more like it.

To acknowledge as much chafed his ego, but as his father would always say, truth was truth.

He raised his wrist to check the time on his smartwatch, and the action of lifting his arm released a waft of body odor. He'd not bathed since they'd gone underground, and now his own stench competed with the fetor of the onion cellar. He couldn't imagine how terrible he must smell.

On rotating his wrist, the watch face illuminated, revealing 0223, nearly the time Léi had estimated she'd return. This was her second outing in as many nights to check dead-drop locations. She'd left coded messages at three spots in Beijing twenty-four hours ago and checked to see if the Americans had recovered them and left coded instructions in return.

She should be back any time now.

His bladder wasn't complaining yet, but he could tell he wasn't likely to make it to morning without relieving himself. Over the past several days, he and Léi had agreed that nighttime bathroom breaks were acceptable so long as they didn't turn on any lights in the restaurant.

I might as well go now, before she returns, he decided, and threw off the blanket covering his legs and torso.

He rolled over, grabbed his personal flashlight, and clicked it on. Next, he dragged three crates of onions aside so he'd have a space to crawl through their wall of provisions. He left the flashlight on the floor to provide enough illumination for his trip out and back. They'd agreed not to use flashlight beams upstairs on bathroom trips.

He crawled through the gap and made his way to the half flight of stairs that led up to the access hatch in the floor. He avoided knocking his head on the low rafters, having done it enough times to cement the lesson. On hands and knees, he ascended the steps to the top, where he cautiously pushed up on the trapdoor with his right hand while steadying himself with his left. The hinges creaked as he raised it, but the noise was not loud enough to be heard outside the kitchen. Careful not to let the door slam open, he climbed out of the cellar, maintaining positive control of it the entire time, before easing it back flush with the floorboards.

Standing in the kitchen, the pleasant olfactory ghost of all the meals the cooks had prepared for the previous night's guests flooded Qin's nostrils. He inhaled deeply, welcoming the change from the stench he'd been immersed in the entire day. The mélange stimulated a powerful urge to rummage through the restaurant refrigerators for leftovers he might snack on.

Why not, he thought, and padded over to one of the commercial chillers and opened the wide steel door.

Unfortunately, he discovered that restaurants do not save "leftovers" in the same manner as people do in their homes. The chiller had dozens of plastic containers, but they all appeared to contain sauces and raw ingredients ready to use for tomorrow's meal preparation. Frowning, he rummaged through the fridge anyway. He was desperately craving meat, but all of the chicken, beef, and pork he came across was uncooked. When he found a liter-sized container labeled SOY-GINGER-GARLIC MARINADE, he pulled it out, pried off the plastic lid, and drank from it like a cup.

"So good," he murmured, savoring the rich, salty tang while wishing he had grilled chicken to go with it.

He put the lid back on, returned it to the fridge, and found a bottle of chilled plum wine. He unscrewed the cap and took several long pulls of the sweet alcohol. Within seconds he felt the calming effect as his brain anticipated the dopamine hit to come. Feeling his spirits beginning to lift, he took another long swallow, wiped his mouth on the back of his sleeve, and returned the bottle to the fridge. Then he padded toward the bathroom in the dark.

The restaurant had two bathrooms, one for the public and one for the staff. The public one, ironically, was much cleaner than the one for the staff, and so he chose the former. Although he was alone, he closed the door. At Léi's request, Jia had purchased a night-light, which she dutifully plugged in by the sink after hours. He walked up to the toilet, unzipped his trousers, and relieved himself. After finishing, he was about to flush the toilet when he heard a noise outside the bathroom.

Qin stood perfectly still and listened.

He heard footsteps and reflexively smiled.

Léi was back.

Thank God.

With a smile on his face, he reached for a second time to flush the toilet, only to stop himself yet again. Something about the footsteps didn't feel right. There seemed an *uncertainty* in the cadence—as if the person walking through the restaurant was unfamiliar with the space. A tentative exploration . . .

Confirmation came a moment later when he saw the fleeting glow of a flashlight beam under the gap of the bathroom door as someone turned the beam down the hallway. Fear blossomed in his chest. He had no weapons. Panicked, he scanned the bathroom looking for something, anything, he could use to defend himself.

Damn it, he cursed silently to himself.

Then his eyes settled on the glazed white lid that covered the toilet tank. Careful not to make a sound, he lifted the thick slab of porcelain that had to weigh close to five kilos. It wasn't anybody's weapon of choice, but a properly directed blow to the head with such mass would be every bit as damaging as a club. He silently stepped into position against the wall beside the door frame and raised the porcelain slab, ready to swing. Whoever was surveilling the Purple Lotus would eventually check the restroom.

I'll get one swing . . . I have to make it count.

He felt his knees begin to tremble and he hated himself for it. How could he, the defense minister of the largest army on earth, tremble in the face of danger like this?

Former defense minister, a voice in his head reminded him.

He watched the gap at the bottom of the door and listened, but the light disappeared, and instead of the footsteps coming closer, they seemed to be moving away.

Then nothing . . .

A heartbeat later he heard the familiar creak of the hinges of the cellar access door.

Oh shit, I left my flashlight on!

On this realization, the soldier in Qin finally woke up. He silently opened the bathroom door and glided out into the hall. He moved with swift and deliberate purpose, and it felt as if some external power seized control of his body as he rounded the corner in a crouch and vectored toward the cellar access. The floorboards creaked and groaned underfoot, betraying him and spoiling his approach. A shadowy torso, dimly backlit from below, turned from where it was descending the cellar stairs. The figure raised a pistol, but it was too late; Qin was already swinging.

The heavy porcelain lid connected with the side of the intruder's head and Qin heard the man's skull crack. The agent crumpled instantly, dropping the pistol and tumbling lifelessly down the stairs into the onion cellar. Qin set down the toilet tank lid, picked up the pistol, and quickly sighted on the unmoving body at the bottom of the stairs. His pulse pounded hard and loud in his ears, and he fought the urge to put insurance rounds into what had to be an MSS agent. He held fast, watching for any signs of movement or life in the body.

Nothing.

His own breath came in heavy and fast huffs.

I'm on the verge of hyperventilation.

This was the first man he'd killed. Yes, Qin was a career soldier, but he'd never been in combat. He'd commanded ships, but never murdered.

A sound behind him caused him to whirl. He scanned for movement and someone hiding among the shadows, but he saw nothing. He leveled his weapon at the back door, which led to the alley behind the restaurant. He put tension on the trigger, adjusted his aim to torso height, ready to unload his magazine into who or whatever came crashing through that door. But instead of a breach, he heard a key turning in the lock.

Léi has a key . . .

He eased his finger off the trigger, but kept the pistol leveled at the door. A moment, later the door opened and the Night Spider stepped inside. Her face indexed through a series of microexpressions as she rapidly assessed the situation—shock, recognition, then fear.

"What's happened?" she whispered, rushing to him.

He swiveled back to check on the man he'd bludgeoned, but the body lay exactly how and where it had before he'd become distracted by Léi's arrival. "*That* happened," he said, gesturing at the body with the pistol.

"You killed him?" she said, her tone clinical, as if seeking confirmation rather than condemning him.

"I think so, but I haven't checked for a pulse. It just happened."

"They usually work in pairs," she said, taking a knee and motioning for him to do the same. "If one is here, the other is somewhere nearby. Maybe waiting in a car. Maybe checking a different shop."

"What do we do?" he said.

"We flee."

He met her eyes. "What about the body?"

She hesitated a long beat, and when she finally answered, he heard pain in her voice. "We leave it."

"But what about Jia?"

"What else can we do? We can't take it with us. Even if we drag it to the alley, it will be discovered."

"We must at least give her a chance to dispose of the body."

He handed Léi the pistol, descended the stairs, and muscled the lifeless body into their hiding place. Then he pocketed his flashlight and moved the onion crates back into place.

"Thank you," she said after he emerged from the cellar.

He nodded and quietly lowered the trapdoor. "Did the Americans get your note? Did they leave instructions?"

"Yes. They gave a code for a location that only I would know."

"Are you sure you can trust whoever put it there?'

A funny smile curled her lips. "Only one other person in the world would know this signal, and he just so happens to be the American I trust the most."

"Okay," Qin said, buoyed by hope for the first time since he'd decided to betray his country. "Let's move before the partner realizes what has happened."

"They left one other bit of news, Hâiyû," she said, and she smiled at him, her hand touching his arm. He was pretty sure she'd never used his given name before, and he looked at her expectantly. "It's your wife and daughters—the Americans rescued them from the Maldives and they are safe."

"Thank you," was all he could manage as tears of relief filled his eyes. Then Qin straightened up, standing tall, a new energy and purpose flooding through him.

Let's hope the American plan for getting us out of China works as well as their Maldives operation.

"We need to go," the Spider said.

He followed her through the dark kitchen back to the rear door, but now buoyed with something special and powerful.

Hope.

42

Ryan listened as Mary Pat updated him on the Qin defection status. Dead drops had been made by Clark, and satellite imagery had clocked a woman checking several of the locations in the middle of the night. Plenty of question marks remained about whether Clark's team and the Spider and Qin would be able to make it to the meet location undetected, but at least communication had been established.

"That's certainly a positive development," he said, crossing his legs and swiveling to a forty-five-degree angle in his chair behind the Resolute desk. "Any updates regarding Sea Serpent and Taiwan?"

"Well, interesting that you ask. The Task Force 25 lead has a compelling theory on a possible false flag that Li will use to launch the invasion."

Ryan couldn't help but feel a personal tug of pride. He knew damn well just who Mary Pat referred to.

"A different false flag from accusing us of assassinating Defense Minister Qin?" he asked, quite interested now.

"Yes," Mary Pat said, "and even more compelling, as it would be almost impossible for us to refute. The photographs they could circulate would drive the narrative . . ."

He listened intently as the DNI outlined Katie's theory that China would insert a covert operations team into Penghu and fire an anti-ship missile at the PLAN fleet. If true, it was brilliant work on Katie's part. An attack on the Chinese Navy would certainly lessen the world condemnation, in fact it might have the opposite effect and rally support for Chinese defense—especially for world leaders looking for an excuse to let Li off the hook for a reunification invasion. Sanctioning China was a double-edged sword, and for most countries punishing the manufacturing giant economically would be a self-inflicted wound on their own economy they'd rather not suffer.

"I need your no-bullshit assessment here, Mary Pat. Do you really think President Li would attack his own ship, possibly kill his own sailors, just to justify an invasion of Taiwan?" he asked.

Mary Pat did something she almost never did—she shrugged. "I don't know, Jack. What matters right now is if *you* think he would."

Ryan let out a long, slow sigh. Did he believe Li was capable of such a thing?

Yes, I do.

Li had become increasingly paranoid and detached from his inner circle and Party leadership, as evidenced by the frequency with which cabinet members were disappearing, and that cold detachment would certainly extend to his military. Ryan was of the opinion that Li had linked his legacy to accomplishing this singular goal; reunification is what Li wanted to be remembered for.

"I do," he said. "And remember, Li doesn't have to actually kill his own sailors or lose a ship. He could fire at his own fleet and bank that the target ship's defensive systems and countermeasures defeat the threat. The Renhai-class cruisers are highly capable and would likely defeat an incoming barrage of Taiwanese anti-ship missiles."

"Especially if they knew they were coming," Mary Pat agreed.

"Probably even if they didn't," Ryan said.

Between China's willingness and aptitude for stealing American defense technology and their lack of budgetary restraints, the Chinese fleet was increasingly mirroring the capabilities of the U.S. Navy. The 055 would almost certainly defeat incoming missiles with or without warning.

Still, what an insane risk, but one Ryan felt sure Li would consider acceptable.

And Katie had proven her instincts more than once already. If she felt strongly enough that this was a possible threat to send it up the chain to where it reached Mary Pat's desk, then he sure as hell best take it seriously.

"What assets do we have on Penghu?" he asked, the thought of his daughter at the center of a Chinese invasion terrifying indeed.

"Task Force 25, of course, with our detachment from Naval Special Warfare Group Eight accompanying them. A platoon from DEVGRU is just arriving, augmenting the SEAL Team Five contingent already scheduled to conduct training with Taiwan's 101st Sea Dragons. The admiral's aide from Task Force 70 is still on the island with a few Navy support personnel."

Ryan paced away from her. If Katie was right, then they would need their operators in the thick of this, augmenting the ROC's version of the SEALs. But they didn't need noncombatant support personnel in the middle of the fight.

"We need to get our noncombatants off Penghu, in case Commander Ryan is right," he said, turning back to Mary Pat. "The operators will be more effective if they don't have to worry about the safety of their support personnel."

"I agree with that," she replied. "The question is whether to secure them on the mainland of Taiwan or not. If this thing goes sideways, they'll be in the middle of coordinated missile and air attacks on any ROC military installations."

"I don't intend to let that happen, Mary Pat," he said. "But just in case, we'll evacuate them to the fleet and have them set up shop with Task Force 70." He glanced at his watch. "We better head to the NSC brief. We'll find out where the *Reagan* is, and if she's still too far out, we'll fly them to the nearest Navy asset. Then we'll get the details of the Task Force 25 analysis and position our Group Eight and DEVGRU assets where they can assist in countering any move by China's Special Forces."

Mary Pat rose from her chair and led him to the door.

Ryan clenched his teeth, following behind his DNI. They were running out of time in a game that, at present, Li held most of the cards in. But it would be a mistake for the Chinese president to underestimate American resolve. Side by side now, he and Mary Pat left the Oval Office suite and headed for the Situation Room.

It was going to be a very long afternoon indeed.

43

CIC
USS *JASON DUNHAM* (DDG 109)
ONE HUNDRED NAUTICAL MILES SOUTHEAST OF THE
  PENGHU ISLAND
ENTERING THE TAIWAN STRAIT
0911 LOCAL TIME

Horrillo stared at the diamond-shaped icon, designated Track 82724, glowing on the port large-screen display at the front of Combat.

With only a glance, he was able to glean a tremendous amount of information about the contact. That was the beauty of the Aegis system and contact management interface—it used color, shape, and lines to communicate the type of contact and threat level. In the case of Track 82724, the yellow color indicated *unknown* status, the diamond shape meant that the track was a *surface* contact, and the dotted-line perimeter of the shape defined it as a *suspected hostile*.

Horrillo and the team in Combat had been monitoring 82724 for nearly an hour. During that period, the track had been shadowing the *Dunham* outside visual range with suspicious postur-

338

ing. The surface contact—which Horrillo and everyone else standing watch in CIC were 95 percent confident was a Chinese warship—was operating with a minimal electronic signature.

Also, noteworthy, it was transiting with AIS secured.

AIS, or automatic identification system, was a maritime navigation protocol that used a shipboard transceiver to broadcast the ship's ID, GPS position, as well as its course and speed. All data was formatted and broadcasted in accordance with a global standard. The purpose of the system was to supplement maritime radar and traffic monitoring by deconflicting contacts in environments with high traffic. In other words, if all ships used AIS, then everyone would know who was out there, where they were located, and where they were going at all times to avoid collision. AIS contacts were automatically populated in a ship's electronic chart display and information system (ECDIS), thereby taking the ambiguity out of contact management.

Track 82724, however, was being ambiguous on purpose.

You don't want to identify yourself, do you? Horrillo thought with a narrowed stare at the diamond icon. *At least not yet . . .*

Securing AIS was not illegal. The *Dunham* did it all the time under conditions where OPSEC deemed it prudent not to broadcast to the world that they were a U.S. warship. An hour ago, the CO, XO, command master chief, and Horrillo had had a debate about whether the *Dunham* should broadcast or secure AIS for their blockade-busting trip through the Strait of Taiwan.

There were pros and cons to both options.

On the one hand, leaving AIS turned on was a show of confidence and strength. President Ryan had personally ordered the *Dunham* to bust the blockade to make an overt statement that the U.S. Navy did not recognize the legitimacy of the blockade. The intent was not for the *Dunham* to slip through the strait under the cover of darkness undetected, but to demonstrate that they did not recognize China's authority to deny them passage.

As the skipper had said, "This ain't supposed to be the midnight ride of Paul Revere."

On the other hand, the XO had made a valid counterpoint: "Turning off AIS doesn't mean they won't see us. We're not a submarine, gentlemen. We're playing in their backyard swimming pool; it's not like they won't notice us. The only thing AIS does is validate their firing solution for them. It's like wearing a ball cap with a forehead patch that says 'Shoot me here.'"

Ultimately, the CO had made the decision to go big or go home and left AIS in broadcast mode. Horrillo still wasn't sure how he felt about that decision.

"Combat, Bridge," the OOD said over Net 15, "crossing inside five nautical miles from the blockade line."

"Bridge, Combat, aye," Horrillo said.

The OOD would give two more similar updates—one at one nautical mile out, and another when crossing the invisible blockade line. When the Chinese defense minister had published the blockade coordinates, he had done so with aggressive rhetoric that any U.S. warship violating the blockade would be considered hostile and treated accordingly.

Horrillo did some quick mental math and with a tight grin thought, *In the next twenty minutes, we're about to find out if they meant it.*

Yesterday the *Dunham* had conducted an UNREP with their Australian oiler escort so they'd have enough gas to transit the strait and join up with TF 70. The Australians had then bugged out and headed south, apparently not so keen on offering up one of their replenishment ships for target practice.

Horrillo got it. He'd have done the same thing in the Aussie skipper's shoes.

"Captain in Combat," the radar system controller announced from his workstation at the port rear corner of Combat.

"Captain, crossing inside five nautical miles from the Chinese blockade line," Horrillo said, turning to face Commander Kreutz, who'd just entered CIC and was dressed in his sea-blue coveralls.

"Roger that . . . Still no ES from this guy?" the captain asked, referring to the contact's electronic signature, which was defined by the number and type of radar and radio emissions.

"No, sir, he's still running stealthy with AIS secured."

The captain nodded, then after a beat said, "TAO, confirm readiness condition."

"Readiness Condition Two Surface is set throughout the ship," Horrillo replied.

On U.S. Navy combatants, Condition One was known as general quarters, or "manning battle stations," and was the highest level of readiness for the ship's crew and systems. During Condition One, the normal four-section, three-hour watch rotation was suspended. Meals and sleeping were suspended. For short durations, general quarters enhanced the *Dunham*'s ability to navigate, defend herself, respond to potential casualties, and conduct combat operations. But maintaining Condition One for a prolonged period eventually had a deleterious impact on the readiness.

Human beings, it turns out, have biological limitations.

They get tired.

They get hungry.

They have to go to the bathroom . . .

No matter how well-trained and disciplined the crew, Condition

One readiness was not sustainable indefinitely. At the *Dunham's* preferred cruising speed of sixteen knots, it would take over fifteen hours to transit the Taiwan Strait and cross the two-hundred-fifty-nautical-mile area encompassed by the Chinese blockade. For this reason, the *Dunham's* CO, XO, and CMC had decided the most prudent decision was to go with a modified readiness posture called Condition Two Surface. This meant manning a portion of the Condition One watches, specifically those necessary to best manage surface threats and promote safe navigation.

As the ship's battle stations TAO, Horrillo would be on watch for the initial ingress past the blockade line and the first several hours of transit in the contested waters. After that, he would be relieved by the ship's weapons officer, rotating on and off in three-hour blocks. Even when he wasn't on watch, he planned to plant himself in Combat anyway . . . except for those times when his own biological needs demanded otherwise.

"TAO, Track 724 has increased speed to twenty-nine knots and changed course to intercept our track. Projected CPA is now inside five hundred yards," the surface warfare coordinator announced from the starboard side of Combat, fresh concern in his voice.

"Surface, TAO, aye," he said, and felt the invisible tension level in Combat jump up a couple of notches.

Horrillo was just about to order the EOSS operator to slew the MK20 Electro-Optic Sighting System to Track 82724 when the watch stander did it on his own. The image on the aux display to Horrillo's left shifted, blurred, and refocused on the horizon where the ship was located, but showed nothing but water. Horrillo checked the range and saw that 82724 still sat outside twelve nautical miles. Even though the EOSS was mounted high and above the bridge, the unidentified contact remained over the horizon, making it impossible to see it.

"A few more minutes and we'll get our first look at our Chinese friend," the captain said.

"Yes, sir," Horrillo said. "Based on Track 724's sonar signature, operating posture, and intercept course, I intend to change track designation from Suspect to Hostile."

Kreutz grinned and let out a little snort at that. "You getting nervous, TAO?"

"Maybe a little, sir."

"Very well."

"Surface, update Track 82724 from Suspect to Hostile," he announced.

"Update Track 82724 from Suspect to Hostile, aye," the SWC said.

A microsecond later, the yellow diamond icon changed colors to red and the dotted line turned solid on all the screens in Combat displaying track data.

"Is XO on the bridge?" the captain asked.

"Yes, sir."

"Good." Kreutz exhaled slowly, then picked up the corded handset mic for the ship's 1MC to address the crew:

"Good morning, *Jason Dunham*, this is the captain. As previously briefed, we have orders to transit the Strait of Taiwan as we head north to meet up with Task Force 70 in the East China Sea. Normally, passage through the strait would be a tense but non-threatening evolution. However, the Chinese have instituted a maritime blockade of the strait. This action is illegal in peacetime and is not recognized by our government. The President of the United States has tasked us to bust the Chinese blockade. We are not at war with the People's Republic of China, but tensions are elevated. There's a chance this thing could get hairy, so I need everyone to be alert and professional. If we all do our jobs and keep our heads, I have every confidence we'll complete our mission without incident and show the world that the U.S. Navy will not let the Chinese rewrite the Freedom of the Seas doctrine on our watch. That is all. Carry on."

"Hooyah," somebody said, and Horrillo thought it was Kip Carron, the missile systems supervisor.

Horrillo turned back to the aux display streaming the EOSS feed. The very top of a mast was now visible above the waves as Track 82724 broke the horizon. He was about to tell the operator to zoom, but as usual, Petty Officer Lynde, who sat at the ROS stack, seemed to read his mind and the image zoomed before he could ask. Horrillo stared at the image—a familiar and distinctive-shaped gray mast.

"Mast configuration on Track 82724 matches the design of the PLA Navy Type 055 Renhai-class guided-missile destroyer," the identification supervisor (IDS) announced. "Recommend updating track classification."

"Very well," Horrillo said, and turned to the captain. "Looks like we have our answer."

"No surprise there. I want to get the hull number so we can hail them by name if necessary."

"Yes, sir."

The Type 055 Renhai-class DDG was longer, heavier, and had more VLS cells than the Arleigh Burke, 112 to *Dunham*'s 96. The Type 055 was also rumored to have longer range, higher top speed, and an electronic-beam-steering radar system that rivaled—if not eclipsed—the SPY-1D. Horrillo and his fellow officers in the wardroom had discussed their adversarial doppelgänger in numerous blood-boiling conversations. The sleek Type 055 was impressive to look at, and its design was undeniably derived from the Arleigh Burke. It was no secret in the surface warfare community that the Chinese pilfered all of the U.S. Navy's best ideas and designs. They were relentless and shameless about it, too. Just in the past year alone, Horrillo had seen news articles about three different U.S. sailors, from three different commands, being arrested for selling secrets to the Chinese. It was bad enough that China's defense industrial complex was pumping out Type 055s like hotcakes—they'd commissioned six in the class in 2022 alone—but the fact that his fellow shipmates were selling out America to help them do it really pissed Horrillo off. For years, the talk in the Navy had been about how the Chinese Navy was closing the gap. Well, looking at the sleek, stealthy Type 055 as it rapidly came into focus on the aux display made Horrillo realize that "the gap" had been closed.

Or worse, maybe they've surpassed us, and the gap is widening in the wrong direction.

"Captain, I intended to secure AIS, place CIWS in Air Auto Hold Fire On, and cover Track 82724 with birds."

"Place CIWS in AAW Auto Hold Fire On, cover Track 82724 with birds, but do *not* secure AIS," Kreutz said. "I do not want to signal an overt change in our posture."

"Aye, sir," Horrillo said, then announced the orders.

Both watch standers acknowledged the orders, then reported the configuration changes. The first order shifted the *Dunham's* Phalanx close-in weapons system to a mode where the mount could move and track potential targets with the safety on. The second command directed the surface warfare coordinator to use the ship's Aegis Combat System to track the Chinese destroyer and ready a firing solution in the event the *Dunham* needed to defend herself. "Birds," which was surface warfare speak for *missiles*, referred to the collective arsenal of missile variants loaded into the *Dunham*'s Mark 41 VLS cells.

Horrillo's go-to missile for this situation was the U.S. Navy's Swiss Army Knife standard missile known as the SM-6—which was capable of targeting surface combatants, aircraft, and even enemy missiles.

"TAO—Track 82724 has been positively ID'd as the *Nanchang*, pennant number 101," the IDS announced.

Horrillo shifted his gaze to the aux display streaming the magnified video feed from EOSS and, sure enough, he could make out a white *101* stenciled on the *Nanchang*'s port bow. The sleek Chinese destroyer was at flank speed and closing fast. In just the last few minutes, they'd gone from only being able to see the top of the main mast to now seeing the entire vessel. The maritime rules of the road determining which vessels are "stand-on" and which vessels are to "give way" were based on vectors and angles. Presently, the *Dunham* was heading north with the *Nanchang* off its port bow; the *Nanchang* was heading east-northeast.

According to the rules of the road, the *Dunham* in this situation was the stand-on vessel, which meant the *Nanchang* was required to give way. However, from what Horrillo was seeing, it looked pretty obvious that the *Nanchang* was in a race to cut off the *Dunham*, with the strategy of trying to physically block their path and prevent entry into the Strait of Taiwan.

"Combat, Bridge—we're being hailed on the bridge-to-bridge by the *Nanchang*," the OOD reported on Net 15. "Do you want me to respond?"

Horrillo looked at the CO for direction.

"Bridge, this is the captain," Kreutz said. "I'll take the call from Combat."

"Captain, Bridge, aye."

"Radio, put the bridge-to-bridge on speaker," the CO announced.

"Aye, sir," the radio supervisor responded, and a voice speaking Chinese-accented English filled Combat.

"U.S. Navy warship, U.S. Navy warship—this is PLA Navy destroyer *Nanchang*," the voice said. "Reverse course and proceed south. Entry is not permitted into Chinese territorial water. Reverse course now."

Kreutz looked at Horrillo and fixed him with a tight grin. "Here we go, TAO."

"Captain, be advised CPA with the *Nanchang* is now calculated at two hundred and fifty yards," Horrillo said, looking at the fire-control system for Track 82724. "They're on an intercept course, sir."

"They're trying to intimidate us," Kreutz said, picking up a radio handset and keying the mic. "*Nanchang*, this is United States Warship One-Zero-Nine, conducting transit on the high seas in accordance with international law. Request you alter your course immediately and maintain a safe distance from my vessel."

A minute passed.

"United States Warship One-Zero-Nine," came the *Nanchang*'s reply, "Permission denied to enter Chinese territorial water. Repeat. Permission denied to enter Chinese territorial water. Reverse course immediately."

From the corner of his eye, Horrillo saw that the ship's CMC, Master Chief Brunner, had entered Combat. "Reverse course my ass," he grumbled. "The strait is international water."

The CO glanced at the CMC and the two men exchanged knowing smiles.

He's enjoying himself, Horrillo thought, having seen that smile enough times during wardroom poker nights to know it well.

"*Nanchang*, this is Commander Kreutz, commanding officer of the USS *Jason Dunham*. I would like to speak to your captain . . ."

Horrillo glanced at the fire-control system. CPA was now calculated at ninety yards in eleven minutes, twenty-five seconds. The damn Chinese boat was on a collision course and the distance was closing fast.

A long pause ensued and the chatter in Combat dropped to barely audible levels as everyone waited for the Chinese destroyer to respond. Finally, an answer came.

"USS *Dunham*, this is Captain Shen," a new voice said over the loudspeaker. "You talk now. I listen."

Unlike the previous radio talker from the *Nanchang*, Captain Shen's accent was thicker and his English less fluid.

"Captain Shen, we intend to transit the Strait of Taiwan in accordance with International Freedom of Navigation standards codified in Article 87 of the 1982 United Nations Convention on the Law of the Sea. We shall remain, at all times, outside the internationally recognized twelve-nautical-mile limit of territorial water from the People's Republic of China," Kreutz said, and Horrillo had the sense the skipper had prepared these words in advance because he spoke them with ease and a practiced cadence.

A long pause ensued . . .

Then the previous radio talker on the *Nanchang* answered. "Captain Kreutz, Freedom of Navigation does not apply to military vessels operating without permission to enter Chinese exclusion zones and territorial waters. Your proposed course violates the Law of the People's Republic of China on the Territorial Sea and the Contiguous Zone. The Taiwan Strait is an exclusion zone. Prior to entry, your vessel must submit a formal request seeking permission. No request was made and so permission is denied. Reverse course immediately."

At this response, Horrillo saw the CO's jaw go tight and his demeanor change. The smug reply from the *Nanchang* appeared to needle him. The skipper wasn't having fun anymore, and neither was anyone else in Combat, as the range to the hostile Chinese destroyer was plummeting by the second.

"Captain, Track 724 is on a collision course with own ship. Calculated CPA is ten yards in eight minutes," the tactical information coordinator announced.

"Very well, coordinator," Kreutz said, his voice a throaty growl.

"Captain, Bridge—I recommend reducing speed to open CPA outside five hundred yards. XO concurs," the OOD, Lieutenant Lewinsky said over Net 15.

Under normal circumstances, the OOD's job was to pilot the ship in the captain's stead. This meant that the officer of the deck was not required to get the captain's permission for every course and speed change necessary for navigation and safety purposes, nor was it desired for him or her to do so. This situation, however, was different. The *Dunham*'s mission was to be a blockade buster and that meant driving assertively into and through the Strait of Taiwan. Chinese intimidation and dangerous seamanship was something that Kreutz had briefed the officers and crew to expect. Because of the elevated tensions and likelihood of the Chinese using dangerous tactics, the OOD was taking the prudent action of checking with the CO.

"Officer of the deck, in accordance with the rules of the road, we are the stand-on vessel. Maintain course and speed," the CO said.

"Maintain course and speed, Bridge, aye."

"XO, pick up channel nine," the CO said, and grabbed a headset, which he tuned to the ordered channel.

"Tuning to channel nine," the XO came back.

Horrillo did not tune to the private channel, but he listened to the CO's side of the call.

"XO, listen up," the skipper said. "Yes, we are the stand-on vessel, but I have a strong feeling these guys don't give a shit about the rules of the road. Looks like we're playing a game of Chinese chicken. If these bastards don't back off or change course in the next five minutes, I want you to take the conn. Collision is not an option, XO, but neither is reversing course. Whatever football move you need to make with this ship to get around these assholes, I want you to do it . . ." the CO said.

As much as Horrillo loved imagining the *Dunham* executing a "football move," the reality was their warship displaced nearly ten thousand tons. The *Nanchang* tipped the scales at thirteen thousand tons. Both ships were the length of two football fields. Despite their massive shaft horsepower and incredible seaworthiness, destroyers were big ships. They did not turn on a dime. The reason that collisions at sea occurred at all was not because the vessels *didn't* turn; it was because they turned too late to overcome the momentum carrying them into each other's path. A collision between the *Dunham* and the *Nanchang* would end badly for both ships, no matter who was technically at fault.

After listening to the XO's reply, Kreutz ended the call, adjusted his headset so it was only covering his right ear, and let out a heavy sigh. He turned to Horrillo. "TAO, set Condition Zebra throughout the ship. Do not sound general quarters. Do not man battle stations."

Horrillo repeated back the order, then picked up the 1MC handset. "Set Condition Zebra throughout the ship."

Condition Zebra was the material readiness condition that provided the greatest degree of watertight integrity to the ship and the highest state of readiness for the ship's survivability in casualties such as fire or flooding. All watertight doors and hatches would be dogged shut and the engineering spaces would transition to the most reliable equipment lineups and secure from any maintenance activities.

Horrillo knew the CO had given the order because of the very real possibility of a collision with the *Nanchang*. He also understood why the skipper had explicitly ordered him *not* to take the ship to general quarters and man battle stations. Transitioning to Condition One would create a frenzy of activity and require turnover at numerous watch stations. To do so now was more risky and dangerous than leaving the crew in the Modified Condition Two stations already set, where they had good situational awareness and control.

"Navigator, Captain," Kreutz said, calling the bridge. "Take over bridge-to-bridge comms with the *Nanchang*. Remind them that we are the stand-on vessel and operating in accordance with international maritime law. No matter what they say, I want you to be a broken record and repeat the message."

"Captain, Nav, aye," the Nav came back.

The CO turned to Horrillo and shook his head.

"Tripwire! Track 82724 crossing inside two thousand yards. Zero bearing rate. Calculated CPA is ten yards," the tactical information coordinator announced.

Horrillo glanced at the aux display streaming live video of the *Nanchang* from EOSS. The fast-moving destroyer was slicing through the choppy waves and dragging a massive white, frothy wake behind it as it barreled toward them. The *Dunham*'s navigator and the *Nanchang*'s radio talker were trading increasingly hard-toned demands that the other vessel alter course and speed.

But despite their insistence and bluster, neither vessel did.

A bead of cold sweat trickled from Horrillo's right armpit and rolled over his ribs as he remembered an eerily similar incident from 2018. A buddy of his had been a JO on the USS *Decatur* (DDG 73) at the time. Just like the *Dunham*, the *Decatur* had orders to conduct a Freedom of Navigation Op in the South China Sea near the Spratly Islands, when the Chinese destroyer *Lanzhou* intercepted and nearly collided with the Flight II Arleigh Burke. The two warships had a CPA of forty-five yards and the *Decatur* was forced to maneuver to avoid a collision.

Was history repeating itself?

A minute passed and Combat was as tense and quiet as Horrillo had ever seen it.

He looked over at the captain.

Kreutz's jaw was set and his fingers were gripping the back of the chair at the captain's workstation in the middle of CIC. How hard and how far was the skipper willing to push the captain of the *Nanchang*? That was the question on Horrillo's mind as the distance between the warships continued to shrink.

"Tripwire! Track 82724 crossing inside one thousand yards. Zero bearing rate. Calculated CPA is five yards," the tactical information coordinator announced.

At five hundred yards, the XO—who the CO had ordered to assume the conn—took action.

Horrillo felt the ship shudder as the XO ordered a backing bell to slow the ship. Horrillo watched the CPA displayed for Track 82724 open to outside a hundred yards. Then, to his dismay, the number began to fall back toward zero as the *Nanchang* adjusted course to maintain a collision vector.

"What the hell are they doing? They really are trying to hit us!" the CMC said.

Even though the *Dunham* was the stand-on vessel, it was obvious the Chinese weren't going to yield.

Suddenly, the ship rolled hard to port as the XO ordered a right full rudder.

Looks like she's performing her "football move," Horrillo thought.

Turning right was the safer option and in accordance with the rules of the road, but it put the Chinese warship behind them. A left turn would have potentially allowed the *Dunham* to "juke" behind the *Nanchang*, but it also would set them up for a head-on collision if the Chinese captain decided to turn at the last second.

Horrillo saw that the XO had now ordered the port shaft to ahead full, while maintaining a backing bell on the starboard shaft. This push-pull configuration created a fulcrum effect, shortening the turning radius and tightening the arc of the turn. He watched the rate of change of the ship's heading increase as the five-hundred-foot-long *Dunham* executed a buttonhook maneuver toward the south. To his surprise, the XO steadied on a heading of 200, letting the *Nanchang* draw east, but after a mere thirty seconds on the southerly course, she ordered a right full rudder.

There's the head fake.

The *Dunham* rolled hard as the bow swung west. He watched the bearing rate skyrocket as the Chinese destroyer—now located a mere eighty yards to the north—zoomed past the *Dunham* in a close aboard starboard-to-starboard passing.

"Way to go, XO," somebody shouted.

The *Dunham* kept turning and swept *behind* the Chinese warship. On crossing the *Nanchang*'s stern, the XO ordered a flank bell on both port and starboard engines. The ship shuddered and thrummed as it accelerated and hammered through the *Nanchang*'s wake. Finally, the list came off the ship as the helm eased them out of the hard turn onto a northerly heading of 350.

Horrillo caught the CO's eye and smiled. "Now, that's a football move if I've ever seen one, sir."

The skipper grinned back at him. "Helluva head fake. I bet that's going to piss them off."

"Captain, Bridge," the XO's voice said over the loudspeaker. "Collision avoided, DDG 109 is on track to bust the blockade in twelve hundred yards."

"Nice driving, XO," Kreutz said. "Let's keep the flank bell on. They can't run into us if they can't catch us."

Horrillo could practically hear the smile on the XO's voice when she answered, "Captain, Bridge, aye."

Horrillo shifted his gaze to the port LSD, where the red diamond for Track 82724 was looping around to pursue the *Dunham* from behind. The XO's maneuver had created much needed separation between own ship and the *Nanchang*. The range between them was now eleven hundred yards and opening, but the Chinese destroyer's speed was increasing as they maneuvered to give chase.

Looks like we're about to find out who's faster—the Type 055 or the Arleigh Burke.

The mood in Combat had shifted from pucker-induced anxiety to something bordering on jubilation. They'd been given orders to bust the blockade and they were four hundred yards from doing it. He looked at the icon for own ship advancing toward the dotted line on the display that represented the Chinese maritime exclusion zone, aka the blockade line. His gaze ticked to the window showing the calculated range to crossing and watched the number fall:

Three hundred yards . . .

Two hundred yards . . .

One hundred yards . . .

"Attention in Combat. Crossing the Chinese Maritime Exclusion Zone boundary and entering the Strait of Taiwan," the tactical information coordinator announced.

Someone whooped and others clapped.

Horrillo took a deep breath, then let out a long, slow exhale. They'd done it. Mission accomplished. But no sooner had the thought crossed his mind, then from the corner of his eye something on the aux display caught his attention. A blast of white smoke and fire from the forecastle of the *Nanchang* as it launched a missile from its forward VLS cells.

Oh, shit . . .

An alarm sounded.

And the air warfare coordinator shouted: "Track 82724 has fired on us! Vampire inbound!"

44

Captain Shen was aware of the political commissar, Colonel Sun, screaming in his face, but in a strange, detached way. It felt almost as if his consciousness existed outside his body and he was observing the confrontation as a third party. It was the spittle peppering his right cheek that snapped him back into himself.

"They're entering the MEZ . . . Why are you just standing there? Do something!" Sun howled.

Shen raised his right hand as a spittle shield and put it between them. It took every ounce of willpower not to shove his counterpart by the face.

"Control yourself, Colonel," he said in a controlled, firm voice, "or I will have you removed from Combat Central."

"You let them get around us. Your incompetence is on display for the entire world, Captain Shen."

"You know nothing about ship handling, Colonel. Our blocking maneuver violated the international rules of seamanship, but I broke the rules and put this ship and crew in danger to service our orders. What would you have me do? Collide with the Americans?"

"Yes, absolutely," Sun shouted, red-faced.

"You really are a fool, aren't you, Colonel? This is a multibillion-dollar warship with four hundred souls aboard. It displaces fourteen thousand tons. A collision with the *Dunham* would sink *both* vessels and kill us all."

The commissar pulled a folded piece of paper from his pocket and waved it in Shen's face. "Have you forgotten our orders? *Deny access. Use of deadly force is authorized.* Right now, the Americans are crossing into the MEZ. Which means, either you've failed to execute our tasking or you've chosen not to. Tell me, Captain, which is it?"

Shen snatched the paper from Sun's hand and slammed it down on the captain's desk. "These orders do not say to use the *Nanchang* as a battering ram. These orders do not say to sink the *Jason Dunham*. What they say is something very different—lethal force is authorized. The *how* and *when* to use such force is delegated to me. I am the captain of this vessel. The engagement with the *Jason Dunham* is far from over. This is just the first encounter."

"Combat Central, Bridge," said the voice of Commander Tong on the loudspeaker. "The Americans are pulling away. Shall I pursue?"

Shen picked up the comms handset and keyed the mic. "Bridge, Captain—pursue at flank speed. Maximum turns."

Commander Tong acknowledged the order and the ship shuddered as the *Nanchang*'s mighty engines answered the call for maximum speed.

Commissar Sun glared at Shen with murder in his eyes.

Shen held the colonel's gaze and glared right back.

Then Sun did something that Shen did not expect. Something Shen didn't even think would have been possible. Something that proved he'd vastly underestimated his political command counterpart . . .

Sun marched over to the missile launch coordinator's console and ordered the junior officer out of the chair. The stunned JO hesitated a beat, then did as ordered, while Sun hunched over the control panel. The commissar turned the missile launch key from SAFE to FIRE, then quickly and expertly began to manipulate the interface.

"What the hell are you doing?" Shen shouted, but it was too late.

The warning tone for a missile launch sounded in Combat Central. The ship shook and the dull roar of a hot-launched missile reverberated in the CCC.

"Missile away," the missile launch coordinator announced, standing helplessly beside his console as the political commissar fired at the American warship.

Shen felt his legs moving, but he didn't consciously remember deciding to run. He felt his arms wrap around the commissar, his chest slam into the man, and his body drive the colonel to the deck with a resounding thud, but it seemed like someone else performing the tackle. It was hearing the crunch of someone's ribs that snapped him back into himself.

"Missile launch coordinator," Shen shouted. "'Safe' your console. I repeat, place the missile control permissive switch in safe mode."

"Placing the MCP switch in safe mode," the junior officer said, retaking his seat at the workstation. "MCP switch is in safe."

A stunned Colonel Sun groaned beneath Shen, but the political commissar was not Shen's most pressing problem at the moment. His ship had just fired an anti-ship cruise missile at the *Jason Dunham* and it would be within the American ship captain's right to return fire with not only a single missile but a salvo, as well as the deadly Mark 45 five-inch naval cannon. At this range, the missile the commissar had just fired would arrive on target in less than a minute.

"Combat coordinator, ready countermeasures and place CIWS in auto," Shen ordered, preparing his ship to defend against a return salvo from the *Jason Dunham* as he climbed off Colonel Sun.

A sharp flare of pain in his right side answered the question about which man's rib had broken in the takedown. Shen winced as he straightened himself up to his full height and turned to look at the large central monitor at the front of the CCC, which was displaying a live video feed of the *Jason Dunham* in a window. In the next few moments, he'd see whether Colonel Sun had started World War III or not.

"Captain Shen, according to Article Two, Section Nine of PLA Navy Governance Doctrine, you're relieved of command," barked Colonel Sun, who was now on his feet. He turned to the ship's XO. "Executive Officer Tan, you are promoted to acting commanding officer. Lock Captain Shen in your stateroom and assume control of the ship."

The captain turned to face his XO, Commander Tan, but he didn't say a word to countermand the commissar's orders. The XO looked at Shen, then at Sun, then back at Shen.

For a long, tense moment, the entire Combat Control Center waited to see where Commander Tan's loyalty lied.

Finally, the XO answered the question by snapping to attention in front of Shen and saying, "What are your orders, Captain?"

Shen, who only then realized that he'd been holding his breath, exhaled and said, "Have the master-at-arms escort Colonel Sun to an unoccupied stateroom, where he will remain under observation until this situation is resolved. Confiscate the commissar's mobile phone and do not give him access to a radio or the ship's internal communications system."

"Yes, sir," the XO said, and snapped his fingers at the master-at-arms, who, along with two petty officers, marched toward Colonel Sun.

"You can't do this! I'll have your command for this, Shen," the commissar yelled as he backpedaled. "You too, Tan. You're both going to prison. Mark my words, you'll burn for this. All of you are going to burn . . ."

Thanks to you, Colonel, your words could prove to be more prescient than you realize, Shen thought as he turned his attention back to the monitor as he awaited the USS *Jason Dunham*'s response.

The commissar's shouting faded into background noise as he was manhandled out of Combat Central. Although Shen was not an overtly religious man, he said a short and silent prayer that the captain of the Arleigh Burke–class destroyer they had just fired upon was no cowboy. Because if the American ship driver returned fire, then Shen would have no choice but to defend his ship and crew with everything at his disposal—all but guaranteeing the mutually assured destruction of both vessels.

45

A terrible wave of déjà vu washed over Horrillo.

Just like the surprise terrorist raid in the Strait of Malacca, the *Jason Dunham* was under attack. Except this time, instead of being targeted by a low-tech, shoulder-launched RPG, the missile screaming toward the *Dunham* was an advanced anti-ship cruise missile.

With only seconds to react, he leapt into action to protect the ship.

"RCS, Hold Fire Off," he shouted. "EW, execute countermeasure PPR!"

"CIWS in Hold Fire Off. Tracking vampire inbound," the RCS operator called back.

"Executing countermeasure PPR," announced the electronic warfare supervisor. "Chaff and Nulka away."

The *Dunham* employed a layered approach to self-defense that utilized multiple different technologies to defeat an inbound threat. The ship's SM-2 missiles with their fragmentation warheads and radio frequency guidance system were highly capable anti-ship missile interceptors, but they were optimized for threats originating outside three nautical miles. Because the Chinese destroyer was inside fifteen hundred yards, the *Dunham*'s entire defense against the inbound cruise missile depended on the combination of CIWS and "soft kill" countermeasures.

The inbound "vampire" would cover the distance between the *Nanchang* and the *Dunham* in less than one minute. The threat transpired at a speed too fast for a human being to calculate and execute a hard-kill response. That's why the *Dunham*'s lone remaining layer to hard-kill the inbound missile functioned autonomously. The CIWS used a close-in search radar designed to rapidly find and track fast-moving inbound threats. The 4,500-round-per-minute Phalanx would send a stream of armor-piercing tungsten rounds at the Chinese missile that would shred it into a thousand pieces.

But, if the CIWS missed, then the *Dunham*'s only hope was a soft kill, using countermeasures. Like all Arleigh Burkes, Horrillo had two types of countermeasures at his disposal—passive and active. The passive variety—chaff—created a cloud in the air with a large radar return. The Nulka, on the other hand, was an active countermeasure designed to interfere with the inbound missile's seeker. In both cases, the goal of the countermeasures was to simulate a large radar return in the air above the *Dunham*—causing the enemy missile to switch targets and fly harmlessly overhead until it exhausted its fuel and crashed into the ocean.

CIWS saved our ass before . . . let's hope it can do it again.

At the same time as he was giving orders, Horrillo rolled the fire inhibit switch, or FIS, key to "green" on his weapons console—turning it clockwise a quarter turn from INHIBIT to ENABLE in preparation for launching missiles and returning fire on the *Nanchang*.

"How many missiles are inbound?" the captain barked.

"One, sir," the air warfare officer answered.

"Are you certain?"

"Yes, sir."

"CIWS engaging . . . Vampire destroyed," the CIWS operator announced with a victorious note to his voice.

"Damn, that was close," the CMC said, speaking for the collective.

Following the skipper's advice, Horrillo forced himself to think two pay grades above his own. To function at a higher level, he needed to think like a ship's captain. Kreutz had just asked for confirmation that only one missile was in the air. At first blush, one might think the captain was just confirming the immediate threat. In other words, validating how many missiles were targeting the *Dunham* so he could keep track of how many needed to be shot down to know the ship and crew were safe.

Certainly, that was part of it, but Horrillo realized there was another level.

He's performing a tactical assessment to determine the timing, nature, and magnitude of our response.

Type 055 destroyers like the *Nanchang* carried both the YJ-18 anti-ship missile and the larger, long-range hypersonic YJ-21. EW had not confirmed which missile had been fired by the *Nanchang*, but Horrillo assumed it was a YJ-18. Also of note, the Chinese ship had only fired one. The *Nanchang* had 112 VLS cells. Had the Chinese captain meant to *sink* the *Dunham*, he would have ordered a salvo.

But firing an anti-ship cruise missile was one hell of a risky warning shot.

What if the CIWS had misfired? What if the missile had hit us and killed people?

Which begged the question, if it really was a warning shot,

why had the Chinese skipper used a missile instead of firing an artillery shell into the ocean aimed a hundred yards off the *Dunham*'s bow? Missiles use seekers, and the one the *Nanchang* had fired at the *Dunham* had been on target.

Warning shots are supposed to miss!

He turned to look at the captain and saw the CO's eyes tick to the live video feed of the *Nanchang*. The Chinese warship was in pursuit, trailing the *Dunham*, but holding position a half mile and thirty degrees off their starboard stern.

"ROS, zoom in on their mount," the captain said.

"Aye, sir," the EOSS controller replied.

The feed shifted, then zoomed on the bow of the *Nanchang* and its deck-mounted 130mm cannon. The Chinese-made H/PJ-38 gun was a reverse-engineered derivative of the Soviet-era AK-130. It had roughly the same capabilities as the *Dunham*'s five-inch gun, the Mark 45 artillery mount. The image zoomed in, then stabilized, showing that the *Nanchang*'s gun was pointing straight forward at 000 relative bearing, as opposed to aiming at the *Dunham*.

"TAO, cover the *Nanchang* with birds, salvo size four," the CO said. Horrillo could see the barely contained fire burning in the man's eyes as the skipper forced himself to react tactically rather than emotionally. "If they so much as flinch, sink them."

"Define 'flinch,' sir?" Horrillo said, needing clarification on this incredibly important point.

"If they move their mount. If they open a VLS door. If they light us up with targeting radar—anything that you deem a prequel to another strike, you let them have it," Kreutz said, his voice a wolverine's growl.

"Understood, sir," Horrillo said, and turned to the air warfare coordinator. "Air, did you hear that?"

"Lima Charlie, TAO," the AWC said. "I've got four birds programmed and ready to launch on your mark."

Horrillo nodded and watched the CO as he grabbed the bridge-to-bridge radio handset.

This oughtta be good, he thought.

"*Nanchang*, this is *Jason Dunham* actual," the skipper said into the handset. "You fired on a U.S. warship in international waters. Most ship captains would consider this an act of war and would have already returned fire. I'm going to give you the opportunity to explain this action before I do . . ."

Horrillo could practically hear the collective inhale in Combat as every watch stander at every workstation waited for the Chinese captain's response. Horrillo, for his part, kept his eyes glued to the aux display streaming the live video feed of the Chinese warship while the captain's last command echoed in his head: *If they so much as flinch, sink them.*

After what seemed like an eternity, the *Nanchang* answered.

"USS *Jason Dunham*, you have entered a Chinese maritime exclusion zone without permission. Your action violates the Law of the People's Republic of China on the Territorial Sea and Contiguous Zone. Reverse course immediately and exit the prohibited area," said the radio talker they'd dealt with previously, undoubtedly the crew member most proficient in English.

"Why did you fire on my ship?" Kreutz said, keying the mic.

Another long pause . . .

"That was a warning shot," the *Nanchang* radio talker replied. "Reverse course immediately and exit the prohibited area."

"TAO, have they moved their mount?" Kreutz asked, holding the bridge-to-bridge mic unkeyed.

"No, sir," Horrillo said, his eyes glued to the video feed, looking for any signs that the *Nanchang* was readying a second attack.

"Do they have any forward VLS hatches open?"

"Not that I can see, Captain."

The captain returned the bridge-to-bridge handset to the cradle and took a seat in his chair at the CO's console in the middle of Combat. Everyone waited in silence for his decision. Finally, after a long moment, he spoke.

"My last order stands, TAO. If they flinch, kill 'em. In the meantime, have radio get me TF 70 on the horn. The admiral—hell, the President for that matter—needs to know what just happened here." Then, in a surprisingly matter-of-fact tone, Kreutz added, "And we need to get hostile declaration from the warfare coordinator. If we have to go to war over this, I might as well make it official . . ."

46

JADE SPRING VILLA OF PRESIDENT LI JIAN JUN
YUQUANSHAN
WEST OF YÍHÉYUÁN (THE SUMMER PALACE) COMPLEX
HAIDIAN DISTRICT
BEIJING, CHINA
1103 LOCAL TIME

I don't care what Captain Shen's excuses are!" President Li Jian Jun shouted, smashing a fist on the conference table hard enough to make the untouched tea service in the center of the small dining room table rattle, and making Han Xuexiang visibly jump in his seat. Li's new acting minister of national defense looked on the verge of collapse. "What I want to know, *acting* minister Han, is why an American warship is currently traversing north in the territorial waters between China and our legitimate territory of Taiwan. And I want to know what the captain of the *Nanchang* intends to do about it."

Beside Minister Han, the head of the MSS, Minister Deng Su Wei, sat stone-faced, his legs crossed at the knee and his hands folded in his lap. With a trembling hand, Han pushed his glasses up on his nose and swallowed hard.

"Mr. President, we gave clear orders to the military that the blockade of the strait was to be strictly enforced. And, as I said, Captain Shen fired on the American warship, which we have identified as the USS *Jason Dunham*, with Captain Kreutz commanding . . ."

"And yet, President Ryan's Navy still boldly travels just miles off the coast of our nation with a warship capable of killing thousands."

Li glanced over Han Xuexiang's shoulder and caught the eye of his head of personal security, who reached inside his suit coat and raised an eyebrow. Li held his eyes and clenched his jaw, but then gave a short shake of his head in the negative. The man withdrew his hand from the gun beneath his coat, just as Han glanced nervously over his shoulder at him, a bead of sweat breaking loose from his forehead and trickling down his face beside his left eye.

"Mr. President, I can leave this room right now and order the destruction of the *Jason Dunham*, if you desire. This was not something I was comfortable—"

"I don't care about your discomfort!" Li snapped. "What part of 'lethal force authorized' was unclear to you and to the captain of the *Nanchang*? Once the Americans crossed into our exclusion zone, we were immediately at war. The captain's response should have been predicated on this." He let the silence linger a moment as he stared hard at the man beside him. Then he let out a long sigh. "However, that opportunity was lost. To destroy the *Dunham* now no longer meets our purpose, as it would represent an escalation by us rather than them. We would be striking proactively instead of reactively, unless we can show an elevated threat. What I *recommend*, Minister Han, is that if this ship makes any aggressive moves she be destroyed. Let me be clear, since it appears you feel clarity was lacking in my last orders . . ."

"Not at all, Mr. President. I did not mean to imply—"

Li held up a hand, silencing him.

"To be clear—I will consider it an aggressive move should the *Jason Dunham* not expeditiously transit and exit the strait. If they loiter, if they conduct missile drills, if they make any aggressive move or threaten the *Nanchang* in any way, lethal force is mandated. Failure to carry out these orders will be viewed as treason on the part of Captain Shen and he will be relieved of duty, court-martialed, and executed. If the Americans do not exit the strait *prior* to the commencement of our exercise—Operation Sea Serpent—then I will consider that to be *your* failure, Minister Han, and I will be forced to punish you for gross negligence and insubordination." He leaned in, fixing Han with his best, deadly stare. "Is there any lack of clarity in my instructions, Han Xuexiang?"

"N-no, sir, Mr. President," Han stammered.

"What is the status of our Special Forces operation, acting minister Han?" he asked, leaning back in his chair.

"We are on target, Mr. President. The team will infiltrate Huayu as scheduled. They are well trained, will have both satellite and drone support in real time, and will no doubt succeed."

"They had better," Li said. "The entire operation depends on their success. And after the firing of the missiles barrage?"

"The batteries on Huayu are already targeted and we will launch cruise missiles to completely destroy the sites on the island once the Special Forces team is clear."

"No. Set a specific time for our retaliatory missile attack. It should happen within a few minutes of the target vessel being hit," Li said, and poured himself some tea from the pot. "It will be the responsibility of the Jiaolong warriors to exfil the island to avoid becoming collateral damage, but the strike must happen expeditiously. Complete destruction of the island is the only thing that erases our fingerprints from this operation. Is that understood?" Li took a sip of tea, then made a *tsk* sound, finding it had cooled more than he preferred.

"It is, Mr. President," Han said.

"You are dismissed, Minister Han," Li said, and waved his hand. "You have much work to do, including letting Admiral Pei know of my disappointment in the performance of the *Nanchang*. It is my hope that Captain Shen will not need to be relieved of duty."

Han rose, bowed in deep respect, and hurried from the room, leaving his counterpart from the MSS still seated across from Li.

Li took another sip of tea, then turned to Minister Deng.

"What updates do you have for me, Su Wei?"

"We have a massive dragnet operation underway, Mr. President," Deng replied, his face and affect much calmer and more controlled than Han's. The man was more an experienced and blooded intelligence agent than a bureaucrat, and his confidence had returned since their last meeting. "Every security agent and police officer in every province has pictures of Qin, and of the Spider, since we have finally identified her as the owner of a taxi company. We are using enhanced interrogation techniques even as we speak to get any information we can from her contacts, employees, and connections. The net will tighten as we learn more, but there is no way they will escape China in time for Qin and the information he possesses to be of any value to the Americans in stopping our operation."

"That is good news, Minister Deng," Li said, but felt anger and irritation rising in him again. "But it is not good enough. Qin and this traitor spy must be found and killed. It is no longer reasonable to believe that Qin is innocent. If the Americans get him out of China, even if it is after a successful reunification campaign, the international repercussions will be devastating. No, this is not a rescue operation. This is a capture/kill mission now—where we should err toward kill. Do you agree?"

"I do indeed, Mr. President," Deng Su Wei said, and his face seemed sincere. "My orders reflect this. The Americans have no viable network inside China now. We will find Qin and this woman Spider and that will be the end of it. Every patriot with a weapon in our employ is now instructed to make finding them the number one priority. Their capture and death are inevitable, sir."

"Excellent," Li said, and he did in fact feel some relief. Deng was right. The Americans did not have the resources and assets in country to succeed at finding Qin, much less getting him out of China. Operation Sea Serpent, ironically the brainchild of Admiral Qin, would succeed, and the loose end of Qin and the Spider would be trimmed off very soon.

I am only days away from securing my legacy.

And despite his superstitious nature, he began contemplating the words of the triumphant speech he would deliver to the nation.

47

What in the hell is this maniac thinking?" Ryan said, resisting with great effort his desire to pound a fist on the table. "If a Chinese warship has fired a missile at our destroyer operating according to maritime law in international waters, then that is an act of war." He scanned the faces of the talented men and women assembled with him. Despite the hour and the long day behind them, all looked fresh, alert, and focused.

"The Chinese claim that we were violating a legitimate exclusion zone ahead of an announced exercise and that by doing so we were provoking war," Admiral Kent said, but his clenched jaw suggested he saw that for the bullshit it was.

"So they targeted and fired upon a ship with more than three hundred souls aboard?" Ryan clasped his hands together on the table in front of him in an effort to remain in control.

"Their stance is that they fired a warning shot, sir," General Kudryk said, but gave a snorting laugh as he did.

"What does the skipper of the *Dunham* say?" Ryan asked.

"He says that the *Nanchang* put itself on a high-speed collision course with his ship to prevent them from crossing into the claimed exclusion zone," Kent said. "When we executed an evasive maneuver and began to outrun the Chinese ship to the north, she targeted the *Dunham* and fired an anti-ship missile at her. *Dunham*'s defensive systems destroyed the incoming missile before it hit."

"Then we are at war already, as far as I'm concerned," Ryan said.

"The skipper of the *Dunham*—Commander Jeff Kreutz, one of our best—agrees with you, sir," Kent said. "He filed a motion of hostile intent and Admiral Urban aboard the *Reagan* agrees as well."

"Well, now we have to decide what to do about it, don't we?" Ryan growled. There was no way in hell he intended to let this act of aggression go unanswered.

"Just so we're all clear, what endgame do you have in mind, Mr. President?" Secretary of State Adler asked softly. When Ryan turned sharply to him, he continued. "What I mean, sir, is we need to know what our goal is to properly advise you on strategy. If the goal is to go to war with China, then that looks completely different from aggressive action to de-escalate and *prevent* war."

"So, you think we should do nothing?" Ryan asked, bristling.

"Not at all, sir," Adler replied immediately. "With China as much as with Russia, peace through strength is the only strategy that works in the long term. But having our desired endgame in mind gives us strategic clarity as we war-game this out."

"But it's little more than war-gaming if we don't know Li's

intent," Kudryk grumbled. "He is becoming more and more un-predictable. If we believe that this incident of muscle flexing is truly his prelude to an invasion of Taiwan, then we have to be prepared to act and act quickly."

Ryan let out a long slow breath and tried to clear his mind. Adler was right. They needed to start with the end in mind. But so was General Kudryk. To do that efficiently meant they had to know what Li had in mind. One thing was sure—this was a clear military escalation from anything they had seen. Flying danger close to American surveillance aircraft, buzzing surface ships, maneuvering in the path of the fleet to disrupt operations—these were all aggressive and provocative actions, but what had just happened with the *Dunham* was different. A Chinese destroyer had targeted and fired an anti-ship missile at an American warship!

"Where precisely is the *Dunham* right now?" he asked.

"In the strait and steaming north," Kent said. "She is being shad-owed by the *Nanchang*, who remains in close proximity. There are additional Chinese warships at the north end of the strait where the *Dunham* will exit and head east to join the *Reagan*."

"And don't forget that she is also in close proximity to main-land China and their gazillion missile batteries and aircraft armed with anti-ship missiles," Kudryk added. "If the Chinese decide to sink her, then the *Dunham* doesn't have enough countermeasures to survive the onslaught."

"Li will know that an attack now," Ryan said, feeling the ana-lytical side of his brain recovering control over his emotions, "with our ship in transit in the strait, already having crossed their fab-ricated maritime exclusion zone, will result in an immediate and overwhelming military response from the United States. He may not know me well, but he knows me well enough to predict that."

He tapped his fingers on the table.

"What is Kreutz's posture?" he asked.

"If the *Nanchang* demonstrates any aggression at all he intends to sink her," Kent said simply.

"Kreutz showed remarkable strategic thinking and restraint when he didn't sink that son of a bitch already," Ryan growled. "He delivers his sailors safely out of the strait, no matter how many Chinese ships we have to destroy—are we clear on that?"

"Crystal, sir," Kent said, his tone suggesting he had already made that decision himself.

"We sent the *Dunham* on a very dangerous geopolitical mission," Ryan said, the weight of his order to run the blockade now heavy on him. "They've performed perfectly so far. We get them home."

"Of course, sir," Kent said.

"One hundred percent agree," Adler said.

Everyone watched him closely as Ryan turned over the problem in his mind. He believed that the intelligence absolutely supported the theory that they were days or even hours away from an invasion of Taiwan. And he had brilliant minds, including his daughter's, working on the details of how that invasion would likely unfold. Originally, the payoff for risking defecting Admiral Qin was getting their hands on the architect of the battle plan for that invasion. But now, even if Clark and his team succeeded in exfiltrating Qin, it would likely be too late to matter. The opening chess moves would be over.

His mind flashed back to the game of Battleship he'd played with Katie at the dining room table—a game where each player is taking shots in the dark at the other player's fleet. The simple game was quite the metaphor for his current situation. He'd always considered the game a "second tier" board game because random chance played as large a role as strategy did in claiming victory. But thinking about it now, he realized that the beautiful simplicity of the game was how it mirrored real-life military engagements. His strategy to counter Li in Taiwan was hampered by incomplete information and also by plain old chance. Li had fired on Ryan's destroyer and "missed." Now it was Ryan's turn to make a move . . .

Do I shoot back? And if so, what is my target?

Ryan felt like he knew Li's mind. What he needed to better understand was the man's heart and strength of will.

"Arnie," he said, turning to his chief of staff, Arnold van Damm.

"Yes, Mr. President?"

"I want President Li on a secure line routed down here in the Situation Room."

"You . . . You want to call him on the phone, sir?"

"That's right," Ryan said. "Get him on the line. Have our people tell his people that the future of both of our countries depends on his taking my call."

"Good lord," one of the DoD staffers mumbled.

"That should get him on the phone, sir," van Damm said, and picked up a handset.

"In the meantime," Ryan said, turning to his chairman of the Joint Chiefs, "I want to expedite the repositioning of Task Force 70 north of Taipei and begin conducting flight operations in the region. And let's get the *Nimitz* into position much closer and southeast of Taiwan. We will not let Li bluff us into taking the bait for whatever false flag he plans to use to justify an invasion, but I don't want to be unprepared, either."

"Immediately, sir," Kent said.

"What else do you recommend, Admiral? General Kudryk?"

The two general officers looked at each other a moment.

"Mr. President, the USS *North Carolina* is deployed with Task Force 70 along with the Australian fast-attack sub HMAS *Perth*," Kent said. "Sir, we recommend repositioning these assets to be ready for either retaliatory or preemptive strikes against both the PLA Navy's northern and southern fleets and fleet headquarters."

Ryan clenched his jaw, but this is where they were now. It was Li who had brought them to the brink of war over Taiwan, but he would neither let their ally fall nor endanger his sailors and Marines any more than was required. If that meant it could be necessary to destroy the Chinese Navy or wipe out their command and control, then the flag officers were right—he'd best be prepared.

"Make it happen," he said.

"Right away, Mr. President," Kudryk said.

"We all need to pray it doesn't come to that," Adler said, and massaged his temples with trembling hands.

"As soon as we leave here, I'll be in communication with our allies," Ryan said. "This isn't just an American problem, it's a world problem. They've supported us covertly with Task Force 99 and now we need their political support as well. The only way to defeat Chinese aggression is with a unified will and purpose."

"I'll reach out now to give their people a heads-up, sir," Adler's chief of staff said, rising and heading for the door.

"Mr. President," the secretary of state said. "They're routing a call from President Li to you here, sir."

"Very well," Ryan said, steeling himself. "Video call?"

"Audio only, sir."

"On the speaker," he said. "To properly advise me, you all need to hear this."

The light on the high-tech phone that the staffer placed in front of him went from amber to green.

"President Ryan, President Li is on the line," Arnie announced.

Li wasted no time and spoke immediately. "The United States has violated the Law of the People's Republic of China on the Territorial Sea and the Contiguous Zone. The Taiwan Strait is a maritime exclusion zone, President Ryan, your warship has violated it," Li said in a measured voice.

Ryan took a short beat to compose his response, then said, "President Li, neither I nor the international community recognize your authority, under any international or maritime law nor any known treaty, to exclude our vessels from safe passage through international waters. I demand to know immediately why you have fired upon our ship operating in compliance with international law, and why I should refrain from an immediate military response to this act of war."

Ryan looked up to see his secretary of state now wide-eyed, the staffer beside him sitting with her mouth hanging open. Apparently, they had expected a different form of diplomacy.

"President Ryan," Li said, venom in his voice. "The act of war here was the murder of our defense minister by American spies operating in China. As we speak, we are on the trail of these assassination agents and when we capture them their trial will be broadcast for the world to see—as will their execution. Perhaps you can explain to me why I should not respond with military action to *your* brazen act of war?"

"I'm sure I have no idea what you're talking about . . ." Ryan looked at Mary Pat, who gave a content and impressed smile and nodded. "We both know full well that Defense Minister Qin is alive and well. Qin is a moral and prudent man who is unwilling to participate in the warmongering acts of your administration that will bring your people shame and economic suffering. Admiral Qin will have a very informed and interesting perspective to share with the world when he reappears at the appropriate time."

Li said nothing for a very long moment, and Ryan wished he could see the expression on the man's face.

"We will see," Li said. "And after the dignified service and proper notifications of loved ones, we will present our evidence—and his body—and it will be the People's Republic of China demanding accountability from those responsible."

"We shall see," Ryan said, "but in the meantime, you have only this call to explain your attack on my ship before I order a military response. There will be no second call."

"This was not an attack, but a warning. We know full well the capabilities of the Arleigh Burke destroyers, President Ryan," Li said, and had the unmitigated gall to laugh out loud. "More than you might imagine. Rest assured that the captain of my ship knew exactly what kind of warning your fleet could defend. If I had desired to destroy your vessel, then it would now be at the bottom of the strait."

Ryan felt the anger surging and clenched his jaw.

"I will not permit you to take such a gamble with the lives of our brave sailors," he said, clenching his fists. "If this was a warning shot, you are now notified that a repeat of such a *warning* will be met with immediate military action to defend our fleet. So much as a warning shot across our bow, a flyby from one of your jets, or even targeting our ship will result in a swift and deadly response. I expect that our ship will have safe passage in her journey north in international waters."

"Your threat against our Navy is noted," Li said.

"In the meantime, President Li, and in response to your aggression and illegal blockade of the Strait of Taiwan"—and now he leaned back, smiling and resting his hands on the table as he played his next card, hoping it would be something he could make happen and not prove to be a bluff—"I will be meeting with international partners in the coming hours. In those meetings, I will be calling for worldwide sanctions in the form of an embargo on all automotive trade with China, to include vehicles as well as parts *and* lithium-ion batteries."

"If your Navy vessel shows any aggression toward our escort or attempts to interfere with our upcoming exercise in any way, including failing to exit our exclusion zone with due haste," Li growled, "we will respond with swift and decisive action."

Ryan heard a click and the line went dead.

"That went well," he said with a grim smile and was met with stunned silence. "All right, people, we have a lot of work to do and not a lot of time to do it. Admiral Kent, you know what needs to be done, including complimenting the commander of the *Dunham* for his restraint, but ordering him to defend his ship at all costs. And you can tell him he should continue passage to the north, but not to expedite doing so. I don't want him to loiter, but I don't want to signal to the Chinese that Li won any sort of concession by the *Dunham* hurrying to get out of there."

"Yes, sir, Mr. President," Kent said, and he and Kudryk rose.

"Secretary Adler," Ryan continued. "Scott, you and I have a lot of work to do to get our international partners on board. We need to build a coalition to put pressure on Li *before* things spiral out of control."

"I'm on it, sir," Adler said.

Last, he turned to Mary Pat, who sat beside him as the others shuffled from the room.

"Bold move, Jack," she said as the door closed. "And the right one. Peace through strength."

"Peace through strength," Ryan agreed. "But it only works if we get Qin out of China before Li finds the man, murders him for real, and blames us. We need Task Force 99 to succeed, Mary Pat, now more than ever."

"If anyone can pull it off it's Clark," Mary Pat said.

Ryan nodded and couldn't help but wonder if the shot in the dark he'd just taken at Li had been a hit or a miss.

48

Katie waited for the salty Group Eight detachment SEAL master chief sitting across the conference room table to respond. She'd just hit him with her theory about the impending infiltration of Huayu island by Chinese Special Forces. Group Eight's role here on Penghu had been about as clear as mud to her since they'd flown out on the jet with her and the rest of TF 25. She'd said as much to Conza, but he'd just chuckled. Apparently, "clear as mud" was how these shadowy, pointy-tip direct-action groups preferred to function.

Conza seemed comfortable with the situation, so she'd told herself to trust the process.

Trusting the process, however, was being stress-tested now that the stakes and risks were rapidly escalating.

"Is this information based on reliable intelligence, or are we talking theory here?" Master Chief Hurley asked, his expression dubious.

Katie was about to answer, but thankfully Conza jumped in.

"Look, Hurley, I get it," he said, giving her a nod. "I've been out there in the suck, with my ass on the line, based on shaky intelligence before. But I can vouch for Commander Ryan, bro. Scenario predictive analysis is what she does, and she does it better than anyone else in the business. I strongly believe this is not only what the Chinese are planning, but where they are planning to do it."

"All right, I'm listening," Hurley said, which Katie took as a good sign. "What exactly is it that you guys are proposing? Because it sounds like a deviation from our charter, which was to support TF 99 and the extraction of the asset from Beijing. That's Group Eight's mission."

"I know, and we're not suggesting deviating from that mission. We have twelve DEVGRU operators who just arrived that we can look to for help. So, to answer your question, what we're proposing is splitting the DEVGRU platoon. We covertly insert half the force onto Huayu to repel the incursion, and the other half remain here on Penghu as a QRF in case we're wrong about the location."

"But if you're wrong, we're leaving an incredibly valuable asset stranded on a remote island," said Commander Beechum, the OIC of Group Eight. Unlike his heavily bearded master chief, the SEAL commander was clean-shaven with close-cropped hair. He shifted his gaze from Conza to Katie. "My concern is that we're leaving Penghu in short order to support TF 99's covert exfiltration of an asset out of Tianjin. Once we leave, DEVGRU will have no organic support to provide them with intelligence in real time. I want to be sure you understand that, Commander Ryan."

"Yes, sir," she said. "Unfortunately, by the time there is any real intelligence to support my prediction, it will be too late to insert a team to repel the attack."

"Ryan has a real sixth sense, Commander," James said, laughing at himself along with the burly operators. "DEVGRU was involved in prosecuting a recent Russian threat to our mid-Atlantic DASH sonar array that Commander Ryan uncovered. If she says the target is Huayu, I'd be inclined to trust her."

"Me too," Drewski added. "I'll volunteer to augment the DEVGRU shooters on Huayu. I'm ground branch and former Army SF, so that adds a gun if DEVGRU wants to hold some Team Guys back."

Across the table, Lorie Tengco gave her nod of approval as well, adding a wink, of all things.

Beechum looked at Hurley and both men reached a silent accord.

"Okay, Ryan," the SEAL master chief said, "I'll talk to the DEVGRU guys and we'll make this happen."

Katie nodded at Beechum and Hurley. It took all her willpower, but she resisted the urge to thank them. This wasn't them doing her a favor. This wasn't them placating her. This was a strategic recommendation, and her doing her job.

"We need to get on this sooner rather than later," Conza said. "It's got be done dark and quiet, since we're sitting right under Chinese planes, drones, and satellites."

"We have some tech that might help provide some cover," Beechum said, and Katie wondered what it might be, "but, John, I think we should talk about how to best infil and exfil the DEVGRU squad to Huayu *before* Hurley and I go give them the bad news."

"Good, I was hoping you'd say that," Conza said. "And after, we need to discuss how we're going to best support the *Capella* operation."

Conza had dropped the bomb on her right before this meeting

that he would be "loaning himself out" to Group Eight to support TF 99's high-stakes, low-probability-of-success defector exfiltration operation. He'd not given her a chance to protest or pull rank on him before making the offer to Commander Beechum. This was something they were going to definitely need to have a talk about, but she'd have to wait until after the brief.

"Ryan, feel free to sit in on both of these if you have the time," Beechum said, it sounding less like an invitation than an order. "Even if you have little tactically to contribute, it'll help for you to be well read in on both operations, since you're leading support back here."

"Happy to, sir," she said, but then turned when the metallic lock of the door clicked, signaling its release.

"Ryan," Sam Bakshi called from the door, gesturing for Katie to join her in the hall.

"Excuse me a moment," Katie said and rose from her chair. "What's up, Sam?" she asked out in the hall once the door clicked closed.

"Thought you should see this right away in case it impacted what you guys are planning in there."

Katie scanned the printed communication Bakshi handed her, the TS/SCI watermark making the desired point. When she was done, she experienced a bizarre mixture of annoyance, anger, and relief. The timing was terrible, but then that was the point, wasn't it? And, more than anything, it suggested that lots of really smart people had read her analysis and thought she must be on to something. Otherwise, why send these orders, right?

"Thanks, Sam," she said. "Sounds like a pretty short fuse, so let everyone know to start breaking down and getting packed. I'll let Lorie and Ted know."

"Roger that," Sam said. "And Drewski and Conza, too, right?"

Katie shook her head, suddenly feeling a sense of dread for the two teammates she'd begun to feel tightly bonded to.

"It sounds like they're staying behind," she said, though she was a little unclear on whose authority Conza was falling in on the operators from Eight. She was his immediate report, right?

"Conza, too?" the CIA spook asked, hands on the hips of her 5.11 Tactical cargo pants, apparently not at all surprised that her ground branch teammate would be staying.

"Yeah," she said, "Conza, too, apparently."

If it was her decision to make, she supposed she had just made it.

She handed the printed orders back to Sam and then punched the code into the magnetic lock and jerked the door handle. She reentered the SCIF and all eyes looked up and conversation stopped when she came in.

"All good, Ryan?" Conza asked first.

"Not sure," she said. "Someone back home must think we're on to something, because they just ordered all noncombatants from the task force to evacuate Penghu."

"I'm not a noncombatant, Katie," Conza said immediately, fire in his eyes.

"Okay," she said. "I'm authorizing you to fall in on the exfil operation with the Group Eight operators aboard the *Capella*," she said. "You'll contribute the most there. And it sounds like Drewksi will stay behind as well to fill out the mission on Huayu, if it's okay with Ted."

"It is," James said. "And Ben is his partner from Ground Branch, so he can stay back as well if he chooses to volunteer to augment DEVGRU."

"Where are we headed?" Lorie Tengco asked. "I assume we'll continue operating as Task Force 25 from somewhere?"

"They want us to fold in on TF 70, but since the *Reagan* is still too far away for a helo op without refueling, we're ordered to evacuate to the *Jason Dunham*."

"Wait," Lorie Tengco said. "Isn't that the destroyer that ran the blockade and was fired on by the Chinese Navy?"

"The same," she said, and felt a nervous flutter in her stomach. Talk about déjà vu, this was setting up to be the *Blackfish* all over again.

"Well, good luck, Ryan," SEAL master chief Hurley said with a grin.

"Thank you, Master Chief," she said.

"No, I mean it," he said, leaning back in his chair. "If the powers that be are pulling you out, just to place you aboard a lone DDG still in the Strait of Taiwan, you'll need luck more than we will."

Katie clenched her jaw.

She'd thought of that already.

49

onza rubbed two knuckles into his left inner thigh just above the knee, where the skin and underlying tissue remained stubbornly numb, despite the more than two years that had passed. It was a nervous habit that didn't make anything feel better, especially since numbness was the opposite of pain, but he found himself doing it whenever he was reminded of his roots.

Sitting here on this slow-ass transport plane, he was indeed reminded of his journey to get here, and that he was a *former* Navy SEAL. However far he'd come, however well he'd mastered his prosthesis, he was not the man he'd been when he had been kicking ass in SEAL Team Five and then augmenting DEVGRU on deployment. Part of him was, literally, left behind on the battlefield. But more than just his left leg had been taken from him. Despite joking with former teammates about being a pirate, and the omnipresent positive attitude he endeavored to maintain, he knew the scars he carried were not just those on his stump of a leg.

His wounds were deeper.

And invisible.

But Sharon had seen them all too well. His former fiancée had gone on the journey of anger and resentment with him for more than a year before giving up. Now they were "friends," whatever that meant, but he would never ask her for more, not after what he'd put her through.

He missed his leg, but he could live with that.

He still struggled to live with the loss of the two brothers who had died in that shitty little compound on the Turkish border that day. That scar still throbbed, red and angry.

"You good, JC?" Hurley asked from across the narrow row between them, and he realized he startled as he looked up.

He smiled back awkwardly at the SEAL master chief. He'd always known Hurley would end up at a place like Group Eight. Dude was a brainiac even way back when they'd made it through BUD/S together.

"Yeah, all good, bro," he said. "Just running through fires for the infil, you know?"

"Yeah, yeah . . . I get it," Hurley said. The SEAL stole a glance at Conza's BDU-covered prosthesis.

"You worried about my mobility, brother?" Conza asked, and felt himself bristle defensively.

Hurley laughed and the laughter cut the tension.

"Nah, brother," the SEAL said. "I trust you, man. You say you're all good, then you're five by for me, man."

He offered knuckles, which Conza bumped with his own.

"Swimming was always such a bitch for me, you know?" Hurley said, smiling. "You remember . . . ?"

Now it was Conza's turn to laugh.

"Swimming is a bitch for you? Jeez, Hurley, you're a friggin'

Navy SEAL for shit's sake. A damn Tier One frogman. And you can't swim?"

"I didn't say I couldn't swim, just that it's a bitch for me," Hurley answered good-naturedly. On their five-mile-long qualifying swim during BUD/S, Hurley had almost not made it—claimed he wouldn't have made it if not for Conza. The freezing water had turned their limbs to noodles, and Hurley started falling back as they swam as a pair. When Hurley started talking about quitting so he could warm up in the safety boat, Conza had turned back to encourage his teammate to push through the wall. When Hurley waved a hand at the boat, Conza had punched him as hard as his own numb arms would allow.

"Damn you, Hurley, if I have to redo this swim because of you I'm gonna kick your ass," he shouted.

Then they'd both started laughing like idiots.

But they pushed through, and finished.

They'd graduated BUD/S, completed SQT, and served at SEAL Team Five together. When Conza had augmented with DEVGRU for a deployment, it was because of Hurley, who had screened for the JSOC unit a year and a half earlier, and his recommendation.

Had he not lost a leg in Syria, Conza felt he likely would have screened for DEVGRU after that deployment. Hell, they might even be teammates at Group Eight together right now.

He felt his throat tighten.

"I'm just sayin'," Hurley continued, snapping Conza back to the moment. "Had it been me, and me being a weak-ass swimmer, I don't think I could have made it back, bro. I have no doubt you're up for the swim, I promise. I'm just in awe, 'cause I still hate doing it with two legs."

Conza laughed again and shook his head.

"Well, we're just swimming from the mini to the *Capella*," he said. "I'm not planning any Ironman competitions anytime soon."

And that was the truth, for sure. If this mission had been to swim a long distance, he would not have insisted on going. But getting from the submerged, autonomous UUV a short distance to the Korean freighter *Capella* would not require much of a swim. In fact, most of the swim would be the ascent.

Getting up the side of the ship would be more work for him with the prosthesis.

But he trained daily, sometimes twice a day, and had no doubt he was up to the job.

Hurley had already leaned back in his seat, popped his AirPods back in, and closed his eyes, and Conza welcomed the silence.

He was glad to be on the mission, where his dual background in intelligence and special warfare made him much more of an asset than sitting with Ryan on the *Dunham*.

He admired the hell out of the quirky lieutenant commander. The entire time on Penghu, not a single person had mentioned her presidential pedigree, which he appreciated. But what he appreciated more was that she didn't wield the Ryan name like a hammer to get what she wanted. She relied on her instincts, intellect, and integrity. She was the perfect spook, if there was such a thing.

I'm just cut from different cloth, he thought, and wondered how long he'd be able to stay in this billet before he got too restless to be a productive contributor.

He looked across the empty window seat and out the window and the puffy white clouds below them. They should be feet dry in South Korea soon, and he glanced at his watch. Less than an hour until they landed in Incheon, where they would be whisked quickly away with their gear to the ROKS *Yulgok Yi l*, a guided-missile destroyer slightly larger and bulkier than her Arleigh

Burke cousin in the States, but fast enough to do the job. The challenge they'd faced during the mission brief was just how the hell to get the team aboard the *Capella*, which was already at sea on her scheduled run from Korea to Tianjin. With Chinese satellites, reconnaissance aircraft, and drones on high alert, they couldn't very well fly out to the freighter and fast-rope aboard without raising suspicion. But when the Group Eight team told him about their favorite new toy, an AI-augmented, semiautonomous, unmanned undersea vehicle—a minisub drone—the plan had fallen into place. They would board the destroyer *Yulgok Yi I*, which would have no problem overtaking the *Capella* before she crossed into the Bohai Sea, putting her north of the border with North Korea, where ROKN operations would raise significantly more suspicions. The UUV could return to the destroyer—or all the way to port for that matter—on her own with the new-generation battery she ran.

Once aboard the freighter *Capella*, they would blend with the crew as best they could, and be available to help with the exfil should the proverbial shit hit the fan.

Quite frankly, they were there more for a late-stage maritime interdiction than to help get the Task Force 99 team and their package out of China and onto the ship. If the spooks from 99 got in a firefight while still in port, there wasn't much a handful of SEALs, no matter how elite, would be able to do to help them. But Group Eight brought advanced communications, cyber, and ISR gear to the fight—much of which Conza knew almost nothing about, and they had chosen *not* to read him in on, other than to tell him it was all very "badass."

How and when those capabilities might come into play was unclear, but Conza was glad to know they were there.

Conza pushed away any remaining worries or doubts, putting

them in a box and placing them at the back of the top shelf of his mind, just as he trained himself to do years and years ago. It was a skill that kept him frosty as an operator, but did very little to improve conflicts in his relationships with women. He pressed his head back into the headrest and reclined the seat the full ten degrees it seemed was available to him by pressing the button on his armrest, and then closed his eyes. He flipped his real leg up on top of his prosthesis to get more comfortable, and then went through the exercise of relaxing his face and neck muscles in turn, knowing it would drift him off to sleep in minutes, just as it always had.

Sleep was a weapon.

And he would need it, since it seemed, somehow, he'd managed to bullshit his way back into the fight.

50

U.S. NAVY MH-60R SEAHAWK HELICOPTER FROM HSM 48,
    DETACHMENT 6
CALL SIGN VIPER ONE
FIVE HUNDRED FEET OVER THE STRAIT OF TAIWAN
FORTY-SEVEN NAUTICAL MILES WEST-NORTHWEST OF TAICHUNG,
    TAIWAN
1123 LOCAL TIME

Katie squeezed her own left thigh just above the knee when the helicopter lurched again, this time hard enough that she felt the four-point restraint securing her to the orange canvas bench seat bite into her clavicle.

"Sorry about that," the pilot said with a slow, southern drawl in her ear inside the "cranium" helmet she wore. "Got some bumps down here low with the winds from that shower ahead. Should settle out in a minute."

So why in the hell do we have to fly so low?

They had waited for the two Navy helicopters to arrive from the *Dunham*, the decision made from the Task Force 70 head shed aboard the USS *Reagan* that if things went bad while they were en route, the Chinese might be less likely to fire on an American he-

394

licopter than a Chinese ROC Air Force bird. For Katie it was worth the wait, since she imagined these aviators were far more experienced at landing on board a moving ship at sea than their Taiwanese Air Force counterparts, but she had no idea whether landing on a ship was particularly difficult or not. Another bump, this one a little less teeth rattling, made her swear under her breath.

"You okay, Commander Ryan?" Commander Hank Endicott asked from where he sat in the seat designed for the port door gunner, straining his neck to see her over the mound of their gear secured with a cargo net to the deck. That crew member who normally sat in his seat sat instead cross-legged at Endicott's feet to make room for the six of them in a helicopter designed for a crew and up to five passengers.

"Yeah," she shouted, then realized how loud her voice was in her headset, since she was on VOX and they were connected via the internal intercom system. "I'm not a fan of flying."

At least they have the damn doors closed . . .

"Didn't they tell me you, like, rappelled out of a helicopter onto a submarine in rough seas once?" Simran Bakshi asked from beside her.

"Yeah," she said with a sheepish smile. "It was the worst experience of my entire life."

She wondered if that was a fair statement, since not long after, she was trapped inside a submarine, deep in the ocean, with a nuclear-tipped torpedo bearing down on them.

"She complained about it for weeks," Bubba said from the other side of Lorie Tengco, who sat on her left. Lydia Temperley, the intel officer from Special Warfare Group Eight, occupied the last passenger seat at the rear of the helicopter. As a non-operator, Temperley had not joined the others from Group Eight on the exfiltration augment mission.

Another bump made Katie's stomach turn, and she leaned forward, elbows on her thighs, to see out the small square window in the hope it would settle her stomach. Instead she was gripped with a new fear at the sight of the second Seahawk, Viper Two, that seemed far too close on the port side. Ted James and Ben Hart, as well as Lou from DIA and the two support personnel traveling with Commander Endicott, the aide to Task Force 70's Rear Admiral Urban, were inside that helicopter and would perish alongside them, if they crashed into each other, she supposed.

Why are they so close? If a gust of wind drives us into each other, we'll all die. I'll drown as the helicopter sinks to the bottom of the South China Sea.

There was very little chance that she would maintain enough calm to remember the emergency procedures she'd learned in the "Dilbert Dunker" on how to escape a sinking, upside-down helicopter when it crashed into the ocean. No, she'd be better off just folding her arms across her chest and sinking to her inevitable death.

"Jason Dunham up ahead," the pilot called into her headset. "On deck in just a couple more minutes."

Thank God . . .

She closed her eyes, hoping the next few minutes would pass quickly and they would be on the deck of the *Dunham.* Never in a million years would she have imagined yearning to be aboard a Navy destroyer at sea. Her brief time at sea on anything smaller than an aircraft carrier—all of it during her three weeks aboard DDG 62, the USS *Fitzgerald,* out of San Diego during the summer midshipman tour after her "youngster" year—had proven beyond any doubt at all that she was not in any way fit for the surface fleet. But even that seemed better than bouncing around in a helicopter that made her flight in the CMV-22B Osprey to join the *Blackfish* at sea luxurious. Thank God she'd received one of only a handful of exemptions allowing her to go directly to intelligence school instead of doing at least three years in either subs, surface ships, aviation, or the Marines, as was required of nearly all Academy graduates. The helicopter hit another invisible bump and she squeezed her eyes shut tightly.

"Hey, what's that?" Lorie Tengco asked, and she popped her eyes open again.

"What? What's wrong?" she asked, leaning over past Bubba to see what Tengco stared at out the square window set in the door.

"Nothing," Tengco said, pulling her long dark hair from her eyes, where strands had escaped her cranium helmet. "I just thought that the *Dunham* was running up the strait alone. Isn't that another destroyer off to the east and behind her?"

"Lemme see," Bubba said, and leaned over, blocking Katie's view. She closed her eyes again, since Bubba's large frame made it pointless to keep them open. "Oh shit. That's no DDG. In fact, that's not an American. That's a Chinese cruiser." Her eyes popped open again.

What the hell?

"In fact," Bubba said, his slow drawl tighter now with tension, "that looks to me like an 055-class cruiser."

"Yep," the pilot said, his calm voice coming over the intercom into her headset as she strained to look past her LPO. "That there is the *Nanchang*. She engaged us as we entered the strait and has been shadowing us ever since. Just sitting out there like she's waiting for us to fuck up."

"Wait," Katie said, not sure she believed what she was hearing. "Are you saying that's the Chinese destroyer that fired on the *Dunham*?"

"Well, we classify it as a cruiser, technically," Bubba said, turning to her, and now she could see the long light gray ship in the distance.

"That's the one," the pilot said. "Hopefully she doesn't decide to get nasty again while we're trying to land this pig. We're on our final approach, so everyone tighten your belts. Seas are a little rough, and with this wind, it'll be a little bit of a ride."

Well that's just fantastic, she thought, and tightened her lap and shoulder belts so tight they hurt. As if tight belts would save her if they were shot down by the Chinese or crashed into the fantail of the *Dunham.*

Omigod I miss my office. And Josie—I miss my little plant Josie . . .

She squeezed her eyes as tight as she could as the Seahawk seemed to slip down and to the left. When the violent maneuver did not result in a crash into the sea, she opened them again, this time staring straight forward to see through the cockpit windscreen, hoping that would drive the nausea away.

"Like a roller-coaster ride at Busch Gardens," Bubba exclaimed, and had the audacity to sound like he enjoyed it, but she knew him well enough to know that was how he coped with nerves.

"What are those yellow lights—the ones that keep switching to red and then back again?" she asked when she saw the lights, like a miniature traffic light, beside the glass of what she guessed to be some sort of flight control room. Definitely not a tower, since it was on the same level as the fantail flight deck.

"Wave-off lights," the crew member seated on the floor at Endicott's feet said after a moment, when the pilot, who now seemed to have his hands too full to answer, failed to reply.

"What does yellow mean?" she asked, but thought she knew the answer.

"Use caution," the enlisted crewman said.

"And red?" she pressed.

He didn't respond.

She watched the wind whip ocean spray across the deck and the yellow light skipped back to red and then found its way to yellow somehow as the stern of the *Dunham* seemed to rush up toward them and then fall away again.

"Well, this seems stupid," Tengco said, her voice tight, and she reached out and gripped Katie's left arm.

Amen, sister . . .

The traffic light beside the control room flashed red again, flickered, went red and then back to yellow, and just as the deck approached them and then began to fall off, the pilot grunted, "Here we go, y'all . . ."

The Seahawk descended rapidly, then leveled out, the rotors whipping through the wind and ocean spray, and Katie reached across and put her right hand on Lorie Tengco's as they rose again, thinking they were waving off. A moment later the sound of the rotors changed abruptly and she realized they were rising *with* the deck, not away from it.

Did we just land?

"That's how that's done," one of the crew members said, maybe the copilot.

"I do what I do," the southern pilot said, bravado in his voice. Through the side windows she saw sailors approaching them, bent over low, securing them to the deck with chains, she hoped.

Moments later, those sailors were leading her and her five teammates across the flight deck toward an open hangar bay on the starboard side of the deck. Inside, the rolling that made her remember how much she hated surface ships didn't stop, but at least the wind no longer sprayed seawater across her face. Along with the rest of the team, she unbuckled her cranium and then her survival vest and handed them to the flight-suited crewman smiling beside her. She glanced past him at the helicopter chained to the flight deck.

"Where will Viper Two land?" she asked.

"Don't worry, ma'am," the young enlisted aircrew member said. "Lieutenant Commander Taylor is just as good a pilot as Lieutenant Peters. We'll get your teammates aboard."

"*Almost* as good," the pilot said as he entered the hangar bay. "Your team will be a few minutes behind you. They'll get our bird into the hangar bay to clear the deck and then they'll land. No worries."

"Okay," she said, wondering if that landing would be as harrowing as hers. "Thanks for the lift."

"It's what we do," Peters said, and then sauntered off.

"Are you Lieutenant Commander Ryan?" a booming voice asked.

Katie turned to see a fit and lean man, bald on top with his remaining hair buzzed close to his scalp, hands on the hips of the blue overalls with a khaki belt and a silver oak leaf indicating he was a Navy commander, or O-5. He wasn't particularly tall, but carried himself with the confidence of the skipper she assumed him to be.

"Yes, sir," she said. "You're Commander Kreutz?"

"I am," he said, and extended a hand, which she shook, his grip strong and dry. "Welcome aboard the *Jason Dunham*, Commander. Glad we could get you off Penghu before the shitstorm hits."

"We appreciate the lift, Captain," Commander Endicott said from beside her.

"Commander Endicott," Kreutz said with a nod and a smile. "Surprised to see you on the flight manifest. Who did you piss off?"

Endicott laughed.

"Just staying on top of things for 70," he said, referring to his boss, the Task Force 70 commander, Admiral Urban.

"Gotcha," Kreutz said. He indicated the woman to his left. "This is my XO, Commander Karen Cook."

"Good to meet you," Cook said, and shook hands all around. "Hank," she said with a nod to Endicott. "How's carrier life?"

"About what you see here, except bigger staterooms and more places to get lost," Endicott said and laughed.

"So, listen, Ryan," the skipper said, "we're glad to have you and your team safely aboard. We would normally roll out the red carpet, offer you a tour and some one-on-one time with the leadership, but I'm afraid our crew has been at a high-readiness state continuously for the last few hours, so that simply won't work today. I hope you'll accept our apologies."

"No apology necessary, sir," she said.

"You may have noticed the Chinese destroyer trailing us off our port stern," the XO said, jumping in before Katie could continue. "Things are a little dicey right now. I'll be on the bridge and the skipper is heading back to CIC, but our intelligence specialist, IS1 Bowen, will help get you squared away. Bowen and the ship's combat systems officer, Lieutenant Commander Horrillo, will be the interface points for your team."

"Understood, thank you," Katie said to the XO. "At the earliest opportunity, my team and I would like to brief you and your department heads on a possible scenario that could lead to an escalation . . ."

Kreutz rubbed his chin.

"Well, that's kind of you, Ryan. But unless you have some insights not shared through the high-side feeds yet, we're pretty sure we know the current threat. Hell, the *Nanchang* has fired a missile at us once already. We're going to hand you over to the command master chief here." He indicated the taller man to his right with the double-starred anchors of a master chief petty officer on his collar. "He'll help get you sorted with temporary berthing and a workspace. He'll also round up IS1 Bowen, who, like the XO, will be your liaison. Once we're safely out of the strait, we'll arrange for your transfer to the carrier at the earliest convenience. I'm sure you'll be much more comfortable there."

With that he nodded to his CMC and spun on a heel, heading out of the hangar bay with his XO at his side.

"He seems fun," Tengco said when the skipper was out of earshot.

"He's got a lot going on," Katie replied, glancing out the hangar door to where the Chinese destroyer still shadowed them in the distance. "I'm surprised he came to greet us in person."

"That's the way he operates," the CMC said. "He wants you to know that we do not consider y'all's presence here a hassle, but safety as opposed to hospitality is his number one priority at the moment. If you'll follow me, we'll get your berthing squared away and we can get your gear to you when time allows."

Katie nodded and followed him forward as the crew of the *Dunham* maneuvered the Seahawk into the hangar behind them. The ship rolled to starboard in the sea state, and Katie swung an arm out to steady herself. She clenched her jaw and felt it pop.

This was going to suck.

For her team to continue to do their job, she needed to brief the skipper and his war council of senior leadership. Unfortunately, with the *Dunham* at high-readiness condition, every member of that war council was standing watch right now.

I guess I'm just going to have to go camp out in Combat and try to bend the CO's ear.

"We can square away berthing later," she said to the command master chief. "Can you take us right to the N2 shop? We've got work to do."

"We don't have a dedicated N2 shop like the big commands do, ma'am," the master chief said, "but we'll get your team a place to work that won't be in the way."

"Thank you," she replied, already feeling like a third wheel.

But that was okay. She was used it.

They still had an exfiltration in China to support, an invasion of Huayu to help repel, and a war to try to prevent.

They didn't have time for a nap . . .

51

Léi drove the sedan with Qin seated in the rear cabin, hidden from sight by dark tinted windows. The car they were in was one of several she maintained as vehicles being repaired or refurbished in two different shops. It would take a deep dive to make the connections between these garages and her business, and so she tried to have a car at each at all times, not yet registered in her company name, in preparation for a scenario such as this. She was quite sure she wanted—maybe *needed*—to be in the driver's seat and had explained to Qin this would help them look more like a hired car service. He had relented and seemed content, but she had little confidence the plan would work. She wore sunglasses, had the visors down, and chauffer's cap, but all it would take was one traffic camera to snap a picture of her face through the windshield at the right angle and the gambit was up.

She glanced in the rearview mirror at Qin, but he didn't no-tice, as he appeared deeply lost in thought. The news that the Americans had safely extricated his family had lifted such a weight from the man that she barely recognized him for his new optimism, energy, and enthusiasm. Qin, it seemed, now had something to run to rather than away from.

Time passed and so did the kilometers, and to her surprise and great relief, they were not stopped en route to the Peking Man museum. As she exited the highway, memories from her past came bubbling to the surface. She remembered the romantic get-away with Larry Sexton at this place—their last. She had no de-lusion that he'd waited for her and that their decades-old love affair might rekindle. She was a realist—pragmatic almost to a fault. For his sake, for his happiness, she hoped he'd made a life with someone else, that he had a loving wife and children per-haps. She would never wish on him a life of solitude and absti-nence. Nor did she harbor foolish schoolgirl expectations that true love waited for her at the end of this adventure. But that there might be a familiar face, a trusted soul to ease the transition from all that she had known to a new life in a foreign land, well, that still offered significant comfort.

"You are sure this is the place?" Qin asked from the rear seat, and she glanced in the rearview mirror to meet his much more curious and empathetic eyes. "You never explained how you knew the message was authentic."

"It contained information that could only have come from someone I trust," she said, giving the same cryptic answer she had when he'd asked the first time. "And yes," she added, "I have no doubts this is the right place."

"What will happen next?" Qin asked.

She let out a long slow breath.

"I'm afraid that part I have far less certainty about. I expect that whatever team the Americans have arranged to facilitate getting us out of the country will make contact with us here."

"There are many different exhibits at the museum. Do we know specifically where we are to go, or do we just wander around, playing tourist, and hope that the Americans make contact before someone else recognizes us as two of the most hunted fugitives in China?"

"I know where to go. There is a specific display inside the museum of a *Homo erectus* family sitting around a fire. That is where we should expect to make contact."

The message had been quite clear on this point.

. . . It sure would be a shame to live a life without knowing love, but that will be up to fate.

Whether it was Larry Sexton or, more likely, someone he sent, that was where contact would be made, but first things first, she needed to get them safely into the museum and to the display without being recognized. Every public landmark and tourist attraction had a security presence, and she suspected both their pictures had been widely circulated. She contemplated having Qin wait in the car, but splitting up and being separated created a different set of risks and potential problems.

She glanced in her rearview again, this time scanning behind them for any cars that looked familiar from their trip south out of Beijing or west along S317. Seeing none, she followed the highway's curve to the right that would take them to the very clearly marked entrance to the Peking Man exhibit. She saw Qin's curious look in the rearview, but he said nothing, having perhaps caught up to the strange world the Spider had spent her life learning. Tradecraft was everything in her world, and the paranoia that had ruled her life for decades would once again determine their survival.

She watched behind them and continued north for a mile. Unlike the more upscale, suburban neighborhoods of Fangshan, this area was mostly industrial. With not a single car in trail, she made a left turn into the large gravel lot of what the sign announced to be a water seal manufacturing business. She made a U-turn in the lot and parked, leaving the engine idling in gear, nose facing out toward the road so she could watch.

"Is everything all right?" Qin asked, his voice concerned, but more confident than it had been that first long day.

"Yes, I think so," she said. "I'm just making sure."

"Did you see something that concerned you?" the former admiral asked, peering south along the four-lane road.

"No," she said. "But we cannot be too careful. They are always watching . . ." Her voice trailed off as she scanned the road.

A moment later, two cars whizzed by, neither familiar to her.

She hated being pitted against technology—unseen cameras, satellites in space, drones so small they looked like birds, all connected to some computer brain processing billions of inputs. The whole concept disturbed her in a way she had trouble articulating. The threat was an insidious abomination, but it was real. Her antiquated practice of scanning for cars in trail was of little value if they were being watched from space.

"I think we are safe," she said, hoping her voice sounded reassuring. "It is time now."

She shifted her foot from the brake to the accelerator and pulled back onto the road heading toward the museum.

"What if the Americans fail to show up, Léi?" Qin asked from the back.

"If they don't show, we leave."

"And then what? How can we possibly make contact?" he asked. "Where will we go?"

She clenched her jaw. Where would they go? With Jia's restaurant compromised, Léi had to assume her entire network, built over a lifetime, would be ferreted out by the MSS. She would not dare go to her other longtime contacts for fear MSS agents would have gotten to them first to lay a trap.

"We would go south and attempt to cross the border into the jungles of Myanmar," she said. "It would be a long and difficult trek, but I will see you safely out of China . . . Or I will die trying."

His face softened in the mirror and he smiled. "And for that, I am eternally grateful."

A black sedan approached, heading in the opposite direction, and she felt herself tense. The driver of the car glanced at Léi as the car passed. Her gaze immediately ticked to the mirror and looked for brake lights, but the sedan did not slow or turn around.

She let out a long, slow breath.

"Is there a problem?" Qin asked.

"No, I don't think so."

"It looks like we have arrived," he said on seeing the sign ahead for entrance to the Peking Man museum. "It's almost time . . ."

"Do you have regrets?" she asked, surprising herself in asking it.

"No," he said after a moment. "President Li believes he can take Taiwan without losses, but I have studied our enemy my whole life. I know this American president and his resolve. War with the Americans will destroy China. I cannot, in good conscience, let that happen to my country."

"You may wish to start thinking of the Americans as something other than your enemy," she said with a soft smile as she maneuvered into the complex. "They did rescue your family and, with any luck, will exfiltrate us, too."

Her gaze was drawn to an enormous statue of a *Homo erectus* caveman that had been built at the entrance to the grounds.

"Yes," he said. "I suppose that is an adjustment I must make."

"May I ask you a question?" she asked.

"Of course," he said, sounding surprised.

"Do you think of me as a traitor, Qin Hâiyû?" For some reason, his answer mattered to her. He no longer seemed like the desperate, impulsive man whose poor tradecraft and decisions had robbed her of her life in China. Now she saw a family man and an officer with integrity, trying to do what his conscience told him was right.

"Did you become the Spider to serve America, to serve yourself, or to serve China?"

She checked the rearview mirror again, but no one entered behind them. She didn't like the layout of the entrance and parking area. With only one way in and out, once they passed through the front gate they could be easily boxed in . . .

"At first, I did it for me—to prove to myself that I was strong and clever. That I could defy those in power and get away with it. But over time, that changed. Eventually, it wasn't about me. It was about trying to balance the scales of power. China could be so much more, if those in power fought for the people instead of the other way around."

"I do not think of you as a traitor, Léi," Qin said, unbuckling his seat belt as she backed them into a spot along the mostly open back edge of the lot. "But unfortunately, so long as President Li is in power, it doesn't matter what I think. We are both traitors, for the rest of our lives."

She put the car in park, but left it idling. She watched the entrance to the lot, glancing at her watch. They still had a few minutes to reach the display on time. No one exited any of the vehicles near them, and no army of black sedans or SUVs screamed in, blocking their exit. She let out one last deep breath.

"I think we are safe," she said.

She turned off the engine, but left the key in the ignition. After opening the door, she climbed out of the driver's seat and stretched her back. Behind her, she heard Qin do the same.

With a nod of solidarity, they crossed the parking lot side by side, heading toward the walkway that would lead them to the front of the main building.

The sound of approaching tires on asphalt made her freeze in her tracks.

The black sedan she'd seen earlier—the one traveling the opposite direction on the road to the museum—had come back and was heading straight for her and Qin. Léi grabbed Qin's arm and turned him, reversing course back to their car, but it was too late. She heard the engine roar and the car speed toward them.

"You there, stop!" a woman called from an open window as the black sedan braked to a hard stop.

Léi glanced over her shoulder and saw the driver, a man, get out of the sedan and pull a pistol from beneath his dark suit coat. An adrenaline dump flooded Léi's veins with liquid lightning. She grabbed Qin by the sleeve and jerked him into cover behind a small tour bus parked along the curb.

"Stop!" the man hollered. "We are state police. We need to speak with you!"

Léi turned to face Qin, but instead of fear in his eyes she saw determination. "They were in the black sedan that passed us on the road?"

"Yes. They must have spotted us and turned around."

"Do you think they were tracking us, or is this a case of bad luck for us?"

"I don't know, but if they did recognize us, the MSS will know soon enough."

"Then we have to kill them," Qin said coldly, and the same blooded military officer who'd killed the agent in the onion cellar was staring back at her.

Léi nodded. "And after, we run."

52

PEKING MAN MUSEUM

P osing as a couple, Clark held Charlie's hand as they walked through the museum toward the exhibit depicting a caveman family sitting beside a fire. They were making mindless, happy conversation while scanning the faces of every guest in the museum, which was not particularly crowded. So far, he'd seen only one woman matching the Spider's physical description, but she appeared to be traveling with a small tour group, so he'd ruled her out.

The unmistakable muted crack of gunfire outside the museum spiked his heart rate.

Charlie's hand tensed in his, then jerked free from his grip.

By the time he whirled, she was already moving swiftly toward the gift shop, which passage through was required to reach the exit. Like him, he saw she resisted pulling her firearm from her waistband under the flowing, shawl-style shirt she wore. He ran to catch up to her, staying a stride back and to her right, as the rest of the museum patrons woke up to the fact that something was wrong. Due to their training and operator instincts, they'd gotten the jump on everyone and were ahead of *most* of the crowd as frightened tourists poured toward the gift shop's twin glass doors.

They exited near the front of the pack, just as fresh gunfire echoed, panicking the crowd. The sound seemed to be coming from the rear parking area, behind the museum. He met Charlie's gaze as she glanced over her shoulder, asking the silent question with her eyes: *Pursue or evacuate?* He hand-signaled the answer, and they both pulled their weapons from concealed carry holsters and vectored toward the danger.

Charlie stopped at the corner of the building, glanced once around, then kept going. He rounded the corner after her, hugging the wall as he moved along a patch of mowed grass beside the sidewalk that cut between the main museum and another building toward the parking lot.

Charlie moved fast through the short breezeway between the buildings, weaving around shrubs and sculptures. She paused at the end of the cut-through, taking a knee behind a square of hedge. He fell in beside her, and she swiveled, giving his shoulder a squeeze, signaling that they were swapping leads for the engagement.

Clark scanned the parking lot, which was about half full of scattered cars. At first he saw nothing, but then movement in his peripheral vision caught his attention and he crabbed around the shrub for a better look. Two figures were ducking and creeping behind a small tour bus parked along the curb. He couldn't make out their features, but they presented as a man and a woman.

Gunfire cracked as an unknown shooter, or shooters, unloaded a volley at the covering pair. Clark shifted right for a better view. The smaller figure, which he was now certain was a woman, popped up and returned fire with a pistol. Beside her, the man peered around the other corner of the bus, pistol in hand, but he did not fire.

"I think that's them," Charlie said.

"Probably," he said, and scanned the line where the woman had been aiming and spied a black sedan, parked blocking the road to exit the rear parking lot. Behind that car another man and woman aimed pistols over the rooftop, sighting on the tour bus.

Shit . . . Could this pair be the package?

The woman behind the black sedan hollered in Chinese, and Clark was pretty sure she was identifying herself as something official and ordering the other pair to drop their weapons, based on his limited working knowledge of Mandarin. Their shooters' aggressive posturing and dark clothing also signaled "agents," which tipped the scales in Clark's mind as to who were the hunters and who were the hunted.

Decision made, he sighted through his optical sight and put a red dot on the side of the female agent's head. But before he could squeeze the trigger she ducked, spoiling his shot. Clark dragged the red dot to the man in the suit sighting over the hood of the car and squeezed the trigger of his SFX9.

The male agent—who thankfully looked *nothing* like the Chinese minister of national defense—pitched over backward as a gory spray erupted from the side of his head. The woman rose, confused, but her confusion was ended quickly when Charlie's 9mm round tore the top of her head off and she collapsed into the dirt.

Clark shifted right, chopping a hand to indicate Charlie should shift left to converge on the other pair sheltering behind the bus, which was hopefully Qin and the Spider and not two drug dealers being cornered by a couple of innocent cops. But when they arrived at the bus, the couple was gone.

"Clear!" Charlie shouted to him from where she had moved beyond the bus. "No joy," she added, indicating she had no visual on their target.

Shit . . .

They had only minutes, at best, before police or MSS agents started tearing through the main gate.

Clark stood and scanned, lowering his weapon to a forty-five-degree angle, signaling his benign intent.

"Qiū Léi!" he shouted in English. "Fate has interrupted our meeting at the caveman family by the fire. Whatever that place meant to you, you'll have to visit it in another life. Come with us now, or we're all dead."

53

PARKING LOT OF THE PEKING MAN MUSEUM

Qin spoke fluent English, and had since his earliest years at the Academy. At the words spoken in unmistakable American English he stopped, reaching out and grabbing Léi by the arm as she maneuvered between the middle row of cars, heading for the dense woods at the far edge of the parking lot.

"It's them—it's the Americans," he said.

The woman he had until just the last twenty-four hours thought of only as the Spider turned to him, the determination in her eyes now mixed with something he'd not seen there before.

Uncertainty.

"It may be a ruse," she said. "They could be MSS. It's possible that the message was somehow intercepted . . ."

"How?" he asked. "You told me you used only dead drops and old-school coded messages."

"Yes," she said. "But they could have intercepted it and then replaced it for us to find. We cannot assume—"

"We're out of time," the American voice hollered again in English. "Come with us now, or I leave you behind."

416

"Léi," he said, meeting her eyes. "They shot and killed the security guards. It has to be them. Your American contacts."

She nodded, remaining in a squat, her back pressed against the green car they crouched behind.

"Tell me the message," she hollered back in English, apparently needing to satisfy the challenge-response protocol before she would commit. "What did it say?"

"It would be a shame to live a life without knowing love," the man shouted.

"It's them," she said, and stood, holding up her hands as she did.

Qin rose beside her and followed her lead.

He spotted the American operator, who lowered his gun and sprinted toward them. An auburn-haired woman followed, but her weapon was still up and eyes scanning the parking lot for threats. A wave of emotions washed over Qin. He was about to surrender himself into the hands of an enemy he had spent his entire life preparing to wage war with. This act completed the betrayal of his country and he clutched the pistol tighter in his hand as the Americans approached.

"Minister Qin, I assume?" said the thin, fit man, who appeared older than Qin had first imagined. When Qin didn't answer, the operator continued. "Admiral, I personally led the team that rescued your wife and daughters in the Maldives. My partner here was on that mission, too, and we delivered Caiji, Diedie, and Beiye to a secure location, where they are now waiting for you. Let's get you to them, okay?"

The guilt, anger, and fear Qin had been feeling were replaced in an instant with relief and gratitude. He handed the pistol to the man.

"No," the American said. "Hang on to it. The fight might not be over."

That was the final act of trust Qin needed and he switched the pistol to his left hand and extended his right to this American stranger.

"Thank you for making my family safe," he said.

"You're welcome," the man said, awkwardly shaking his hand in a cross-handed grip with his left, not wanting to let go of his weapon. "Now we have to go."

"I am Qiū Léi," Léi said from beside him. "And I wish to come also."

"Of course you're coming," the woman said. "I'm Charlie. Your reputation precedes you. Your name means Autumn Thunder, I believe, and it is fitting. Decades of covert operations behind the lines. You are my hero."

Qin watched Léi smile at this.

"And I'm John," the American operator said. "Now let's get the hell out of here before we all die."

They ran as a group to a blue crossover SUV at the rear of the lot.

"Wait," Léi said. "Are you operating in the country under the cover of being an American businessman?"

"Yes," the man called John said over his shoulder.

"Then we should take our car. Yours will be under state surveillance if you are an American in our country."

"And yours just got attacked by two MSS agents," the woman said.

"Perhaps," Léi said. "But I think these were two police investigators who simply recognized us from the nationwide manhunt. I don't believe they are Guóānbù, or there would be helicopters and agents swarming this place . . ."

The man nodded. "Okay, we take your car, but I'm driving."

They ran to Léi's gray sedan. Qin and Léi jumped into the back and ducked low, while the Western woman with a man's name slid into the front passenger seat. Engine roaring and tires shrieking, they sped out of the museum parking lot. The driver, John, whipped around the black sedan—jumping the curb with two wheels and fishtailing wildly as he recovered and maneuvered to flee the museum complex.

"Shit," John cursed, and Qin leaned forward to look out the front windshield.

A police car sat angled across the exit, a uniformed officer directing fleeing people toward the grassy area beside the statue of the Peking Man, where two other officers stood. The American maneuvered the sedan left, around the throngs of people, but the policeman saw him coming and stepped into the other lane not blocked by his police car.

The officer raised his hand, commanding them to stop.

When John pressed on the gas, the policeman pulled his pistol and hollered to the other officers. At the last moment, the officer dove clear, narrowly avoiding being run over.

"Everyone get down!" Charlie barked.

Qin ducked, throwing himself on top of Léi, who was reclined on the rear bench. Glass shards rained down on them as a bullet exploded the rear window.

"We need to get off the road, ditch this vehicle, and find new wheels," John said to his partner, and Qin got the gist of the American vernacular.

"What is the exfiltration plan?" Léi asked, sitting back up and looking out the large hole in the rear window.

"Step one is to get away from here," John said. "Are we being pursued?"

"Not yet," Léi said.

John swerved the car off the main road and onto a dirt access road, weaving behind a series of blue-roofed warehouses. Toward the rear of the small complex sat an open garage with road repair equipment inside. John maneuvered the sedan into the garage and skidded to a stop.

"They can't see the car from the air," John said, looking back at them over his shoulder. "Wait here."

In a flash, he was out of the car and sprinting away. For a terrifying moment, Qin wondered if the American was abandoning them to save himself.

"Trust me," Charlie said with a tight-lipped smile. "I haven't known him long, but I've seen him in action. He'll get us out of here."

Moments later Qin heard the growl of a diesel engine, and looked up, gripping the pistol he'd nearly forgotten he had in his hand. Instead of a military vehicle, Qin saw a dump truck rumbling toward them, dust kicking up from the dirt road, and John grinning behind the wheel.

The truck groaned to a halt outside the open garage door.

"Qin, can you drive one of these?" John shouted as they all piled out of the sedan.

"I can figure it out," Qin said, hoping he could. He had commanded a billion-dollar warship, surely he could figure a dump truck out.

"Good," John said. "Because it'll look strange to see an American behind the wheel."

Qin stepped up onto the tall metal step as John flipped himself over the front seat into the rear.

"Everyone else back here with me," John commanded.

Qin took the wheel and studied the gearshift a moment.

"Put these on," John said, handing him a work hat and a pair of sunglasses. "The service road runs parallel to the main road for less than a mile, then heads west along the mountains. Follow it until we hit Highway X030 and then head south. When we come to the next town, we'll change vehicles."

Qin nodded, getting the main idea.

"Well," Charlie said from behind his seat. "That went well."

The American laughed.

How one could laugh at such a time seemed inconceivable to Qin, but then he thought back to the times he'd made jokes in the heat of a crisis at sea to ease the nerves of his men.

We are all not so very different . . .

He ground the gears as he put the truck into first and they jerked away from the shed. Moments later he had the feel for the clutch and the stick shift and shifted smoothly out of second and into third gear, pulling the truck onto the service road, heading north.

"What is the plan for getting out of China?" he asked over his shoulder, looking back to see Léi and the two Western spies crouching on the floorboards.

There was an uncomfortable pause before John spoke.

"Step one is to survive the next hour. Then we find a new vehicle and survive the hour after that." The American let out a long, slow breath. "If we pull that off, we make our way to Tianjin . . ."

Qin shifted into fourth gear and clenched his jaw.

This plan was far from reassuring, but at least he wasn't trapped in a smelly onion cellar any longer. And, most important, Caiji and his girls were safe. For that, he owed this American his life.

54

President Ryan listened carefully to German chancellor Aneke Schultz, trying to decipher any unspoken concerns, but hearing none. He had a strong working relationship with Schultz, and winning her commitment was critical to having European support. She was tough, fair, and courageous, and Ryan had worried the least about this call.

"You can count on Germany, President Ryan," she said.

Ryan smiled to himself. They had become Jack and Aneke whenever they met face-to-face, but for the purposes of this official call she was sticking to the formal.

"I know I can, Chancellor Schultz," he said. "I appreciate your leadership and courage on this. I know that the economic implications here are not insignificant."

"That is true," the German chancellor agreed. "But we have no one to blame but ourselves, I'm afraid. This moment was inevitable and demonstrative of the risks of allowing too much power, whether political, military, or economic, to be achieved by any one nation. As they say about absolute power . . ."

"Indeed," he agreed. "Still, an attack on our ship . . ."

"Is an attack on all of us, Jack," she said, and now smiled. "Is that not how it is supposed to work? And, in any case, the fall of Taiwan would give China even more economic leverage, as it will grow their monopoly in semiconductor exports as well as increased military control in the South Sea. Offering our support is in our own self-interest as well."

"Thank you, Aneke. We are stronger together," he said, glad to be working with someone who saw the truth so readily. Not all of his calls had gone so easily, though in the end a consensus had been reached and alliances had been shored.

With that they said their goodbyes and the video chat was ended and he was left with only two calls left to make. But before he could reach for the phone to alert the Oval Office secretary to have his chief of staff make the next call, the phone rang on its own and he pressed the speaker button.

"Yes?"

"Mr. President, I know you have a tight schedule with two remaining calls, but Director Foley is here with CIA director Stephens. They say it is urgent."

"Send them in," he said and felt his pulse quicken.

The door opened and Mary Pat led CIA director Ben Stephens into the Oval.

"Sorry, Mr. President, but we have an update we felt you would want to hear immediately."

Ryan studied their faces, trying to discern whether this was good news or bad.

"That's what I always want, Director Foley," he said. He stayed at his desk instead of walking them to the sitting area of the office, conveying the message he still had much work to do. "What's going on?"

"It's kind of a good news/bad news situation, Mr. President," Stephens said, and Ryan waited for the shoe to drop.

"The good news is that it appears that Task Force 99 now has Minister Qin and our CIA asset in their possession, and appear, for now at least, to be safely away."

"Well, that's great news," Ryan said. "What's the bad news?"

"The bad news, sir, is that the meet did not go as hoped. Qin and the Spider were either followed or otherwise detected and confronted prior to the meet. There was a gun battle . . ."

"Did we lose anyone?" Ryan asked, his friend John Clark's face filling his mind suddenly. He was a man who had given far more than his share to his country.

"No, Mr. President," Mary Pat said. "But they killed two national security officers in the parking lot of the Peking Man museum prior to getting away. We were able to monitor the entire event via a satellite we had tasked in position at the time of the meet. At present, we don't think that the MSS is on their tail, but it could just be a matter of time."

"So they went after the two most wanted people in China with just two officers?" Ryan asked. It made no sense, unless . . .

"We think it was just bad luck, sir," Stephens said, confirming his guess. "Obviously every cop and agent in China is on the lookout for them. We think these two were following up on a random sighting or something. Otherwise . . ."

"Our guys and Qin would be dead already," Ryan said, finishing the thought.

"That's our read, Mr. President," Stephens said with a nod.

"Where are they now?" Ryan asked.

Mary Pat shook her head.

"We're not sure," she said. "We saw them exfil the museum and then disappear into a warehouse district. The car never came out. There were a number of cars that could have been them departing the area over time, and one large dump truck, but nothing panned out. We lost them."

Ryan smiled.

"If we lost them, *knowing* the where and when, then it was pretty good odds the Chinese lost them, too," he said, feeling the glass was now well more than half full. "How much time until the exfiltration?"

"Plenty of time for them to make it," Mary Pat said.

Stephens grimaced and looked at his feet.

"You seem unsure," Ryan said.

"No, not exactly, sir," his CIA director said. "It's more a cost-benefit analysis."

"Explain," Ryan said, but he knew what Stephens would tell him.

"Sir, at this point the risk of getting Qin out may exceed the potential benefit. It seems the timeline is too tight for any intelligence he could share to be of any benefit whatsoever. We have ideas and even evidence now of what President Li is planning, and Minister Qin, whether he's the architect of the plan or not, can add very little, and none of it in time to be of help. On the other hand, sir, the risk of Qin being picked up by the MSS along with our field agents . . ."

"I understand what you're getting at, Director Stephens," Ryan said, holding up a hand, "but Qin risked everything to prevent this war. Our people are coming out either way. I'm inclined to bring Minister Qin out with them."

"Understood, Mr. President," Stephens said. His face suggested he knew Ryan well enough that he'd predicted this response. But, as irritating as it was, Ryan respected that it was the man's job to show him all the options and balance them with the risks.

"We're gonna do the right thing, Ben," he said, putting a final point on it.

"Yes, Mr. President."

"How is the exfiltration plan shaping up?" he asked, shifting his eyes to Mary Pat.

"Everything is in place," she said. "We have a team aboard the South Korean cargo ship *Capella* and we believe the remainder of Task Force 99 has made it to the Tianjin area. Once the *Capella* docks, we need to get everyone aboard without being detected and embark the ship. If we can make it to international waters without being interdicted . . . then the South Korean Navy can escort them to Incheon."

"What could possibly go wrong?" Stephens asked, and chuckled.

"Right," Ryan said, trying to summon a smile but failing. "Keep me in the loop," he told them, signaling that the meeting was over.

"We will," Mary Pat said, and he watched his intelligence leadership leave the Oval.

As soon as the door shut, his desk phone chimed and he pressed the speaker button.

"Yes?"

"Mr. President, I have French president Carayon standing by for a video chat, when you're ready."

"I'm ready," he said.

Ryan leaned back in his chair, closed his eyes, and said a short prayer for the safety of the team in China. Then he pushed all thoughts of Clark and Qin from his mind. Clark would do what he did best.

Now I need to do everything I can to head off this war.

But Ryan's plan would only work if he could get buy-in from his international partners.

The screen of his desktop came to life and the French president gave him a tight smile.

"Thank you for making time for me, Laurent," he said.

"No thanks required, Jack," Carayon replied, his accent thick and tone serious. "These are dangerous times, and we must stick together. I received the briefing from Secretary of State Adler, and it appears the situation has become dire. Is it true the PLA Navy fired a missile at one of your ships?"

"It is and I'm afraid there's going to be many more missiles fired by both navies if we can't find a way to de-escalate and stop Li from crossing a line he can't come back from."

"What can France do to help?"

Ryan smiled and launched the prepared pitch he had already made a half dozen times today to other world leaders.

"We must be unified to face down this threat, Laurent, and that will require us standing as one. That will mean sharing what might be a heavy economic burden . . ."

55

Xu Chao, secretary general of the People's Republic of China, stared at President Li Jian Jun. Inside Xu harbored great concerns, but on the outside his face was a mask. He had watched Jian Jun's gradual but undeniable transformation over the years. Li had always been ambitious, but that ambition had once been tempered by a patient and pragmatic approach to problem-solving. Not anymore. Like waves on a beach, the power of his position had eroded those traits until all that remained was raw ambition. Li meant to become the most powerful man in the world, and he was tired of waiting.

Xu was not afraid of President Li's wrath, because Xu did not fear death. His concern was only for his country. The PRC was on the verge of achieving superpower greatness, but like all good things, such an achievement took decades in the making. Li had once understood this, but not anymore. And now Xu was beginning to worry the man may have lost his mind.

"Perhaps you can explain to me how it is that Minister Qin and his abductors—or perhaps, it would now appear, his *accomplices*—were able to escape?" Li shouted at the minister of state security.

To his credit, Deng Su Wei kept his calm and appeared fatalistic in the face of the knowledge that he might not survive the day. The only other man present, Deputy Minister for Foreign Affairs Bai Ming, wisely remained silent.

"That Qin and the Spider were found was as much good fortune as good tactics, President Li," Minister Deng said gently. "The local agents were, we believe, following up on a possible sighting when they encountered the two in the parking lot of the Peking Man exhibit. There was but one witness we could find—a man sitting in his car in the lot at the time—and he reports that both Qin and the woman, whom we believe to be Qiū Léi—"

"The Spider," Li said, spitting the words out as if they left a horrible taste in his mouth.

"Yes, the Spider," Deng continued. "He reports gunfire was exchanged, and that both the Spider *and* Qin were firing at our agents, confirming in my mind that Qin is indeed a traitor. Then there were two others who arrived, killing our agents and escaping with the first two. Our witness is not certain if they were Chinese—"

"Can he not tell the difference between Chinese and Westerners?" Li shouted, pounding a fist on the table.

Xu pursed his lips, his concern and his irritation increasing. This was not how one got things done.

"He was seeking cover on the floor of his car," Deng said calmly. "But he saw them leave in a gray sedan. We have archived satellite coverage of the area that shows this vehicle traveling north until coverage was lost. We did not have a dedicated satellite in position, since this was opportunistic, obviously, but we have not been able to identify the vehicle more precisely nor find it again."

"And why in the hell were only two agents sent?" Li demanded.

"Again," Deng said, and Xu saw the intelligence professional's patience thinning, though he suspected the man was far too savvy and controlled to let it slip entirely, "they were not sent. They spotted a suspicious vehicle and were following up on it, we believe. Their suspicion may not have been very high, since they did not request an additional response."

Xu watched Li struggle to regain control. The president was staring daggers at his minister of state security as he let out a hissing breath through clenched teeth.

"They were heading north when we lost them," Li said, narrowing his eyes at Deng. "That is a data point we can build from. Find them, Minister Deng. Find them and kill them while there is still time."

"I've diverted all available resources to working this problem," Deng said. "They will be found."

"In the meantime, President Li," Xu said, finally finding his moment. "We must discuss ways in which to de-escalate the situation in the Strait of Taiwan. With Qin now in direct contact with the Americans, we cannot know what details about Operation Sea Serpent he's shared. Couple that with President Ryan's clear unwillingness to back down on his support of Taiwan, and I fear that the opportunity for a swift and relatively bloodless reunification campaign has been lost. It seems prudent to conduct our exercise as planned to save face, but we should postpone the invasion until a later date, when we will once again have the element of surprise on our side."

Li turned to him, his eyes burning coals of anger.

"Save face?" he growled. "Is that your concern, Secretary General Xu? I am trying to raise our nation up to its place in the world as a superpower, a deserved move that absolutely requires the reunification of Taiwan for both the increased economic advantages it gives us over the world's hunger for semiconductors, and for the strategic presence in the South China Sea. I could care less about saving face. Are you a man or a mouse?"

Xu chose his words carefully, as the manic look in Li's eyes brought his level of concern to an all-time high.

"I am simply pointing out that patience is often our greatest ally, Mr. President," he said. "Waiting is far less costly than failing—"

"And succeeding requires courage and strength," Li interrupted. "China has both. *I* have both. We are presented with a once-in-a-lifetime opportunity here. Ryan's Navy will make a mistake and we will capitalize. And even if they don't, they will be too slow and too disorganized to intervene effectively. Mark my words, once Taiwan has fallen and we are in control, the pundits will complain, the politicians will saber-rattle, and the financiers will move money, but ultimately the world will do nothing. We will let their greed and desire for self-preservation win the war for us."

Xu watched Li carefully, but said nothing.

Timing would be everything here. The only thing worse than the risks of the situation Li had placed them in was to combine it with a failed coup.

He gave the president a nod and folded his hands.

"We are a short time away from victory, Secretary General Xu," Li said, and now his face had returned to the calm but charming look that had seen his rise to power. "I know these are trying circumstances and that there is risk and that brings fear. But we must be brave enough to continue. Great gain often requires such courage."

"Of course," Xu conceded.

"That is all," Li said, rising quickly from his chair and hurrying out the private door from the room, his two goonish foot soldiers from his security detail in tow.

Xu glanced at Deng, who had risen from his chair also and now gave him a slight bow of both deference and thanks. Deng was a good man in an impossible situation. Deputy Minister Bai was already hurrying from the room, his attaché case clutched to his chest, no doubt just happy to have survived.

As Xu made his way to the door, his mind already swirled with questions—and a few answers—about what he must do next. He had the will and courage to do what must be done, but he worried if he, any longer, had the assets and support necessary. They had, perhaps, let the President Li problem fester too long. He had to choose very carefully whom he could now trust.

His thoughts went back to the sage words of the wisest man he knew. His father had served under Mao and had been a true believer. He has also been pragmatic. Some of the last words he'd shared with his son, of whom he was quite proud, came to Xu now.

"Do you know what the greatest danger of capitalism is, my son?" Xu's father had asked.

"Tell me, Father," young Xu had replied, in awe of his legendary father.

"That it can be so easily corrupted by men seeking power and

wealth." The old man had then smiled and looked him in the eyes. *"And do you know what the greatest danger of Communism is, my son?"* When young Xu had simply shaken his head, the old man had whispered, *"The same thing. Never forget this. Communism only works when it serves the people, not asks the people to serve their leaders."*

This memory filled the secretary general with a powerful sense of purpose . . . and a plan for how to stop war with America.

56

F rom the front passenger seat, Clark used a spotter scope to scan the rows and rows of stacked shipping containers that stretched into the distance in both directions. Despite the late hour, the port wasn't dark. Halogen floodlights on tall aluminum light poles provided good illumination along the service roads and piers. There were gaps, however—dark corridors between the thousands of shipping containers stacked three, four, or five units high. Something about attempting to navigate the warren of passages in the stacks between their current location and the ship waiting for them at pier 117 taunted and teased his tactical mind.

"Damn, this port is huge," he mumbled as he looked for security guards and roving patrols among the containers and possible snipers perched in the metal lattice structures of the massive cranes that lined the waterfront.

"It is the biggest port in China, and one of the largest in the world. It has over a hundred and fifty berths and covers one hundred and twenty-five square kilometers," Admiral Qin said from the back seat of the stolen sedan. "Half a billion tons of cargo moves in and out of this facility every year."

Charlie let out a little whistle. "I've never seen anything like it. You could probably combine all the ports in Australia, and they still wouldn't have that capacity."

"What do you see?" asked Léi from the driver's seat.

Clark had happily delegated the driving and navigation duties to the Spider after they ditched the truck. His Mandarin sucked and he couldn't read the signs.

"Nothing. I see *nothing* and that's what's bothering me," he said, letting a little of the concern he was feeling creep into his voice. He shifted his gaze to the ROKS *Capella*, the Korean vessel waiting on them to exfil. He noted the smudge in the air above the exhaust stacks, indicating that the ship's diesel engines were running. Tugs be damned, they would be departing as soon as Clark and his team were aboard.

"You think this is a trap?" she asked, more statement than question.

"My gut tells me it's too easy, but common sense says if they were onto us, they would have already picked us up. Why let us get all the way to the finish line?"

"Can I take a look?" she said.

He passed her the monocular dual-band scope. "Be my guest . . ."

She took it and began a scan of her own, talking while she did. "You are right to be suspicious . . . There is an advantage to setting a trap for us to walk into. They have more control that way. It would be a very Guóānbù strategy."

His imagination gave form to her words. He visualized himself leading their four-person squad in a diamond formation through the darkened corridors between stacks of shipping containers four and five boxes high. Charlie would take the rear position with Léi and Qin in the middle, all of them without body armor, helmets, NVGs, or rifles. And when they got to the middle of a row, he imagined two squads of black-clad Chinese SWAT operators blocking their path front and back with shooters popping up on top of the containers, taking aim from above. There was no combination of marksmanship, dexterity, and luck that would allow them to persevere in that geometry.

Clark studied the woman as she surveyed the loading docks with the scope. In only the short time that he'd known her, he'd become a big fan of Qui Léi, *Autumn Thunder.* Her pedigree and knowledge of tradecraft from decades of working undetected in Beijing spoke for itself, but there was another layer that he appreciated even more working with her in person. She was intuitively tactical and methodical. The same qualities Clark credited for his own success in the world of clandestine operations. Not to mention her balls of steel taking on the MSS unaugmented and alone for God knows how many years while living twelve blocks from their headquarters in Beijing . . .

I could use a woman like Léi in Operations at The Campus, he thought, his mind already working on his recruitment sales pitch to her. But he was getting ahead of himself. *First, we get out of this alive.*

"Do you see anything?" he said when a full minute of silence had passed.

"No," she said, and lowered the scope. "Do you have confirmation that the other task force members are on board the *Capella*?"

He nodded.

She handed him the scope back. "Even if we make it aboard, it must be three hundred kilometers of ocean travel to reach the Yellow Sea and international waters."

"Three hundred and fifty," Qin said from the back seat. "That is a long time, in which the PLA can mobilize assets to board and commandeer the vessel."

"I know," Clark said, "but it is what it is. This is our exfil plan. Don't worry about after. Our focus now is getting aboard the *Capella* without detection."

She nodded, but her expression looked cynically dubious.

And rightfully so . . .

"Let's assume Léi is right and our friends at the Ministry of State Security have set a trap for us, then the logical play would be for them to position shooters so that, when they spring that trap, we're stuck in a kill box," Clark said, working out the details as he spoke. "We need to take that option off the table."

"Yes, yes, this is very good thinking," Léi said. "They will expect us to sneak between the shipping containers and take the most direct path. We should not do this."

Clark pulled out his mobile phone and opened a satellite image of the area of the port where they were now. The image was dated because they didn't have real-time cyber support due to OPSEC restrictions, but it was better than nothing. He set the phone face up on the center armrest console so everyone could see it.

"I wish I had a printed copy, but we're stuck with this," he grumbled, hating how his thick and callous sausage fingers blocked out a fifth of the screen when he pointed at something. "The *Capella* is berthed here at slip 117. Thankfully, the captain had the foresight to have the tugs turn her around before snugging up to the pier so she's pointed nose out. We've got this service road that runs along the entire jetty between the dock cranes and the container stacks. What if instead of cutting between the stacks, we loop around and approach from the east by car? That's the long way around, so they wouldn't expect it. Also, it keeps us out of the stacks."

"So, you're saying, drive past this corridor, this corridor, and this corridor, skipping all the cut-throughs between the stacks and go to the end of the jetty where we chuck a Uey and come back to the *Capella* on this service road here?" Charlie asked, tracing with her fingernail the exact path that Clark was proposing.

"Precisely," he said.

"If we come from the east," Qin said, "we have no option to abort and reverse course. We trap ourselves between the water and the capture team . . . Assuming there is a capture team."

"That's true," Clark said, "and the disadvantage of the plan."

"If there's a capture team, we're already buggered," Charlie said with a laugh, "but I'd rather have a fighting chance than serve their snipers my head on a platter, thank you very much."

"So, we're all in agreement," Clark said. "We go with this plan?"

He got nods of consent all around.

"All right, it's settled," he said and texted the number *1* to Lee Hyori to let the other members of Task Force 99 on the *Capella* know he'd arrived at the terminal with the package. Then he pulled his suppressed pistol and scooted down as low as possible in his seat. "Everybody get low. It's showtime."

57

His lower body crammed in the footwell and torso pressed uncomfortably into the seat of the front passenger seat, Clark gripped his pistol and waited. He watched Léi's face intently as she piloted the sedan along the looping service road on Jetty 1. A change in her expression would be the first indicator that something was wrong.

Or a sniper round through her forehead, he thought morbidly.

"Halfway there," she said, barely moving her lips.

"Check," he said as the cabin of the sedan alternately brightened and dimmed as they passed under the halogen dock lights.

Ten seconds later, she started the fishhook turn that would take them around the tip of the jetty. After passing a pair of east-facing piers, they would loop onto the southern leg of the road, which served the mile-long row of berths for deep draft vessels. The *Capella* was parked five births down, in number 117.

He could hear the defense minister's nervous breathing from where the man was ducked down in the back seat. Beside him,

439

Charlie seemed ready for action. And Léi looked as calm and unflappable as Ding or Adara or any other Campus teammate, had
they been in the driver's seat instead of this woman he barely knew.

The sedan's tires thudded rhythmically over the seams between the concrete sections used to build the massive man-made
jetty. With every *ka-chunk, ka-chunk*, they were three yards closer
to freedom. He watched Léi ease up on the wheel, then straighten
it out as they came out of the turn.

Ka-chunk, ka-chunk.

Ka-chunk, ka-chunk . . .

In his mind's eye, he pictured their westward progress down
the service road toward berth 117. And just as he was beginning
to dare to hope they might actually make it, he saw her frown.

"What?" he said, fresh dread in his stomach.

"Security guard with a flashlight ahead," she said, barely moving her lips as she eased off the accelerator. "He's waving me to
stop."

"How's he dressed?"

"Black tactical clothing."

"Helmet and rifle?"

"Yes."

Shit, we're fucked.

His mind shifted into high gear as he war-gamed out the inevitable confrontation.

"What should I do?" she said.

"Wave at him, but keep moving. Do not accelerate, but do not
stop. Passive retreat is our only option."

"I understand," she said, and he watched her smile and raise a
hand in greeting.

The sedan kept rolling.

Ka-chunk, ka-chunk . . .

440

"Do you see any other guards?" he asked.

"No," she said through a clench-jawed smile.

Having been in countless situations like this, Clark had a well-calibrated internal clock for how they unfolded. If the guard was port security doing a routine check, there was a chance he might let them drive on by. But if he was part of a capture team, he would call her bluff and—

Léi cursed in Mandarin, mashed the accelerator, and ducked.

Well, that answers that question, Clark thought with a fatalistic frown.

The sedan's engine roared as the vehicle screamed forward. The guard opened fire and she jerked the steering wheel to the left. The volley of gunfire was cut abruptly short by a loud and jarring thud, as she plowed into the guard using the sedan as a weapon. She corrected after impact, steering back to center as the sedan raced down the service road.

Ka-chunk, ka-chunk . . .

Ka-chunk, ka-chunk . . .

Fresh gunfire erupted, fracturing the windshield and blowing out the passenger window above Clark's head, showering him with chunks of glass.

Ka-chunk, ka-chunk . . .

"Just keep going, Léi," he shouted over the roar of the engine and the report of gunfire.

"I am trying, but I can't see," she said, doing her best to stay low and drive.

Gunfire blew out the back window and then the driver's-side window. He watched a fresh scarlet trickle run down her right cheek from a glass nick above her right eyebrow. A gunshot blew out the right front tire, jerking the car hard to the right.

Léi blindly course corrected.

Ka-chunk, ka-chunk . . .

A heartbeat later, a second gunshot blew out the left front tire and the sedan lost all momentum as the front tires ripped off the rims.

"They want to take us alive," Qin called from the back seat.

Clark agreed with the comment because the snipers were not putting rounds through door panels or the roof.

Not yet, that is.

"Now what?" Léi said, looking at Clark as the front rims spun, sparked, and grinded on the concrete to no avail.

"Qin is right, they want to take us alive, at least some of us," Clark said. "We wait for them to advance on the vehicle. We make them open the doors. When they do, we put rounds in faces and fight like hell."

Léi removed her foot from the accelerator, and everything fell silent. Clark resisted the urge to lift his head to look around, knowing they'd pop his melon in a second once they saw he wasn't Qin. He gritted his teeth in frustration and knew he'd have to shoot with the precision of a Navy sniper in the zone for them to have any chance of surviving. And even if every one of his rounds was perfect, the odds were still grim.

If this is how I go out, then I'm doing it in a blaze of glory, the old SEAL inside decided.

His mobile phone vibrated in his pocket.

What the hell?

He fished it out and took the call—because at this point, it didn't matter if the Chinese intercepted it.

"Yes?" he said, answering on speaker.

"JC, this is JC," said an unfamiliar American voice on the phone. "How's it going down there in the suck?"

From the tenor of the voice and the word choice, Clark knew

he was talking to a fellow operator. "I'm not gonna lie, I don't like our odds."

The dude chuckled. "Yeah, your odds are shit. You have a circle of shooters closing ranks around your sedan. Four up front. Three converging behind you. Your vehicle is twenty-five yards from the *Capella*."

"That's helpful visuals, thank you."

"Is the package with you?"

"Check."

"So, here's the deal, sir. I'm a frogman with a God's-eye view of the situation," the man with the initials JC said. "Leaving people behind just ain't in my DNA. With your permission, me and my pals would like to drop the hammer."

A salty smile curled Clark's lips. JC was talking a language Clark well understood. *God* was a common sniper call sign used in the teams, and by using it JC was communicating that he and "his pals" were set up in perches with long guns.

"Drop the hammer."

"Hooyah," JC said. "Hold the line . . ."

The next thing Clark heard was a trio of long guns going to work. Return fire from the enemy capture team followed in a chorus of prolonged bursts from all around the sedan . . . But in short order the Chinese machine guns fell silent one by one until it was dead quiet on the pier.

"You're clear to move the package," JC said. "Go now."

Clark shoved the phone in his pocket, pulled the door handle, and kicked the door open with his boot. He slid out of the car and into a low combat crouch, scanning a wide arc over his pistol for threats. Unmoving black-clad bodies littered the pier. The American snipers had done their jobs well, using precision headshots to make sure none of the Chinese agents could get back in the fight.

"We're clear—go, go, go!" Clark barked at his three compan-
ions, and chopped a hand at the metal brow linking the *Capella*
to the pier.

Charlie, Léi, and Qin—who had all exited the sedan on the
driver's side—sprinted toward the ship. Clark took off after them,
ten yards behind. As he ran, his Spidey sense began to tingle; he'd
been in the game too long to ignore it. He turned and looked over
his left shoulder, just in time to see the guard that Léi had hit
with the car getting into a kneeling firing stance twenty yards
away. Clark whirled, sighted, and unloaded half his magazine at
the shooter. He could tell some of his rounds connected, but the
Chinese shooter squeezed off a volley, strafing the pier.

Clark got low as a high-velocity sniper round pierced the night.
He watched the Chinese operator's head jerk back, ending the
engagement. The threat neutralized, Clark spun back to front to
see both Léi and Qin down on the pier, the former lying partially
on top of the latter. Charlie, who'd been in the lead, ran back to
help as Clark arrived simultaneously from the other direction.
With a quick survey, Clark saw that Léi had taken a round in the
upper thigh.

"You saved me," Qin said, sitting up and looking at Léi with
incredulous eyes.

Léi winced, but managed a tight smile. "Only because I knew
they don't teach you how to duck in the PLA."

Clark performed a quick scan for new threats and, finding
none, shoved his pistol into his waistband.

He squeezed Léi's upper arm. "I'm going to carry you. Lay on
your back."

She did and Clark performed a Ranger roll to hoist the Spider
into a fireman's carry. His right knee cracked, his left shoulder
popped, and his back complained loudly from the strain, but he

executed the maneuver and had her up and across his shoulders in two seconds flat.

Thank God she's as thin as a board, he thought as he jogged toward the brow with Qin running in front and Charlie protecting his six.

The exhausted, embattled foursome crossed the metal gangway to the deck of the Korean vessel, where a team of three American operators were waiting.

"Where's she hit?" one of the kitted-up warriors said, stepping up to Clark.

"Left upper thigh. It's a bleeder, too," he said, because he could feel the wet on his upper back already.

"How about I lighten your load, old-timer?" the SEAL said with a punchy grin.

Clark, who realized that he was huffing like he'd just run a half-marathon, said, "Only if you promise to take good care of her."

"Bo is an Eighteen Delta," the other operator said. "Don't worry, sir, she's in capable hands."

Clark lowered himself to a knee and the two SEALs eased Léi off his shoulders. As they carried her away, she shot him a weary, grateful smile. He smiled back at her and mouthed the words Thank you.

As he pressed to his feet, the *Capella* shuddered and began to move. Clark looked for tugs pulling them away from the pier, but he didn't see any.

The lone remaining operator standing on deck said, "The *Capella* has thrusters . . . A little secret not on the register."

Clark nodded as he turned to look at the brow, which normally required a crane to remove prior to disembarking. As the *Capella* powered away from the pier, the brow began to drag and scrape as it was pulled away from the concrete ledge. When the gap between the ship and the dock exceeded the span, the metal footbridge tumbled into the water with a resounding splash.

"Oops," the operator said with a grin.

Clark raised an eyebrow at the man. "JC?"

The operator nodded and stuck out his hand. "John Conza."

Clark shook it. "Nice shootin' back there."

"Easy day," Conza said, then turned to Charlie and Qin. "You guys need to get belowdecks with the others. Especially you, Minister Qin."

"Thanks for having our six," Charlie said, extending her fist to JC as she turned toward the hatch the other SEALs had disappeared through with Léi.

"Happy to help," JC said.

Qin nodded in wordless thanks to JC, then turned to Clark. "You are a very brave man. Thank you for everything you risked."

Clark nodded. "Same to you, Admiral. Now, you need to get belowdecks."

The defense minister turned and jogged after Charlie, leaving Clark and Conza as the lone two people topside. The two former SEALs stood side by side, looking aft as the *Capella* slowly accelerated under full power away from the pier toward Bohai Bay.

"How far do you think we'll make it before they board us?" JC asked.

Clark scratched at the two days' stubble on his neck. "Seven nautical miles."

"Sounds about right," the spooky operator said. Then, after a beat, added, "I've never done time in a Chinese prison before. What about you?"

"Nope, can't say that I have . . . but it's on my bucket list, so at least I've got that going for me."

This comment got JC laughing, which got Clark laughing—the gallows humor tempering the dread each man was feeling about the inevitable horror show of interrogation and torture that lay in their future. They'd just killed eight Chinese operators and left the bodies on the pier in front of berth 117. There was no way in hell they'd reach the Yellow Sea before the Chinese sent an overwhelming force of SOF operators, helicopters, and PLA Navy warships to seize the *Capella*.

We were so damn close to pulling this off. His thoughts went to his family he would never see again. *Sandy is never going to forgive me for this.*

Conza reached into his left chest pocket and pulled out a pack of gum. "Wanna piece?" the operator asked, extending a foil-wrapped rectangle.

"Thanks," Clark said and took it. He wasn't a chewing gum guy, but in service of solidarity, he popped it into his mouth.

The two "retired" warriors folded their arms across their respective chests and watched as the Port of Tianjin began to slowly shrink.

"So . . . what do you think about the new head coach of the Commanders?" Clark asked, because it was what men like them did in situations like this. "Think he'll be able to turn things around?"

"Ah, hell no," JC said with bravado. "To do that they'd need a new quarterback, a new offensive line, and a new linebacker corps . . ."

Clark smiled as he listened to Conza go on a football tirade, while the lights of Tianjin seemed to wink at him . . . *Until I see you again.*

58

Andrew "Drewski" Miaoulis raised his head above the gentle waves of the South China Sea. With the rest of his body and his weapon still beneath the surface, he scanned the rocky beach ahead, feeling very, very much alive. As one of a handful of Army SF Green Berets who'd been selected for and completed the elite Combat Diver Qualification Course, Drewski was at home in the sea. After being delivered close to the island by a UUV minisub with his Navy SEAL DEVGRU brethren, he'd completed a grueling underwater infil to the beach. With most of his combat deployments in SF being in the Middle East, he'd had no real-world opportunities to put the skills learned in combat diver school into practice. For Drewski this felt like his first real "FTX."

The night vision embedded into his mask was a thousand times better than what he'd trained on a decade and a half ago in the Army, and the dark world of the remote island lit up in full color.

He saw no movement in the rocks nor beyond in the sector he scanned. A squeeze on his shoulder told him that his teammate, JSOC Navy SEAL Scott Todd, was in position beside him and had also cleared his sector. Just ahead, SEAL senior chief Max Harden, who led their three-man stick, scanned to the south. A beat later, Harden signaled with a hand over his head that they were clear and should continue into the beach.

Drewski slipped back beneath the waves, finning powerfully forward until the water was too shallow to remain submerged. At that point, he slipped out of his closed-circuit rig, secured it beside his left leg, and raised himself into a kneeling firing stance. He scanned the shore over his rifle and, finding no threats, advanced silently forward in a combat crouch, dragging his rig beside him. On reaching the rocks, he doffed his mask, fins, and rig. Next, he shed his tank and shoved everything into a break in the rocks, where he could find all his gear later if necessary. Finally, he traded his dive mask for a helmet with even better color-enhanced NVGs, and climbed on steady legs up the slippery rocks—his combat dive boots gripping the slick surface with ease.

He took a knee again behind and to the left of Harden, while Todd mirrored him to the right in an arrowhead formation. After a moment, Harden chopped a hand forward and they quick-stepped across the rocky beach to the scrubwoods they would use as cover on their approach. There were three missile batteries on the tiny island, and their target was the one most inland—which wasn't too daunting on a hunk of rock barely a half mile across. The two other three-man teams would assault the other two batteries, one on the south end close to the single marina servicing the military ferry to the site, and the other on the northwest. The plan was to reach all sites simultaneously and ambush the Chinese infiltrators. If Katie Ryan was wrong, and they found only missile batteries manned by Taiwan's ROC soldiers, then they would assess the defensive readiness and support and augment the ROC soldiers until the threat window had passed.

If only we end up being so lucky . . .

Drewski had come to the opinion that the quirky female naval intelligence officer was rarely mistaken. He tightened his grip on the rifle that felt like an extension of his body and scanned the scrub for threats, his footfalls all but silent on the mossy ground. As they churned across the next hundred yards, his thighs burned in familiar protest. Still nothing—which included any "blue" patrols, though they were not expecting any security except right at the fence line of each site. They reached the edge of the woods, and took a knee in near unison, studying the battery fifty yards beyond.

"Neptune One is Cadillac," Harden whispered over comms, announcing they were in position to make their final advance on the site.

Like clockwork, the other two sticks checked in, confirming they, too, were in position.

Drewski scanned the site, a small trailer building sat beside the launcher itself, twin boxy missile housings elevated forty-five degrees and pointed west. Drewski knew the box contained four separate Hsiung Feng IIIB supersonic anti-ship missiles, programmed and launched from inside the trailer that contained both the weapon control systems and the living quarters for the six-man team assigned there. Two of the team members were missile control technicians and the other four were security. They manned the site on a rotating three days on/six days off cycle, and today was day three of their shift.

The first thing that raised Drewski's antennae was the absence of any exterior activity.

"Where are the sentries?" he whispered.

"They should be in position left and right, one beside the missile trailer and the other on the roof of the building," SO1 Scott Todd said.

Drewski rose slightly to get a better view and saw a booted foot and part of a leg sticking out from behind the building. "Man down beside the building. Southeast corner."

At that exact moment, the boxy launcher began to move, a loud mechanical whirring sound signaling its response to electronic inputs as someone programmed a target from inside.

"Neptune, execute!" Harden commanded.

Drewski and Todd were up in a flash, sprinting in a low crouch toward the fence line, rifle scanning for targets. A green beam of light appeared suddenly in Drewski's NVGs as an enemy shooter's IR targeting beam reached out from the rooftop, followed by a muzzle flash.

He activated the IR designator of his own PEQ-4, and put the green light on the face of a shadowy figure on the roof. He squeezed the trigger just as green light filled his NVGs and a muzzle flash blinded him.

The impact of the enemy bullet felt like getting hit with a baseball bat and he fell forward as pain exploded in the right side of his chest. Then he heard two three-round bursts from his right as Todd engaged the enemy.

A flame burned deep inside his chest and a strange numbness extended up his neck and into his left jaw, and Drewski knew he was hurt bad. Five combat deployments to Iraq and Afghanistan as a Green Beret, two more to Syria as CIA ground branch, and countless covert operations since, and he'd never had so much as a splinter. He'd begun to believe he just might be bulletproof, but now, as he felt a heaviness growing that made it hard to pull in a breath, he realized that had been a lie. A coppery taste filled his mouth and with his left hand he straightened his helmet and NVGs, and then struggled to his knee, raising his rifle.

He saw no targets, but the mechanical whirring continued, the missile launcher shifting toward whatever target the Chinese saboteurs had selected.

If I'm gonna die in this job, it's gotta matter . . .

Despite the pain in his chest and the wooziness in his head, he surged forward, rifle up and legs pounding the rocky dirt as he made for the fence. Already he could see where the Chinese operators had cut a large hole in the black chain link, and he angled in that direction as more gunfire lit up to his left, with Todd returning the fire from behind him.

Drewksi dropped and rolled through the hole without slowing, feeling a sharp edge of the cut fence ripping deep into his right cheek as he did. He ignored the wound as he finished his roll and popped back up onto his feet.

"I'm coming up on your six, Drewski," Todd called behind him. "You're clear left."

The whirring noise ended abruptly with a loud, metallic *clunk* as the launcher locked into place. Two more steps and Drewksi was at the door, which he now saw was cracked open, allowing a stream of light to escape. He flipped his NVGs up to protect his vision, and flung the door to the control trailer open.

A black-clad operator stood over two dead ROC operators at his feet, his rifle up at port arms and his right hand turning a missile key on the control panel. The saboteur whirled, his eyes went wide, and his hand reached quickly for a red launch button beside the key, set into the panel with an LED screen.

Drewski squeezed the trigger and the side of the man's head evaporated in a gory cloud of blood, bone, and brains. The enemy shooter collapsed to the ground just as a suppressed rifle shot sounded behind Drewski. He looked over his shoulder to see Todd standing beside him, holding a smoking rifle. Drewski followed the SEAL's muzzle line just in time to see a second saboteur sliding down the wall to the ground, leaving a smear of gore on the wall.

"Thanks, bro," Drewski said, realizing it took great effort to do so.

"You CIA bitches are crazy," Todd said, his eyes deep with concern. He moved past him, clearing the room behind the man he'd just shot. "Clear," the SEAL announced. "Two more dead back there."

A profound heaviness was tugging Drewski down now, and he felt like his knees were about to give out.

I need to sit, he thought, and made for a nearby chair.

Unable to make it to the chair, he sat straight down on the floor instead, his rifle cradled in his lap.

"I'm jacked up, bro," he said, his voice sounding tinny in his ears.

"I gotcha, buddy," Todd said, moving toward him as he pulled a medical blow-out kit from his cargo pocket.

"Poseidon, this is Neptune One," Harden said, appearing at Todd's side. "Site Alpha secure. I have one urgent surgical. Request CASEVAC."

Drewski realized that he was the urgent surgical.

"Poseidon, this is Neptune Four," another voice said on comms, the team leader from another stick, Drewski's cloudy brain decided. "Site Bravo secure, but we have one angel."

Oh shit, we lost someone . . . But at least we stopped World War III.

He realized that Todd had laid him on his back, but he didn't recall him doing so. Gloved hands felt around his bare skin

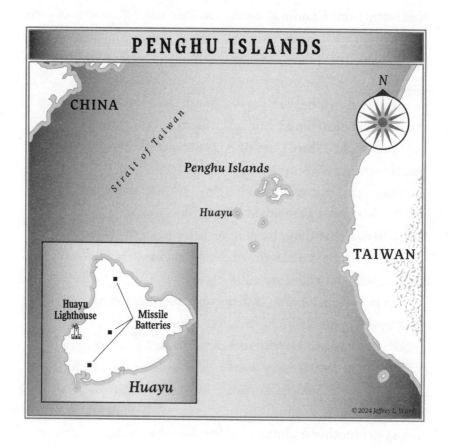

PENGHU ISLANDS

CHINA

Strait of Taiwan

Penghu Islands

Huayu

TAIWAN

Huayu
Lighthouse

Missile
Batteries

Huayu

© 2024 Jeffrey L. Ward

beneath his kit and the ripping of Velcro was followed by his kit being pulled up over his head.

"Where's my rifle, bro?" he asked the man kneeling beside him. He couldn't remember the man's name. Was it Terry Brubaker from Charlie Platoon?

No, that's not right. Terry died years ago in Iraq. What is this guy's name?

He tried to take a deep breath, but his chest felt like someone was giving him a bear hug.

Where the hell am I?

"Did we do it, bro?" he asked the stranger, who was now pouring something cold on the bare skin of his left chest.

"Poseidon, this is Neptune Seven. Charlie is not secure. I repeat, Charlie . . . Oh, shit . . . Poseidon, two missiles away from site Charlie. Say again, two birds in the air . . ."

Drewski closed his eyes even as he felt a new but far away pain in his chest just below his collarbone.

I'm in Taiwan. And I got shot for nothing, because those assholes just fired two missiles from the Charlie site.

"Poseidon, I need CASEVAC right away," the SEAL above him said. Harden something was his name, he thought. "Reed, I need you here, bro. Neptune Three has a chest wound. Round went in around his body armor under his left arm. We just put a tube in for a pneumothorax, but I need you here."

Son of a bitch. I should have gone with Ted and the Navy lady. What was her damn name? . . . Ryan. Yeah, the hot girl was Katie Ryan.

Drewski smiled as a warm envelope of darkness engulfed him.

59

Katie could tell from Captain Kreutz's body language that her presence in the CIC was neither needed nor desired.

But he hasn't kicked me out yet, she thought. *So, I've got that going for me.*

In the surface Navy, Combat was the electronic hive mind of the ship—the central nervous system where all information flowed in service of executing the ship's mission. Unlike the conn of a submarine, where piloting, navigation, and warfighting activities happened in a single space, on destroyers, the CIC was physically separated from the bridge. This meant that Combat wasn't as cramped as the conn of the *Blackfish*—the fast-attack submarine on which she'd spent her last underway.

I'm still in the way here, but at least people aren't bumping into me every five seconds.

Having earned her surface warfare pin during her tour on the

456

Eisenhower, she was no stranger to the "controlled chaos" of the CIC. To an outsider she could see how it would be overwhelming, but she'd stood watch as TAO many times, so the rhythms and routines happening all around her felt nostalgic and almost comforting. What was *not* comforting, however, was the drumbeat of impending doom that seemed to thrum in her very bones. Like a storm looming on the horizon, conflict with the Chinese PLA Navy felt inevitable. Except she didn't have the luxury of a tornado cellar she could hide in to ride out the storm. She, and the crew of the USS *Jason Dunham*, would have to sail straight through this particular hurricane when it hit.

I've got to read him in on what I know, she thought, watching Kreutz talking with his TAO, LCDR Horrillo. *He needs to know what we could be up against.*

Steeling herself, she left her spot and walked to the middle of Combat to stand next to Kreutz and Horrillo. When they stopped talking and both looked at her, she took her shot.

"Captain, I'm sorry to interrupt, but if I could bend your ear for five minutes, sir, I would really appreciate it."

Like a passing shadow, she saw a brief wave of annoyance ripple across his face. For a moment, she was convinced he was going to scold her and kick her out of Combat, but to her relief that didn't happen.

"You've been very patient, Commander Ryan," he said with a tight smile. "What's on your mind?"

"Captain, the reason my team was on Penghu island is because we believe that Operation Sea Serpent is not an exercise. It's a cover story to allow the Chinese to mobilize their Navy, Air Force, and Marines to take Taiwan by force. The maritime exclusion zone they announced was a precursor event to the invasion.

The goal of the MEZ was to create a clear path—free from the civilian ship traffic and the U.S. Navy—to minimize interference and collateral damage during the blitzkrieg when their forces from the mainland shoot across the strait," she said.

The look on Kreutz's face told her that he'd probably pieced this together already himself, but that hearing it confirmed succinctly like that from her made it real.

He looked at Horrillo and they both laughed.

"What's so funny, Captain?" she asked, a little confused by the reaction.

"The timing of your arrival, for one," he said, grinning at her. "Commander Horrillo and I were just talking about the fact that the President—who I've just come to learn is your father—would allow his daughter to take up residence on the very ship he ordered to bust the Chinese MEZ, knowing the PLA Navy is about to invade Taiwan . . ."

She gritted her teeth at this comment but didn't interrupt.

"Which tells me that either your dad doesn't like you very much, or you're a helluva brave woman who heloed out here on purpose, daring the Chinese to fire on us again. My gut tells me it's the latter, Commander, but regardless, we're glad you're here."

"I wish I could give you that comfort, Captain, but the Chinese don't know I'm here, and I'd prefer to keep my family pedigree out of the tactical calculus if it's all the same to you."

Kreutz's smile dimmed, but it didn't disappear. "I apologize. You'll have to excuse me, Commander, I'm seriously sleep-deprived, so my brain-to-mouth filter is offline."

This response won him points with her, because his using that particular expression made them kindred spirits. "My own malfunctioning brain-to-mouth filter is the reason I ended up on

Penghu island in the first place," she said with a chuckle. "So that's something we have in common, sir."

"I have a question, Commander Ryan," Horrillo said, prompting them back on topic. "What's the catalyst for the invasion? The PRC has been saber-rattling about reunification for years. Why now?"

She was just about to answer the question of all questions when the air warfare coordinator announced:

"TAO, ACS has a new track, designated 82843—probable supersonic anti-ship missile. Range thirty-nine miles. Based on speed and trajectory, probable target is own ship."

"Where was it launched from?" Horrillo asked, shifting his attention from Katie to the tactical displays at the front of Combat.

"That's odd . . ." the ACW said, not finishing his sentence.

"Is it Huayu island?" Katie asked.

"Yes, how did you know that?" the officer said, turning to look at her from her console.

"Captain, that missile is not intended for us," Katie said, meeting the skipper's intense stare. "That missile was fired at the *Nanchang*. At the current range, ACS can't distinguish the trajectory between us and the Chinese destroyer, but trust me, it's meant for the *Nanchang*."

"TAO, ACS has a new track, designated 82844, second probable supersonic anti-ship missile. Range thirty-nine miles. Based on speed and trajectory, probable target is own ship," the ACW said, reporting a second inbound vampire.

"Okay, so this is it—the invasion has started, and Taiwan is launching a defensive salvo," Kreutz said, nodding at Katie. But then he suddenly screwed up his face and turned to the port forward corner of Combat. "EW, have you picked up anything indicating the Chinese are launching an offensive with coordinated surface and air assets?"

"No, Captain. Quite the opposite, it's been very quiet," the electronic warfare supervisor reported.

"This was what I wanted to talk to you about," Katie said, grabbing Kreutz by the arm. "This is how my task force war-gamed the beginning of the conflict. PLA Special Forces infiltrate Huayu island, which has missile batteries, but is otherwise an unpopulated rock. They launch missiles at a Chinese warship, giving the PLA Navy justification to retaliate and turn Operation Sea Serpent into an invasion."

"Captain, I intend to kill Track 843 and 844 with BIGSTICKS," TAO said, interrupting, his voice urgent.

"Not yet, TAO," Kreutz said, holding up a hand to Horrillo, but keeping his stare fixed squarely on Katie.

"Are you saying the Chinese are going to use a false flag to justify their attack?" the skipper asked.

"Yes. They don't want another Crimea. They want it to look like Taiwan was the provocateur on the world stage."

The captain of the *Jason Dunham* held her eyes for a long moment, then said, "I believe you. And the situation is extra fraught by the 'warning shot' the *Nanchang* fired when we busted the blockade."

"Captain, vampires are inbound at Mach 3.5," Horrillo said. "We don't have all day."

"I know that, TAO, but Ryan's thrown a monkey wrench into the calculus here," Kreutz snapped.

"Captain, it's imperative that *we* shoot those missiles down before the *Nanchang* does," Katie said, holding his gaze. "We cannot give the Chinese the opportunity or excuse to claim they were fired upon and launch a war because of it."

Kreutz nodded and quick-stepped over to the bridge-to-bridge radio and grabbed the handset. "I agree, but before we launch missiles—even if we're launching them to protect our enemy—I need to make sure there is no confusion about who and what we're shooting at."

60

COMBAT CONTROL CENTRAL (CCC)
NANCHANG (101)
TYPE 055 GUIDED-MISSILE DESTROYER
STRAIT OF TAIWAN IN TRAIL OF THE USS *JASON DUNHAM*

No matter whether he was standing or sitting, Captain Shen could not find a comfortable position. The rib he'd cracked tackling Colonel Sun was really bothering him and the unyielding pain was making it difficult to concentrate. The pain also was putting him in ill temper, which was only exacerbated by the anxiety he was feeling over breaking ranks with his counterpart and incarcerating the political commissar like a mutineer.

"Captain, here is your tea and the other item you requested," the on-watch messenger said, handing him a saucer with a teacup and two painkiller tablets.

"Thank you, Seaman Peng," Shen said, wincing as he shifted positions in his captain's chair.

The young man bowed and stepped back.

Shen popped the two pills into his mouth and dry swallowed them because the tea was still too hot to drink.

"Attention in Combat Central—missile launch detected," the

combat coordinator announced. "Bearing one-three-two, range thirty-nine miles. Classification is probable supersonic anti-ship missile. The system is calculating the missile's trajectory . . . Estimated target is either the USS *Jason Dunham* or our ship."

Shen turned to look at the large display showing the missile's current location and projected track over water on the bird's-eye-view contact management display known as the tactical geoplot. The *Nanchang*'s Type 346 active electronically scanned array, aka Dragon's Eye, was tracking the inbound missile flawlessly.

"It looks like the missile was launched from Huayu island," Shen said, squinting at the screen.

"Yes, Captain," the coordinator said, then added, "Second missile launch detected. Bearing one-three-two, range thirty-nine miles. Classification is probable supersonic anti-ship missile. Trajectory matches the first missile."

Shen shifted his gaze from the tactical geoplot to the streaming video of the *Jason Dunham*, which the *Nanchang* was trailing at a range of one nautical mile off the Americans' port stern quarter. He did not see any outward signs of activity on the U.S. destroyer, but he assumed the Americans were seeing the same thing with their SPY-1D radar and readying a response.

"Captain, we have an incoming bridge-to-bridge radio hail from the *Jason Dunham*," the communications officer, Lieutenant Kwok said in a loud voice.

"Answer the hail, Lieutenant," Shen said to his Commo, who was fluent in English and had handled all of the communications with the *Dunham* thus far.

Shen tightened his core muscles to brace himself as he prepared to rise from his chair. A flare of pain shot up into his armpit as he got to his feet. The messenger, who was always hovering within several meters, lunged forward to help him.

"I'm fine," he said, stopping the young man with a wave of his hand.

"USS *Jason Dunham*, this is PLA Navy warship *Nanchang*, go ahead," Lieutenant Kwok said into the handset as Shen walked up to stand beside the communications terminal.

"*Nanchang*, this is *Jason Dunham* actual," the voice of the American captain said over the speaker. "We are tracking two inbound supersonic missiles. Based on velocity, trajectory, and altitude, we have classified them as Hsiung Feng III anti-ship missiles. It is my intention to shoot these missiles down, and I am informing you of this action in advance. The *Jason Dunham* will fire a two-missile salvo targeting the inbound threats. If the first salvo does not achieve kills, we will fire a second salvo. This is not offensive action against the *Nanchang*. I repeat, this is not offensive action against the *Nanchang*. Confirm you copy and understand."

Lieutenant Kwok swiveled in his chair and translated the message, then waited for Shen's response.

Shen took a moment to collect his thoughts before responding. It was smart of the American captain to notify the *Nanchang* of their intent to take defensive action against the missile launch. And it was also a gesture of respect. But why would the ROC Navy fire missiles at the American destroyer?

It wouldn't, he realized. *Which means that the inbound salvo is meant for us . . .*

"Captain, how do you want to respond?" Kwok asked, feeling the pressure as the seconds ticked by.

"Tell the American captain that we appreciate his offer to shoot down the inbound missiles, but that the *Nanchang* is fully capable of defending itself. Tell him that *we* will shoot down the Hsiung Feng III missiles targeting our ship, and that his assistance in this matter is not desired or required," Shen said.

"Yes, sir," Kwok said, and began relaying the message in English.

"Combat coordinator, prepare a defensive salvo to down the inbound Taiwanese missile threat," Shen said, which would be his next move as soon as Kwok delivered the message to the Americans.

The combat coordinator acknowledged the order and got to work prepping the salvo.

Shen turned back to the comms terminal expectantly, awaiting the American ship driver's response. But instead of responding on the radio, the *Jason Dunham* took action.

"Attention in Combat Central—missile launch detected from the American warship. Contact 27 has fired a two-missile salvo," the coordinator announced. "Classification is SM-6 surface-to-air missiles based on velocity and trajectory."

Shen turned to look at the tactical geoplot and saw two missile tracks heading southeast away from the *Jason Dunham* on an intercept course with the inbound Hsiung Feng III missiles. He shook his head, but a smile curled his lips.

Well played, Captain Kreutz . . .

"Captain, two missile salvo is ready, targeting inbound missiles designated tracks 49 and 50," the coordinator said.

"Very well, coordinator. Hold fire," Shen said. "It appears the Americans are first to take action."

"Captain, a word," said the ship's XO, Commander Tan, and motioned that Shen join him where he was standing a few meters away.

Shen nodded and walked over to caucus with his second-in-command.

"Permission to speak freely, Captain?" Tan asked.

"Always . . ."

"Why would the Americans shoot down missiles that are clearly fired by the ROC Navy targeting our vessel?" Tan whispered. "I fear it could be a trick."

"A trick how?" Shen said, his curiosity piqued. He'd not expected this line of reasoning and was intrigued to see what Tan might have thought of that he'd missed.

"Maybe they are making us think they will destroy the missiles, but plan to miss on purpose. Then it will be too late for us to launch our own counter salvo."

Shen considered the scenario, but quickly dismissed it. "The SM-6 has a seeker. It uses active-radar homing for the terminal kill phase of the engagement. What you describe is not possible. Also, they reacted very quickly. I estimate the intercept will happen at ten nautical miles from our position. If the SM-6s fail to do their job, we will still have time to launch."

"But why would they defend us? And why has Taiwan fired? Operation Sea Serpent is still hours from commencement."

Shen nodded. *These* were the questions and concerns he had been wrestling with himself. Then, possibly sparked by Tan's skepticism, a germ of an explanation was beginning to form in Shen's mind.

"It's possible this is a false attack orchestrated by the Americans in conjunction with the ROC Navy. Maybe the plan is for the *Jason Dunham* to take credit for shooting down a pair of rogue missiles *accidently* fired, thereby saving the *Nanchang*. It would help validate the narrative of our ship as the aggressor and the *Dunham* as the de-escalating actor in the strait. This could be the American's clever response to politicize our warning shot and turn it into an international incident."

"So, what do we do?"

"Nothing," Shen said with a pitiful smile.

Tan arched an eyebrow. *"Nothing?"*

"Yes, nothing. Thanks to Colonel Sun's rash stupidity, we find ourselves in this difficult position. So, we accept the American captain's generous offer to use two missiles from his inventory and waste ten million dollars of his countrymen's tax dollars to protect us, while we save our complement of missiles to service our next set of orders."

Tan pressed his lips together into a hard line, then nodded. "A wise choice, Captain."

Shen gave a little snort. "We will see, XO . . . We will see."

"Captain," Lieutenant Kwok called from his console. "We have new orders. Flash traffic from Southern Theater Command."

Shen walked over to Kwok's terminal. When he looked at the message on the screen, a lump immediately formed in his throat.

Oh no . . . If I do this, it guarantees war.

61

A s much as Katie enjoyed being right, she was also beginning to hate it.

The fact that the ROC Navy had fired missiles from
Huayu island meant that Chinese Special Forces had infiltrated,
taken over a missile battery, and conducted the false flag operation
to serve as the spark for war of reunification. It also meant that the
squadron of SEALs she'd dispatched to stop that threat had either
arrived too late to stop the Chinese SOF element, or, even more
troubling, that they had failed.

Her heart ached at the possibility of the latter.

She forced the thought out of her head so she could focus
on the immediate situation.

The pair of inbound missiles traveling at three and a half times
the speed of sound were ship killers, designed to sink ships like the
USS *Jason Dunham*. They employed sophisticated flight patterns
to improve survivability and avoid being shot down. They also
had internal CPUs with programming to help them *not* get out-
smarted by passive and active countermeasures and maintain a

lock on the real target. There was no guarantee that the *Dunham*'s SM-6 salvo would down the Hsiung Feng III missiles. And if they didn't, there was no guarantee the Taiwanese missiles would correctly target the *Nanchang* instead of the *Dunham*, which were only operating a mile apart.

"Well, Commander Ryan, it appears as though you were right," Captain Kreutz said, turning to face her after hanging up the bridge-to-bridge radio handset. "Anti-ship missiles were fired from Huayu island without provocation or warning. The ROC Navy would never, in a million years, launch an offensive strike on the PLA Navy, especially with us operating in the immediate vicinity of the target warship. So, my question to you, Commander, is what happens next? Are we about to go to war alone and trapped in the middle of the ultimate kill box? Because the Strait of Taiwan is the last place I want to be when a war between China, Taiwan, and the United States kicks off."

"I wish I could answer that, Captain, but unfortunately all I can do is speculate," she said.

"Then by all means, Ryan, speculate."

"Well, sir—"

"BIGSTICK 1 is entering terminal homing on Track 843," the air warfare coordinator announced, cutting her off.

During the bulk of the intercept flight, the SM-6 fired by the *Dunham* was receiving continuous midcourse guidance from the ship's Aegis radar and targeting system. Only during the terminal phase of the engagement would the SM-6 take over homing duties. At the very last moment, the missile's directional blast fragmentary warhead would explode in the direction of the target and throw shrapnel out to destroy the inbound vampire. The announcement by the AWC let everyone in Combat know that transition had just happened.

"Very well," Kreutz said, then turned back to Ryan. "You were saying?"

"If I was the Chinese theater commander, I would direct the fired-upon asset to retaliate with decisive and overwhelming force," Katie said, meeting the CO's gaze. "In other words, I'd order the *Nanchang* to level Huayu island and turn it into a smoldering, useless hunk of rock, thereby eliminating any and all evidence of the false flag."

"I was afraid you were going to say that."

"Mark India," the AWC announced, indicating the SM-6 was at the intercept point.

"Battle damage assessment?" Horrillo said.

"Assessed as probable kill based on deceleration, sir . . . Now hold multiple new tracks on ACS at India. Confirming debris fall. Good kill, TAO."

"What about BIGSTICK 2? We should be terminal on Track 844 any second," Kreutz said, turning his attention from Katie to the AWC.

"Yes, Captain. BIGSTICK 2 entering terminal homing now on Track 844," the air warfare coordinator replied.

Katie realized she was holding her breath as she waited—along with the rest of Combat and the world, or at least the few unlikely world dwellers in the know—to learn the fate of the second missile.

The seconds ticked by, but felt like minutes to Katie . . .

"Mark India," the AWC announced, his voice triumphant. "Stand by for battle damage assessment . . . Tracking debris fall. Good kill, TAO. Vampire destroyed."

A cheer erupted in Combat and Katie exhaled with relief, but they weren't out of the woods yet. Not even close.

"Great work, everyone, but stay frosty. This isn't over," Kreutz said, stealing the words straight out of her mind. He turned back to face her. "You were saying, Ryan?"

"We just neutralized the *actual* threat, but that doesn't prevent the *Nanchang* from taking action," she said.

"How so?"

"We have to assume the CO of the *Nanchang* is read in on the false flag, Captain. And we just monkeyed with that plan. If my orders were to fire on Huayu, and I was keen on executing those orders, I'd find a way to twist the narrative to support it. Yes, the *Dunham* shot down the ROC missiles, but the *perceived* threat still exists. The PLA Navy's narrative will be 'Taiwan fired on a Chinese warship, so action must be taken to prevent additional strikes' . . . Or something like that."

Kreutz nodded, then looked at Horrillo. "What do you think, TAO? What's our play?"

Horrillo tapped a finger on his chin and thought for a moment before saying, "Get the skipper of the *Nanchang* on the radio and make a compelling case that the threat is neutralized and no further action is required . . . That's what I'm thinking at least."

She sensed Kreutz wasn't looking for advice but rather giving his TAO an opportunity to contemplate a command decision without actually being the one in the hot seat.

The CO nodded in agreement, then turned back to Katie. "Anything else before I make the call?"

"We have a SEAL team tasked to defend and secure Huayu. Does the fact that two missiles were fired mean the mission failed, or are the SEALs hitting the island now? I can't answer that question, but either way I refuse to let them be collateral damage. We can't let the *Nanchang* fire on Huayu. I need you to buy us time so we can get an update on the operation. Better yet, try to get a pledge from the Chinese captain that he will not fire on the island."

"I understand," the skipper said with a wry smile that she interpreted to mean *Sure, and while I'm at it, I'll ask him for the keys to his ship.* Kreutz picked up the radio handset and raised it to his mouth. "*Nanchang*, this is *Jason Dunham* actual, over . . ."

"*Jason Dunham*, this is *Nanchang*, go ahead," the Chinese radio talker replied.

"We have neutralized the inbound missile threat. I repeat, we have neutralized the inbound missile threat . . ."

A longer than expected pause ensued before the *Nanchang* came back. "We concur the two inbound missiles have been neutralized, but that does not mean the threat was neutralized. The ROC Navy has taken aggressive action and fired anti-ship missiles at our vessel. They could fire more at any moment. Be advised, *Jason Dunham*, we have received orders to destroy the missile batteries on Huayu isle."

Kreutz winced at this and looked at Katie.

"Tell him that we have confirmed the missiles were *not* fired at the *Nanchang*, but were fired at the *Dunham* as part of a training exercise," she said, pulling the idea out of God knows where. "We need to change the narrative back to them being the aggressor rather than defending themselves."

"Oh, that's good, Ryan," Kreutz said with a grin, and keyed the mic. "*Nanchang*, your last statement is in error. The *Jason Dunham* was conducting a training exercise with the ROC Navy. The missiles were not fired at the *Nanchang*. They were fired at the *Jason Dunham*. It is for this reason that we shot them down. The United States, on behalf of the ROC Navy, apologizes for the irresponsible nature of the exercise. The training missiles never should have been fired while the *Nanchang* was in such close proximity to the *Dunham*."

"Nice, Captain," Horrillo said with a crooked grin when the skipper released the mic.

Kreutz shrugged. "We'll see if it works."

The pause this time lasted even longer than before. Finally, the *Nanchang* came back:

"Captain Kreutz, this is Captain Shen, commanding officer of the *Nanchang*," a new voice said, speaking English less fluently than the radio talker, but doing an admirable job of it nonetheless.

"Go ahead, Captain," Kreutz answered.

"What is name of the training exercise?"

"Operation Battleship," Katie said, blurting out the first thing that came to mind as the memory of her and her dad playing Battleship together popped into her mind.

Kreutz shot her a screwed-up look, but said it anyway. "The name of the exercise is Operation Battleship."

"I document and report this to my superiors. If you end exercise now, I have no requirement to act. If more missile fired, I will know this not an exercise. Do you understand this message?" the Chinese ship captain said, the subtext crystal clear despite the language barrier.

"I understand, Captain Shen."

"You . . . You are . . ." Shen started to say, but stopped. A pause ensued, then the voice changed back to the fluent radio talker. "Captain Shen would like to acknowledge that this is the second time the *Jason Dunham* has been required to defend against a missile fired in error. The first time was our mistake. This time was your mistake. Now the status quo has returned."

Kreutz met Katie's eyes. "Are you thinking what I'm thinking?"

"We scratched his back, now he's scratching ours," she said.

Kreutz nodded and raised the mic to his lips. "Copy all, *Jason Dunham* actual out."

Katie felt a wave of relief flood over her. "Good job, Captain. Looks like you've just negotiated a ceasefire."

"Not necessarily," Horrillo chimed in. "They could strike Huayu with air-to-ground missiles or fire ground-attack missiles from batteries on mainland China. The strait is only a hundred nautical miles wide."

"You're right," she said, "but we've bought the SEALs time."

"What's our next move, Commander?" Kreutz asked.

She hated what she was about to say, but she said it anyway because it was the truth. "We cross our fingers and hope that diplomacy wins the day. Because I think at the pointy tip of the spear, we've done all the de-escalating we can possibly do."

62

Navy SEAL Scott Todd glanced at Chief Reed—the team's Eighteen Delta SEAL combat medic—as Reed leaned over Drewski and listened to the wounded operator's chest with a stethoscope. Todd watched Drewski's IV bag drip twice, before he returned to his scan, looking for tangos who might challenge their exfil off this fucking rock. Teammates from the squad that had hit Bravo site, Del and Arnie, were scanning their sectors as well. But Todd noticed Del kept glancing down at their dead teammate and brother, a SEAL named Skip Anderson, whose body lay wrapped in a silver thermal blanket on the beach.

If the crazy CIA ground branch guy died, it would make Skip's death all the worse. Drewski, like most ground branch guys, was a Green Beret and combat diver, and that made him a part of the SOF brotherhood. Losing two on an op was as unusual as it was terrible.

"Neptune One, Seven—sitrep?" came a call in his ear from their

475

teammate Wild Bill, who was leading the other stick to a water exfil off the northwest corner of the shitty little hunk of rock.

"One," Harden answered, his voice a growling baritone. "Bro, a water exfil is gonna be damn near impossible. Our Urgent is unconscious now . . ."

"Hemodynamically unstable," Reed added.

"And unstable. We can't swim him out, at least not underwater."

A long uncomfortable pause ensued . . .

"Dude, swim him out as best you can on the surface. CASE-VAC by air is on hold. We might be in the middle of a fucking naval battle right at any second. Poseidon is having Eight position the UUV to get you guys first. We'll swim all the way to fucking Wangan if that gets your guy to the docs sooner," Bill said, referring to what would be an eight-mile swim to the island of Wangan due east of them.

"One," Harden said in acknowledgment, clearly not happy with that answer, but the situation was what it was. "Let's move it, guys."

With Harden on point, Todd and Reed each took a corner of the poncho liner underneath Drewski and began to drag him in the direction of the beach. Behind them, Del hoisted Skip's limp body into a fireman's carry on his shoulders for the trek to the surf. Scanning for threats, they crossed the quarter-mile distance to the surf's edge at what felt like a snail's pace, but was in reality only minutes. Todd took a position on the slippery wet rocks, checking their six over his rifle, the landscape presenting in full color, but eerie in the new NVGs he was still getting used to. The TOC had reported no enemy thermals left on the island after the SEALs won the gun battles at the missile batteries. But . . . this was the Chinese. Who knew how deep into the U.S. satellite network the PLA could hack.

Todd watched Reed check Drewski's breathing, then used two fingers to check for a pulse in the man's neck.

"Son of a bitch," Reed said. The SEAL medic leaned back on his heels, tilted his face skyward, and let out a long, rattling sigh. Then he collected himself and turned to Harden. "He's gone, boss."

"Damnit," Harden said, clenching his jaw and shaking his head. "All right, we bring him anyway. No man left behind."

"Hooyah," Todd said, the battle cry a reflex. He was suddenly aware of a tear on his cheek, but gripped his rifle tighter and let it trickle into his beard.

"Poseidon, One," Harden said, his voice tight. "One is Chevy. We are now four plus two angels. Say again, now two angels. We're inbound to Corvette."

Todd covered his teammates while Reed secured the CIA man's body tightly into the poncho liner and then he continued to watch their six as his teammates pulled dive gear from the rocks and suited up. Then, with Reed covering him over his rifle from the water, he slipped down the rocks, quickly donned his gear, and submerged.

Towing the body of the dead former Green Beret turned CIA operator behind him, Todd finned deeper and deeper as they headed through the dark water out to sea. He hoped Drewski's lifetime of service and selfless sacrifice on the island of Huayu would never be forgotten.

Navy SEAL Scott Todd sure as hell would never, ever forget this day.

63

Jack Ryan closed his eyes and gritted his teeth as the makeup team touched up his graying hair and tucked tissues into his collar as they put makeup on his face. He hated every minute of this process and struggled not to let his discomfort be taken out on the hardworking staff performing what, he supposed, were necessary duties.

"You can't present on worldwide television looking like a disheveled hobo who doesn't know how to comb his hair. Looking in control of the nation starts with looking like you're in control of yourself . . ."

His wife Cathy's words from the very first time he'd been through this—what now seemed both yesterday and a lifetime ago—came to him and he relaxed.

"Almost done, Mr. President," the woman dabbing something on his cheeks said.

"Thank you, Darcie," he said, and smiled as her name came to him.

Arnie van Damm emerged from the mayhem, and folded his hands in front of him, waiting for Ryan to say something.

"Everything good, Arnie?" Ryan asked.

"I think so, Mr. President," van Damm replied. Ryan stole a glance at his chief of staff, causing Darcie to make a little *tsk* sound as he messed up her work somehow. Van Damm looked nervous.

"What's bothering you, Arnie?"

The man he trusted with his day-to-day in the White House sighed.

"It's a lot of moving parts, Mr. President. We have simultaneous feeds that have to stream via satellite from France, Germany, the UK, Australia, and South Korea."

"Is that what really has you worried?" Ryan asked as Darcie finally, mercifully, removed from his collar the tissues meant to prevent makeup from staining his shirt.

Van Damm held his eyes.

"Well, sir, to be honest . . ." The man shifted uncomfortably. Ryan had always made it clear that he wanted open, honest, and unfiltered advice from his team. But he got how hard that must still be. "Scott and I are concerned about our partners. We're taking a real risk here, Mr. President. We have no control over what these other leaders might or might not say—"

"Unfortunately, we can't control what they say or do, Arnie," Ryan interrupted. "They don't work for me . . ."

"I know, sir, and I understand. But to the world—to *China*—whatever the others say during this address, we're married to."

"Which, I believe, is outweighed by the benefit of sending the world the message that we and our partners are together on this. There is strength in numbers, Arnie. Li needs to know that the fallout from his aggression will be global, not just a scolding from the United States. This accomplishes that task."

"Yes, sir, Mr. President," van Damm relented.

Ryan ground his teeth. The truth was, van Damm and Scott Adler were right. This plan had significant risks and their concern about what partner leaders might say represented only one of them. But these were well-calculated risks, and he trusted the relationships he'd fostered over the years with their partner nations. In any case, this was their last play. Showing a unified, international front was the only thing he had left to pull them from the brink of a shooting war in the South China Sea. The very thought filled him with a renewed urgency. Missiles could be in the air toward Taiwan or the U.S. fleet any second.

"Are we ready?" he demanded.

"Yes, Mr. President," the technical production head, Micah Young, said and lights came on, blinding him until his eyes adjusted. He took one last glance at his notes, but then he was never really a script kind of guy.

"One last feed to merge, Mr. President, and we're ready," Young said. "Okay, here we go. Are you ready, sir?"

"When you are, Micah," he said, and folded his hands in front of him on the desk.

"Five seconds, sir," Young replied. "Four . . . three . . . two . . ."

"Good evening," Ryan began, looking directly into the camera and imagining it to be the face of a father or mother from somewhere in the Midwest, a trick he'd used since the beginning of his presidency. Cathy always said he was a natural at this, but he sure as hell never felt that way. "Many times now I have sat at this desk and addressed the American people as the President of the United States. Tonight, things are different. Tonight, I'm addressing the country and the world as a member of a coalition of world leaders who, together, have decided to stand up as a united voice against an aggressive bully that threatens us all. As my good friend, German chancellor Aneke Schultz, said to me earlier today—an attack on one is an attack on all. In a world where technology and international commerce connects every person on the planet, I am grateful for America's friendships and global partners."

In his mind, he could now see a family, somewhere in Texas perhaps, crowded around the television and listening to his every word. He spoke to them, trying to be honest and to give them hope.

"After my brief words, you will hear from other world leaders—including Chancellor Schultz—but I have been given the honor of speaking first. And so, my fellow Americans and citizens of the world who love and cherish peace and freedom, I'm here to inform you that the People's Republic of China—under the leadership of President Li Jian Jun—has launched an illegal and unprecedented attack against the United States Navy. After firing an anti-ship missile at an American destroyer operating freely in international waters, the Chinese military has launched a sneak attack against Taiwan, targeting the isle of Huayu. We have evidence that this was an intentional and coordinated attack, designed to take control of Taiwan's maritime missile defense system and make it appear that Taiwan had launched an attack against the Chinese Navy. President Li directed this insidious false flag operation, resulting in the deaths of both Taiwanese and American military personnel. Why would he do this, you might ask. Because he hopes to trick the world and justify an invasion of Taiwan. President Li is counting on ordinary citizens, like you, to believe the lies he's told about American spies kidnapping Chinese ministers. And to believe the lies he *plans* to tell about Taiwan attacking China, and not the other way around. President Li hopes that you are too busy, uninformed, or suspicious of political rhetoric to care. He hopes that you will stay silent and that he can exploit your apathy and get away with his plan. But I know none of those things are true. I know you care, and I also know you deserve to know the truth. When he invades Taiwan, Li is gambling that our friendships and bonds as freedom-loving citizens are not strong enough to unite and take the hard path to stop his unjust war . . ."

Ryan continued, no longer even glancing at his pages, the confidence in him swelling, the anger growing. He no longer pictured the faces of everyday Americans, crowded around televisions and iPad screens. Instead, he pictured the faces of his sailors, airmen, soldiers, and Marines performing their duties bravely in harm's way against a lethal adversary. He pictured the SEALs on the rocky beach of Huayu carrying their dead to sea. He pictured Captain Jeff Kreutz and the crew of the *Jason Dunham* bravely transiting the Strait of Taiwan . . . The Marines standing by to go to battle . . . The aircrews aboard the *Reagan* and the *Nimitz* readying planes to launch from catapults on the flight deck . . . Lastly, he pictured the face of his daughter Katie, resolute and brave in the face of danger.

He could feel the power of their honor, commitment, and courage. He could feel them counting on him to lead, to stand up for what was right and just and to defeat Li without firing a single shot. He felt all these things and more, transmitted across the globe, all the way into his very bones.

He took a deep breath, and buoyed by their strength, he made his case to the world . . .

64

JADE SPRING VILLA OF PRESIDENT LI JIAN JUN
YUQUANSHAN
WEST OF YÍHÉYUÁN (THE SUMMER PALACE) COMPLEX
HAIDIAN DISTRICT
BEIJING, CHINA
0632 LOCAL TIME

Li Jian Jun, president of the People's Republic of China, strode quickly across the foyer of his luxury villa, his expensive Italian shoes clicking out a staccato beat on the rare white Carrara marble floor. He entered his office brimming with irritation. No, far more than irritated, he was livid. He had risked it all to bring his country to a new level of power and prestige. He had done so by having the balls that no one else possessed to make the hard choices necessary to defeat an enemy like the United States. And now, as he worked hard to cover all traces of their actions in the Strait of Taiwan and protect China from devastating economic blowback, Secretary General Xu Chao had the audacity to call him to a meeting at Zhongnanhai.

Who is he to summon me?!

This was an insult Li had every intention of fixing.

483

He had no time to indulge the questions of those beneath him. He had work to do. He had calls to make. For one thing, he needed to know if the missile barrage from the *Nanchang* had achieved the tactical objective of devastating the isle of Huayu and destroying any evidence that the Chinese Special Forces had been there. This was the most crucial piece of information that he needed before he could respond to President Ryan's infuriating global address.

If Captain Shen did his job, then this is still salvageable . . .

There would be satellite imagery demonstrating the missiles fired from Taiwan at his ship. Their response, not knowing if additional missiles might be inbound, would be understandable and defensible.

Ryan and his international coalition of self-important tyrants could cry and bloviate all they wanted about the invasion of Taiwan, but under the circumstances, China's military action would be justified. He would prove America had provoked China by crossing his blockade and directing Taiwan to fire missiles at the *Nanchang*. He would make *them* the aggressors.

He glanced at his watch—the limo should already be here—and then leaned over the desk to tap the keyboard of his computer. But the screen did not come to life. Instead he simply stared at his screen saver and the horribly annoying spinning circle that suggested the connection had been lost.

"Damnit!"

He didn't have time for this. He needed desperately to know whether the attack on Huayu had been successful. Even more urgent, he needed to know whether Admiral Qin had been found and was in MSS custody. Every hour of delay only bolstered the credibility of Ryan's lies.

There may even be a version of this aftermath that still allows us to make a move on Taiwan, in the name of our own safety and national security.

The thought made him smile.

This is not over yet, Jack Ryan. You will not win . . .

But the damn spinning circle in the center of his screen saver just kept spinning.

He slammed his palm on the desktop, turned, and stormed out of his office.

He crossed the foyer, picked up his leather attaché case, which he'd set on the black and white Lenzi Eva console table by the door, then, remembering it was forecast to rain, grabbed his Bottega Veneta trench coat and slung it over his shoulder. Jaw clenched, he stepped outside. The black Hongqi H9 luxury sedan was already idling in the circle at the bottom of his stone steps, so he hurried toward it. The first few drops of rain—from what he was certain would become a downpour—spattered against his face, irritating him. Somehow the driver must have failed to see him, because the fool remained in the driver's seat instead of hurrying around to open Li's door. Li opened his own door and ducked into the passenger compartment just as the sky opened up, the rage he already felt now boiling to a whole new level.

"What the hell are you doing, you idiot?" he demanded as he slipped into the leather seat and slammed the door behind him. "You leave me in the pouring rain? I could have you imprisoned for such disrespect . . ." He stopped.

The eyes in the mirror were not familiar to Li.

"My sincere apologies," the man in the mirror said, his voice neither sincere nor apologetic.

"Who in the hell are you?" Li demanded. "I will have your ass for this. Where is Wong?"

"Comrade Wong is unavailable, I'm afraid," the driver said,

pulling the car away from the villa and accelerating rapidly around the drive, making Li fall backward into the plush seat. Still pressing hard on the accelerator, the driver piloted the Hongqi down the hill at a reckless speed. "Secretary General Xu sent me to take care of you."

There was something—something in the man's voice and also in the eyes—that felt suddenly very wrong.

"Stop the car immediately," Li demanded. "Take me back to the villa. I . . . I have forgotten something."

"There is nothing else you will need where you are going, Mr. Li," the man said, and now laughed.

"*President* Li," he corrected the man, but all of the rage was gone from his voice, replaced with realization and fear.

"Right," the driver said, still laughing. "Our secretary general wished me to share something with you. A quote . . ."

"What quote? What are you talking about? Stop the car immediately or I will have you killed."

"He said to tell you, 'Only an Army of the People is invincible.' He wanted to be sure you heard these words."

"You are making a terrible mistake," Li said, his voice trembling. "Xu does not know what he is doing, the cost of what he is attempting . . ."

"I have my own quote from Mao Tse-tung to share, Mr. Li," the driver said as the bulletproof partition between them began to rise. "Mao also said, 'It is always darkest before it becomes totally black.'"

"Stop!" Li screamed. He tried both door handles, but they were locked. Then, in a panic, he grabbed on to the partition glass as it rose. "Wait, listen to me. I can help you."

"I don't need your help, Mr. Li," the man with the dark eyes said as the glass made it to the top. Li pulled his hands away, but a moment too late, and his left middle finger was trapped.

"Stop!" he screamed now, as much in pain as in fear as the heavy glass crushed his finger behind the first knuckle, then severed it. He watched in horror as his fingertip slid down the other side of the glass, like a tiny piece of chewed food, leaving a little bloody trail behind it.

He clutched his bleeding left hand against his chest. He fell to his back and with all his might began to kick the heels of his Italian shoes against the right door window, feeling the jarring pain all the way up to his hips with each failed kick. Finally, his right foot impacted at a funny angle, and he felt the tendons in his ankle snap with a nauseating pop as his foot twisted inward and pain shot through his foot and leg.

"Please stop," he sobbed as he fell over on the leather seat in agony as the Hongqi H9 made the last turn and headed toward the gate of Yùquán Shān. "Someone, please help me."

But he knew that no help was coming.

Mao was right. It is darkest before it becomes totally black . . .

65

President Jack Ryan was not a pacer, but he simply couldn't sit any longer. The minutes that passed felt like hours as he watched what felt almost like static images on the large-screen map of eastern China, Taiwan, the Strait of China and, to the north, the East China Sea. Now and again the green square labeled DDG 109 would flicker and reposition a tiny click north, the red triangle labeled NANCHANG moving in mirror image just to her west, so close the images almost overlapped. What *wasn't* moving mattered as much or more—none of the red triangles to the north and south of the strait were converging on the *Dunham*, nor were they moving toward Taiwan. No new icons were appearing, marking the paths of incoming missiles or aircraft. The only airborne assets on the map were combat air patrol aircraft from the *Reagan*, which circled over the mainland of the island nation, and a similar CAP flying oblong donuts to the south and east.

"This is almost unbearable," Arnie van Damm said from across the table, staring at the same screen as Ryan.

"Almost?" one of the SecDef staffers said, and the tension was broken for a moment by laughter from around the table.

"I gotta say, that captain of the *Jason Dunham* has balls of steel," Robert Burgess, his secretary of defense, mumbled. "When do we make him admiral?"

Kent smiled knowingly. "Kreutz is a rising star . . . But for the moment, he's right where we need him."

"When did we last get an update on the SEALs exfilling from Huayu?" Ryan asked the room.

"Not since they entered the water, sir," answered a young woman seated beside the SecDef. "They are estimated to rendezvous at the pickup coordinates in another fifteen minutes, but might be late because . . ." She paused and looked up, her eyes wet when she met Ryan's. ". . . Because of the, you know, load they have to carry."

Ryan felt his throat tighten.

The human toll . . .

"Mr. President?" said Alexis Wilkins, the secretary of state's deputy for communication, her voice urgent.

Ryan looked to the monitor to see what was going wrong now, but everything appeared the same. He turned to her and raised an eyebrow.

"Sir, there is a direct call for you from Beijing . . ."

"This ought to be good. I can't wait to hear what Li is going to threaten us with now," Ryan growled.

"That's just it, Mr. President. It's not Li," she said, her face full of surprise and worry. "It's the secretary general, Xu Chao."

"Well, that's unexpected," Ryan said, shooting a look at Adler.

"Don't look at me," Adler said. "I'm just as surprised as you."

"I'll take it in room two," Ryan said, and paced away from his chair to the second of the three smaller breakout rooms along the wall behind him.

Inside he forced himself to sit and let out a long, slow breath as he waited for the call to encrypt and then connect to the desk phone. The light turned green and then a voice came through the speaker saying, "Line is secure and call is connected."

Ryan pressed the button beside the flashing green light and leaned toward the phone.

"This is President Jack Ryan," he said in his most presidential voice. "Who is this?"

There was a short beat, either a delay in the signal or a pause as the caller took a moment, and then a voice answered.

"This is Secretary General Xu Chao of the People's Republic of China," the confident, and familiar, voice replied. Ryan had met Xu more than once—a quiet and reserved and apparently serious man. Xu tended to defer to Li, but when Li was out of earshot, Xu had surprised Ryan by being both candid and funny. "Thank you for taking my call, Mr. President. It is most urgent that I speak to you."

"What is urgent is that you cease your aggression toward our forces in the region and the territories of Taiwan immediately. Why are you calling me and not President Li?" he asked, but had a feeling he knew the answer. If he was right, he suspected this call to be good news.

"President Li is unavailable, Mr. President."

Xu let the words hang a moment.

"I assume that it is unlikely he and I will have another opportunity to converse, then?" Ryan pressed.

"Very unlikely indeed, Mr. President," Xu said. "I wish to convey to you that the People's Republic of China deeply regrets that the desires and poor decisions of one man have caused such damage between our countries and that lives were put in danger . . ."

"Lives were *lost*, Secretary General Xu," Ryan said with heat, then clenched his jaw as the faces from the service records of Special Operations Chief Skip Anderson and CIA officer Andrew Miaoulis filled his mind. "Good men."

"I regret this most of all," Xu said after a brief pause. "Mistakes were made. I wish for you to hear this first before I make an address to the world. The recent aggressive actions were not the will of the Chinese people or the government in Beijing. These actions were directed by one man, and that man no longer serves as president. In China, we believe that our government serves the people and not the other way around. Please accept my apology on behalf of the nation of China and its people."

Ryan considered the olive branch he'd just been given, something the wolf warrior Li Jian Jun would never have extended under any circumstance. But as satisfying as this moment was, Ryan needed more.

"I sincerely appreciate that, Secretary General Xu," he said. "But your ship the *Nanchang* has been operating dangerously close to our destroyer transiting the strait, and we have special operators requiring rescue . . ."

"The *Nanchang* has been ordered to stand down and reposition. We have dissolved the maritime exclusion zone, and as such, the USS *Jason Dunham* has free and safe passage through the strait. If there is anything we can do to assist in the rescue or recovery of your soldiers . . ."

"That won't be necessary, Mr. Secretary," Ryan said, and through the window gestured for Kent to come into the room.

"All I ask is that our air assets be allowed to operate safely in the area to recover our men."

"It will be done," Xu said, and Ryan pressed the mute button when Kent opened the door.

"Get air assets spun up right now to recover the DEVGRU operators, Larry," he said. "And confirm that the *Nanchang* is disengaging."

"Their ship is literally reversing course as we speak, Mr. President," Kent said, wonder in his voice.

"Get it done." Ryan unmuted the call and into the speakerphone said, "This action will go a long way toward restoring the trust that has been lost, Secretary Xu."

"I can also guarantee something else," Xu said.

"What is that?" Ryan asked.

"The American spies currently aboard the South Korean–flagged cargo ship *Capella* will also be given safe passage to Incheon," Xu said, and Ryan grinned and closed his eyes. "We will not interdict the vessel as she leaves the Bohai Sea en route to South Korea, nor will we interfere with any operations to extract your military and intelligence personnel from the vessel. We will, of course, deny any future entry of the *Capella* into our ports, but this is something we will discuss with South Korea directly."

"Understood," Ryan said, and felt the last and final presidential weight he'd been carrying lifted from his shoulders.

Clark and his team were coming home.

EPILOGUE

Beer bottles in hand, Ryan paused at the glass slider door before opening it to take a mental snapshot of the scene. Katie stood on the deck, palms on the railing, looking out at the water. She had her back to the house and didn't notice him looking. Her caramel-blond hair danced in the wind as she stood motionless and lost in the moment.

How did I get so damn lucky to have her as a daughter?

Once again, she'd proven herself as both an analyst and tactician under fire. She'd been on the front lines of a potential war with a Chinese superpower, and she'd played a critical role in anticipating an adversary's response and inserting strategic exit ramps to help him outmaneuver President Li and de-escalate the situation.

If she keeps on at this rate, she'll be the one sitting behind the Resolute desk in the not-too-distant future.

Grinning, he held the two beer bottles in his left hand while

493

yanking the slider door handle with his right. A gust of sea breeze greeted him, as did Katie's smile as he stepped out onto the deck to join her.

"Brought you a beer," he said, presenting her a Sam Adams Wicked Hazy.

"Thanks," she said, taking the bottle and holding it out to toast. "Cheers."

"Cheers," he said, clinking bottles and taking a swig. He stepped up beside her at the railing. "In case I forgot to say it already, you did real good out there, kid. If it wasn't for you having the guts to pull out your crystal ball and let everyone up the chain know what you were seeing, I think President Li would have pulled it off. They were one step ahead of us, and you closed that gap and allowed us to take the lead."

She smiled at the compliment. "Thanks, Dad . . ."

"Apparently, the captain of the *Jason Dunham* gave a heckuva glowing report about you. Something about how you didn't wilt under pressure and came up with the response that stopped the *Nanchang* from launching missiles at Huayu island."

"I don't know about that," she said, taking a sip of beer. "I just reframed the narrative, is all. It's not like I negotiated the Treaty of Versailles."

"No, but you made a decision that affected the lives of millions. If the captain of the *Nanchang* had leveled Huayu, then Taiwan would have had no choice but to defend itself. That would have given the Party ample reason to let Li launch the war of reunification rather than ousting him from power. Your insight protected the sovereignty of an island nation of twenty-four million people, which includes thousands of American expats, and a squad of Navy SEALs on Huayu. *You* did that, Katie."

He saw her blush a little at this, but she didn't comment, just stared out at the water.

They both sipped on their beers for a long comfortable moment before she said, "So . . . Admiral Qin. Was he reunited with his family?"

Ryan nodded. "Yes, and from what Mary Pat tells me, they are contemplating returning to China."

She turned to look at him, eyes wide. "What? That's a death sentence."

"I'm not so sure," Ryan said. "Qin didn't actually turn over any confidential information to us. By the time we got him out with the battle plans for Operation Sea Serpent, the gambit was over. He didn't turn traitor to sell us secrets. I believe he's a patriot who was trying to do the right thing to stop an unjust war. With Li out of power, we might be able to broker Qin's safe return."

She shot him a dubious look.

He chuckled. "I'm serious. It could mark a new direction in U.S.-China relations."

"If you say so."

"Just pinned on lieutenant commander and you're already a cynic, huh?" he said.

"I think there's compelling evidence to support my position. If he returned, I think he'd be disappeared within three months. And even if they don't punish him, he certainly won't be given his job as defense minister back. You don't break ranks in China and get to keep your reputation or your job."

Ryan took a sip of beer. "We'll see . . . I'm hopeful. And not because I'm naive, but because it's a better philosophy than the alternative." Now it was his turn to stare out at the Chesapeake. "I couldn't do the job otherwise."

"What about Léi, the Spider?" she asked.

"Now, she's a different story. There's no going back for her. The MSS would dissect her into a thousand pieces if she tried to return. And she knows that."

"I assume we're going to repay her courage and sacrifice by helping her start a new life?"

He gave her a reassuring smile. "Mary Pat is taking care of the details."

"Good," Katie said, seemingly satisfied and letting the matter rest.

Since this morning, he sensed there was something she wanted to talk to him about, but she'd yet to bring it up. He got the feeling now that it was on her top of mind, but she was still holding back for some reason.

"Kay-kers, what's on your mind?" he asked, using the family pet name for her that had been around since she was a little kid. "I get the feeling there's something you want to ask me?"

The rosy in her cheeks turned a shade darker. "How do you always do that?"

"Do what?"

"Read my mind!"

"I'm an analyst," he said, grinning large. "Reading minds is what I do."

"It's annoying sometimes. Has anyone ever told you that?"

"Yes, your mother. Every damn day."

They both laughed at this.

"Now that you mention it, there *is* something I wanted to ask you . . ."

"Yes," he said, drawing out the word playfully.

"Do you remember Commander Knepper, the XO on the *Blackfish* I told you about?" she said, her cheeks now beet red.

496

"Yes," he said, drawing out the word again and still grinning.

"Well, um, the *Blackfish* is back from deployment and going to be in port for the next couple of months and so, I was wondering . . . if we could have him out to the house for dinner?"

"Him who?" he teased.

His daughter blushed.

"Oh, I guess I haven't talked about it much, but . . ."

"Commander Knepper seems like a fine man."

She punched his arm, her face now crimson.

"You're doing it again," she protested.

A dozen possible zingers popped into his mind that he could use to tease her, but he stayed his tongue and simply said, "I think that's a great idea, so long as he's okay helping out in the kitchen. If you're going to roll with the Ryans, you gotta earn your keep."

A giant grin stretched her cheeks and put her dimples on full display the likes of which he hadn't seen since she graduated the Academy. She leaned into him, which was code for "Give me a hug." He wrapped his right arm around her shoulders and gave her a squeeze.

"I think you're going to really like him, Dad," she said. "He's smart and funny and brave . . . Just like you."

A warm, wonderful feeling blossomed in his chest at hearing her so excited. "Well, that all sounds well and good, but before I can authorize the two of you dating, he's going to have to pass vetting."

At this comment, she pulled away from his one-armed hug and gave him the stink eye. "Dad! No . . . That's *so* not cool."

He shot her a mischievous smile. "I'm not talking about Mary Pat vetting; I'm talking about Milton Bradley."

"Milton Bradley?" she echoed, confused.

"Battleship, Katie," he said. "Milton Bradley is the toy company that originally invented the game."

"Ah . . . gotcha. So, Battleship is the bar that Dennis has to clear?"

"That's right, until he can beat me at Battleship, you can't date him."

She gave his upper arm a little pat, then snugged back in for her hug. "In that case, I'm golden. He'll dispatch you before we even get through appetizers."

He laughed at this and took a sip of his beer.

Then he put his arm around her shoulders, and they stared out at the sea together in silence.

THE UNMISSABLE
JACK RYAN, JR. SERIES

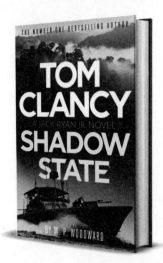

Surviving a helicopter crash in the Vietnamese Highlands is only the start of the challenges facing Jack Ryan, Jr.

The vibrant economy of the new Vietnam is a shiny lure for Western capital. Companies are racing to uncover ideal opportunities. Not wanting to be left behind, Hendley Associates has sent their best analyst, Jack Ryan, Jr., to mine for investment gold. And he may have found some in a rare earth mining company, GeoTech.

But a trip with a Hendley colleague to observe the company's operations takes a treacherous turn when their helicopter is shot down. Some things haven't changed, and Vietnam is still the plaything of powerful neighbours. The Chinese are determined to keep Jack from finding the truth about what exactly is being processed at the isolated factory.

Now Jack is in a race for his life. He's got to stay one step ahead of a pack of killers while supporting his wounded friend. And he'll get no help from the government, because in the jungle, it's the shadow state that rules.

OUT NOW

READ THE PULSE-RACING
JACK RYAN SERIES . . .

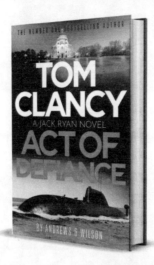

When a Russian superweapon is let loose under the waves,
it's up to President Jack Ryan to find a countermove.

US intelligence is reporting turmoil in the Russian navy. Their deadliest
submarine, the Belgorod, has unexpectedly launched. Who authorised
the departure? What mission is it on? And, most disturbing of all, what
weapons do the giant doors on the sub's bow hide?

It's been four decades since a similar incident with the Soviet sub, Red
October, ended happily, thanks to a young CIA analyst named Jack Ryan.

Now, President Jack Ryan finds himself with fleets of ships, squadrons of
jets, and teams of SEALs at his command, but what he doesn't have is insight
into the plans of the Belgorod's commander. It falls to a younger generation
of Ryans to do the dangerous work that will reveal that information.

But there's always a price to be paid. When the final moments tick
away, will Jack Ryan have to choose between the safety of
his country and the safety of his child?

OUT NOW